LUTHIEL'S SONG
DREAMS *of the* RINGED VALE

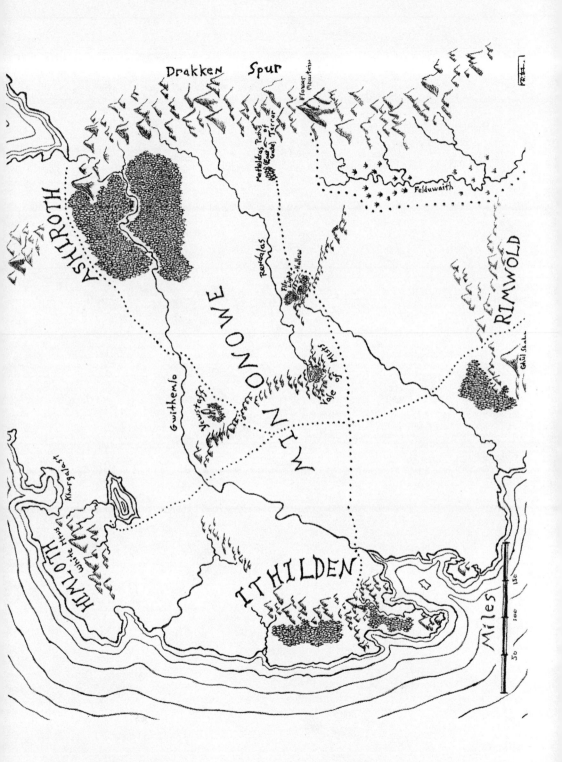

LUTHIEL'S Song

DREAMS of the RINGED VALE

ROBERT MARSTON FANNÉY

DARK FOREST
PRESS

Edited by Matthew Friedman

www.luthielssong.com

Cover art and interior art by Siya Oum
Cover design by Matthew Friedman

Library of Congress Cataloging-in-Publication Data
Fannéy, Robert
Dreams of the Ringed Vale/ Robert Fannéy
p. cm. (Luthiel's Song ; bk. 1)

SUMMARY: In the elfin land of Minonowe, a fifteen-year-old orphan named Luthiel embarks on a dangerous journey to save her beloved foster sister Leowin. On the way, she encounters sorcerers, werewolves, dragons, monstrous spiders and Vyrl. Through her adventures—both in the world of Oesha and in the world of dreams—she learns that nothing, not even her own life, is what it seems.

ISBN 0-9764226-0-3

To all of those women ~
Strong enough to be heroes;
Fair enough to be ladies.
This song is for you.

CONTENTS

APPENDICES

THE LILTING

Silver slips that ringed Vale
The mists that curled the air
Cupped in stone like snowy fists
All wreathed in gossamer

Lunen danced,
Her silken beams
A gauntlet to the night

And nine they rode
Their fiery steeds
To brave false mornings' light

Hey ho! Said he
The grim faced god
Whom winds named Vlad Valkire

His fist clenched strong
His sword—slim, long
Cold—wrought
Dubbed Cutter's Shear

Which clove the air
And set the night
Ablaze with starlight fire

Shear clove to heart
Undid Undeath
Damned Vyrl
And slew desire

The nine danced
Sacred lilting shades
To Vlad In rebel's song

Who reigned over Vyrl
Brought death to life
And freed the cursed chained long

When all was won
The battle done
Of nine
But three remained

A pact they made
An oath of blood
To purge the murderer's stain

So they grew
Again to shine
Like angels
Of Ëavanya and Ëavanar

Aedar
Of old,
Daughter of Elquellia
And sons of Evanestar

From his charred glass throne
Vlad reigned O'er all
Goblin, elf and Vyrl

For three hundred years
Summer to summer
With neither blight nor quarrel

Till black moon dreams
Scarred his nights
And in winter's nightmare
He roamed

So he returned
To Lenidras of old
To craft
His last two stones

Of wyrd they were
Of dreaming sighs
Of fancies strange and light

Dim colored one
Cool as breezes
A drifting rim of night

The second danced
Like starshine lingers
Upon the ocean's hair

One for his sire
One for his mother
Both old wounds to repair

But with her first touch
The lady fell to sleep
And dreams of Gorothoth

Where she yet fights
The strange lord's spell
Of winter cold and dark

But with her loss
Into madness
His grim sire fell

His cry pierced the forest
Aroused the Sith
His words a demon's spell

From tree and vale
From crag and rock
His might flew out to do battle

But Vlad received him
Cast down his Shear
Ordered his soldiers
"Bare no metal!"

So Vlad Valkire
Met the rage of his sire
Whose name may never be spoken

Vlad gave up his Shear
With words of love
With words of wrath
The cold wrought blade was broken

Now Shear all shards,
His hand once strong
Now weak in dying strains

Unleashed blood,
And his wraith
Cries out to kin
From those gleaming stains

For now my friends
Of Vlad Valkire
And his Love
Merrin of ocean waves

We know but this—
She sleeps in grief
As he lingers
On tongue of father's blade

The three they grieve
With starving wail
The loss of their boon lord

And twist to bind
Their long held oath
Sealed by the bite and sword

To dance in mists
To hunt their bond
To grant, guide and receive

And sing with songs
The dance lilt long
With kin and sow fate's seed

PROLOGUE: A DISPATCH
OF THE LORD TUORLIN

Mithorden ~

*Old friend, if there were ever a time when I had need of your counsel then
it is now. My trouble comes from the Vale of Mists where a great vapor builds,
boiling over the hills that encircle it, creeping out into the land, molding the flesh
of every beast or branch it touches. Now, creatures of strange magic walk
abroad both day and night. I fear that this anger in the mists is merely a sign
that the Vale's terrible gods ~ the Vyrl ~ have become enraged. They dispatched their messenger to Ithilden only yester-eve demanding us to send
another child. She will be the fourth sent this year ~ as though one a year were
not enough! Now they demand four! When word gets out, I'll have all the
swords in Ithilden screaming to me for war.*

*The Vyrl have brought too many years of loss. Too many mothers weep
over children sent, far too many, who now lay dead in the vapor. Far too few
returned, and those like me, who have, bear scars that serve only as angry
reminders.*

*In all my years, I've never seen such fury among the lords. They call upon
me to loose the Blade Dancers, to bid them hunt the werewolf Othalas before
he takes another to the Vyrl's waiting mouths. The Kingdoms who received the
message just tonight send emissaries of war to Ithilden. Zalos, Lord of Ashiroth,
sends word that he is coming to address me, personally, and has already pledged
a thousand of his most fierce wolf-riders.*

My friend, I have long dreaded this day! For though I hate the Vyrl more than most and I judge Valkire's promise to them for what it was ~ the last desperate act of a dying god, I, of any, should know that to fight them is folly.

The lords, I fear, will not be turned. When they look at me, they see only what the mists have marred. But with the Vale's gift I have glimpsed a danger, more terrible than any I have yet foreseen, rising up from the ashes of this war. My counsel will be for peace but I fear that even my voice will be silenced.

So it is, in this darkening hour that I call you, my friend. Your wise words and steady hand are needed, more than ever. Perhaps you, who walked with Valkire, could sway the lords. Zalos' mind is already set and to my advice its windows have long been shuttered. So I ask you to come with all speed to Ithilden! I will wait and watch. Come soon! Though it is summer, I fear the light is already starting to fail.

Yours in need,

The High Lord Tuorlin
Master of Ithilden, Keeper of the West Wind,
Bearer of the Sacred Eye, Who sits on the Starlight Throne

BOOK I

LUTHIEL

To be me is to be different, she thought as she watched them, from her place apart from them, upon the hillside.

And there was much to watch. For everywhere across the Minonowe, and where she lived in Flir Light Hollow, elves were preparing for celebration.

They were festooning trees with glowing flir bug bulbs, baking delicious almorah cakes, and rolling out giant gourds filled with the best summer's wine. Master Alderdalf's pixies were hard at work under the woven canopy of his voluminous fae holme turning out specially prepared fireworks. Loud popping tindersnaps, eek-eeking neekerbeeks, bright flaring fizzleflashes, and the scaly Romas Dragons lay in red, green, orange and silver stacks outside. Lady Lutendrah was busy tying ribbons to her famous pandur's boxes (you never knew what would pop out). Even the otherwise grim-faced elves of the Dark Forest seemed to brighten as they drank toasts to the day—First Summer's Eve.

As she watched them, a lively wind rose up, dancing through the trees, swatting gold and silver ripples across the lake shore, before riding up the hill on which she stood. The breeze played in the branches about her, but the swaying of her arms and the gentle curves of her neck were just as graceful. From her head flowed hair the color of moonlight. It spilled over leaf-shaped ears before falling down shoulders so supple they belied the gentle strength that lay beneath. Clothes of forest green embroidered with silver lay across skin as fair as a cloud. Eyes, which shone like green-blue stars, rested beneath softly sloping brows.

Even elves thought of her as beautiful—if a little strange. And sometimes she would hear them teasing that she'd arisen from the wyrd of sea foam or was born to earth in the cradle of a crescent moon floating down upon the gloaming. For she was an orphan and no one knew her parents.

Though the elves welcomed her, accepting her as one of their own, she could always sense that they held her apart. She bore it with a kind of sad resignation. But she always wondered:

Why do they treat me this way?

Am I not an elf like them? she would think. *Why can't they see me as Leowin does?*

For her foster sister Leowin was the only one who treated her as though she were no different.

Luthiel smiled at the thought and sniffed the air. She sighed and let all the happy sounds, all the various smells, wash over her. It was going to be quite a party. Fitting, because this was the day she turned fifteen, or near enough as her foster parents Glendoras and Winowe could reckon. Some asked her if she cared that her birthday also fell on the night of First Summer's Eve. But she only laughed.

"Can you think of a better day?" she would ask them in return. And what better day to be born than on the day that the world shook off the darkness? What happier time to celebrate than when everyone else was celebrating?

She secretly fantasized that the reason for all the hubbub, the cause for all this happy commotion, was her birthday. And she smiled to herself when the first thing they said to her was—"Happy Birthday, Luthiel!" followed by "Happy First Summer's Eve!"

LEOWIN

Luthiel felt a hand tap her shoulder and turned around just in time to glimpse Leowin's ruddy face before she sprang up into the leafy canopy.

"You're tapped!" she could hear her cry from her hiding place among the leaves. A shower of laughter soon followed.

Her sister, though a year older than Luthiel, was three inches shorter. Wild strands of gold spilled down to her shoulder blades and light blue eyes shone at her from the shadows. Leowin wore colors that made it easier for her to hide—green and brown—and her sure footed, supple frame was well practiced in the arts of jumping, climbing and hanging.

"Leowin you flutterfler!" Luthiel cried and bounded up after her.

Leaves smacked her face as she sprang, faster than a tree frog, from branch to branch. Some of the branches were more than ten feet apart. Luthiel's springs were long and her balance sure. Her tiptoes found purchase on each branch for only an instant before she was flying off through the air again leaping as surely and gracefully as a bird on a rope.

When it became plain to Leowin that Luthiel had found her, she shot up from her hiding place like a thrush flushed from the bushes with a happy cry bounding from limb to limb as if they were stairs.

"Can't catch me!" Leowin taunted.

"You're not getting away!" Luthiel cried back, then leapt gracefully through the air skipping two of the branches Leowin had just used and landing on a third. Luthiel was catching up to her fast. Soon now, she'd tap Leowin and then it would be her turn to run.

Leowin loved to play tap-and-turn and she'd found a hundred little tree hollows and crevices to hide in. Luthiel was often surprised by Leowin's cunning; by the sly tricks she'd play and by a hundred planned escapes. But Luthiel was faster. So each played to their advantage. Luthiel was almost within reach of Leowin. She stretched her hand before her— mere inches away from Leowin's back.

"No you don't!" Leowin gasped.

Sudden as raindrops, Leowin leapt off the branch she was standing on and into mid-air.

THE WYRD STONE

Luthiel felt her heart rise into her throat. She watched helplessly as Leowin's body rushed toward the ground, more than fifty feet below.

She lunged, stretching out a hand to grasp her, but the plummeting Leowin was already out of reach. Before she hit ground, Leowin lifted her arms above her head and pointed her toes. Her face, staring up at Luthiel, bore a wide grin.

What was she doing?

Suddenly, Luthiel's eyes refocused and she saw the lily pads beneath Leowin part as her toes touched them, revealing a sparkling pool of water.

Splash! Leowin disappeared beneath the surface and didn't come up. Luthiel sighed.

"That puk," she said.

Luthiel didn't give up easily, though, so she ran along, hopping from tree-limb to tree-limb, tracing the lily pads that were disturbed as Leowin swam beneath the water. Luthiel hid herself in a thick patch of leaves, watching from the shadows as Leowin pulled herself from the water, made her way through a moss patch, then turned toward East Wind Road.

Luthiel was quiet—silent as any ghost fly—but Leowin was quieter.

Luthiel dropped from branch to branch like a shadow. Staying within sight of Leowin was the real trick. She dared not to even blink lest she lose the sneaker. Little by little, she closed the distance between them. Within a hundred heartbeats, she was a mere ten feet behind and above Leowin, gathering her legs beneath her for a pounce.

She shot through the air, spreading her arms wide like wings. An instant later, her arms encircled Leowin and they tumbled through the underbrush.

"Aaaaeeeeeaaaaaaa!" Leowin yelled in surprise and fought to escape. Luthiel struggled to grasp the flailing Leowin. Head over heels they tumbled, rolling back and forth, this way and that, until; at last, they somersaulted onto the speckled cobbles of East Wind Road. Luthiel ended up on top. She grabbed Leowin's shoulders and pinned her against the stones.

"Caught you!" Luthiel cried.

With those words, Leowin stopped wriggling and looked up at Luthiel with a big grin on her face. With her free hand, she started digging at her belt.

"Not even Lorethain can catch me," she said. She seemed to have found what she was looking for and balled her hand around it so Luthiel couldn't see.

Leowin's face, though still happy, suddenly became more somber. She placed a hand on Luthiel's chest and gently pushed her away as she stood. She took a moment to brush herself off with her free hand.

"You sure made a mess of me," Leowin said.

"I can only take half the blame," Luthiel replied. "You're the one who jumped into that muddy pond."

"That I did," Leowin said with a grin.

Then, she stepped forward and embraced Luthiel.

"Happy birthday Luthiel," she breathed into her ear, pressing something round and cool into her hand.

Luthiel laughed. "So I had to catch you before you'd give me a birthday present?"

Leowin's eyes twinkled with mischief as she nodded her head. "I wanted to make you earn it."

Luthiel shook her head and laughed. "Well, it certainly is an odd way to get a present."

"Odd? It's a surprise," Leowin said and then motioned at Luthiel's hand. "Aren't you going to take a look at your present?" she asked.

Luthiel's eyes dropped and she opened her hand. In it she held a perfectly round crystal. The Stone was clear as glass but the light that fell through it somehow came out brighter, more like silver. It was as if it washed the light. Luthiel's mouth fell open in wonder.

"Leowin, it's beautiful," she said, her voice touched with awe. "I've never seen a thing do that to light. What is it?"

Leowin smiled at her mysteriously.

"I'm glad you like it. Here, let's get off the path a bit," she said, grabbing her wrist and walking her over to the side of the road.

Luthiel nodded, still staring at the treasure she held in her hands.

Far in the distance Luthiel could hear the shriek of a Romas candle. Soelee had started to set. The festivities would begin soon. For the moment, though, she didn't care. She was captivated and surprised by Leowin's gift.

Leowin guided Luthiel away from the road, finally sitting her down on the wide roots of an oak.

"Just sit here and watch the Stone," Leowin said.

Luthiel couldn't have done otherwise; it was as if some spell had captured her eyes.

Suddenly, unexpectedly, Leowin began to sing. The words of the song were simple; the tune, one she'd never heard before.

More graceful than willows, more lithe than the birds
Softer than Silva, she's the kindest of words
For she's wise as the ocean, a great mystery
And her love is as endless, with depths I can't see
Luthiel! Luthiel!
Her name is for water both gentle and strong
Like the waves on a seashore she sings her own song
No mountains may bar her she carves her own path
And her timeless will no thing can outlast
Luthiel! Luthiel!
No truer one I've known!
Luthiel! Luthiel!
The water through stone.

The song lulled through the forest and surrounded Luthiel like a pair of loving arms. She felt her cheeks become hot as her sister sang and in her heart she felt a deep, aching warmth. Then, as Leowin stopped singing, the Stone trembled in her hand. A note, so pure and forlorn that it drew a tear from her eye, rose up from the Stone. The sound seemed both loving and full of sorrow. The note became louder and the aching in her chest grew until it seemed unbearable. She couldn't restrain it any longer. Before she knew what she was doing, she opened her mouth.

The sound that came out was both loud and pure. It blended with the music of the Stone, coming into harmony with it. The song continued, drawing all the air from her. When she could sing no more, the Stone's music abruptly stopped.

Luthiel gasped for breath, but she still couldn't take her eyes away from the Stone.

Then, a brilliant light bloomed from its depths, bathing the forest in a silvery-white glow, making the trees cast long shadows in a ring around them. As Luthiel watched, breathless, the light shone on for about three heartbeats and then slowly dimmed until all that remained was a small silver glimmer in the center of the Stone.

Finally, she was able to tear her eyes away.

She felt different—as if something had changed her.

Luthiel didn't know what to say.

"What is it? What's it done to me?"

Leowin, who'd been watching Luthiel with a fascinated gleam in her eye, grabbed her hand.

"Luthiel, it's all right, don't be afraid. What just happened is wonderful," she whispered in excitement.

Luthiel could only stare back at her.

The Stone rested in her trembling palm. But she kept her eyes from it. She felt an urge to let it roll over her fingertips and off her hand. But she didn't. Instead, she blinked her eyes and licked the beads of sweat off her lip.

What has Leowin done? she thought.

"The Stone is a secret thing," Leowin continued, "I didn't know what it was when I found it. Sure, I had my suspicions. I've read a bit in the libraries at Ithilden about such things."

Leowin had taken a few trips to Ithilden with Father Glendoras and Uncle Hueron. Often she would brag of her exploits there in the late night when most of the flir bugs had dimmed into slumber. Her most daring were her forays into the forbidden halls of Imûl.

A great library of lore long considered dangerous was secured there. Only those with special permission could enter and study. Except, of course, for Leowin who was exceptionally good at getting into places she shouldn't.

Leowin was quite proud of her exploits.

Luthiel, whose voice had been taken from her only moments earlier, was having difficulty finding it again.

"You!" Luthiel said finally. "You've got me wrapped up in some Secret Finder's game. Why?"

Leowin looked at the Stone and then smiled up at her. There was mischief in that grin—but there was also wonderment.

"Well, I've always wanted to be one," she said. "Maybe discovering this means I am." She motioned to the Stone. "There's only one type of thing that can do what it does to light," she explained. "I spent days gazing at it, watching it turn flir bug's glow from yellow to silver. So I thought I'd give it a test. Now I know."

"What do you mean, a test? What have you gotten me into?" Luthiel asked.

"No, Luthiel, you don't understand—this is wonderful!" Leowin said. "It's a treasure! A Wyrd Stone, one of the few crafted by the hands of Vlad Valkire."

Luthiel felt her mouth fall open in disbelief. She knew of Vlad Valkire only from the old ballad called the Lilting. It was just a myth— telling how Valkire freed all of Oesha from the Vyrl and how, in the end, his father killed him. She didn't believe in it. It was just a sad old tale, one that tried to explain things for which there were no explanations.

Luthiel looked at Leowin.

"How can this be? I never even believed in the old song." She held the Stone before her eyes as though seeing it for the first time all over again. There was dismay in her voice. "I am not Valkire. I am only Luthiel. Why should I keep his Stone? It should stay in the fairy tales with him."

Leowin put her hand on Luthiel's shoulder.

"Don't worry, Luthiel. 'Truth's existence never depended upon belief.' If Valkire left us with it, then it is a gift we should not refuse."

"He also left us with the Vyrl," Luthiel said.

Leowin sighed. "The Stone is not a creation of the Vyrl, Luthiel. It is a good thing and it chose you." She was smiling at Luthiel again. "I had to give it to you the right way, though—with love and with a song. And I did."

"What's it for?" Luthiel asked.

Leowin looked at her with a level gaze and a serious expression. "Luthiel, it's whatever you want it to be for. But don't worry about all that right now. Just accept it."

Luthiel gazed at the Stone for a long time before she spoke again. It was such a simple thing—so smooth, so round. But it had a way of holding her eyes. It was like staring into a pool of water so clear she couldn't tell if the bottom was near, or very far beneath. Something about it drew her—making her want to dive inside. "I don't know what to think of your gift. It feels light in my hand but when I look at it, it seems a strange weight has been laid on my heart. It's not a good or a bad weight, though, just something that is."

Leowin only smiled knowingly.

Luthiel felt apprehensive, but she didn't want to refuse Leowin's gift. She was still trying to take it all in when a sudden thought rose to the surface of her muddled mind.

"Leowin, where did you find this? You said a number were made but I've never seen one."

Leowin stared off into the distance for a moment and then met eyes with her. "There weren't many even to start with. Now there are only a few."

"But where did you find this one?" Luthiel said.

A nervous grin spread over Leowin's face.

"I stole it from Elag."

"You did *what?*" Luthiel's back stiffened and her head jerked upright. "Leowin, that's just too far! The sorcerer is dangerous. You remember what happened last time!"

Leowin shrugged her shoulders. "But we only took carrots."

Luthiel waved the Wyrd Stone in front of her. "This is more than carrots!"

"He'd locked it up." Leowin nodded at the Stone. "So I spied on him. I saw him trying to use it, over and over again. But so long as he held it, it darkened. He was doing it all wrong. He needed to sing to it and then give it away freely to the right person before it would work properly. Instead, he kept it locked in an iron box and never let even the dimmest light touch it. Even without all the secrets I've discovered over the years, I'd have known that the magic within the Stone was starting to die. But you don't just go telling someone like Elag that they're making a terrible mistake."

Luthiel wondered if it was a mistake at all.

"One thing's certain," Leowin continued. "He wanted to keep it for himself. You should have seen the things he did to protect it! Didn't work, though. It was much happier after I'd saved it from him. In his hands it was all dull and cloudy. But I knew how to turn it back to silver. It was very relieved." Leowin seemed quite pleased with herself.

Luthiel looked down at the Stone with wonder and, for a moment, set aside her fear. "You speak as if it were a feeling thing."

"Well, it's supposed to be." Leowin replied. "I read that if the Stone is around someone who is in extreme pain, or has fallen into madness, or has bad thoughts it darkens."

Luthiel wondered once again if it would be wise to keep the Stone. Valkire, Elag, and its magic all implied a business she did not want to become involved in.

"If Elag ever finds out, Leowin, he'll have us both thrown out of the Minonowe or worse. He's very well respected in Ithilden. Besides, he doesn't like you and he hates me. He'd take any excuse he could get."

"Will you stop worrying about Elag? I know all about him and there's no reason for Ithilden to respect him. Why, with all the things he's been dabbling with, he's the one who should be exiled. All the more reason why I had to take it."

"Do you realize what you've done? I can't keep this." Luthiel said, trying to press the Stone into Leowin's hand.

Leowin pushed it back toward her.

"Luthiel—you don't understand. It's yours now. Others may keep it but it will be yours for as long as you live. Likely it would find its way back to you even if you did return it to Elag." Leowin leaned closer and her voice became a low whisper.

"Besides, Lorethain said that it was with you when you came to the Minonowe and that Elag took it from you then." Leowin's lips formed a half-smile. "Lore was drinking too much honeywine again. He'll talk about anything when he's like that."

"What are you saying?" Luthiel said, her voice catching in her throat. "It came with me?"

"Well, Lorethain didn't say much. But yes, it came with you."

"Then it could be from my parents," Luthiel said, staring at the Stone with renewed interest. "But Elag took it?"

Leowin nodded.

"What did he do? Snatch it from my bower?" Luthiel said hotly. "Did they just stand by and let him?"

"Well, I don't know," Leowin stammered. "Lore was really drunk and he mumbled a lot. I don't know how it happened."

"Then how do you know that it's mine?"

"Well, Lore was clear on that part. I'm certain it was yours."

Luthiel looked at Leowin for a long moment, unsure whether to believe her. It seemed so improbable.

"Does Lorethain know you stole it from his tutor?" Luthiel whispered. Though no one was around, she felt the sudden urge to be quiet.

"No, of course he doesn't. He'd feel obligated to tell Elag. Luthiel, I'm just returning what was yours. Your mother or father must have left this with you. I can only imagine who they were." Leowin's eyes fell to the ground.

Luthiel felt anger rising in the pit of her stomach. She didn't like such talk. It made her feel like she didn't belong.

"I never knew them. Leowin, *you* are my family," Luthiel said.

Leowin returned her gaze sadly. "Luthiel, it's not wise to disregard who you are—whatever that may be."

Luthiel sighed and looked down at the Stone apprehensively. *It's just a stone,* she told herself. Still, she carefully placed it in a silken pouch and tied it to the silver chain that hung around her neck.

"I don't know if I understand what it is that you've given me, but I wish you'd stop talking about me like that. I'm not ever going to leave the Minonowe. There's no place in all of wide Oesha I'd rather be than here." Luthiel paused for a moment and then looked directly into Leowin's eyes.

"I want you to know that I'll always cherish the gifts you've given me—both the song and the Stone," Luthiel said.

Leowin stepped forward and put her hand on Luthiel's shoulder. "You're just a mystery. Sometimes, I'm afraid that whoever brought you here might come back and take you off again."

"What are you talking about? Why would I leave?" Luthiel asked.

Leowin shrugged and shook her head. "I don't know," she said. "I'm glad you like your birthday present, Luthiel." Then she smiled at her. "Oh, and I almost forgot to tell you. If you want to use the Stone, just sing to it but also think of someone who loves you very much. You could think of me!" Then the smile faded and she placed both hands on Luthiel's shoulders and looked her directly in the eyes. "Understand?"

Luthiel nodded stiffly, wondering at Leowin's sudden mood changes.

"Good," Leowin said. "Now let's go back before we miss all the fun!" She laughed and Luthiel managed to smile back at her.

A BLADE DANCER COMES

I don't understand anything, she thought to herself as they turned down the East Wind road toward Flir Light. While they walked, she found her thoughts returning, as they often did when strange things happened, to the sorcerer.

Luthiel couldn't remember a time when the sorcerer didn't scare her. Her brother Lorethain, who was Elag's apprentice, always laughed at how she'd jump at just the mention of his name. She used to chide herself for her fear. But that was before she and Leowin got it into them to steal some of Elag's carrots.

She remembered the sickening sensation of a tree branch slithering around her ankle just before she was jerked upside-down and then hauled into the heart of Elag's Fae holme. Once inside, the great tree split open and began stuffing her and Leowin into a gaping fissure in its trunk. Gnarled knobs in the wood ground into them like great wooden teeth. Her right arm was pinned between two of the knobs. She cried out as it was slowly crushed.

Elag was there, but he only stood and laughed.

"My, my, see the great rabbit my tree has caught!" He grabbed Leowin's foot and gave it a painful twist. "And look at this weird one!" he said to Luthiel. "A fine bit of fertilizer you'll make!" His laughter was cold and he just sat there watching with a gleam in his eye as the tree began to close about them.

The nobs crushed against her, forcing the breath from her lungs and wrenching her arm. She could feel the bones grinding together. She cried out again, but Elag just stood there, watching.

Then one of Elag's wind charms tinkled, announcing a visitor. Elag made a quick wave of his hand and Luthiel was spat out of the tree's maw as it sealed itself behind her. Luthiel cradled her painfully twisted arm close to her body.

Lorethain walked in briskly and handed something to Elag. He raised an eyebrow when he saw them laying on the floor all covered in sap.

Elag chuckled. "See the two rabbits my tree caught? Trying to pilfer carrots from the garden. They're fortunate I was here. Who knows what could have happened if I wasn't?" Luthiel gasped at the disappointment in his voice.

He and Luthiel had locked eyes then. There was something cold in his gaze that she couldn't shake from her mind. It kept coming back to her, like the ache in her arm when the weather changed.

"Well, you'd better take these carrot thieves home for a bath," Elag said with a sneer and a dismissive wave of his hand.

Luthiel remembered how she'd limped home. Remembered how she'd made Leowin swear never to set foot under the twisted branches of Elag's fae holme again. But Leowin wasn't much for promises when there was a bit of mischief to be had.

She should have never gone back. Especially not for my Stone, she thought. Elag will kill us. The thought hung in her mind and she could see his cold eyes staring at her once more.

"Leowin?" she said.

"Mmmm?" Leowin smiled at her.

"I just had a thought about Elag."

"Not him again!"

"This is serious. I think I just realized something important."

"What?"

"I really think he would have let it eat us."

Leowin laughed. "Oh, enough! You're just worried because of the Stone." She turned so that she was looking Luthiel in the eye. "Don't worry, we'll keep it secret. He'll never find out."

Luthiel shook her head. "I'd hate to think what would happen if he did," she said.

But Leowin only smiled back at her and laughed.

Luthiel fell silent.

No use talking to her. She never listens, she thought with a sigh.

They continued to walk down the road in silence. Leowin would, on occasion, make a face or crack a joke. But Luthiel was too wrapped up in her thoughts to do anything other than look and smile.

Not the birthday I expected, she thought.

They had only been walking for a few minutes when Luthiel heard something. She came to an abrupt halt.

Her fear returned but this time it was stronger. She felt a tingling over her body and her arms were covered with gooseflesh. A sudden, unreasoning, sense of dread fell opon her.

"What?" Leowin exclaimed.

"Shhhhh." Luthiel hissed. Leowin quieted down and she listened as the sound grew louder. She could hear the fall of boot heels on the road behind them.

"Somebody's coming." Luthiel whispered. "I don't want them to see us."

"Why?" Leowin whispered back.

"I don't know, I've just got a bad feeling."

"This is absurd," Leowin laughed.

The sound was growing louder and Luthiel was certain that at any moment the walker would come round the bend.

"Get out of the road," Luthiel whispered.

"Luthiel, you're scaring me."

"Get out!" Luthiel hissed as she grabbed Leowin and pulled her into a nearby thicket. She felt immediately embarrassed. Why should she hide from a traveler on the East Wind? Perhaps she was just worried about Elag or maybe she was still agonizing over what Leowin said about leaving. She tried to shake the sense of foreboding, but it stuck with her growing until it became a nagging worry, which was enough to keep her hidden.

"Where is it?" Leowin whispered to Luthiel. Luthiel motioned with her head toward the East Wind. Orin's Eye was turning a brilliant purple and orange as it set in the west casting long shadows over the road. She peered into them, eyes scanning for any hint of motion. At first, the only sign of the stranger's approach was the growing sound of boot heels against stones. Then, she saw a dark figure moving on the road. Beneath a gray cloak that draped to the tops of snug black boots, she could see armor plates shaped like leaves rippling over his tall form. Girded to his left shoulder was a ring of blades that seemed to flex with every footfall. His gauntleted hand rested on the black and silver hilt of a longsword. In spite of the evening's warmth he wore a hood that overshadowed his face, but she could see the gleam of his eyes as he scanned the path.

Her breath caught in her throat. She was frozen, unable to tear her eyes from him.

The figure came abreast of where they were hiding and stopped. His head moved slowly from side to side as though he were listening. Luthiel felt her heart quicken.

A branch jabbed her in the side, thorns pricked her, a fly landed on her hand. But she didn't dare to move. Out of the corner of her eye, she saw that Leowin had gone stiff.

The figure turned toward them, walked to the side of the road near where they were hiding and sat down with his back to a tree. Luthiel's heart was beating so loudly, she was certain he would hear it. She tried to soften her breathing. Beside her, Leowin squirmed.

The fly on her hand crawled over to her thumb and then bit it. She flinched, ground her teeth. Repressing an urge to smack it, she brushed it away with her forefinger. It flew off, only to land again on her cheek. She blinked her eye furiously hoping to scare it off. But she didn't dare to raise her hand.

He pulled out a waterbulb and took a couple of gulps. He then opened another pouch at his belt and started fishing out pieces of dried fruit with a small knife. The ring of blades at his shoulder suddenly swirled away. It cut through the air, flipped itself upside down and then landed on a tree branch.

The fly bit her again.

Luthiel almost jumped. She felt like screaming in fear and frustration. Instead she slowly raised her shoulder and brushed it against her cheek. The fly buzzed off only to land on the bare flesh of Leowin's arm.

Leowin looked at her with a pained expression, but she didn't dare move.

He was so close to her she could reach out and touch him. What if Leowin suddenly sprang up? Would he kill her?

She could see Leowin's face flinching with pain.

Suddenly, his hand shot out and snatched the fly from Leowin's arm. He held it in his fist for a moment and then opened his hand. The fly buzzed off down the road.

Startled by the sudden movement, they jumped, tangling themselves up in the thicket.

"Happy First Summer's Eve," he said without looking at them.

Her cheeks flushed. She could hear Leowin's quick breathing beside her and felt her hand grab the fabric of her shirt. She felt Leowin's breath on her ear.

"He's a Blade Dancer." Leowin whispered. "Let me handle him."

"Oh," she said hollowly.

A Blade Dancer? She'd heard of them but she'd never seen one. They were the solitary guardians of the Minonowe and most elves shared a feeling of unease about them. They were necessary—defending against a thousand horrors both from the outside and from within. But often, they seemed as dark and dangerous as the things they fought. Violence was a way of life for Blade Dancers. Luthiel found that even talk of them was worth avoiding.

As she picked her way through the bramble, Luthiel wondered why he had come. Blade Dancers only came to a place for two reasons—either to root out some danger or to name a Chosen. The second task was reason enough for their infamy. Chosen were sent to feed Vyrl in the Vale of Mists. A more horrible doom Luthiel could not imagine—die by having your blood consumed or return horribly disfigured by the magic of the Vale. Lately, the Vyrl had been demanding more and more Chosen. One a year was normal. But this year was different. So far, they had demanded three and it was barely summer.

Maybe the Dancer is just here to deal with Elag, Luthiel told herself. *Leowin said he'd been dabbling in things he shouldn't. Or maybe there is some other danger?* She found herself hoping that this was true and that the Blade Dancer was not here for a Chosen.

Luthiel's face flushed hot with embarrassment and fear when she finally stepped out of the bramble. Leowin popped up with twigs in her hair and seemed to tremble.

Luthiel felt Leowin's hand squeezing her shoulder.

"Happy First Summer's Eve." Leowin replied.

The Blade Dancer looked up at her. His face warmed into a smile and he nodded.

"You've still got something in your hair," he said, motioning with his hand.

Leowin combed her fingers through her hair, but missed it.

"Ah, here, let me help," he said as he stood. He lifted his hand and gently plucked the last twig from Leowin's hair. "There, that's it," he said as he tossed the twig aside.

He picked up a bag from his pack and offered it to them. "Hungry?"

Luthiel looked at Leowin, who nodded. "Then have what you like. The orange ones are especially good." He motioned with his knife at some of the orange pieces of fruit that were peeking up out of the open bag.

Luthiel crouched down and picked up a piece. She recognized it as dried Yewstaff fruit. At any other time she would have happily eaten it. Yewstaff was a tree of life and his fruit was both delicious and healing to the body. Even dried, it was a gift beyond compare. But her hunger of a few minutes before had been replaced by a sick feeling in her stomach. So she just looked at it.

Leowin sat down beside her and pulled out a piece for herself. She looked at it for a moment and then nibbled at the corner.

"Just wanted to know if I was in the right place." The Blade Dancer said softly after they had eaten a bit. His gaze lingered, for a moment, on Leowin. "Is this the town of Flir Light Hollow?"

Leowin nodded her head. "Yes, Blade Dancer, you've come to Flir Light." She looked as if she was going to ask a question and then thought better of it.

Luthiel understood. She, too, was curious about why the Blade Dancer was here. But it was a sort of dreadful curiosity. She would almost rather not know why he had come. Blade Dancers only came for two reasons. Even if this one was kind, it couldn't change that simple truth. He was here to sentence someone to likely death or he was here because something dreadful had come to Flir Light.

She rolled her untouched fruit in her hand and wondered how Leowin could stomach any of it.

"Blade Dancer, what's your name?" Leowin asked.

"Vanye," he said. "And you two?"

"I'm Leowin Valshae and this is Luthiel, my sister."

The Blade Dancer paused and stared down the road. Then, he turned to Luthiel. The look in his eyes was sad—full of sympathy. It was just a glance, but there was such a depth of remorse within them that she stood staring for long moments even after the Blade Dancer had turned away.

She opened her mouth, but nothing came out.

"A lovely name. They're both lovely," he said. Leowin's face flushed and she laughed nervously.

"Vanye, a heart-gift to meet you." She extended her hand making the sign for Orin's Eye. Vanye covered her hand with his, but his face had darkened and he seemed to be fighting off a frown.

For long moments he sat there, still as a stone. There was a gentleness in his sad gaze that belied his hard form. Then his eyes dropped and his face set into grim lines. He withdrew his hand, stood up, and turned his eyes into the sunset. The gentleness of a moment before was replaced by desolation.

Luthiel's unease deepened as she watched him. *Why's he acting this way? Why did he look at me like that?* she thought.

She watched on with growing discontent as Leowin stood there struggling to find the right words to say. It was absurd, like trying to talk with a thunderstorm. She just wanted to leave, leave the Blade Dancer be and forget they ever met him.

"Vanye. It's First Summer's Eve. All of Flir Light Hollow is celebrating. Why don't you come and join us?" Leowin invited. But he just stood there. Leowin wrung her hands. "Let us at least have this night," she pleaded. "Tonight is Luthiel's birthday."

The Blade Dancer was all harsh lines and sharp angles. Then, he almost sighed. It was a simple movement, a slight flaring of the nostrils, a slow breath. Even though Vanye scared her, Luthiel felt a twinge of pity for him. Here he was doomed to bear these horrible tasks, to face and defeat one kind of monster only to have to tell families and loved ones that one they cherish will be sent as food for another.

Leowin saw the Dancer's sigh as well and appeared to be moved by sympathy. She lifted her hand, hesitated, then laid it on his arm. He was stiff and impassive as a statue.

"Please," Leowin said.

Vanye's eyes flashed with what Luthiel thought was anger. Luthiel felt the urge to take Leowin by the arm and run. What was Leowin doing? Touching a Blade Dancer!

Again there was a pause. She could see Vanye's jaw clench.

"Perhaps tonight is not the best time, perhaps it is. Flir Light is where I'm bound. Lead on. You'll forgive me if I don't celebrate."

He turned and started walking down the road. The ring of blades lifted away from the tree upon which it rested and landed, once more, on Vanye's shoulder.

"What are you doing?" Luthiel whispered.

"Making the best of a tight spot," Leowin replied. "We'd better follow him."

"What do you mean? Why don't we just get out of here? He doesn't need us."

"I don't think it's a good idea to keep a Blade Dancer waiting."

"What?" But even as the word escaped Luthiel's lips she could see the Blade Dancer standing among the lesser shadows on the road. His gleaming eyes were on them and they didn't waver. She could tell by the way he watched them that Leowin was right.

So without another word, they started back toward Flir Light. The Blade Dancer's strides were long and it was all Luthiel could do not to break into a run as she tried to keep up.

"I've heard of him," Leowin whispered as they walked behind him. "It's Vanye, the Hunter of Nine Trolls Army."

"Oh," Luthiel said hollowly. But the only thing she could think of was the way he'd looked at her with his hard, sad eyes.

The road wound its way across the backs of three hills that skirted Flir Light. As they walked, the trees to either side fell away and were replaced by conical fae holmes. Festooned with flir bug bulbs, each fae holme looked like a galaxy and, from a distance, it was difficult to distinguish treetop from starry night. Their feet followed the road as it bent downhill, flowing into a meadow crowded with elves dancing and merrymaking under the fireworks' spider light.

All about the meadow trees were decorated with wreaths and vines of living flowers. The wind rustled softly through the vines and a constant rain of petals dusted the ground and nearby revelers. The meadow sloped in a natural amphitheatre and tables were set in rows about it. In a clear space beneath them elves danced and swayed before a hillock upon which minstrals played. The hill drooped upon the shores of a lake—Aewin's Wet—sparkling with both the lights of the elves and those of night.

Halfway around the lakeshore, elves were bending their great bows in a competition of archery. Shafts hissed through the air, diving upon targets hung from trees or propped between boulders. Even though the elves were grimly serious about their archery, tonight there was laughter among the competitors and the large crowd that watched them. Wine was passed around freely and even when money changed hands it was with a laugh or a slap on the shoulder.

When they reached the rocky shores of Aewin's Wet, Luthiel's dread increased. She felt a pang of envy for the other elves as they made merry, still happily unaware of the Blade Dancer walking beside her. Perhaps it was her mood, but even by the light of four moons—silver Silva, pearl Lunen, gray Sothos, and blue Merrin—he looked dark and hard.

Tables of all kinds heaped with every sort of food ringed the meadow and all forms of fae were eating, singing, dancing, or sneaking by pairs into the wood of Eaven Vole. There were the tall and noble Ithildar, the strong and proud Gruagach, short, flame haired red-caps—goblin-kin from Rimwold in the south—and here and there were elves from the Dark Forest that lay far beyond the Gates of the East across the great Drakken Spurr Mountains. Luthiel might have grinned, or laughed out loud, or danced over the damp grass, were it not for the Blade Dancer. Instead, she looked at her feet. Leowin turned to her and gave a wan smile.

"Let's take Vanye and get him some food," she ventured. Again, Luthiel wondered at her courage.

"I guess I could eat something," she lied. Her stomach churned at even the thought of food.

"Are you still hungry?" Leowin asked Vanye.

He only nodded in reply.

At first, as they walked out onto the meadow, the merriment around them continued. Then, one by one, the elves took notice of the Blade Dancer. The music quieted as they paused to stare or whisper nervously to one another. Elves parted before him as though afraid he might, without warning, lash out at them. Even after he was well past, they stood still and somber and were slow to return to their merrymaking. But the elves near-est to him stood straight as grass blades and hushed when he passed, watching him with wary eyes. After, the merriment was never as lively as before.

Leowin gave simple greetings. But Luthiel noticed that their eyes were always drawn back to Vanye. Yet they never spoke to him or acknowledged his presence other than with their fearful eyes.

They made their way to one of the tables scattered about the mead-ow. A large group of faerie was gathered around it, helping themselves to every variety of food.

"Vanye, come here, this is Eolas, and Tarna, and Galdin," Leowin said as she grabbed Galdin by the hand. He'd seen Vanye and was walk-ing away just as Leowin caught him. Now he nodded his head in greeting to the Blade Dancer.

"It is—it is good! An honor!" he said awkwardly then hurried off before Leowin could catch him again.

"I'd introduce you to my parents but you must be very hungry!" Leowin said. "Ah but here is Minelwe! Min, come here! This is Vanye!"

As Min curtsied awkwardly and Vanye nodded in return, Luthiel grabbed Leowin by the elbow.

"Leowin, are you all right?" Luthiel said.

"I'm fine," Leowin said with a small laugh.

She squeezed Luthiel's arm as if to reassure her.

Luthiel flinched. Leowin was squeezing hard!

She opened her mouth to say something, but Leowin had already spun around—returning to Vanye before Luthiel could say another word.

Luthiel rubbed her arm where Leowin had squeezed it. It stung.

It looked as though Leowin was determined to make Vanye less threatening and she seemed to think that a bowl piled high with food might do the trick. Luthiel admired Leowin's efforts, but thought the wooden bowl Vanye held—laden with all forms of puddings, breads, fruits, both cooked and raw meats, vegetables and every kind of spice, candy and pastry imaginable—only made him look ravenous.

Vanye poked an inferno rock with his fork, watching as it toasted one half of his slice of almorah bread. Leowin picked it up and popped it into her mouth. "You eat them! Oooo! Hot!" she exclaimed, waving her hand in front of her mouth from which a thin stream of smoke was curling. Inferno rocks didn't actually burn your mouth but they sure felt hot. They were also very good—tasting of cinnamon and honeygrass. "You should try one." She motioned to the sizzling rock candy on Vanye's plate.

"I think I'll decline," he said. Leowin did her best to smile.

Luthiel was impressed by Leowin's gestures toward the Blade Dancer. Everyone else was giving him wide berth, eyeing the ring of blades on his shoulder. Luthiel felt a bit odd being so friendly with the Dancer. It was like having a dragon over for dinner.

She almost felt relieved when Galwin walked over with a shy look on his face. Like everyone else, he cast nervous looks at the Blade Dancer. But he was brave enough to approach them, which was more than most. When he asked her for a dance she felt as though a weight had lifted from her. The food on the plate in front of her was untouched and her neck was beginning to grow stiff with tension. She looked at Leowin who, for an instant, seemed to be terrified—but the moment passed and Luthiel slowly nodded her head.

"I'd love to dance," she said.

Even in the moonlight, she could see his face flush. "But, you've never said yes before," he stammered. For the first time since she met the Blade Dancer, she smiled. Galwin seemed more afraid of her than of him.

"And would you rather I said no?" she replied.

"Well no, but, you see, uh, I'm not very good at dancing," he blurted.

Luthiel tried not to laugh. She knew Galwin fancied her. She'd started to notice it about a year ago. Though she didn't share the feeling, she liked Galwin all the same and considered him a friend. What she really wanted was some time away from the Blade Dancer.

Let Leowin deal with him.

Glancing over her shoulder, she saw her chatting with him and shook her head. She still felt apprehensive but wanted to shake off her unease and enjoy herself. Perhaps dancing would help.

"Don't worry, I'll teach you," she said.

In the dim light she saw Galwin's face glow even brighter and she couldn't help but laugh at him as she dragged him out to dance.

A group of musicians were playing the stringed allatars with accompaniment by the ethereal sound of lulutes and the banging of kal-sticks. Tinae was singing, her musical voice filling the meadow with its full-bodied tones. It was a passionate song with a good beat for dancing. She grabbed Galwin's hands and led him. Soon, he'd managed to build up some confidence and was doing rather well. They danced together until green and golden-banded Tiolas rose above the horizon. A loud hail of fireworks ascended to greet the wild moon, bursting into patterns like flowers and trees. Everyone stopped to watch. Luthiel stood beside Galwin throughout the sparkling display. When it ended, Tiolas was completely free of the horizon and was joining the other moons in the sky.

Luthiel turned to Galwin with a grin on her face.

"A fine dancer you've turned out to be!" she said. "I'll be leaving now though, so you'll have to find another partner."

"Wait," Galwin said. He was fumbling with his pockets. He opened one, grabbed what was inside, and handed it to her. "A present for you, Luthiel."

"Galwin, you didn't have to."

"Please take it," he pleaded. "I wanted to give you something for your birthday."

Luthiel opened her hand. It was a pandur's box. Out of the corner of her eye, she could see Galwin's smile start to fade. Luthiel laughed quietly. She couldn't help but find it to be funny. He had probably just pulled out whatever was in his pocket.

"That wasn't–" he stammered.

"Oh a pandur's box!" Luthiel interrupted. She was having fun watching all of the conflicting expressions dance across Galwin's face. "Hmm, I wonder what's inside?" she taunted.

Galwin was turning three shades of pale. "You don't have to–" he blurted.

Before Galwin could mouth the word "open," with a quick flick of her wrist, Luthiel popped the lid. From out of the box shot a long-stemmed rose. Galwin was blushing furiously.

"Now that's very sweet," Luthiel cooed. At that moment, the rose exploded with a loud "pop!" and a flash. A brown cloud of smoke filled the air around them. The cloud stank terribly. Luthiel coughed, laughed, held her nose and waved her hand.

"Luthiel, I'm so sorry," Galwin apologized.

Luthiel reached out and grabbed his shoulder.

"No Galwin. I loved it. I needed to laugh," she said, smiling.

This time, he smiled back at her sheepishly.

"Happy birthday," he managed as she smiled and laughed once more. She was surprised at all the fun she was having. Galwin was normally so shy he couldn't even speak to her.

As she turned to leave, Luthiel glanced at the table where she'd left Leowin and Vanye. They weren't there.

Where could they be? she wondered.

Revelers passed in front of her, blocking her view. She pushed through them, standing on a stone as she looked out into the crowd.

Then she saw them. They were standing not too far away beside a group of elves that were joining the dance. For all the movement, Vanye's eyes stayed fixed on Leowin. She was talking and kept waving her hand at the dancers, and then she leaned close to Vanye.

Luthiel, who was walking toward them, could hear her last few words.

"Will you dance with me?" Leowin said.

"No, lady," he replied.

Leowin only grinned at him and stepped out among the dancers. Soon she was arm in arm with a handsome young elf. But she often looked at Vanye whose eyes never left her as she skipped and turned.

Luthiel watched the Blade Dancer for a few minutes before she felt brave enough to join him. It was awkward standing beside him. She didn't know what to say. So she stood for a while in silence.

"Vanye –"

"Your sister is very beautiful," Vanye interrupted.

In shocked silence, Luthiel watched as he walked out among the dancers and caught Leowin by the hand. She stepped away from her partner and turned to face Vanye, taking his other hand in hers. Neither said a word and for a moment they stood still, face to face, among the swirling revelers. Then, slowly, they began to dance.

Luthiel could feel her heart pounding in her throat. Her sister in the arms of a Blade Dancer! Vanye moved with an almost otherworldly grace and Leowin seemed to float like a thread in his hand.

She stood there alone, caught up in disbelief, watching as her sister and the Blade Dancer swirled back and forth. A sick fascination fell over her and she was unable to do anything other than watch the dance. It was somehow both beautiful and terrible. Leowin and Vanye were by far the most graceful and daring of all the dancers and they seemed only to grow more so as they continued. Were it not for the Blade Dancer, Luthiel would have clapped and laughed. But instead, a melancholy fell over her and she felt that, somehow, something about it was sad.

"Luthiel! Luthiel!" The loud calls snapped her out of her reverie and she turned her head to see Lorethain sitting on top of a small hill waving at her.

THE CHOSEN

As she walked away from the dancers, she noticed Winowe and Glendoras sitting beside Lorethain. They had all gathered round a flat boulder and were busy eating, drinking and talking with uncle Hueron— a muscular Valemar who looked as if he might be at least half Gruagach. Luthiel jogged up to where they were sitting. Lorethain was drinking from a tall tankard of honey wine and Winowe was looking at him crossly.

"Where's Leowin? I thought she was with you," Lorethain said.

Luthiel, whose eyes kept darting toward the crowd gathering around her sister and Vanye, suddenly felt her ears go hot.

"I don't know," she said.

"Well, I'd like to know where she is," Winowe said. "You'd think she'd take more interest in her little sister's birthday." She smiled at Luthiel before she turned to Lorethain with a scowl on her face. "If you keep gulping it down like that, it'll crack your skull come morning," Winowe said, motioning to his tankard.

Lorethain waved his hand absently. "Ah, mother, I know how much I can handle," he said.

"So do I. And I can tell you're well beyond it," Winowe said.

Lorethain grinned and took another long pull at his tankard.

Luthiel frowned. Normally, Lorethain's drinking upset her but she hardly heard them talking as her eyes kept drifting back to the gathering crowd below and the two figures at its center. The dancers around them were laughing and cheering at the pair.

Maybe I'm worrying too much, she chided. *I need to be strong—like Leowin.*

"Luthiel, why don't you take a seat?" Glendoras asked gently. She looked into his kind eyes, sighed and sat down.

Lorethain glanced at her and then looked out at the crowd. Something caught his eye and he frowned as he peered down at the swaying figures. Luthiel could feel her heart in her throat again and her eyes were drawn once more to the dancers.

Lorethain stood up. "Is that a Blade Dancer?"

Hueron choked on his drink. "What did you say?" he sputtered.

Luthiel was watching again. It was terrible, but she couldn't help herself. How could they be cheering? He was with her sister.

"Vanye," she whispered.

Now they were all looking at her. Even Glendoras' eyes seemed to take on a harsher cast. She shrank from them.

"What did you say?" Winowe said softly.

But Luthiel didn't want to say anything else. She just sat there, not daring to meet her family's eyes, unable to keep from looking at the crowd that had now blocked her sister and Vanye from view.

"What do you know about Vanye?" This time it was Lorethain who asked. But she couldn't bring herself to speak. It was just too much.

Lorethain took a step toward her.

"If you know something, then tell us," he said grimly.

They were all looking at her now and though Lorethain had said it, she could tell by their furrowed brows that Glendoras and Hueron were thinking the same thing. She couldn't find her voice.

"I can't–" was all she could manage.

Winowe placed a hand on Lorethain's shoulder, gently turning him away from Luthiel.

"It's her birthday," she said softly, meeting his eyes.

"But you heard what she said," he snapped.

"Even so, show a little kindness. She is not so ready as you, Lorethain, to face the grim things of this world."

Lorethain sighed.

"I'm sorry," he said. "It's just that—" he glanced back at the dancers but Leowin and Vanye were out of sight.

"We shouldn't be jumping at shadows," he said with a shake of his head. "Especially not on First Summer's Eve—your birthday!" He motioned to four packages tied with ribbon that were sitting on the blanket they'd draped across the stone.

"Happy birthday," Lorethain said.

His happy birthday was followed by echoes of the same from the others. If a little subdued, they sounded sincere all the same.

"Thanks," she said.

Lorethain tapped a long thin present wrapped with black and silver thread. "This one first," he grinned at her. "I spent a year making it." He winked. Luthiel grinned and threw her arms around his shoulders.

"All right you bear!" She replied and reached for the present.

Her hand had just touched the paper when Glendoras said, "Is that Leowin?"

Her hand hovered over the paper. She opened her mouth to reply, but nothing came out.

A loud cheer suddenly rose up through the crowd of elves below. As one, they turned their heads toward the noise. Below, the elves had formed into a ring. At its center were Vanye and Leowin. The Blade Dancer moved as though he'd caught fire. Leowin flowed with him like an accompanying cloud of white smoke. And on both of their faces, she saw a look of utter surrender.

In the faces of her family, Luthiel saw only shock.

She didn't need to say anything. They all saw Leowin now. They stared on unbelieving.

No one spoke as Vanye and Leowin continued their dance. They watched on, unable to tear their eyes away. Finally, the music stopped. Vanye lowered Leowin to the earth. She looked into Vanye's eyes for a moment longer, then blinked and glanced around as though suddenly self-conscious. Everyone was watching them.

Vanye, who had seemed warm and gentle a moment before, became stiff and returned the onlookers' gaze with his hard eyes. They backed away from him. The cheers stopped and where there was clapping before now all was silent.

Leowin quivered like a moth, darting glances here and there. Vanye stood motionless beside her.

"Storm crows every one," Hueron said. "Nothing good ever comes from 'em." He nodded toward the Blade Dancer.

"Remember Nine Trolls' Army?" Glendoras said.

"That's what I'm talking about. We didn't need the Blade Dancer. We had our *Cauthrim* blades. We handled that army just fine," Hueron said.

"After he killed the nine trolls," Glendoras said. "We fought a broken army."

"*Him?*" Hueron stared down at the harsh figure. A few lonely notes rippled through the air as someone tried a tune on a lulute.

"The same," Glendoras replied.

Lorethain stared blankly into his tankard for a moment and then seemed to come to himself. He turned to Luthiel with his eyes flashing and grabbed her by the wrist.

"We're going down there right now," he said.

"Rushing won't help," Winowe replied, placing a hand on his arm. "The Blade Dancer's news won't change now or in an hour."

Lorethain turned to Luthiel. "So you knew he was here?"

She nodded.

"Why didn't you tell me when I asked you?"

Luthiel started talking suddenly, without realizing what she was saying.

"We were playing tap-and-turn near the East Wind when we saw him. We were scared and we tried to hide, but he stopped next to us and started talking. He said he was trying to find Flir Light so we led him back here," she said in a rush. She couldn't help but feel that all of this was somehow her fault.

Lorethain shook his head. Then he turned and looked down into the meadow.

All was still. The elves seemed to be waiting, holding their breath. Vanye stepped away from Leowin. As he withdrew, he seemed to grow darker. Leowin saw them and, with a last glance at Vanye, started walking up the hill. Vanye came on behind her.

Glendoras and Winowe locked eyes for a moment.

"Is he?" Winowe said. But Glendoras only placed his hand behind her ear and nodded. Winowe raised her hand to cover her mouth but Luthiel could see her fearful eyes. Glendoras kissed her on the forehead, then left her side to join Lorethain who bristled before the approaching Blade Dancer.

Lorethain nodded to Glendoras.

Luthiel felt her heart sink even lower and she drifted away from her family.

Of all days, why did he have to come on this day? She asked herself. But she realized it didn't matter. Regardless, the Blade Dancer would have come and, for such arrivals, there were no good days.

Leowin rushed up the hill and came to stand beside her grabbing her hand. Vanye's eyes were intense, his face like a statue. Luthiel watched him approach, unable to move.

"Vanye, is that you?" Lorethain asked.

Vanye nodded his head. "Lorethain," he said.

Lorethain gestured to the Blade Dancer with his hand. "Father, we know him."

"Indeed, how could I forget the hunter of Nine Trolls Army," Glendoras said.

Vanye just stood there like a great bird of prey. The ring of blades glistened on his shoulder.

"You were right," Hueron said under his breath.

"You doubted me?" Glendoras said arching an eyebrow.

"Hello Vanye." Hueron said with a nod.

Happy First Summers and other simple greetings made their way around the small gathering. Lorethain pursed his lips as if carefully considering what to say.

Then everything grew quiet and they all watched Vanye. The silence stretched on. The lulute players had started again.

"Let's not play games with words," Glendoras said after a long pause. "We all know there are only two reasons why a Blade Dancer would come to a place like Flir Light. So what danger are we in, Vanye? Or have you come to claim a Chosen?"

Luthiel flinched at Glendoras' words.

Vanye paused and frowned as though unwilling to speak.

"Your daughters have shown me rare kindness." For a moment, his sad gaze lingered on Luthiel. She stared at her hands.

Vanye continued. "This is the part of my duty that makes me wish I had never found *Li*." Again, he paused.

Why's he taking so long? Luthiel wondered.

"Enough," Glendoras said. "Name the Chosen."

Luthiel felt herself letting go of Leowin's hand and falling back against the tree behind her. There it was right before her and she never noticed. The way Vanye acted around her, the way he seemed surprised when he heard her name.

The way he looked at me with sad eyes, she thought. *That's why he danced with Leowin. To get away from—*

"It's me." Luthiel mouthed the words but hardly any sound came out.

She felt nubs of tree bark making small indentations in her back. They stung, but not enough. She pressed harder. The nubs bit deeper and she was reminded of Elag's tree.

She grabbed the bark with her hands. Her legs tensed. She wanted to run.

But where could she go that the werewolf wouldn't find her? She was breathing heavy—as if she'd already run a great distance even though she was standing still.

She stood there for long moments, unable to raise her eyes to the Blade Dancer who'd come for her.

She slowly lifted her chin. There were tears in her eyes but she brushed them away before they had the chance to fall. Finally, she looked at him.

But he wasn't looking at her.

"It's–" she whispered again but she couldn't speak anymore. She couldn't say it.

No one noticed her; all eyes were on Vanye who was standing there with his eyebrows lowered.

"It's Leowin." Vanye said.

Luthiel felt her legs give way. She slid down the tree and sat on the ground with her face buried in her arms. She felt as though she would laugh and cry at the same time. An incredible sense of relief washed over her. She wasn't the one! Then, she raised her head from between her arms.

Lorethain gripped his tankard hard. The cup clattered against the stone table. Winowe was crying. Hueron growled. But what shocked Luthiel the most was Glendoras. In all her fifteen years, she'd never seen him angry. Now his face contorted into a look of utter rage. He clenched his fist so tightly that cords of muscle in his forearm stood out.

"How dare they," he said in a quiet tone that carried more force than any shout.

Hueron locked eyes with Glendoras and seemed to share his rage. "Four in one year. It flies in the face of their promise!" He spat on the ground.

Then she looked at Leowin. She was deathly white. Her eyes fluttered, she was trembling. Even the tips of her ears seemed to quaver. Luthiel grabbed the little pouch around her neck.

How could I have possibly felt relief? she thought. *I won't see her again, not in a thousand years.*

She recalled Leowin as a child, laughing as she splashed in the puddles of a summer shower, making garlands of flowers in the springtime. Leowin had stolen her journal again. She was angry then, but now it made her feel sad. Then she saw an older Leowin, her body like a limp doll. Blood spilled from a gash in her neck and trickled out of two eyeless sockets. Dark forms stood above her—with blood in their mouths.

Leowin is going to die and I felt relieved? It terrified her. She returned her gaze to Leowin who was doing her best to remain composed. She could see the determination in her eyes as she gave a stiff nod. But her face was pale, like frost touched by moonlight.

Hiding her face in shame for her cowardice, Luthiel slipped into the shadows beneath the tree and scampered off under the cover of darkness. She climbed until she found a quiet shadow between two boulders. Below, she could see her family clearly and she watched on as she cried. Catching a glimpse of Leowin's tear-streaked face, she punched the boulder in frustration. Below, her family was silently watching on as Leowin buried her face in Lorethain's cloak.

"I can't let them take her away," she muttered to herself. Her mind raced.

I could sneak away with her into hiding.

But even as the thought crossed her mind she shook her head.

And then what? Wait to be hunted down by Blade Dancers? Or worse? She held her head in her hands.

"No! No! No! That won't do at all. The Vyrl have a werewolf. They'll send him."

She rocked back and forth on her heels, punched the boulders and the dirt, pulled her hair but none of it seemed to help.

"It's no use!" she growled to herself in frustration. "Why did it have to be her? Anyone but her!" She tossed a rock down the hill but as she watched it fall into the darkness a chill passed over her.

"Anyone but her," she whispered. Then she sat for a while, listening only to her breathing, afraid to continue down the path which her thoughts were leading her.

"It could be anyone but Leowin," she said finally and then in a barely audible whisper—"It could be me."

She looked up at the moons. She wanted nothing more in that terrible moment than to fly away to some other place. But even the moons seemed to reject her, blazing down on her with a stern glare.

"I don't even belong here, do I?" She looked around at Flir Light as though seeing it for the first time. "It's not even my real home. I don't even know my real home." Then she cast her eyes out to the rolling hills of the Minonowe.

"If there's anyone who should be going, it should be me," she said. Though she was still and nearly silent, her heart was pounding so hard her fingertips throbbed.

Below, her family gathered around Leowin. Winowe put an arm over her shoulder and Glendoras patted her back as they slowly walked off, leaving Vanye alone. He stood still, like a black spike thrust up from the earth, casting long shadows.

If she was going to do anything, it would have to be now. But her body didn't seem to want to move and it took great effort just to stand. Her legs didn't feel right and they wobbled as she made her way down the hill. It was unreal, as though she were watching herself.

I must be mad, she thought. *No sane person would do this.* But her feet continued along their path until they carried her to Vanye. He was standing alone with a frown on his face, his left hand clenched into a fist. At first, it seemed that he didn't notice her. She just stood there a few feet away from him, staring at the ground.

He motioned with his left hand.

"Your family's down there if you want to join them." His hand fell back to his side and his eyes seemed to unfocus. She started at his bleak tone and it took her a while to gather the courage to speak.

"Vanye, I came to talk with you." Her throat felt tight and dry but she continued regardless.

Vanye shook his head.

"I know what it is you're going to ask me." His eyes flashed dangerously but in them she also saw sadness. "I wish I could give you another answer."

She took a step back, almost ran. But something, she didn't know what, held her there.

"It's not what you think. I just wanted to know if—"

The Blade Dancer glared at her. Her voice broke, her legs wanted to run but somehow she managed to stand her ground.

"I just wanted to know if you'd let me go to the Vale instead."

Vanye turned so that she couldn't see his face. His sharp form loomed over her like a barricade. Again she felt the urge to run, again she resisted. Then the Blade Dancer let out a low chuckle.

"Well, you certainly have surprised me. Brave, though, and very foolish." His eyes reflected the moons' glare. He reached out, and before she could flinch away, caught her shoulder in his firm grip. He pulled her closer till they were almost nose to nose. His eyes bored into hers, searching.

"No one has ever made such an offer." His grip tightened and the gleam in his eyes grew even more intense. "You know that what you say is against our law?" he said.

She felt her breath catch yet within her there was a small spark of defiance.

"But the Vyrl have also broken the law. Leowin will be their fourth." She stood beneath the intense gleam of his eyes for a few more moments wondering if she'd said too much.

"Perhaps I've drifted just enough to take you up." For an instant, he seemed unsure of himself.

"You will?" she asked, not knowing what to hope for.

"I will?" His eyes wandered for a moment toward the path Leowin had taken. His hand tightened yet again, and then his eyes returned with an even greater intensity in them.

"No."

Luthiel froze. One last time, she almost turned away. But, somehow, she stood fast.

"I could go anyway," she said.

"You don't understand," Vanye said. "You can't. I can't. No elf can. It cannot be done."

"Please," Luthiel said. "She's my sister."

"You're asking me to kill you."

"I'm asking you to save her."

Vanye stood still for a moment. His breath steamed in the night air.

"Did you like dancing with her?" she asked.

The Blade Dancer's eyes flashed.

"This is ridiculous. You're not going," he said resting his hand on his sword hilt.

"Well, then, you'll have to kill two people tonight," she said, making a move to walk around him.

His arm shot out, catching her across the shoulders. He must have meant to grab her but his blow fell heavy, knocking her off her feet and onto the ground. She used her hands to break her fall. But when she struck the ground, her pouch slipped out from under her shirt. The draw strings must have loosened, for her Stone rolled out of the bag and onto the ground. It bounced once, twice, and then rolled along the ground before coming to rest in front of Vanye.

It glimmered, the small spark at its center shining in the darkness.

Luthiel stared, disbelieving, at the Stone. How had it popped out like that? She shifted her eyes, glancing fearfully at the Blade Dancer.

Vanye stood still for a moment, staring at the Stone. He stooped, reached out his hand. It opened above the Stone, closed, opened again. Then, in a fluid motion, he scooped the Stone into the palm of his hand. Cradling it, he walked over to her and gently returned it to her pouch.

"I am sorry," he said.

Luthiel's breath caught in her throat. But she nodded her acceptance as Vanye helped her stand.

"Now listen to me carefully." He waited until he was satisfied he had her full attention.

"You are going to have to move fast. The Vyrl will send their were-wolf Othalas for your sister. You're going to have to pass into the Vale and reach them before he returns. I may be able to delay him. But it still doesn't give you much time. So you have to leave tonight. Do you under-stand me?"

She did her best to control her fear. *Now you've really done it, Luthy* she thought. *Like it or not you're going to the Vale of Mists.*

"I—I understand," she stammered.

"You are a child. If you knew what this thing is that you're doing you would not be doing it."

"I choose to," she replied, a little steadier.

"Good. Now the fastest way is to turn west and follow the Rendalas. It spills into the Vale at Withy Wraith falls. Beside the falls is an old stair-case. The staircase leads to the floor of the Vale. From there you will have to find your own way to the Vyrl."

This time, she couldn't bring herself to speak so she only nodded. The fear was nearly overwhelming and she was having trouble meeting the Blade Dancer's gaze. Vanye seemed to notice and grabbed her chin, lifting her face till their eyes met.

"Every thousand years or so, someone lives to return. I've met two. When I asked them how they made it, they both told me the same thing. They didn't give up. I hope to see you again, Luthiel, so don't lose heart." He paused for a moment.

"The only reason I will help you," he glanced off toward the depart-ing Leowin "the only reason, is that I believe you might have a chance."

He let go of her chin and she looked away.

"You probably tell that to all Chosen," she said.

"Only those I think will hear it," he replied.

"I'll try to remember what you said."

"That will just have to do for now. I'll do what I can to delay the werewolf." He slapped her on the shoulder. "Now, you'd better get going."

She turned, took a few steps, then stopped and looked over her shoulder. "Thank you," she said.

"I should thank you. What you're doing has never been done; it is a far better thing than you know." He drew his sword and touched it to the ring of blades on his shoulder in salute. "You won't be forgotten." Then he lowered his sword as he spoke the ancient farewell. "May your feet always walk in the light of two suns."

"May the moonshadow never fall upon you," she replied.

"Now go!" Vanye said and she was off, pausing only long enough to gather her unopened birthday presents. She laughed grimly at herself for running toward the danger; she was so afraid she couldn't help but run.

SILENT FAREWELL

Luthiel rushed toward her fae holme. She skirted the revelers, hurrying past those who tried to talk or held their hands out in gestures of comfort. Friends and acquaintances alike were left staring after her as she fled down the hill.

"Wait! I thought we'd talk!" Galwin shouted as he ran after her. But she only ran faster.

"Can't talk," she muttered.

"I thought we'd–" he sputtered as she outdistanced him. "Well, thanks for the dance anyway!" he yelled after her.

Near the bottom of the hill, she spotted her family. They were in the middle of a large group of elves gathering around Leowin. Those closest to Leowin were laying their hands on her, murmuring quietly. She peered through the crowd, hoping to catch a last look. But too many were blocking the way.

Despite herself, she stopped running and took a few steps toward the crowd. But even standing on tiptoe, she couldn't see Leowin. She stood there for a moment longer, then started pushing her way through them. She was jostled but somehow she got closer. Soon, she was standing less than twenty feet from her sister. Peering through a break in the crowd, she watched Leowin gracefully accept each gesture of comfort. Though Leowin's voice was calm, Luthiel could see the fear in her eyes, the trembling of her hands.

Luthiel couldn't move. She wanted to give Leowin comfort, to let her know she was going instead. Wasn't there something she could say?

Luthiel stood there for a time, worrying over what she could do or say. To her, it seemed only a few moments. But it was actually much longer. Minutes passed as Luthiel stared into space trying to think of something to say to her sister. But she never found anything that would suit.

Just leave, she thought to herself. *I'm only making it worse.*

Then, as she was about to back her way through the crowd, Leowin saw her. Their eyes met. The crowd seemed to notice Luthiel as well and the quiet murmuring fell into silence as they turned to stare at her.

"I saw you running down the hill. Why were you running?" Leowin asked.

Luthiel stood there not knowing what to say. "I was afraid–" her voice broke.

Leowin's eyebrows lowered and she frowned.

"So am I," she said. "Even though everyone is here, I feel so lonely."

Luthiel ached. If only she could hug her. If only she could explain.

"I can't," she whispered, more to herself than to anyone else. She stood for another moment, torn. Then she realized she couldn't stay an instant longer. She could lose her resolve, or worse, tell them what she was planning. She wanted to tell them even now. If she did, they would try to stop her. She remembered Vanye's words.

"You know that what you say is against the law?" he had said. Hardening herself, she looked back into Leowin's eyes.

Leowin gasped, mistaking Luthiel's firm look for anger.

"Luthiel?" she asked. Luthiel could see tears welling up in her eyes.

"I have to go," she said simply. In the quiet, her voice seemed to carry far up the hillside. She almost broke again. How could she treat her this way?

"I love you so much!" she said in a rush. She turned away and ran up the hill.

"Don't leave!" Leowin cried after her. "Don't go! I'm afraid! I need you!" There was a hysterical edge to Leowin's voice. A sharp pang ripped through Luthiel's chest and tears streamed freely down her face. But she didn't turn around. She knew if she looked into Leowin's eyes again she wouldn't be able to stand it. She would break and everything—her decision, her dim hope that she could save Leowin—would melt away. She would be helpless again, able to do nothing more than comfort her until the werewolf came.

Then, anger rose in her. She wouldn't let it happen. She would do something. Her heart pounded and she ran faster.

"I love you, Leowin," she whispered as she ran. But no one heard. Behind her, Leowin struggled against the arms of Winowe and Lorethain.

"Let me go! I want to see my sister!" she cried.

"Leowin, let her go. Can't you see she's afraid too?" Winowe whispered into her ear.

"Let her!? She's a coward. A COWARD!!!" she yelled.

Luthiel flinched. But she didn't turn around.

She'll understand, she thought. *She'll understand when I tell her.* But a horrible dread fell over her and she feared she'd never have the chance. Luthiel ran as fast as she could away from the crowd, away from her family, and away from Leowin. Fae holmes slid by her in the darkness as she sprinted up a trail she'd walked a thousand times. Afraid of more encounters with friends or family, she was careful to stick to the shadows and the trail led her home without further mishap.

Out front, she was met by her moon-hound Kindre. He nudged her. But she was so preoccupied by her thoughts of Leowin that she didn't notice him at all. With a hurt expression in his eyes he loped behind her as she entered the front wind-hole.

Flir bug light streamed down onto her, making small white circles at her feet. It was a comfortable place filled with arching branches and a high ceiling of green. Carpets of moss were shot through with pebble pathways and water ran in furrows down the great tree to collect in basins of living wood that kept it ever fresh. Hanging white ivy and skeins of fine cloth divided rooms that were roofed by intertwining branches. High above, a breeze rustled through the leaves. Small bells hung from wind charms tinkled softly. It was a sound slightly changed from that of the open wood, a sound that reminded her of rest and happiness.

Will I ever hear it again? Luthiel thought. The pain in her chest hadn't gone away yet. She figured it wouldn't until she saw Leowin again—*if* she saw Leowin again. She exhaled, trying to calm herself. Then she bunched her body up and leapt onto one of the lower branches. She sprang from one to another until she came to her loft near the leaf-roof some fifty feet up. It was a wide row of interwoven branches jutting from the trunk. For walls it had brightly colored cloths that were bound to the branches arching up from the boughs that made the floor. It reminded her of a cocoon. When it rained she loved to sit and listen to it pitter-patter on the leaves above her.

She stopped for a moment and her eyes fell to the heartwood basin Winowe had shaped for her. In its water she could see her face reflected. She stepped closer. A small and afraid girl stared back at her. Her eyes were red, her hair rumpled and the dry streaks of tears were plain on her face. Disgusted with what she saw, she splashed the water.

Falling back onto her bed, she let out a long sigh. She wanted to fall asleep, curl up and forget it happened. But the longer she lay there the more the aching in her chest grew.

"What am I doing!" she snapped. Sitting up, she looked over her loft. "I don't even know what to take," she said. For a time, she just sat there, staring at her plate shaped shelves, feeling the ache in her chest spread down into her stomach. She'd never been more than a few days from Flir Light and that was always with Glendoras or Lorethain or uncle Hueron. They helped her pack, so she had little idea of what to bring with her on the long journey to the Vale.

Finally, she stood. Rushing frantically back and forth, she grabbed things at random throwing them into a pile on the floor. Slowly, she sifted through it considering each object carefully before she chose it or discarded it. Soon she had a pack from this corner and some shoes from another, a wind charm from her windows and a water gourd from beside her bed. A small coil of rope—light but strong, and plenty of socks soon followed. Her brow furrowed as she tried to remember all the things Lorethain took when he traveled.

When she was halfway through, she noticed what a horrible mess her room had become. So she started meticulously putting everything back in its place and from that point on, she was careful not to disturb her loft. It seemed almost a sacred place to her now that she would likely never see it again. She didn't want to leave it ransacked. So she was careful and when she was finished, her bed bundle was tidy and all her things were in order.

As she looked her loft over one last time, she ran through what she'd packed in her head. Two pairs of boots, a nice thick bedroll, a spare cloak, three tunics, socks and more socks, rope, enough food for two weeks—mostly nuts, cheese, dried fruit and almorah cakes—two wind charms, good for keeping the rain off, and her best map were all stuffed into her pack. With them were some of her birthday presents—a vial of honeywine from Lorethain, a knife from Hueron and her Wyrd Stone, which rested in the pouch around her neck.

On a second thought, she pulled the knife from her pile. She was going to strap it to her belt when she noticed the sheath—made of blued steel—was warm to the touch. Curious now, she drew it.

The blade, a little more than a foot in length, cleared the sheath with a low chime. It was a bright metal, highlighted with tints of red and blue. Its single edge ran down the blade in waves and just above the hilts a round stamp, textured like the face of a moon, was pressed into the metal.

Wanting a better look, she held it close to her face.

She could feel heat against her skin and through the hilt upon the palm of her hand. A thin line of smoke rose from it. In the metal stamp and along its edge she could see dancing flecks of red and blue fire. Her eyes were drawn at last to the stamp. It was round like a moon but it looked like a—

"Dragon eye," she whispered. "Of all moons save Gorothoth, I fear you most. Cauthraus dragon eye."

Everything, the heat, the smoke, the shape of Cauthraus stamped on the blade told her one thing.

Hueron has given me a blade made of metal from the red moon—Cauthraus.

It was a very valuable gift. But it was a weapon, and very grim. It made her feel ill at ease as she strapped it to her belt.

I may need it where I'm going, she thought.

Satisfied that she'd thought of everything, she walked over to the shelf beside her bed. On it rested her journal. On the journal's cover, in silver letters, was her name—*Luthiel Valshae.*

Valshae was Luthiel's adopted last name. Her first name was given by her true parents who had written it on a note. The note, which was fastened to her carriage when she was abandoned in Flir Light Hollow, read *Please care for our Luthiel as if she were your own.* At the bottom of the note was the letter M. in common script beside its equivalent in the high speech ⚹.

The note was still folded, yellowed and dew smattered, into the inside front cover of her journal.

For a moment, she considered taking it with her. With a sigh, she decided not to. She'd leave it, something for people to remember her by. She turned to the first blank page, grabbed a quill from her shelf and wrote:

First Summer

Leowin, Lorethain, Mother, Father

I could not stand the thought of losing you, any of you. So I've left for the Vale of Mists to take the place of Leowin. You've treated me better than I deserve—as one of your own—and I will love you always.

Luthiel

P.S. If I do not return, please give this journal to Leowin.

She considered it for a second longer and then tucked it beneath the cushions of her bed.

"It will have to do," she said, giving her room one last look.

She hefted her pack and glanced at her reflection in the basin again. She looked a little better. Her eyes were clearer, less afraid. But she felt stretched and strained. With a curt nod to her reflection, she turned on her heel and bounded down from her loft. Kindre was waiting for her. She stopped to give him a hug and tousle his ears before hurrying out the front wind hole.

"Good-bye Kindre," she said, trying to keep her voice from catching.

Head cocked to one side, Kindre watched as she walked away.

She found the shortest road out and then skirted Flir Light, careful to choose the paths that weren't well traveled. When she was some distance away, she turned around taking a final look at the lights twinkling through the trees.

"Good-bye," she said. Then she turned and started making her way into the woods of Eaven Vole. In the east the sky was starting to brighten.

INTO THE WORLD
OF DREAMS

As Luthiel walked, worries began to gnaw at her. How long would it take the werewolf to reach Flir Light? How would she find the Vyrl? What if she became lost? The more worried she became the faster she walked. Presently she broke into a jog. Her pounding limbs, her breathing, the slight burn in her muscles all helped. But the sense of anxiety hung with her.

She was so wrapped up in her thoughts that she nearly ran headlong into Marl. At the last instant, she turned aside. Still, her shoulder brushed him and she spun, trying to keep her balance.

Marl grimaced at her touch, as though it had hurt him, then glared down at her.

She froze.

Though an elf, Marl looked more like a creature of nightmares. He stood a head taller than most elves; his limbs were long, ungainly, ending in massive hands and feet. But by some defect of blood or birth, his bones were overgrown. The tips of his finger-joints penetrated the skin, sharpening into claws. His elbows clove through his flesh in wicked spikes and his mouth was a nest of long teeth.

While still only a child, Marl had lived alone, away from the other elves who feared him. But a family from Flir light had pitied the deformed boy and took him in. For a time, besides the occasional taunt from other children, Marl found acceptance. But that was before Marl got into his first fight. Armed with spines like knives, Marl left the bully badly cut and bleeding. Winowe, even with her gift for healing, was barely able to save him. After, Marl's horrified parents sent him to live with Elag. To Luthiel, it seemed that being Elag's ward had only made Marl more aggressive. But there were no further instances of violence to prove her misgivings.

Elag's other ward, Vane, was never far from Marl and her heart sank as she heard his voice.

"Where are you going Luthiel?" Vane said as he stepped from behind a tree. Vane was the older than Luthiel by almost two years but unlike Marl, his features were perfect in every way. His skin, his golden hair, his light-blue eyes. He was almost too perfect, like a flower locked in ice.

"Ralith, go! Tell Elag we found her," Vane said over his shoulder.

A third elf, this one tall and long limbed, sprang from the tree line.

"Strangeling's in real trouble this time," Ralith said as he rushed by Luthiel and back toward Flir Light.

'Strangeling' was a name Vane had given her years before. Many of the other elves, who thought her odd, had picked it up. Just hearing it made her stomach ball up into knots.

He's gone to find Elag! I've got to get away from them!

With a growing sense of dread, she turned her eyes back to Vane.

Vane Rauth was another rarity—a prince from a noble family in the southlands of Rimwold. It was said that a Rauth who did not demonstrate talent for sorcery could not become a lord. Vane had failed to show talent. So his father Tannias sent him to Flir Light to study under Elag.

For Vane, it was exile. In the Rimwold, he was a prince; here he was barely an apprentice. Vane loathed his exile, but Tannias, who was a skillful politician, was grooming Vane to be his heir—should he show even the barest touch of Wyrd. From time to time, Tannias would visit Vane while on one of his trips north, lavishing his son with extravagant gifts.

Vane jealously guarded his family secrets, which Luthiel only knew about because of Leowin. The way Vane took charge, you'd think he was Elag's chief apprentice—and half of Flir Light did! Vane, not one to show his soft underbelly, disliked Luthiel and Leowin even more for what they knew about him.

She recovered her composure and sidestepped around Marl who fell into pace with her. He frowned as he walked, flinching with each step. She found it difficult not to feel sorry for him.

"None of your business, Vane," she replied as she kept walking.

"Elag told us to keep an eye on you and to let him know if you do anything strange." He said the word without emphasis, but it jarred her nonetheless. "A good thing too, because last night we followed you on your chase. You remember, with Leowin?"

Luthiel kept her pace, pretending to ignore him. But her heart quickened.

Vane and Marl continued to walk beside her in silence for a few moments.

"I think it's sad what happened to Leowin. You always hear about Chosen, but you never think it would happen to someone you know. I don't know how the lords decide these things, but if I were Tuorlin, I wouldn't just choose at random. No, I'd choose unwanted people first— like girl orphans. What do you think about that?"

Her ears burned and she glared at Vane.

Careful, she cautioned against her rising anger. *He's as polished as a rill-adder and just as treacherous.*

She took a deep breath and kept walking.

Vane studied her, eyes glinting like smooth stones.

"You and Leowin took something that doesn't belong to you," Vane persisted.

"So you followed us. Doesn't surprise me at all. A couple of stalkers like you wouldn't think to respect a person's privacy," she said hotly.

"We saw you Luthiel," Vane said softly. "We know what you stole from Elag. Something old and precious. Theft of such a thing, I'm certain, would carry a heavy penalty."

Luthiel stopped, turned toward Vane and glared up at him. Vane smiled back at her.

"It was mine, Vane. It was with me when I was a baby and Elag took it then. I'm just claiming what was mine!"

"I don't think Elag will see it that way." He grinned, but his eyes flashed dangerously. "No, he's not at all forgiving, is he Marl?" Marl gave a short laugh and ran his tongue over his teeth. There was blood in his mouth and Luthiel wondered if he'd bitten himself. "You know how unkind he can be, don't you?"

"He keeps cruel company. You would know better," she said.

Vane's perfect face suddenly became very cold.

"You'd find out if we took you to him," he said. "But I'll offer you better than you deserve. If you give me what I ask, I'll let you go."

Vane reached out as if to touch her. She backed away stumbling as she rushed.

"Woah! See how she starts!" Vane and Marl both laughed at her. "All I want is the Stone and—" his eyes seemed to take on a distant, glazed look. "And one lock of your hair. A small price to ask in return for my silence."

Luthiel involuntarily touched her hair. "You've asked me this before. But you never told me why."

"Why? I have shown you kindness you do not deserve and you bother me with questions. Luthiel, it is a small price. And the Stone—whatever Leowin told you was a lie. What would a girl orphan be doing with a Wyrd Stone?" He laughed. "Can't you see? It's absurd!"

"They are mine, both of them. You won't have anything from me, Vane! No hair, no Stone. Go away! Having you around is price enough!"

Vane flexed his hands. "If you don't hand it over, we'll have to take it from you. I would like nothing more."

She stood there paralyzed, looking from Vane to Marl, not sure what to do. Both were taller than her and much stronger. She was sure, given a chance, that she could outrun them. But they were too close to her now for her to just run off.

She didn't have time to think long, though, as Vane stepped closer to her and put his hands on her shoulders.

"So what is it, then?" he said.

Luthiel nodded her head slowly. She reached for the pouch at her chest and began undoing its strings.

Vane's eyes flashed with alarm.

"Don't take it out!" he snapped. "Just give us the bag!"

Vane's grip tightened. Her skin crawled underneath his fingers.

Don't take it out? She was surprised by the alarm in his voice. *Is he afraid of it?*

Ignoring Vane, she pulled the silvery crystal out of the bag and held it before her. Beside Vane, Marl eyed her warily, wiping the blood off his mouth. Something about the way they shrank from it made her skin prickle.

"Just put it back in the bag," Vane said slowly and with force.

Luthiel's heart pounded in her ears. It was going all wrong. She didn't believe they would let her go, even if she gave them the Stone. But the way the Stone seemed to give them pause gave her a faint surge of hope. In desperation she thought of Leowin—trying to remember. What had she said about the Stone?

"If you want to use the Stone, just sing to it but also think of someone who loves you very much. You could think of me! Understand?"

Use the Stone? But what did it do? Make light?

Vane's fingers dug into her shoulders. "Give it to Marl!"

Instead, she thrust the Stone out, almost striking his nose. Vane grabbed her wrist, trying to shake the Stone loose. But she held firm. She was trying to think of Leowin. As she struggled, she began to sing the song Leowin made her. She was afraid and shaken and her voice cracked as she forced the words.

"Stop singing!!" Vane commanded.

With his other hand, Vane latched onto her elbow, which he wrenched in an impossible angle. She tried to keep singing and barely managed. The pain was so intense, her eyes started to water. Vane wrenched again. Fire shot through her arm and she feared that it might break.

This is it, she thought. *If he does it again, I'll scream.* But despite the fiery pain shooting up her arm, she sang and thought desperately of her sister.

"Marl! Stop her! She's trying to use magic!" Vane yelled as he twisted her arm a third time. It felt as though her arm was breaking. She clenched her eyes shut. Pulling deep, she sang with all her strength.

Then, suddenly, it was as though a cool blanket fell over her and the pressure on her arm subsided. Her lips moved and somewhere, far away, she heard singing, but she could only half-understand the words. She opened her eyes. Silver light was gushing from the Stone. Everything the light touched wavered like seaweed in a strong current. There was a rushing in her ears like the sound of water or fire. Vane stumbled backward and he held his hands in front of his face to shield his eyes from the light. At first, he looked no different. But as she watched, he seemed to change. His eyes became sunken and a green light shone in them. His body seemed to grow thin, the flesh stretching tight over bone—his skin like polished rock. With one hand before his face, he leaned into the light as if it were a gale. With his other hand, he grasped at the Stone. Before he could touch it, he jerked back. His hand fell limp at his side. She heard him cry out, but the sound came to her as over a great distance.

Still, those green eyes stared at her.

"It is beautiful," Vane said with a hoarse voice.

Afraid that Marl would grab her from behind, she lurched sideways, looking over her shoulder. When she saw him, she froze for a moment in horror. She could see through his flesh and beneath the skin she saw where his bones stabbed him each time he made a step toward her. He moved slowly, pushing against the light.

Terrified, Luthiel stepped around Vane and fled.

She ran and the forms of trees, wavering and elongated, passed on either side as she rushed down the trail. She ran hard but she barely felt her legs move. Blurred forms of trees flashed past her. She rushed on, afraid to look back and see Marl and Vane behind her, terrified of this strange world she'd entered. In the silver light, her legs seemed tireless and she fled for an unknown time. Overhead, the suns seemed to climb, impossibly fast, into the sky.

Finally, she came to the shore of a river—broad and fast flowing. Still afraid she was pursued, she glanced over her shoulder. But she saw no trace of Vane or Marl. Still, she looked around her in every direction, not trusting her senses.

Above her, the suns and moons gleamed with eerie brilliance. Everywhere there was light save for the western horizon, which was blanketed in a curtain of darkness. For a moment, she wondered at it. It lined the whole rim of the western sky and no light escaped it. It seemed to her that even though the suns stood at mid-sky, night had returned and was now eating the edge of day.

Shivering, she tore her eyes from the blackness. In her hand, the Stone blazed like a beacon, illuminating even the undersides of clouds. She felt suddenly exposed.

How far away can I be seen? she wondered even as the fear inside her grew.

Even as she thought this, the western darkness rippled and was pierced by a great mote of shadow, blacker even than the darkness that surrounded it. Knifing through the sky, it cast its cold arm over the day, dimming the suns and eclipsing a moon. It sliced back and forth, as though searching.

Fear became terror, and she threw herself on the ground, shielding the Stone with her body. Still the shadow searched, licking some of the taller treetops.

She had to get out. She tried to stop singing. But she had the odd sensation of not being entirely in control of her voice. It was as though something compelled her to sing. Her lips moved, she could feel them, but the song was far off. It seemed to issue from the air around her and not from her mouth. She tried again, and for a moment she thought she had succeeded but the singing kept on.

Her terror became panic.

What if I can't leave this place? she wondered. Finally, in desperation, she scrunched her eyes and held her breath, struggling to stop singing.

For what seemed like a long time, nothing happened. She struggled and struggled. All the while the day about her seemed to be growing colder as the light faded into grays and browns.

Then, she drew a great breath of air and the silver light suddenly faded, melting back into the Stone from which it had sprung. When the light was gone, so too was the shadow. Everything looked normal once more. But a terrible cold had fallen over her and she trembled.

Quickly, she stuffed the Stone back into her pouch.

"Leowin! What have you given me!" she cried as she fumbled with the strings. If only Leowin hadn't given her the Stone! If only the Blade Dancer hadn't come! And, not for the last time, Luthiel wished it was all some nightmare that she'd wake up from on a beautiful, normal, First Summer's Eve morning.

She peered at the western sky afraid that the cold and the dark would return. She cowered on the ground for a few moments longer, and then forced herself to stand. What if Vane and Marl were hunting her? She needed to keep moving. So she turned left and ran west beside the river Rendalas.

It was then that she realized it was no longer morning. Soelee hung in the western sky, about four hours away from setting. Of course! She'd reached the river. It was at least twenty miles from Flir Light. And she'd run almost the entire way.

But she didn't feel tired. There was no ache in her muscles nor thirst in her throat to signal that she'd exerted herself all morning and part of the afternoon. Even though she wasn't hungry, she forced herself to sit down and have a bite to eat.

RACE TO THE VALE

Luthiel settled beside a massive old tree. Unshouldering her pack, she pulled out one of the water gourds and emptied it. She bit into an almorah cake and held it in her mouth while rummaging through her pack. Other than looking at maps, she knew nothing of the lands surrounding the Vale.

Pulling out the map, she unrolled it, orienting it north to south as Glendoras had taught her. She studied it, occasionally looking up to peer at the surrounding countryside. Finally, she thought she was able to find where she was.

"There," she said, placing her finger on the spot. Her best guess was that one hundred miles lay between her and the Vale. She traced her finger over a blue line on the map—the river Rendalas. It wound like a watery highway straight into the Vale.

"Just like Vanye said. But what's along the way?" She peered intently at the map hoping that at least the journey to the Vale would be simple.

The river flowed through mostly flat, uninhabited, woodlands before it fell into rapids as it crested the rocky hills called the Mounds of Losing. There it finally plunged over Withy Wraith falls. The falls spilled into the Miruvoir—a large lake at the heart of the Vale of Mists.

But her finger stopped at a bend in the river. There, plainly marked on the map a dwelling labeled—Sorcerer's House—overlooked the Rendalas on a high bank some twenty-five miles from the Vale.

"What's this?" she asked herself, straining to remember anything.

"He's an old sorcerer," her sister had said. "Older even than Elag, if the rumors are true. And it is also rumored that he likes to be left alone and that his house is tended by goblins, almost as old and wicked as he."

"Doesn't he have a name?" Luthiel had asked.

"Not one he's giving out freely. Sure there are rumors—a retired teacher from Tirnagûl, one who was kicked out on bad behavior long ago. That's what people say. I don't know, but I'm going to find out."

For a moment, she thought about crossing the river to avoid the sorcerer's house. But the nearest ford was more than twenty miles upriver.

She didn't have much time—the werewolf Othalas was coming for Leowin. A normal wolf could cover the distance from the Vale to Flir Light within a single night. Othalas was no normal wolf. If the tales were to be believed, he stood as tall as a horse. He was probably able to run the same distance in half the time. Sometimes Othalas arrived mere days after the Chosen was named and once he made it to the Chosen before the Blade Dancer messenger was able to come with the news. But for some reason—perhaps a grim sense of courtesy—it normally took about a week. She hoped she had that much time.

She pored over the map, worried. Since she didn't know when Othalas would start out, she decided to give herself no more than five days, including today, to reach Withy Wraith falls. That gave her one more day to search for the Vyrl. One day. She hoped it was enough. The Vale was large—about twenty miles end to end and ten or so top to bottom and it was always in a constant fog.

"How am I going to find anything in there?" she asked herself. "I'll be lucky if I can just make it in and out alive."

Luthiel stared at the map a moment longer and then shook her head.

"I've got to stop thinking like this." With a sweep of her hand she rolled it up and stuffed it back in her pack. "Worry about it in six days."

It left her with little time to be overcautious about sorcerers.

Luthiel sighed. "So it's going to be a race then, a race between me and the werewolf Othalas." The only thing she had going for her was Othalas didn't know he was in a race yet.

Looking up at bright yellow Soelee riding the mid afternoon sky and Orin's Eye, white with blue lashes, behind, she suddenly felt tiny and insignificant. In that moment, a desolation settled over her heart and she was afraid.

"Why must people be sent to the Vale of Mists?" she lamented. "I surely don't want to go and be food for a Vyrl."

She wanted to talk to someone, to at least feel the comfort of a hand on her shoulder, or better, melt into a reassuring embrace. She felt like a soldier who volunteers to fight in an impossible war if only to protect someone she loves.

Leowin.

"Remember why you're here, Luthiel," she said to herself.

She forced herself to stop worrying about the Vyrl and the Vale of Mists. Instead, she packed up her things, took another drink from the water gourd, and started jogging.

Determined to beat the wolf, Luthiel pushed herself. Muscles straining, her fear for herself became distant. She thought only of Leowin imagining that, even now, the great wolf was bearing down on Flir Light Hollow. With these thoughts, a strange sense of doom settled upon her. A part of her—a grim, hard, part that, before now, she hadn't thought existed—stared straight into the teeth of what lay before her and accepted it.

I cannot change what will happen, she thought. *I can only change how I act in the face of it.* So she ran onward, for the moment, untouched.

The river flowed along beside her as she ran. She had the odd sensation that its current pulled her.

As the day wound on, the river entered a wetland and she had to pick her way carefully through a marshy place. The river had tossed rocks and boulders up on its banks and she was able to make her way easily through the shallows or across slick beds of pebbles. She was careful to keep a watchful eye out for the packs of wild Urkharim that roamed the wilderness of the Minonowe. Though less frequently than in their home forest of Ashiroth, the giant wolves sometimes ranged this far south as they hunted. During the spring, they could be found on the far bank searching the shallows for fish spawning in the river. Once, she saw a lone Urkharim watching her from the far bank. But the river was wide and too swift for even the great wolves to cross. After she passed the wolf, she was glad she hadn't given in to her fear of sorcerers.

Possessed of a frantic energy, Luthiel continued long into evening and three moons had risen by the time she finally stopped to rest. She found a great old tree and clambered up among his boughs. There she made her camp. Two other trees grew beside him and his branches spread wide and low—providing her with many paths for escape, should she need them. After a quick meal, she collapsed into her bedroll and was soon fast asleep.

She woke up once during the night, troubled by a dream of the shadow in the sky and a sound like the cold cry of wolves in wintertime. When she broke from sleep, she sat upright and trembled with chills. Even though the night was warm, she drew her blankets close about her. For a time, she stared into the western sky, fearing that the dark would come again. After a while, though, the sensation passed and she fell, once more, into deep sleep.

She awoke before first light and continued at a fast pace. Morning dawned gray and dreary. Soon a steady rain was falling. She hung a wind charm from her hat to keep the rain off, but it blew sideways into her or splashed up from puddles on her path. Soon she was damp and cold. Her sense of doom deepened.

She wondered if the elves of Flir Light had sent anyone after her or if her family was, even now, following her trail. It was enough to make her quicken her pace. She even took a long leafy branch with her and used it, from time to time, to brush out her tracks.

Am I doing this right? she would wonder as she swept the ground.

But her determination of the day before faded and her efforts were half-hearted. She'd grown so lonely and homesick that not an hour passed that she didn't think of turning back.

"Oh, curse this weather!" she would say in a moment of annoyance and think longingly of mother Winowe's tea kettle singing or of a hot bath in their Fae Holme's rock basin. The rain, which she thought at first might help clean the dirt off, only seemed to soak the grime into her skin.

By the time the day ended, Luthiel was wet, dirty, and exhausted. Only two days had passed and the worst of it was still ahead of her.

The land steadily rose into shallow banks even as the river cut lower. These banks were mostly rock and pebble. Boulders were strewn on both sides. The hills were topped with trees and here and there she saw small clusters of Fae Holmes twinkling in the distance. For a while, she thought longingly of approaching one of these settlements and begging shelter for the night but she was afraid of what they might ask her or of what word they might send to those in Flir Light once she left. So she found another tree and with her wind-charms was able to make for herself a somewhat dry spot among its branches. Luthiel even attempted a small fire, but the twigs were too damp and wouldn't hold a spark. She thought jealously of Lorethain and his talent. If only she could conjure a small flame, then she might eke some comfort out of this desolate place! But if she possessed any sorcerous gifts they remained unknown to her, and so she tried her best to sleep, soaked though she was.

The next day dawned warm with Soelee and Oerin's eye burning off the cloud cover and drizzle. Soon, Luthiel was dry and her mood rose a bit. Flowers hung over the river and a few dropped into the flood making a petaled pathway through its many swirls and eddies. Fish played and jumped and she managed to catch one in the shallows. She even took the time to make it into a nice lunch before continuing on.

The warmth and food cheered her a little but Luthiel felt, in her heart, a growing dread for what lay before her. As she jogged she wondered about Vane, Marl and Elag. She never understood why they had taken such a dislike to her. What had she done to earn it? Sure, there was that time in Elag's garden, but she didn't understand the malice. What confounded her most was that they were so well respected. Or maybe she was mistaking respect for fear?

Beneath it all was a growing curiosity for what she had seen in the light of the Stone. And horrible though he was, a part of her felt saddened for Marl. She wondered what it would be like to live with the constant stabs of pain; her own bones made out to hurt her. Where Marl made her sad, Vane puzzled her—the way he'd seemed to harden under the Stone's light.

What did it mean? And what was she seeing? She wished Leowin was here to answer her questions. Leowin would know.

As she continued, the land became darker, wilder. The hills to either side of the river continued to gradually rise and the sparse settlements gave way to ruins of stone castles and towers that seemed to her dark and wicked. The sorcerer's house was only a day's journey away from her now. It was the last dwelling between her and the Vale. She became more alert, staying out of the open places near the river, careful to leave no trace for it was rumored that foul things had gathered here away from the lights and singing of the elves.

Finally, in the late night, Luthiel stopped and made camp among the boughs of a grandfather tree. The stars shone bright through his branches and there was only a sliver of moon in the sky. Even though she was very tired, she had difficulty sleeping. A hundred eyes seemed to stare up at her from the darkness. Some were clearly animal but others seemed oddly elfin except for a faint green glowing and an almost insect-like roundness. When these passed, she would hear a soft clicking sound. An unexplained fear would fall upon her and she would draw her blankets close about her in spite of the early summer warmth. How could people sleep easy when there were such strange things in the world? She lay awake for a time staring out into the woodlands, watching the eyes as they passed beneath her. By the time she finally drifted off it was completely dark, even the sliver of moon had set.

The next morning dawned much the same as the day before but there seemed to be a heavy charge in the air. Warm winds blew up from the south and she sniffed them wondering if a storm was brewing.

But the sky stayed clear long into the day. With the wind in her face she made good time.

THE SORCEROR'S HOUSE

It was early evening when Luthiel came within sight of the old house. High swooping eves overlooked a wide bend in the river and round windows twinkled with the light of Soelee as it set. A long stairway led from a pair of big, red-painted, doors all the way down to a stone landing that met the river at its bend. On either side of the landing stood two trees and from their branches hung flir bug bulbs. At its center sat a brown-haired man.

He wore robes of light blue and in his hand he held a fishing pole. His dark hair was long and flowing and a beard grew on his face. His head was nodded, his body hunched, the pole limp in his hand. His eyes were closed beneath thick brows that bristled like flame. From where she stood, she could hear the soft sound of his snoring.

She stood there for a moment, uncertain what to do next. Could it be the sorcerer? He didn't look threatening. He didn't even look like an elf. Maybe it was a servant. But something in his features—both youthful and yet seeming to carry the weight of a great many years—made her doubt it. She could just slink by, quiet feet on the stone, and he'd never know.

So she took a breath and started out, moving silently on the balls of her feet. She crossed the distance to him fast and was nearly past him when suddenly the line on his rod went taught. With a snort, he awoke and fumbled with his pole, almost dropping it.

Startled, she crouched down, hoping he wouldn't see her, cursing herself for not crossing further up the path where she wouldn't be so close.

"Thought you'd steal the bait with me napping, did you!" he cried then gave the pole a yank. "Oh-ho, no!" and with another tug a fish easily as long as her arm came sailing from the water. With a smack it landed on the quay flapping its broad tail back and forth. "Who's the crafty one now?" the man chuckled as he chased the flopping fish. "Would you mind lending a hand here?" he said to her without even looking. She stared at him in surprise.

Did he know I was here all along? she asked herself.

"Well, don't just squat there like a frog on a lily pad!" he cried as he struggled to hold the fish.

Shocked, she stumbled forward and grabbed it.

"Ahh, that's much better," he said after he'd removed the hook. "Now just look at her—beautiful." He held the great fish before him reverently.

Then, to Luthiel's surprise, he walked to the edge of the quay, leaned over, and gently slid it back into the water. With a great swish of her tail, she was gone.

"You let it go!" she said despite herself.

"Of course I let her go! What else would you have me do?"

"Well, you could eat it."

"Eat it! And waste the best fish in the entire river! Monstrous!"

"But that fish could feed five!"

"There are other things to feed than just your belly and there are other things to catch, than just a meal, Luthiel Valshae."

"How did you—?"

"How did I know your name? How could I not? Just four days ago you sang it loud for all who have ears to hear such things. Not all are as friendly as I. But let us eat first, before we speak. All your talk of meals has made me hungry and I could eat as much as five men! Fishing makes you hungry. Come, follow me, what I have is better than fish!" He turned to walk up the stairs.

Listening to him, she hadn't a doubt that he was the sorcerer. She hesitated, suddenly unsure of this man and cast her gaze toward the river. She could run now and he would have little chance of stopping her. But just as she was about to spring away he spoke again.

"If you wish to leave, go along. But be careful! For snares far more cunning than fisherman's hooks are laid across your path. Those that tend them are far crueler than I. No, they don't let anything go once they catch it."

She stopped in mid-stride. "What do you mean?"

He looked her straight in the eye and there was such an intensity about him that she took a step back.

"Just what I said," he replied. Then he seemed to brighten and he smiled. "Do you like cheese? I have the finest cheese in all the Minonowe and bread and honey from its best bees! You've traveled hard. Rest for a while and then we'll speak of such things, as we must. But for now I'm offering you some good cheer—take it if you like!" With that, he sprang up the stairs and she was left with the choice to leave or to follow.

"Not at all like Elag," she whispered. She took one glance down the river past its bend and into the distance where strange shadows seemed to play across the water. In that land, the shadows seemed to fall longer, twisting away from whatever cast them in black spirals.

You're just afraid, Luthiel, she thought. *Now your eyes are playing tricks on you.*

For a moment, she considered going on. But at last her will failed her. Perhaps it was her fear of what lay ahead, or maybe it was just the kind voice of the sorcerer. It seemed so long ago, though it was less than a week, since she'd laughed or shared a moment of companionship.

"Well, a little help wouldn't hurt," she said, then mounted the stairs behind him. In truth, she was lonely and desperate for company and a friendly voice. With what lay before her haunting her every thought, she wanted nothing more than to enjoy the time that was left to her. Who knows, maybe the sorcerer could help her after all.

"Ah, so you've decided to come," the sorcerer said looking over his shoulder. "Good!" He smiled and spread his arms. "Welcome to Lenidras, as it was known of old. Elroth helped me lay the first stone more than three thousand years ago."

"Lenidras," she said. "I've never heard of it."

"Few have," the sorcerer said. "At that time there was reason enough to keep the school hidden. Here, I taught the ancient mysteries to promising young sorcerers."

"A school of sorcerery? Here?"

"Yes. Though small and secret, the greatest sorcerers of that day came from Lenidras. Those who knew it would say it surpassed even Tirnagûl."

"Why was it kept a secret?"

"It was a dark time. In that day the study of sorcerery was forbidden to all but those who were hand selected by the Vyrl. Tirnagûl existed because it stood at the heart of a cunning maze. Lenidras existed because it was secret."

They had reached the top of the stairs. The red doors stood before her. Upon the walls, long necked gutters styled in the shape of dragons heads opened their mouths as though in a cry of greeting. Each round window bore at its heart a small work of stained glass—a flower, a flame, a dragonfly. The roofs swooped high reaching spires up like fingers tipped with workings in the shape of suns, moons, stars. Through the windows, one by one, lights were winking on.

"It is a beautiful place," Luthiel said.

"Yes, Lenidras has a way of making its own light. I come to it, now and again, for rest from the road. It is seldom, though, that I have the pleasure of introducing it."

The sorcerer rapped gently "Warlin! Come! We've a guest!"

The doors swung wide and Luthiel was greeted by a stately goblin who bowed, then offered to take her pack even as he swept the fishing pole from the sorcerer's hands.

"It is an honor, Lady–"

"Lady Luthiel," the sorcerer supplied.

"Welcome to Lenidras, Lady Luthiel. I am Warlin, the groundsmaster. Will you be staying for dinner?"

"She will," the sorcerer said before she could answer. "Best pour a bath first, though, and ready a room for tonight." He turned to Luthiel. "You would like a bath wouldn't you?"

Luthiel stood there a moment. A bath? She would like nothing more, but she didn't have time to linger.

"I'm in a hurry. I really shouldn't."

"Nonsense! You'll travel faster after a bath, a good meal and some decent rest. When was the last time you slept in a bed?"

It was then that she realized how tired she was. She had traveled hard for four days and often late into the night. Still, she worried. The werewolf was coming for Leowin.

"I really shouldn't."

Warlin nodded. "Take a bath at least and scrub the road off. You'll have to wait for dinner in any case."

She found herself nodding. "I suppose a bath would be nice."

Warlin put his hands together and smiled. "Well, now that that's settled, if you would please follow me Lady Luthiel, I'll show you to your bath."

Warlin led Luthiel down a wide hallway. At the end were two giant statues carved in the likeness of unicorns. But at their sides were folded great wings and from their hooves and horns shone a light like blue fire. Though they appeared to be carved out of stone pale as the face of Lunen, their manes fell in hues of every color. Their eyes were closed, their heads bowed as though in a deep sleep. For a moment, she thought she saw one move and reached out in wonder to touch it.

Warlin grabbed her hand and, embarrassed, she returned it to her side.

"They're beautiful," she said.

Warlin nodded. "Yes, but do not touch them, it will disturb their slumber."

"So they're real?"

"As real as you or I."

"What are they called?"

"Keirin. They are spirits of light, storm and air, but they slumber in stone. Come along, your bath is waiting."

But she couldn't take her eyes off the beautiful creatures slumbering in stone and she stared at them long after she'd passed that archway and into the great chamber that lay beyond. Finally, she looked away and noticed that in front of her stood two large tables running parallel to one another. Intricately carved seats were set along the lengths of each table. She craned her neck to look above her and saw circles rimmed with light or fire painted on the ceiling. Within them she could see a sun, the moons, and stars shining. The ceiling took on the hues of evening and she saw Orin's Eye setting from the ceiling and into the west-facing window. The circles, though plainly painted, were moving as they followed the heavenly bodies they depicted.

The hall was lined with swooping poles, from which hung glimmering flir bug bulbs, and large half-circle windows looked both east and west over rolling fields and gardens. Far away she could see the silvery line of the river Rendalas winding over the Minonowe.

On the walls were portraits of mysterious figures and paintings of vivid landscapes. Her eyes were drawn to the pictures and she couldn't help but stare at the beautiful and fierce faces. One, she recognized as that of the sorcerer. She was about to step closer to read the caption beneath when Warlin caught her by the arm.

"Lady, your room is this way," the goblin said.

She nodded politely and let herself be guided to a south facing archway, then up two flights of stairs and finally to the end of a long hall. Now and again, they passed other goblins involved in various tasks. Occasionally one would stop and whisper briefly to Warlin before hurrying off again.

"You sure do keep the place nice," she said.

Warlin walked on for a few moments silently as though in thought. "Sometimes, old students or masters of Lenidras come to meet or do research. Our library is quite extensive. It is less a school now and more a place where old things are kept or where, on occasion, great meetings are held."

"Leowin would love this place," Luthiel whispered.

"Ah here it is." Warlin said and with a quick step to the right he pulled the latch on a beautifully carved stone door set with crystal. On the other side was a warm room with a wide bed, a desk piled with books, a beautiful round window that overlooked an orchard and an open door leading to a marble floored bath. Towels and a white-and-gray robe with a silver brooch were laid on the bed.

"While you're here, it is traditional to wear the robes of a sorcerer of your order," Warlin said.

Luthiel almost laughed. "But there must be some mistake, I'm not a sorcerer."

"Nonsense, I have it on the highest authority. Now, I'll leave you to your bath. Dinner should be ready in the great hall in about an hour. If you need help, just ask one of us." Then, he turned on his heel and quietly shut the door.

With a sigh, she sat down.

The bath made her feel much better and by the time she was toweled off a quick look at the sky told her she still had a half an hour before dinner. She collapsed into the bed and soon fell into a light sleep. It seemed only moments later that she woke up, somewhat refreshed after her little nap. She sat up and looked at the robe spread out beside her.

It took her just a few minutes to put it on. She regarded herself in the mirror. The robes were simple, made up of a tunic with leggings underneath and long, flowing robes over top. The undergarments were white and the over garment was gray. It took her only a moment to fasten the silver brooch. The robes felt free and easy to move in.

Once ready, she walked into the hall where she found a goblin waiting patiently for her.

"Lady Luthiel, your place has been made. If you would please follow me?"

She fell in behind the goblin who turned and hurried his way up the hall and down the two flights of stairs.

Once there, she was greeted with the smiling faces of some fifty goblins. The lights on the wall were warm, but dim enough to allow the moons and stars to shine through the windows or the strange drifting globes on the ceiling. Everywhere goblins were eating, drinking, singing, playing instruments or telling tales. A steady flow of platters laden with food or bottles of wine came from the kitchen. The general hubbub was festive and she was quite surprised to see so many jovial goblins all in one place. They were usually dour and seeing them this way lightened her heart.

Her guide led her to one of the long tables and sat her down on the right side of the sorcerer who rose and helped her into her chair. Aside from herself and the sorcerer, almost everyone else was goblin. Across from her sat two ladies whom the sorcerer introduced as Listelle loremaster of Lenidras and Aerdara huntress of Lenidras. A great white fen-hound named Grim sat beside Aerdara, saber-like tusks glittering in the dim light. The tall goblin to her right was Morjin armsmaster and Keltrin the minstrel sat beside him tuning his lulute. They had a refined air about them that oddly complimented their half-bald heads, gleaming eyes and hooked noses and she found herself immediately impressed by their grace and stature.

A plate heaped with fruits, breads, cheeses, nuts, and vegetables of every variety was laid in front of her and she happily began eating.

"Thank you so much!" she said with sincerity. It was the best meal she'd had since before First Summer's Eve. The goblins and the sorcerer politely talked amongst themselves or engaged her in small talk as she ate. Plate after plate was offered to her and soon she was sampling pastries from one, tasty gum fruits from another and a delicious quiche from yet another. Soon she was stuffed and her ears were starting to feel warm from the wine.

As the plates were taken away, Keltrin rose from his place, walked to a raised platform at the end of the hall and to loud clapping began to play a lively tune. Luthiel joined in the clapping as most of the goblins had left the table to dance.

She watched on, clapped her hands and sang the chorus when she knew the words. Keltrin played for a while this way and then settled into softer music. The new song was in a tongue alien to her. But she couldn't help but be caught up in its enchantment. The goblins who listened or sang along seemed to be holding the words in reverence.

"What is it? What song is this?" she said, grabbing the arm of a passing goblin.

"It is the Lay of the Lady of the Dark Wood," he whispered with a bob of his head, then strode off before she could ask him any more questions.

When the song was over, the wine stopped and one by one, the goblins started to leave. A cup of clear, honeyed water was placed in front of her and, presently, she found herself in the great hall alone with the sorcerer.

"I'd thank you if I knew your name," she said. "You've given me what you said you would—a nice place to rest after a hard road."

"Name? I am many things that are more or less than my name. For now, sorcerer will do. A sorcerer's name has special significance you see. It should not be given freely, nor should it be taken lightly.

"Your thanks are welcome all the same," the sorcerer said. "It is my pleasure to give what I am able. I, too, understand the hardships of the road." His eyes sparkled and his neatly brushed hair seemed to shine under the flir bug light. He had exchanged his blue robes for ones of midnight and gray the same style as hers except for the brooch which had a rippling border and depicted a large M rune in its center.

"But let us talk about you first, Luthiel."

"How do you know *my* name?"

"How indeed? I could ask you the same question, how is it that I have come to know your name?"

He paused and she sat uncomfortably.

"A little help then?"

She nodded, a bit confused.

"Let me see your Wyrd Stone."

"I don't know what you're talking about," she said.

Involuntarily, she put her hand to where it hung at her neck.

"Even if I had one, what would it have to do with you knowing my name?" she asked, pensively.

"Everything," he replied.

"How did you–?"

"How did I know? Well to some this kind of thing is obvious, no matter how well hidden."

He waited but she didn't move.

"So cautious, now, that you would not show me this thing, if only for a moment?" he asked. "Then you should be even more cautious when you use it. A Wyrd Stone can reveal many things. Where it takes you, dreams have power and nightmares take on life. When you touch that world, there are those with eyes to see, ears to hear, and minds to know a great deal about one who stumbles about in the dark shining a bright light and making such loud noises!" His eyes held a harsh edge to them, but then they softened. "You are not so unlike those that came before you. But you must be careful! There are things in this world and the other that are better left undisturbed."

His words awakened a fear within her as she recalled the terrible shadow in the sky. What was it? Was it still searching for her? Could the sorcerer tell her? He seemed very wise. Again, Luthiel struggled with herself. What if the sorcerer's kindness was faked? What if he wanted to take her Stone? But again, her desire for help and friendship finally won out.

"I think it is too late," Luthiel said in a hushed voice. "I saw a shadow in the sky. It kept getting closer, as if it were searching for me. It made me feel—cold."

The sorcerer nodded and steepled his fingers. "The dark moon has a will and sight all its own. It is now a creature of the enemy. Count yourself lucky that you didn't use the Stone a day earlier. Then, beneath its black face, you would have surely been discovered. For though the enemy sleeps in this world, in the other, he is awake and alert—the black lord of nightmares."

"The *enemy?*" Luthiel asked. "I thought the enemy was defeated long ago."

"If you mean the Vyrl, then you are mistaken. Their king is long dead and even he was only a lieutenant to the great enemy. But if you thought of Gorthar the great, then you were wrong only in thinking that he was wholly overcome. Though cast down, he still lives. Now, he lies sleeping on the black moon where he fell so long ago, dreaming strange dreams."

"I—I didn't know," she croaked. To her people, the black moon was a mystery no one understood and myths of the ancient enemy were seldom told and less often believed.

"Have the elves so easily forgotten the elder days?" the sorcerer asked.

"We are not as old as the elves of Ithilden and they keep their secrets. What we know, we know only by myth," she replied.

The sorcerer's eyes flashed and he stood, slamming his fist into the table. "If the elves weren't so busy staring at their feet they would realize what it is that hangs in the sky above their heads! Oesha never knew winter before the black moon rose! And the day may soon arrive when summer won't come back!" Luthiel jumped, rapping her chair against the floor. She began wishing that she hadn't stayed. This sorcerer seemed to have gone mad. She turned her eyes to the doors and windows wondering what her chances were of getting out without the sorcerer stopping her.

But as quickly as the rage came upon the sorcerer, it subsided. He drew a long breath and sat slowly back into his chair.

"Luthiel, I am sorry. I am not angry with you. You are blameless. My ire is for those who know better and still do nothing. There are few who will listen to such black news coming from this old fool of a sorcerer. I doubt there are many even in Ithilden who still believe that Gorthar lives. And those that do have grown complacent."

As she watched him, it seemed as though a great weight settled upon his shoulders. Seeing this, she felt a pang of pity for him. Reaching a hand across the table, she laid it over his.

"Though I can see your cares," she said, tracing the gentle lines of his hand. "You don't look so old to me."

He picked her hand up, squeezed it and laid it back on the table in front of her. His smile returned but the sad look was still in his eyes. "I am far older than even my cares may tell," he said.

She looked away from him. "I don't understand everything you're talking about. And what I do understand of it, I wish I didn't," she said. "It *is* hard to hear."

"There are many things I would change now that I cannot," he said. "So I ask you to take what advice I have and then be very careful. There is a reason why many of the sister Stones to the one you possess have disappeared. We live in a time when the dreaming lord of the dark moon holds sway over many creatures on Oesha. It is a mystery how this has happened. It started with only a few feeble shadows. Then the fell races began to spring up.

"Luthiel, unlike those that went before you, you do not have the luxury to make big mistakes. You should only use this gift when you have great need."

"I didn't know what would happen when I used it. I was terrified," she said. Her hand clutched tighter around the Stone. "It was a gift from my sister. She made a song." A flash of pride swelled through her as she remembered. "Besides, there was nothing else I could do. I'd do it again if I had to."

"Really?" the sorcerer chuckled. "Are you so certain? Or are you too afraid?"

Luthiel still clutched the Stone but her eyes wandered and she opened her mouth, unsure what to say.

"It was not meant to be this way. Awakening into such a place should be a wonder. But ever since the rise of the dark moon it has become very dangerous," the sorcerer said. He held his hand out. "I promise you, I will return it after I am finished."

She nodded, slowly pulling the Stone out of her pouch and holding it before her. "It is dear to me and yet, I cannot tell you how afraid I am for what happened. Still, I remember my sister each time I touch it. Leowin gave it to me for a reason. Though it may be a hard gift, she gave it out of love."

One of the sorcerer's eyebrows rose at the mention of her sister's name. "Did she? Good, very good. That love protects you even now." He looked away again, as though puzzling something over in his mind.

Then he turned to her with a reassuring smile and gently laid his hand on the Stone. "May, I? It would be an honor to hold such a gift. I do not take your confidence lightly."

Luthiel nodded and with an effort she let it go.

The sorcerer held it before him and suddenly the light inside it seemed to flicker and grow. In that flash he seemed greater, more than the man that sat before her. The shadow he cast on the wall grew until it loomed like a great storm cloud. Then the light faded and he was only a man once more.

"*Methar Anduel*," he whispered. "I have not seen this Stone for a long, long time. I thought it was lost, taken or worse—much to my despair. But here it is." He smiled, and placed the Stone on her palm, folding her fingers around it. "Now in good hands. Let's make sure it stays that way."

He winked at her. Then he stood and walked over to the window, holding his chin and staring out into the night.

His intensity was such that she was afraid to interrupt him. Carefully, she placed the Stone back into the pouch that hung from her neck.

"One night is too short," he whispered and then "I am rude. I would have told you the first time you asked but I have grown suspicious in this uncertain age. But as I said before, a sorcerer should not be careless with *her* name." He turned around and walked back to the table placing both hands on its end and looking her straight in the eye. "I, for my part, have many names, but the one most know me by is Mithorden."

"Mithorden!" she stammered despite herself. Leowin had loved to tell the tales of Mithorden in the late night, and Luthiel had loved to listen.

Mysterious even for a sorcerer, danger and adventure cropped up along the path of his life like weeds in an untended garden. His name was in a hundred stories, each hinting at a hundred more, and he was old, older than Valkire. But none knew the years for it was said he came to Ithilden during the time of the Vyrl on a ship from some faraway land.

He laughed and the sound was merry. "Don't start so, you look as though you'd seen a ghost! Don't be afraid! I am only who I am; no more, no less. Besides, we don't have any time for stammering and staring, the night is short and I have much to ask you and more to tell. So if you'd be kind enough to finish, I'll continue."

"Yes, yes," she managed. "But, sir, I mean, Mithorden, if you don't mind, I'd like to ask you a few questions about my Stone." The way he talked about the lord of the dark moon and her Stone seemed to hint at a danger she couldn't quite grasp.

Mithorden laughed. "Good, I see that after all I've said and all you've been through that you've kept your wits and your courage. You'll need more of both, though, before this business is through, Luthiel Valshae. But be brief, if you can. Neither I, nor you, have time to waste." His eyes glinted underneath his bristling brows.

Luthiel nodded gathering her thoughts. "You said a name—Methar something. What does that mean?"

"Ah, you *were* listening. Long ago, thirteen Wyrd Stones were made. Each has a name. This one is called *Methar Anduel*—the dreaming song."

"*Methar Anduel*," she repeated, letting the words roll off her tongue. "So how does it take me to that strange place? And I still don't understand how you came to know my name." She said the last part only as an afterthought.

"Now, that's two questions at once, but I'll answer the first one first." He crinkled his brows together. "There is a world very near our own. In that place everything that was ever dreamed of or feared has life. From there come many things. Wonders are born. Strange things that few understand slip over. Or terrible things of want and hunger rend the veil in search of lives to devour. For the dreams and nightmares will sometimes pass into our world. When this happens, it is called Wyrd or, as most say, magic."

"But what does all that have to do with my Stone?" Luthiel asked. A tightness and a chill had settled upon her. But now that she was asking questions she wanted answers, even if she didn't like them.

"If you sat still and listened, you would know sooner." He glowered at her and fire seemed to bristle in his eyes.

"Sorry," she whispered.

"Apology accepted," he replied. "There are very few things that live in both this world and the world of dreams. Most are gods, angels and demons. The Stone you hold was made by Vlad Valkire the son of an angel and a demon. By the divine blood that ran in his veins, Valkire could see the light and hear the song of creation—if only as glimmerings and whispers.

"Over time, he became aware of the light and the music and as he grew so did his understanding of it. At the age of twenty two, he began his greatest labor—the making of the Wyrd Stones. In them he captured the light and song of creation and by them some of the powers of gods, angels and demons fell into the hands of elves and men. A sorcerer who knows its secret may—like a god, angel or demon—stand with one foot in this world and another within the world of dreams.

"Your Stone is a gateway into the world of dreams, Luthiel. When you sing, it opens and you are, in part, taken there. Others who hold a Wyrd Stone like yours may know when someone crosses into dream. When you sang, I could hear you quite clearly."

"You have a Wyrd Stone?" Luthiel asked.

"Of course I do! Don't ask silly questions."

"But how did you know my name?" Luthiel asked.

"I already told you," the sorcerer said somewhat irritated. "I heard your song."

"You heard me sing my name?"

"Isn't that what I just said?"

"I suppose, but it was very roundabout the way you said it," Luthiel replied.

"You should learn to listen better," he said. "You'll hear more. Now where was I? Ah yes. There are things that would notice you even if they didn't hold a Wyrd Stone. When you used it, your Stone cast a light that could be seen for many miles in both worlds. On both sides of the Veil there are creatures better left undisturbed. Some you might scare, others you might anger—as a sudden loud noise might anger a beast of the wood. Still others would hunger for what you hold and hunt you."

Luthiel shuddered, remembering his talk of the dark moon. "What are they?"

"We have already spoken of the enemy. So I will only remind you of him by telling you of his creatures. A few, I know of only through hints and rumors, these I cannot name. Some, I will not speak of. Seven, who are still called fair by some, hold Wyrd Stones that were taken and corrupted by black art. Those who possess them are bent—body, mind and spirit. I will not name them here. Consider yourself warned! Though they have been forced to live in secret for a time, that time, I fear, is now coming to an end. If for nothing else, be wary of using your Stone for them. They are perilous!

"Others are no less dangerous. Some you may have heard of—Vyrl, Widdershae, Dimlock. Indeed, the Vyrl who rules the Dark Forest possesses a Wyrd Stone—which he has bent to his will. All these may have noticed you."

She sat for a moment, blinking with fear.

"I've only heard of Vyrl," she whispered.

"Widdershae are spiders—wicked, merciless and always hungry. They haunt a ruined land called Detheldris—the Paths of Terror. These were the monsters that devoured the mountain elves long ago. It is because of them that the Gates of the East are now closed and that elves have grown estranged from men.

"Dimlock are all that remain of spirits the Vyrl consumed. Stripped of dreams they live in shadow, always hungering for what they lost. In sunlight or beneath the bright moons, they have no form, but in the dark under the black moon they become solid and roam the night—cold killers for a cold season.

"You would be wise to avoid all I've mentioned. Don't think that you are too small a concern. They would hate the light you bear, or worse, covet it, seeking to turn it to darkness."

"Are Vyrl creatures of Gorthar?" she asked in a voice that to her ears sounded very small.

Mithorden considered her for a moment before answering. "It is a good question. They were once angels, but long ago they fell under his sway. Since then, they have been ruled by terrible hungers. Valkire, alone, was able to soothe the hungers of a Vyrl. For a time, a few of those who followed him recalled their grace. I am afraid, though, that since his death they are once again creatures of hunger and want. With each passing year, they care less and less for their promise to Valkire and for the lives with which they are entrusted."

Luthiel shivered. The flir bug light suddenly seemed too dim and the shadows at the corners of the room hid too much.

Mithorden, noticing her distress, made a broad gesture.

"*Lumen*" he uttered and five golden flames appeared in the air above the table, chasing away the shadows.

"Here, drink some of this." He held her cup to her lips and she gulped the honeyed liquid down.

The cool, sweet drink refreshed her somewhat and the golden light warmed her.

"How do you feel?"

"Better. For a moment there, it was as though a shadow fell over me. But it's gone now."

She took the Wyrd Stone from around her neck and held it before her. The thoughts of the enemy and his creatures of nightmare still swirled in her mind. But they still seemed remote to the immediate danger of the Vyrl.

"Here. If Leowin knew, I'm certain she wouldn't have given it to me. Take it; I will have little need of it. Tomorrow, I leave for the Vale. I—I probably won't return. You should give this to someone who is better able to bear its danger."

The sorcerer stared at her for a few moments. The Stone swung from its string between them. Then, he snatched the Stone and hung it around her neck.

"No, Leowin chose well. The Stone is yours—it is a part of you. Unless you are broken or killed, it cannot be taken from you. Even if you cast it away, it would return to you. For good or ill, it has bound you to the world of dreams. It is best that you learn to accept it and live with both its dangers and its blessings."

"Leowin would have probably said the same thing," Luthiel said.

"She sounds like she is very wise."

"She's always known much for her age. Now, I think I've learned a few things that even she doesn't know, though I wish I hadn't."

"It is always easier to deny the things you fear," the sorcerer replied "But there is always something to be gained in facing it. We only have tonight, but I will try to help you on your dark and lonely journey."

"Help?" Luthiel whispered the question. She'd grown accustomed to the idea of having to face the Vale alone and without aid. Loneliness and despair gnawed her, becoming more unbearable with each passing day. Now a hope and longing rose within her. "Would you please come with me?" she asked. She wanted help but more than anything she didn't want to be alone.

The sorcerer put a hand on her shoulder. "There now," he said.

"So you'll come with me?"

"I would, if other matters were not so urgent. Tuorlin of Ithilden has sent for me. My meeting with him must come first. Yet even if I were to go with you, I doubt I could do more than deliver you safely into the hands of the Vyrl. No matter what I do, you will still have to face them alone."

"Oh," she said.

"I'm sorry, Luthiel. But there is other help I can give. There is still more for you to learn about your Stone and I know a thing or two about the Vale of Mists that may also be of use. In turn, you could help me. It would be very useful to know how your sister found the Stone and you could satisfy an old sorcerer's curiosity by telling him why you are traveling to the Vale. So you see, even a sorcerer needs help sometimes." He smiled at her.

She sighed and did her best to compose herself.

"Well, a little help is better than none at all. I just thought that I might have a chance if you'd come with me. It is hard to think of things as being inevitable, especially bad things. I guess I'll just have to get used to it in the little time I have left."

The edges of Mithorden's mouth turned down and a sad look filled his eyes. He took her in, then stood up and walked to the corner of the room—staring out into the night. For a minute, he stood there with his fingers thrumming on the chair's back.

"It is true," he said, "that what lies ahead of you is dangerous. I don't know why you have decided to risk the journey. But if, for your own reasons, you're determined, don't resign yourself to an end that hasn't happened. There are entire races that lack elfin immortality. But instead of giving in to despair, most find hope in life even when it leads to death. You have more hope than they for your end is not so certain."

"I understand the sense in what you say, though it gives little comfort. Yet I will listen and do what I can," Luthiel said.

"Fair enough. Now listen to what I have to say about your Stone. Though it is dangerous and should be used only when in great need, it is still a very useful thing to have. When used, the Stone takes a part of you into the world of dreams. To those in this world you become ghostly—both less substantial and at the same time filled with light. The transformation has certain effects. First, it makes you less susceptible to harm of all kinds.

What would kill a normal person might only be a scratch to one under the spell of the Wyrd Stone. Fatigue and hunger are of no concern.

"As you are, in part, within the world of dreams, you perceive more. People are revealed as their true selves—their hurts and ambitions become plain to see. Wyrd is also easier to learn and use. Simple spells are as natural as breathing, difficult spells become simple and enchantments undreamed of by sorcerers who cannot touch the second world are within reach. The Wyrd Stone is a powerful aid to any who wish to learn sorcerery and even you, though still a novice, may discover how to use simple enchantments."

"But I'm not a sorcerer," Luthiel said.

Mithorden only laughed. "Using a Wyrd Stone is sorcerery. If you didn't have the talent, your Stone would be of no more use than any other pretty gem."

Luthiel blinked. "But I've never done anything before."

"That is no matter. Sometimes it takes many years for the talent to develop. Now, if you're quite done with this silliness, I'll continue."

Luthiel nodded still not believing what she was hearing. How could I be a sorcerer? she asked herself.

"When using a Wyrd Stone," Mithorden continued, "there are many dangers. One, we have already discussed—you might draw attention to yourself. But there are others. Moonsteel is tied to both worlds and it will hurt you. Dimlock, Widdershae, Vyrl and other spirits or creatures of nightmare are as deadly in dreams as they are in the world. And while in the world of dreams, you are subject to all enchantments that affect spirits. So have a care when dealing with strange sorcerers!"

"Why are you telling me all this? I said I wasn't going to use it again."

"You might change your mind. Your Stone may become very useful in the Vale. Its Mists cannot harm you in the world of dreams."

"I could use it the entire time?" she asked.

"Indeed, you could. But this brings us to the last danger of using a Wyrd Stone."

"I thought you told me everything already. It draws the attention of dark things, sorcerers can influence you, moonsteel and other spirits can harm you. Isn't that all?"

"Not quite. The world of dreams was not a place meant for the conscious minds of men or even elves. By their nature, they live in one world only, not in both at the same time. The longer you are in contact with the world of dreams, the more difficult it becomes to leave. Some have been trapped there and can never again return. They are forever doomed to wander the boundary between worlds as lonely spirits—never fully belonging to one place or the other. More than an hour is risky and no one who has stayed for longer than a day has returned."

Luthiel remembered her struggle the last time she entered the world of dreams, how she had to exert all her will just to get out.

"I must have stayed for many hours. I didn't know," she said. "Time seemed not to pass at all while I was there."

"Your sense of things is altered but if you pay attention to the suns and moons it will help you. They still move in the sky and will give you a good idea of how much time has passed. Don't fixate. It is easy to become fascinated by things while in contact with the world of dreams. In order to return, you must remain aware of yourself.

"So, it is wise to enter for short periods. You will attract less attention. Also, if you sing quietly your Stone will cast less light. It is like tip-toeing."

Luthiel nodded. "I think I understand."

"Very good, now something about Vyrl—though many mystical creatures covet Wyrd Stones, the Vyrl above all desire them. If your Stone is open, it is likely that they will discover it and then try to kill you so that they can claim it."

"Oh I wish I could be rid of it. It is more trouble than it's worth," Luthiel said.

"Don't be so hasty. It may prove useful yet. It has already gotten you out of one tight place, though at great risk."

"But if the Vyrl kill me for it, of what use will it be to me then?"

"These Stones were carefully crafted with the Vyrl in mind. If you wish to close the Stone all you must do is utter the words *Nin Alhandra*. It will appear to be little more than a normal crystal and even if the Vyrl were to discover that you carry it, they could never use it until you opened it once more by singing your name. You should try closing it a few times, so that you will remember when you have need."

Luthiel undid the strings to her pouch, pulled the Stone out and held it before her. "Tell me the words again?" she asked.

"*Nin Alhandra*," Mithorden whispered.

"*Nin Alhandra*," Luthiel repeated. At first, there was no obvious change in her Stone. But then, the light within it flickered and went out.

"Now sing your name, but very softly."

Luthiel nodded and sang. Suddenly, her Stone erupted with brilliance and she felt her body go cool. Everything in the room wavered. Mithorden seemed to be cloaked in white fire and a light like a star shone at his brow.

"Stop singing," he said.

In sudden horror, Luthiel realized she'd entered the world of dreams. She concentrated on stopping her voice. Again she had to struggle, but this time it was easier and she made it on the second try.

"That was better than the last time. But it was still rather loud. You need to learn to be gentler. It will come with practice. Let's hope it's sooner rather than later."

Luthiel was gasping, trying to calm down. "I don't think I'll ever get used to it. You looked different, splendid and shining."

Mithorden laughed. "Thank you. Now try it again."

Luthiel took a deep breath and nodded.

After about four times, she'd gotten it somewhat under control and managed to only drift into the dreaming world for a second.

"Good," Mithorden said. "You're learning fast. But remember that you can't close the Stone while you're in the world of dreams."

"I'll remember," Luthiel said. "What else were you going to tell me about the Vale of Mists?"

"Ah yes, the mists of the Vale can change you. But if you use the Stone just as you feel your body starting to change it will remove the Mists' hold over you for a time. You must be certain to use the Stone as soon as you feel it happen. Some have described a feeling like worms beneath the flesh—which is not far off. When you feel this, sing to the Stone, you only need to sing for an instant. Understand?"

Luthiel nodded her head.

"It is probably best to keep the Stone closed once you enter the Vale of Mists. The Vyrl are matchless hunters and it is possible that they could come upon you unawares. If you use it to fend off the mists, make certain you close it immediately after."

"Thank you Mithorden," she said sincerely as she tied the strings to her pouch. "I feel like I have a better chance now."

"I'm not finished. You should listen to my directions. The Vale is not a good place to be lost and the Vyrl are, by nature, reclusive hunters. By day, they roam the wilds of the Vale but by night they gather in their castle—Ottomnos—on the northwest side of the Miruvoir. If you enter the Vale, you can reach them by following the lakeshore. It is said that there is a ring of standing stones on the far shore. There you may find them come sunset. Do not stray from the lakeshore. The mists are treacherous and you will become hopelessly lost."

"How do I find the lake?" Luthiel asked, not liking all this talk of the Vale.

"The Rendalas spills directly into it. Once you climb down the stairs you will see it." Mithorden watched her for a few moments more then pulled something from beneath his robe and laid it before her. "Here is an old map of the Vale. It may help you somewhat. But remember, the mists are thick. It is unlikely you will see the land around you much less the hand in front of your face."

Luthiel felt grateful. She'd had a good meal and the sorcerer was doing the best he could to help. She stood up and gave him a big hug. "Thank you!" she said.

Mithorden, taken off balance, let out a guffaw. "There, there," he said, patting her on the back and then holding her out at arms length. "You are welcome!

"Now that that's finished, I have a few questions of my own." He stroked his beard with the tips of his fingers. "You see, your song surprised me. It has been long since I have heard the rumor of *Methar Anduel* in the world. So I made a point to journey to Flir Light as soon as possible to meet you and help you. But then, just this afternoon, I saw you running along the banks of the River Rendalas. By the presence of the Stone, it was plain to me who you were and by your path, there could be no question where you were headed. There is nothing in the lands beyond Lenidras but the Vale of Mists. But it is clear that you are determined to make the journey. What do you hope to accomplish there?"

Luthiel pursed her lips, wondering if she could tell him the truth. But what else could she say? No one went to the Vale by choice.

"I—I decided to go in place of my sister," she croaked.

Mithorden raised his eyebrows. "Indeed?" He leaned back in his chair, stared at the ceiling and sighed. "What you are doing is bold and selfless and therefore something to be admired. It is also exceptionally dangerous, not to mention against the law."

"But you don't understand. I am only an orphan. Leowin is a part of a family. She has so much more to lose than I."

"Does she? Are you not also a part of that family? Do you love life less than her? Or is your life of less importance simply because you are an orphan?"

Luthiel looked away. She didn't want to say it, but she felt that her life wasn't worth as much as most.

Somebody didn't want me, she thought. *I was just a castaway.*

"Even if I weren't, I couldn't bear to lose her. Please don't try to stop me; I don't want the Werewolf to take her away. You don't understand, the thought of her dead, and–" she stopped abruptly not certain if she should continue.

"And?" Mithorden asked.

"A Blade Dancer told me he thought if anyone could make it back alive, then it would be me."

Mithorden's eyebrows lowered and his face became very serious. "A Blade Dancer? Which Blade Dancer? I know many of them and this is highly out of character. They have strict instructions."

"It was Vanye."

"Vanye, now that doesn't surprise me as much. He's been known to, ah, shall we say, bend the rules from time to time."

"Please, don't make me go home. Don't make me go back and see Leowin taken."

"I understand the tradition for what it is—a tribute, a bribe in exchange for peace with the Vyrl. It is something I have never been able to accept. The Vyrl have always taken advantage, killed where they were supposed to protect. Don't worry, I am not going to hold you for the benefit of an unjust law. I was only curious. You are a rare person, Luthiel. You should value yourself more than you do. I wish I knew ten more like you."

Luthiel didn't know what to say so she only nodded at the compliment.

"So how did you and Leowin come to possess *this* Wyrd Stone?" he asked.

Again she paused, wondering if she could tell him the truth. "I already told you," she said finally. "My sister gave it to me."

"Yes, yes, but where did she find it? How did she learn how to sing a name-song? And how did she know that you had the gift? She couldn't be much older than you, how did she come to know so much?"

Luthiel again chose her words carefully. "My sister has always wanted to be a Secret Finder. She's been collecting secrets ever since I can remember and she's only a year older than me. She said the Stone was with me when I came to Flir Light and that my foster parents had kept it ever since. I didn't know about it, but she did. So one day, she took it from them and gave it to me as a present on First Summer's eve." It wasn't entirely true, but she didn't want to tell him about Elag.

The sorcerer's eyes twinkled as he listened. "This is very interesting. And you have no idea who your real parents are or where you came from?"

"There was a note with me. It was short, giving only my first name and asking the people of Flir Light to care for me. It was signed simply with one initial M."

At the mention of the initial Mithorden's eyebrows raised. "Indeed? Well, this is most unexpected."

"What do you mean? Do you know my parents?"

"Well, I may. I don't know." He stared off into space but his eyes held a knowing gleam.

Luthiel's heart pounded in her throat. "If you know anything at all, please tell me."

"Luthiel, I can guess, but that doesn't do you any good does it? No, I'd like to be certain before I tell you anything that might give you false hope."

"I would like for you to tell me now. You won't have the opportunity later."

Mithorden grinned at her and patted her on the shoulder. "I think I will. There's a strength in you that even you don't see. Vanye saw it, and so did Leowin. But such strength shouldn't be squandered! It has been a long night full of dark and heavy talk and you have a very hard road before you. I strongly suggest that you rest now, Luthiel. Try not to worry so much about your past. I promise you, I will help you as best as I am able." With that, he stood and helped her out of her chair.

A NIGHT TERROR

Together, they walked out of the great hall and into the wing toward her room.

She suddenly felt very tired and thought of the nice comfortable bed in her room. It was late and she wasn't going to make it any further this night. There was little point in leaving now. As she walked, she thought about her family, wondering.

"Mithorden, I'm sorry if I pressed you. I just thought that you, out of anyone, might know something about my real family."

The sorcerer laughed. "Ah Luthiel, it would be so much easier if I knew only half of what people expected me to know."

"It must be hard having all that expectation piled on you. How do you manage?"

"I carry on in my own way. Often, it is despite what is expected of me." He smiled at her and winked. "It helps, sometimes, to have a few friends with you along the way. Ah here we are." They had arrived at her room.

"Sleep sound. I will meet you in the early morning for a brief breakfast and to see you off."

"Good night," she said. But before she turned to her room she suddenly felt afraid. All the things they had spoken of returned to haunt her and she didn't want to be left alone with her fears. "Um Mithorden?"

"Yes?"

"This place is well guarded?"

"Do not worry, there are protections here you cannot see but they are as strong as any. You are safe; you may rest easy."

She felt embarrassed for her fear. "Thank you, good night," she said

"Good night, Luthiel," he replied and then he disappeared down the hall.

She hadn't laid her head on the pillow for a minute before she was deeply and contentedly asleep.

But her sleep was disturbed. Late in the night, she heard a clicking at her window. The sound was sharp and she awoke with a start. Huddled in her covers, she peered out through the window. There, she thought she saw a shadowy mass and at its center were two ichorous green lights. She stared at it for a few seconds and then she could hear the loud baying of Fen-hounds. The lights seemed to slowly fade into the shadows and then they were gone. Outside her window, she could hear the snuffling of dogs.

For a time, she lay awake terrified of the apparition she had seen.

What was it?

She wondered and her mind danced with the terrors Mithorden had described. She kept staring into the shadows at the corners of her room, expecting them to come crawling up to her. Finally, she pulled the covers over her head, undid the strings to the pouch around her neck and let her Stone roll out into her hand. Its soft light comforted her and soon she was fast asleep with it clutched in her hand.

She awoke in the early morning to the sound of Warlin rapping at her door.

"Luthiel! Luthiel! Wake up Luthiel!"

"Stop yelling, I'm awake," Luthiel said groggily, wiping the sleep from her eyes. She slid from her bed, walked over to the door and opened it a crack.

"Yes?" she said.

Warlin was still wearing his night-cap, red robe and slippers.

"Mithorden sent for you. He is waiting in the great hall with breakfast."

Luthiel nodded. "Tell him I'll be there in a moment," she said.

The goblin bowed as she closed the door and noticed that her things had been repacked and a clean set of her traveling clothes were draped over the chair by her bed.

"Now that's nice," she said. "Must have done it last night while I was talking to the sorcerer." She slipped her clothes on, grabbed her pack and set out into the hall. As she walked, she remembered her vision of the night before and decided she'd probably had a nightmare. After all the things the sorcerer told her it was a wonder she didn't have bad dreams all night long.

When she entered the great hall, she noticed that Soelee was rising amidst an explosion of red and orange. It looked like a volcanic eruption. She slowed down to stare. She'd never seen such a sunrise.

"Doesn't bode well for the weather, does it?" Mithorden said from across the hall. He was the only one sitting at the table. There were a couple plates of leftovers from the night before on the table and he held a pitcher of some kind of red juice in his hand. "Come, have some breakfast. It's best you get off to an early start if you're to have any hope of beating the storm," he said.

She walked over to the table and sat down across from him, grabbing some fruit, a pastry and a wedge of cheese.

"How did you sleep?" the sorcerer asked.

"Good, considering all you told me last night. I only had one nightmare."

"Well, we won't mar the day with talk of nightmares!" he said washing down a mouthful of pastry with a gulp of the juice. "You should have a drink, excellent stuff, made from the berries in our own orchards. Makes even better wine. But the juice is a nice way to start the morning." He poured her a glass and she took a drink.

It was smooth and sweet with a hint blossoms and honey. The sorcerer was right, it was delicious.

"Mmmm. Thank you," she said.

Too soon, breakfast was finished. Her insides felt raw with anticipation of the day. Slowly, she gathered her things.

Mithorden watched her and when she was done, he stood.

"Come, I'll walk you down to the river," he said.

"Thanks, I'd like that," she replied.

They walked down the stairs in silence. When they reached the bottom, Mithorden turned to her.

"I have a final word of caution for you. These past few nights, our huntress has chased Widdershae off the grounds. It would seem, large numbers of them moved into the lands around the Vale of Mists sometime within the past few weeks."

Luthiel felt her stomach clench. "Maybe it wasn't a nightmare," she whispered.

"What did you say?"

"I thought I dreamed it. Last night, I saw something at my window. It was too dark to make out. It seemed darker than the rest of the night. Like a pile of black clothes in the corner of a dark room. But I could see two green lights like eyes peering through the glass. The hounds seemed to scare it off and I didn't see it again."

"You've seen them then, good."

"Why do you say that?"

"You would probably see them sooner or later. It is better that you weren't surprised on the road. They've laid snares along all the paths that lead to or from the Vale. For some reason, it appears they don't want anything entering or leaving. You must be very careful. Widdershae are vicious predators."

"What has made them come here?"

"I would like to know! But for you, the why doesn't matter. I would suggest that you stay a little bit away from the river and out of the open. You may want to pick your way carefully and not run blindly onward. There is the matter of their webs."

"Spider webs?" Luthiel's skin crawled. The thing she saw last night was big—probably three times her size.

"Not normal webs! These webs are spun out of shadow. They are very clever, looking like masses of shade cast by tree branches or outcroppings. If you are careful, you can find them because they don't move with the suns like regular shadows. Worse, these webs stretch into the world of dreams. They will bind you there sure as they do in this world. If you see one it is best to circle around it. If you pass underneath, you will almost certainly be spied by the Widdershae that made it."

Luthiel felt sick. "I'll be careful," she said. She stood there for a moment longer staring down the river toward the Vale of Mists. Overhead, the sky was the color of paste.

"This stretch is very dangerous. I would not suggest resting until you reach the Vale. Once there, you may use the Stone as I taught you." Then he put his hand on her shoulder. "Here," he traced his finger on her forehead. "*Ethelos,*" he chanted.

"What was that for?" she asked.

"Good fortune. You will need it!"

He looked up into the sky. The unease in his eyes made Luthiel tremble.

"I little like this weather. It rises on an ill wind," he said, then turned back to her. "Have a care, Luthiel, and remember what I told you. It could save your life."

He stood there for a moment, watching her.

Her feet never felt heavier. Lenidras had provided her with more comfort than she cared to admit—making it all the more difficult to leave.

"You'd best set out now," the sorcerer said.

"Farewell, Mithorden," she replied as steadily as she was able. "Thank you for all that you've done. I hope it is enough to get me through."

He gave her shoulder a squeeze.

"As do I," he said, then turned to walk up the stairs. He stopped at the last step to give a final wave and then stepped back through the red doors.

SPIDERS AND WEREWOLVES

She was alone. It took her another minute to gather the courage to start. When she finally did, she took the Sorcerer's advice. She kept out of sight of the river and continued at a walking pace, careful to inspect any out of the ordinary masses of shadow before she crossed through them.

Now and again, she would stop and look at the sky.

Oh if it would hold! she thought.

When she sat down beneath a willow tree for a bite to eat, she saw something that made her ears prick. Far off, in the northwest, she saw a small gray smudge near the horizon. It looked like a patch of haze just a shade darker than the pasty sky.

It wasn't until after she repacked her things and started walking again, that she realized the smudge was no mere patch of haze, but the topmost fluff of a behemoth storm cloud. By midafternoon it had grown until it covered a full quarter of the sky. Thankfully, it was moving very slowly. But by evening, the entire sky was covered in clouds the color of clay. In the northwest, where the smudge first appeared, the sky was black. She could still see Orin's Eye, though, dimly through the pall. Soelee had set like violence through a tear in the clouds almost an hour before.

She was so focused on the storm that she almost missed it. Digging her heels in at the last second, she backed carefully away, and then hid behind a tree as she watched. The thing that had caught her eye was a bear. It was suspended among the shadows some two feet above the ground. It was no longer alive. In fact all that remained was a desiccated husk. The carcass was so dry that in places it was crumbling away to dust. It was as though all its fluids had been sucked out.

Around the bear, tree-shadows seemed to bend toward one another. They formed a rough circle criss-crossed with the jagged shades of branches. Now that she looked closer, she could see other creatures, some of them still alive, caught within them. There were birds, small rodents, and insects of every kind. A flutterfler flapped its wings wildly as it tried to pull away from the dark thing that had snatched it.

The breeze shifted, blowing out from the Vale. It was cold and on it was the stench of dying things.

A shadow web! She pressed her back against the tree and trembled.

She was close to the web, too close for her liking. She glanced around trying to guess the most likely places for a spider to hide. Then, very carefully, she tiptoed away from the web.

It was only the first of many shadow webs. Soon she'd slipped by another two. She was beginning to get very nervous. The third was laid parallel to the ground and so low that she didn't see it until she was almost on top of it. Soon it would be dark and she'd have almost no way of seeing the webs. In the gloom of twilight and the growing storm she was already having trouble.

But it looked like she was getting close.

Beside her, the river Rendalas rumbled over rapids. Dimly she could hear a low roar that she hoped were Withy Wraith falls. Beyond lay the Vale of Mists. A shiver of fear ran like spider legs up her spine. The Vale of Mists. Its name whispered through her mind like the breath of a nightmare. She wanted to run all the way back to Flir Light and its comforts, to hear mother Winowe's tea kettle whistling or Leowin's chattering.

She still couldn't shake her memory of the night she left. Of how Leowin had screamed at her. *"Coward!"* She could hear it even now. She grit her teeth forcing herself to move. She still had the shadow webs to worry about and they seemed to be all around her now.

The darkness was growing deeper and deeper. She was forced to walk beside the river where the light was the brightest and on the way, she snared her cloak on a web. She untied it and left it hanging, scampering away as fast as she could, heart pounding in her ears.

That was too close, she thought. *Are they near?*

Her skin crawled. Her eyes darted side to side.

Could be all around, hiding in the deep shadows, and I wouldn't even know.

She thanked Ëavanya that Gorothoth was not riding in the sky adding its own murk to the night. She crouched low and made her way cautiously along the bank, ducking through the webs that she could now barely see. There was no help going under them now. They were strewn everywhere she looked as though a mad weaver had run through the forest, spinning out black thread wherever she went. It was darker here and cold, as though the webs would let neither light nor heat pass. Eerie, though the trees danced in the storm wind, the webs were still.

Then her eyes caught movement. Behind her, no more than fifty feet, she saw a pair of green eyes drifting down among the webs. They were strange—bulbous, like those of an insect, but almond shaped and elongated, like those of the fae. Black orbs glittered around them. It moved with a horrible, slow, deliberateness, all its limbs in uncanny coordination.

The movement was accompanied by a low clicking. It was choppy and it took her a few moments before she realized the thing was talking to itself.

"Hard to see is it? Soft and sneaky is it? But I saw it, oh yes! I saw it first," the clicking said. "It's mine. Nice fair elf-flesh, yes? Just a little further. No pouncing!"

Luthiel froze in panic.

It was talking to itself wasn't it? She didn't want to think about another of these things. One was terrible enough to watch. She couldn't keep her eyes off it as it continued its deliberate progress, legs questing toward her. She fumbled with Hueron's knife. Her hand trembled, but on the second try it snicked free of its sheath.

"Does it have a fang?" it twittered. "Does it now?" It stopped for a second and tilted its head as though it were taking her into account. "May leave this one to you, nobble knees, may be tougher than it looks. But won't be tough after it's dangled for a while, will it? Just one prick! That's all, then it'll be soft. Nice elf, soft elf, put away your fang. No, we wouldn't want to have to hurt you. Would we, nobble knees?"

The forest was quiet but for the distant rumbling of the oncoming storm.

Luthiel started to walk sideways down the riverbank, careful to keep the knife between her and the advancing spider. Her eyes darted everywhere. What was it talking to? She looked around frantically but a sudden movement drew her eyes back to it. It was pulling its legs tight; its body quivered.

"That's close enough!" she yelled, brandishing the knife before her. "Or so help me, I'll stick you!"

"Stick you! Stick you!" the thing chattered back. "We'll see who gets stuck and who does the sticking now won't we nobble knees? Not too fast is it? All alone is it?"

But it seemed, for the moment at least, that Luthiel's display had worked. The great spider stopped moving and chattered to itself as though it were having some lengthy internal debate.

"I am going to walk right down this river and then I'm going to go down the stairs beside the waterfall. I don't want you following me. You'll just have to find easier prey."

"EEEEEEeeeeeeeeeeerrrrrrrrrrrrrrrrrriiiiiiiiiiiiiiiiiittttttttttttttttttttttttttcccc- ccccccccchhhhhhhhhh!" It screamed. "NO IT WON'T!" The chittering was shrill and screechy like the scraping of metal on metal. "No one can go there. We're to take those that try. Take them and taste them!"

It seemed to have resolved itself and it started moving toward her again, rapidly making up the ground it had lost.

"Stay back!" she cried, brandishing her blade.

"Oh it's close nobble knees! I can almost taste it. It's mine nobbles, no nibbles for you this time! No no!" It poked one of its long legs at her.

She didn't know what it intended—to push her over or to prod her like a piece of fat meat. But she was going to have none of it. With a yell of fury that surprised her with its ferocity, she lashed out with her knife. It was a good blade and it must have been made with the last of Hueron's *Cauthrim* for it sparked as it cleaved clean through the insect's appendage, flashing briefly with blue flame. The first three feet of its leg fell to the ground. Immediately, it balled itself up around its wounded limb.

"EEEEEEERRRRRRRRIIIIIIIIIIIIIITTTTTTTTCCCCCHHHHHH-HHKILLL IT! KILL IT!" It screamed.

The attack was swift, brutal and came without warning. The hidden thing lashed out with a speed and force never seen in nature, except perhaps, in the white sharks of the ocean. Such was the strength released in such a bound that it could tear creatures much larger than itself in half. That was its favorite way to fight—to sting from the shadows, to leave its prey bleeding and poisoned as it leapt back into the safety of darkness waiting until the victim was helpless. Then it would return and collect the hapless thing for its larder.

As it leapt, its glossy body tipped with fangs like axe heads, it was certain of the outcome. It was not like its mate—a careless male half-wit. No, it would not fail or risk itself; it had attacked from behind in that instant when its prey was least aware. In anticipation of the blow, poison flooded into its fangs.

At the first sign of movement, Luthiel sprang away. Out of the corner of her eye, she saw a vast creature pounce from the shadows, grasping for her with its barbed legs, fangs poised to plunge through her flesh but striking instead on the rock beneath it. It missed her by a thread's width, front leg tips slicing through her tunic, cutting her chest. In the place she was standing, two deep furrows scored the rock.

She jumped in the only direction she could—toward the river.

With a splash, she landed waist deep and was soon swept away by the strong current. She let it happen. The brutality of the attack overwhelmed her. How could something so big move so fast? How could she not have seen it? So close! It was only ten feet from her and she hadn't seen it at all. She felt a great sense of relief as the spiders disappeared behind her—one in a ball and the other bobbing its bulbous body up and down in rage.

She twisted and tumbled in the river, trying to stay near the left bank but still afraid to leave the water. The spiders could be chasing her, or worse, warning others. So she did her best to avoid the rocks while staying close enough to shore to get out if she needed to. It wasn't long before the roaring around her grew louder and the current became a raging rapid. She was jostled up and down, side to side, banged against rocks and held under the water for longer than she liked. She began to struggle in earnest—fighting for the bank but the current tossed her like a bit of deadwood. She was hauled under again and when she finally broke the surface she could see the river arching up into a great wave about four hundred yards ahead and then disappearing into a cloud behind. The roar now was deafening.

The falls! She'd already come to the falls!

She struck out with renewed effort but it did her little good. Then, she was swirled around in an eddy that shot her closer to shore and she had a glimmer of hope. She pushed hard but couldn't make any progress. The eddy started to pull her back out toward the middle of the river.

This is it, she thought. *If I can't make it this time, I'm finished.* She fought with everything, her muscles strained. Then she saw a black blur in front of her. *Another spider,* she thought and despair flooded into her limbs. She'd let the river take her before the spiders. But, suddenly, it was in the river beside her and she felt sudden pressure around her neck. To her amazement, she was lifted bodily from the water by a great black wolf.

She was unceremoniously dumped on the bank and found herself with her back against the ground, with a single paw the size of a small tabletop on her chest. A pair of large yellow eyes stared down at her.

He was black—like a piece of starless night cut in the shape of a wolf. And he was huge—at least six feet tall at the shoulder. His yellow eyes gleamed wickedly in the blackness. Those eyes regarded her and she froze.

"Othalas," she whispered.

She was stunned. Her heart leapt up into her throat and she trembled like a rabbit.

She'd heard the tales, listened on in disbelief as elves boasted that Othalas was larger than a horse, had laughed when they told her his coat was the night itself and turned her head in disgust as they bragged about how he could snap off an elf's head with one bite. She'd never believed the stories. Even now it was difficult for her to accept her own sight. Othalas was massive, more than twice the size of even the greatest of the Urkharim—the mighty wolves of Ashiroth—but he moved with a grace like the roll of a powerful wave. And he had plucked her from the river as though she were little more than a cork bobbing in the water.

The claws of the paw on her chest unsheathed and then retracted. "It seems you've wriggled your way off of one plate and onto another. Tell me. How did you get past them?"

His voice was like a boat bottom grinding over rocks. The sound of it grated through the woods and was answered by the distant rumble of thunder.

Luthiel squirmed with fright.

"There–there were spiders," she said, doing her best not to stutter. She was still coming to grips with having nearly been swept over the waterfalls just after a narrow escape from two monster spiders. Now she was cowering beneath the very Othalas that would take Leowin to the Vyrl if she didn't stop him.

"I know. They just keep weaving their webs. I'd like to know how you got through so fast."

"Jumped in the river." Her lips trembled and she could do little more than utter dumb phrases.

"Mrrrrrrhurrrr! River's not fast enough until you get close to the falls. Spiders are out much further. How did you get—ah, I think I see now. Very cunning."

Now it was her turn to stare. "Wha—what do you mean?" she stammered.

"There's the remains of a cunning enchantment," he said pawing her clothes. "But you lost something. A cape perhaps?"

Luthiel started when he pawed her. She cowered, trying to make sense out of what he was saying.

"Might prove useful if you could do it again. If you lay it upon me, I won't eat you. Agreed?"

"Enchantment?"

"Don't play stupid." The werewolf growled.

"But I didn't make any—" and then it dawned on her. Mithorden had whispered something just before she left. He must have enchanted her so that she could slip by the spiders. They noticed her only after she lost her cloak.

"I didn't do it," she said finally. "It was a friend."

"That doesn't help me," the great wolf growled.

"Sorry," she said.

"Sorry! That doesn't help me either!" he growled. "And I thought you were a sorcerer!" He opened his great maw and started to lower it over her.

"Wait! I know why you're going! And you don't have to! I'm here to see the Vyrl!"

The werewolf stopped, closed his massive jaws and peered at her with his great, yellow eyes. She trembled beneath that terrible gaze waiting for the snap of teeth that would end her. But the wolf seemed to be regarding her with curiosity.

"You're to see the Vyrl?" he growled.

"Yes," she replied. It wasn't entirely a lie.

The werewolf pulled back a bit and showed his fangs. "Is your name Leowin?"

She wriggled out from under his paws and stood before him. The top of her head didn't even reach the tip of his chin.

She took two steps back from him. He eyed her, calculating.

"Are you?" he growled.

"No," she said. "I'm Luthiel. I came to replace her." She felt that she should be lying. But something told her the wolf would know if she did.

The wolf's muscles seemed to tense themselves into a hundred knots.

"Please," she pleaded. "She's my sister."

"Chosen don't choose themselves." He crouched low, jaws unhinged, ready for the bite that would end her. "It is not done."

"I chose!" she yelled, drawing her knife a second time. "I'll fight you if I must!" With one yank, she ripped the Wyrd Stone from the bag that hung around her neck and clenched it tightly.

"*Luthiel!*" she sang and felt the cool rush flood over her as she passed into the world of dreams. The fury and fear inside of her spilled out in a gout of white fire, illuminating the wood around her. Othalas changed too. His teeth and claws gleamed like silver in that wavering light and inside of him, beneath the black of his fur, she could see a shape in the outline of a man.

"I have endured Blade Dancers, sorcerers' cronies, a grueling journey, and spiders with nothing better to do than kill elves to come here. I don't doubt you could kill me as well. But I might hurt you. What do you care if I die trying to reach the Vyrl? I know that I am no match for you, but my blade might find you first. It has already tasted spider blood. Why not werewolf's blood as well?"

Her voice seemed to echo in the dreaming world as she spoke and to her the sound of it was terrible—more like a rising storm wind than the sound she was so used to hearing. She brandished her blade, singing soft but angry.

Othalas' eyes narrowed—shining like embers in the Wyrd Stone's light. But he waited, searching for some weakness.

"*Methar Anduel,*" he growled. Then, slowly, his muscles relaxed.

"Hah! If you can make it to the Vyrl, you're welcome to offer yourself. But I'll let you know something. I'm not going to be easy on Leowin. No, I think I'll make it harder on her."

With that, he turned and plodded off toward the shadows.

Luthiel followed after him.

"But the spiders are keeping you," Luthiel sang, the strength gone from her voice.

"Then I will hunt them all." His yellow eyes burned like twin torches.

"It would be much easier if you just took me." She was pleading now and she was too strained to conceal it. "Why can't you?"

"Because it's not what's done, it's not our law."

"That's no good reason," she sang.

"Who are you to judge the reasons of Vyrl!" He growled, snapping his jaws at her.

"Someone who wouldn't see her sister's life thrown away for an unjust law."

The rumble in Othalas's chest was indistinguishable from the thunder. He paced from side to side, his great flanks walling her in. With each passing moment, she felt smaller, less capable. Finally, with a snort, Othalas lowered his head.

"I'm taking you to the Vyrl."

"You'll take me to them?"

"I will. I want to see them drain you with my own eyes. Then, I'm coming back for your sister."

Luthiel stood for long moments in shock. She hadn't thought it would happen this way. Why not? The Vyrl were hungry—hungrier this year than ever before. In that moment she felt as though everything she'd endured had added up to nothing.

I will die and so will she.

"Well, what are you waiting for?" he growled. "There's a very bad storm coming and we should find shelter soon."

She nodded once, impassive. The world of dreams swirled around her. She turned her attention to the Stone. After two tries, she awoke from the world of dreams and shoved the Stone into her pouch. But she kept her knife out.

The wolf stretched his legs out and lowered his body so that she could climb up.

"Get on."

Grabbing the tuft behind his ear, she clambered onto his broad back. She'd barely seated herself when he bounded off and she was left holding on with only one hand. She almost dropped her knife and after three tries she managed to put it away. The second hand helped and she finally regained her balance.

In only a few great bounds of the werewolf, the Vale of Mists suddenly loomed into view. It was all she could do to stay atop Othalas as she stared in horror.

INTO THE VALE OF MISTS

They came to a halt on a high precipice overlooking the Vale. Storm winds howled over the lip. A couple of raindrops stung Luthiel's skin. Beneath a flashing sky, the Vale lay before her. It was all covered in roiling mist that rose and fell like waves driven by a hurricane. Even in the darkness between the lightning's flash, she could see the mist. It was speckled by a thousand tiny green lights drifting within it. By this light, she could glimpse rock outcroppings, treetops, even the glitter of water before the next surge of mist swallowed it. In places, it spilled over the Vale's rim. As she watched, a great swell climbed the cliff before her and in a moment she was covered by it.

Within the mist, all sounds seemed sharper—the wind, the crash of thunder, the groaning of the trees. At the same time, Luthiel felt confined as though the mists were pressing in on her. The green lights flashed by her, moving as though pulled along by the tide of mist. One struck her arm and where it touched her, her skin tingled. The light wound around her arm in a spiral. Then, there was another light, and then another until, within moments, Luthiel was surrounded by a swarm of them. They swirled around her each brushing against her, each leaving behind that strange tingling sensation. Then, as suddenly as the lights appeared, they were gone. The mists had withdrawn, taking the firelights with it.

"What are they?" Luthiel whispered.

For a time, the great wolf was silent. Luthiel was beginning to think he would ignore her when he finally answered.

"Once, they were like you but they stayed too long in the mists. Now they are only wanderers who have lost their way. Stripped of both form and memory they are doomed to roam the Vale living a wretched half-life—spirits that can no longer remember who they were or where they came from."

"How could such a thing happen?"

"All who come to the Vale of Mists are changed. Some, lose only their bodies. Others lose everything. What happens depends on how well you know your true self. The lights you see are those who, in life, lost clear sight of themselves. When they came to the Vale, and the mists started to change them, they had no sight of themselves no vision of who they were or what they could become. So they became nothing more than the tiny lights you see. Now, they move from one impulse to the next, hardly remembering the last. Their old lives are no more than a half-remembered dream."

"But some remain unchanged." It was more a statement than a question.

"Only those who are in touch with the world of dreams." Othalas looked over his shoulder at her. "Very rarely, a sorcerer is born who is aware of the source of his power. Those who are able to open a window to the dreaming world at the time the mists come upon them may pass through the Vale unharmed. It is very rare. But you know this already."

"I did not understand it the way you explained it."

"Words. What are they but shadows on a page or howling on the wind? They are as ever changing as the mists below us and it is just as easy to lose sense of yourself among them. I am older than most sorcerers so what I know may, indeed, be close to the truth. Magic, wyrd, words, dreams, they all come from the spirit. Within them lie both power and peril. For to misuse any is to warp your sense of self. To lie in words, or in magic, or in dreams—that is how you become lost. The lights you see, they were lost long before they came to the Vale."

"And what of you? You were once an elf—were you not?"

The great wolf chuckled. "Yes, but that is no matter. There are other things than mists to lose yourself to in the Vale. Things with a taste for blood that care nothing of whether you know truth or not. That is where you're going. So you needn't concern yourself with me."

"But how did you remain yourself even though you were changed?"

The wolf growled this time and, for a while, Luthiel waited as the storm grew about them. Finally the great wolf answered.

"To survive, you have only to know yourself. But to go on unchanged, that takes more. It takes being in touch with the world of dreams. I was not. So I became only how I saw myself but not how I was *intended* to be."

With that, Othalas clambered onto the first step of the stairway that descended into the Vale of Mists. In two flights, the mists were all around her again and the green flames returned, swirling around her like a robe of dancing light. Soon the mist around her was suffused with a bright green glow as more and more of the ghostly fires gathered near her. She wondered why they were drawn to her and not the wolf—whom they seemed to take no notice of.

About halfway down the stair, lightning flashed through the mists and with a dull roar the skies opened up. It was only a few moments before both Luthiel and the black wolf were drenched. Luthiel pulled up the hood of her cloak and hung a wind charm from a braid of her hair. It helped some, but the downpour was so great she doubted that even a wreath of wind charms about her head would have stopped it. The wind whipped at them and, more than once, Othalas was forced to crouch to avoid being ripped from the ledge.

By the time they made it to the floor of the Vale, small hailstones were falling amongst the raindrops. The wind had risen to a howl and the trees about her swayed back and forth—branches snapping in the gale. To Luthiel, it sounded like a hundred wolf voices crying out in the deep dark of winter. The sound swelled, then dipped, then sustained a high pitch before dropping again into a growl. She trembled, remembering her dream of only a few days before.

A large piece of hail fell among the small ones, pelting Luthiel on her back. She screamed in pain and surprise. A second hailstone exploded in a shower of fragments beside them.

Othalas moved into the woods, but their way was no easier among the trees. They were slashed by branches ripped from the straining trees and once, a tree, rotted with age, snapped in half before them and fell across their path.

"We cannot go further in this storm!" Luthiel yelled. "Don't you know of any shelter nearby?"

The wolf growled. "None that is less perilous than this storm!"

"Surely, some cave in the cliff face–"

"There is but one cave in the Vale of Mists that is near! But I would not go there unless there was no other choice!"

Luthiel shielded her face from a flying branch with her upraised arm. "It will do us no good to be beat to death out here by hailstones or crushed under a falling tree!"

But the werewolf only growled and pressed onward.

Soon, the small hailstones had turned into balls of ice the size of hammer heads and Luthiel was forced to hold her wind charm above her head in order to keep from being battered by the massive chunks of ice. Even so, her legs and knees were struck many times. Othalas fared worse and after a few minutes of harsh punishment he suddenly turned with a loud growl she could barely hear over the storm.

"This storm will be the death of us!" he roared. "But there is only one place where we can find shelter nearby! That way may prove even more dangerous!"

"Anything is better than being beaten to death!" Luthiel yelled.

"Some deaths are worse than others! But, for once, I agree with you!"

Othalas bounded through the falling ice, sprinting across a forest floor carpeted with shattered tree limbs and fallen trunks. Luthiel noticed that his back was bloody from the heavy pelting and counted herself fortunate for the glancing blows she'd suffered. Still, her legs were raw, bruised and bleeding in a number of places before they reached the gaping mouth of a cave in one of the Vale's cliff walls.

THE CAVE OF
PAINTED SHADOWS

Othalas padded just far enough into the darkness to shelter them from the falling ice. But he didn't go far enough to find shelter from the wind.

"Stay here," he growled as she clambered off his back. His voice was hushed and she could barely hear it against the cacophony of the storm outside.

"We could go a little deeper."

"Quiet! Deeper? Don't you know where you are?"

Luthiel shook her head.

"This is the Cave of Painted Shadows!"

Luthiel sat stunned for a moment and then whispered—"Why would you bring me here?"

"It was the only shelter nearby. Would you rather we stayed in the storm and were beat to death?"

But Luthiel was looking over her shoulder. She noticed, now, that the green lights—which were so thick about her moments earlier—had all gone and she was left alone with the werewolf in the dark of the cave. It was cold in the cave—much colder than the outside air—and against the harsh winds of the storm a chill breath seemed to push up from the depths. She trembled and averted her eyes afraid of what she might glimpse upon the wall.

Instead she rummaged through her pack for a dry change of clothes. She found some beneath her second wind charm and quickly changed out of her soaked clothing. Even so, the chill of the cave seemed to be seeping into her with each passing moment.

Othalas was lying on his side, staring out into the storm. His tongue lolled and his breaths came in rapid pants. For a while, she thought she would leave him to his misery. Hadn't he threatened to take Leowin even after she was delivered to the Vyrl? Would she give aid to one of Leowin's killers? In the end, she found herself unable to refuse him help and stepped closer to examine his back. About his shoulders, it was a bloody mess and with a few quick probes of her hands she found that two of his ribs were broken.

"What are you doing?" he growled.

"Tending to your hurts."

From her pack she pulled a clean cloth and some of Winowe's ointment. She dabbed at the mangled flesh with a cloth, then smeared the salve liberally over his wounds before looking after her own. All the while, he lay there allowing her to tend to him. She wondered at this and at how, only hours before, this great beast was about have her for dinner.

"This should help the pain and speed healing. I think two of your ribs are broken, so you should be careful about how you move."

"How do you know these things?" Othalas asked without moving from his side.

"My foster mother is a healer."

Othalas grunted.

Then she sat beside him, dabbing at the cuts and bruises that covered her legs and at those the spider had left on her chest. The storm was still howling not twenty feet away and, occasionally, she could hear a loud snap as another tree fell.

The chill in the cave continued to grow and soon she was shivering all over. Othalas' breath misted before his face. Laboriously, he turned his head toward her, fixing her with those great yellow eyes.

"If the shadows come, will you face them?" he whispered.

"I?" she asked and her voice quavered.

The wolf nodded.

She sat still for a while in the growing cold that seemed to be drawing about her like the fingers of a great cold hand.

Othalas, afraid! Of course he is! And so should you be, Luthiel.

"How many did the Vyrl kill here? You would know," Luthiel asked the werewolf, laying a hand on his shoulder.

"More than counting. They drove any they suspected of disloyalty here. Then the Vyrl summoned fell beasts from the depths—creatures of living flame called Malcor—who burned them with the fire of their bodies. The heat and light was so intense that it burned their shadows into the walls. It looks as though they were painted there by demons hands. Ever since, this place has been—dangerous."

"I've heard the stories," Luthiel said. "Is it true that only Valkire has entered this place and returned?"

"No. The Lord of the Dark Forest came once. But he and Valkire are the only two. Valkire came twice—once in life to try to still the restless shadows and once in death. His remains are buried here. The shadows— they jealously guard his grave."

"And all the others who came here?"

"The shadows kill them, or worse, drive them into the depths of the cave. It is said there is a black hole like a wound in the air. The shadows push them through and they are never heard from again."

Luthiel sat there for a few moments watching her breath. Disquieted by Othalas' story, she walked to the very edge of where the rain and hail were still falling and sat down. Othalas looked at her and, seeing the fear plain on her face, let out a long rasping laugh, then fell silent. The cold felt as though it were sinking into her bones so she pulled a blanket out of her pack and wrapped it about her.

The rumbling thunder and pounding hail continued unabated. Despite this racket, the chill of the cave, her fear, and the aching of her legs, she felt drowsiness creep over her. She didn't realize how exhausted she was until she sat still for a moment. Her body ached with need of rest. She could just sit here with her eyes closed for a few minutes. She'd listen— yes that's what she'd do—she'd keep her ears open while she rested her eyes. It wasn't long until Luthiel's breath steadied, her head fell to her knees and she was sound asleep.

Beside her, Othalas, wracked with pain from his rapidly healing wounds, noticed she'd fallen asleep.

"Hrrummmph!" he muttered. "I should just bite her head off and save me the trouble."

But for some reason, the werewolf didn't bite her. Instead, he pulled his great body up beside her. His ribs were already mending. The healing was worse than the hurt and the fire of it burned through him as if he'd swallowed a mouthful of hot embers. But despite his pain, he felt a drowsiness fall over him. Soon his head nodded and his nose touched the ground. He jerked his head up with a start and blinked his eyes.

How long had he dozed? He glanced around him. Were those shadows deeper down in the cave moving? No. It was just the dance of lightning. Soon the drowsiness was upon him again. If he just rested his head so—here on his paws—he'd close his eyes and let his sharp ears tell him of danger. It wasn't long until Othalas's breath steadied and he fell into a deep, dreamless sleep.

Far off, in the depths of the cave something void of light stirred. It moved with a silence possessed only of ghosts for it had no flesh with which to brush the earth or kick a stone. Oh it could, if it concentrated enough, touch a thing. But it was easy as breath to the living for it to slip across or through solid things as though it were little more than smoke. It was drawn, as its kind are, to heat of living flesh—whose memory is only a bitter ache that for such a thing is distant kin to hunger. Quieter than the lightest breath of air, it began to chant an ancient spell of the grave. A spell of sleep—which to the living is a little death. Oh they wouldn't hear. Oh no! Better chance would a man have of hearing the step of death itself. And so the song was called Footsteps of the Little Death among the wraiths called Dimlock—which the shadow was.

Aroused by the heat of life, other shadows moved beside it. In the cave. In their cave. In the cave bought by their pain, by the dust of their flesh blasted black upon the wall.

They would kill. Kill so that no life would leave the body. Kill so that the spirit was trapped. For they were stranglers and by their murderous art both spirit and breath was trapped within the victim's body. When the heads finally hung from wrung necks, they would bear the bodies down, down into the dark at the twisted end of the cave, to the black tear. Into that black hole they would cast the bodies. Then there was no hope for the spirits trapped within those horribly strangled bodies. For the tear was an opening to the Black Moon. Upon that dead world walked creatures who would consume the dead—body and spirit. Such was the Dimlock's revenge against all living things that came to their cave. For Dimlock hated the living if only for the fact that they still knew the joy of life.

By the sound of *The Footsteps of the Little Death*, Luthiel and Othalas slept. And all the while the shadows advanced. They crept until they could touch the wolf, swarmed over his chest and squeezed, waited for the next exhalation, and squeezed. Slowly the air was crushed from him. So too they came upon the elf and six shadowy hands clamped round her neck, crushing.

Luthiel gasped for air. She was having a nightmare in which she couldn't breathe, couldn't wake up. She was paralyzed and she couldn't breathe. Her neck was being twisted and she couldn't breathe.

The dark things craved nothing more than terror. It was their custom to wake their victims when the end was near to let them see. So it was with Luthiel. The chanting stopped and the weight of the dark spell lifted. And Luthiel, who could feel the life fading within her, struggled to wake.

Her eyes fluttered open and she saw them, rank upon rank of white-eyed shadows. There were hundreds all around her, their cold hands pawing, pulling, crushing the life from her throat. She scrambled, fought to breathe, felt the terror well within her. She wanted to scream. But thrash and roll as she would the hands of shadow remained upon her—choking. She slashed at them with Hueron's blade, but it only passed through them. The shadows pressed closer. Their pin-prick eyes seemed to mock her. Those horrible, cold eyes were growing dim and she knew, soon now, she would die.

In desperation, she tore the Stone from its bag around her neck. It was the only thing she could think to do. She knew it was hopeless. She couldn't sing. The breath was trapped within her. Nevertheless she swung the Stone around her and then held it high.

Within the Stone, there was a small spark and in the dark among the shadows it made a light like a candle. Seeing this light, she struggled harder, making one final, desperate, attempt before she fell into darkness.

Methar Anduel, that great Stone of old, held in it more magic than any of the other Wyrd Stones. It bore the songs of Valkire, and of Merrin his wife, and of the Vyrl he bent to his will and it had rested in the pommel of Valkire's sword—*Aeowinar*. As any Wyrd Stone, it held within it some of the spirit of those who bore it. Those spirits slumbered, only to awake in times of great need.

By Luthiel's desperate act, the spirits within *Methar Anduel*—of Valkire, Vyrl, Merrin, and of Luthiel herself, awakened. And when the Stone touched a shadow it burst in a flash of white flame.

Luthiel felt hope rise again within her and she swung the Stone around her, catching the Dimlock unaware. With three swings and with three brilliant flashes the stranglers crouched upon her chest were gone. She drew a long rattling breath and blinked her eyes to clear them of tears. Her chest burned, and even though the cold hands were no longer about her throat, she labored to breathe. But she didn't let her guard down and as the spirits gathered to rush her, she brandished the light above her head. Looking at the light with their pinprick eyes, the shadows came to a stop just outside the ring of light. Beyond the light, their numbers grew and to Luthiel it seemed as if a vast black cloud full of cold white lights was gathering to smother her once more. In the few moments it took for the Dimlock to gather, her breaths came more easily. Then swinging *Methar Anduel* in a circle above her head, she sang out.

Nani! Nani! Lumen eni Methar Anduel! Lumen eni Luthiel!

Which in the elder tongue means, "Here! Here! Is the light of
Methar Anduel! The light of Luthiel!" And upon singing the word *Luthiel!*
the small light within the Stone grew into a radiance like a sunrise.
Luthiel felt that lightening sensation that she associated with crossing
over into the World of Dreams and the lines of the cave seemed to waver.
But the shadows remained as they were. Except where the light touched
them, they seemed to diminish. They fled from the light, seeking refuge
among the shadows in the corners, deeper within the cave, or cast by the
jagged walls. Those that didn't find the shelter of shadow diminished into
small points of black and then vanished.

Now Luthiel stood alone beside the body of Othalas. She strode
around him, driving off those Dimlock that were still cowering in the lee
of his body. Bending over, she laid her free hand over his chest. When her
fingers brushed his flesh she was suddenly overcome by a powerful sense
of rage. She heard a 'twang' as though a string was snapping and the sleep
spell that was laid upon him broke. The great werewolf sprang suddenly
to his feet with a hoarse howl. She snatched her hand back and it came
away tingling.

Even though she stood beside him, his howl came to her as if from a
great distance. The sound of her singing also came to her as though it was
carried on the wind and not coming from her moving lips. There was a
third sound as well. Though it was less distinct, after a few moments of listening, Luthiel was able to make out a sound like the tinkling of broken
glass upon stone. As far as Luthiel could tell, that sound was coming from
deep within the cave.

"The storm still rages," Othalas said.

"I can keep this up for a little while yet," she sang in reply.

Though the shadows cowered at the edge of *Methar Anduel's* light,
they were gathering again, pressing in where they could, attempting to
make their way along tiny paths of shadow cast by the large stones scattered throughout the cave. She strode to a tall rock beside them and the

shadows cast by the stones diminished even more. Touched again by her light, the Dimlock fled to the deeper shadows. A few didn't make it and diminished into nothing. She stood for a few moments longer thinking about what she was watching.

"Does the cave grow larger as it goes deeper?" she asked.

"No, it narrows steadily the further in you go."

"Stay with me," she sang. Holding *Methar Anduel* high she advanced upon the Dimlock, driving them into the ever-narrowing space of the cave. Now and then, she'd trap one within the glow of her light and it would dwindle into nothing. Beside her, Othalas walked. His yellow eyes glowed like twin flames in the brilliance cast by her Stone taking in everything. Occasionally, he would point out the hiding place of a Dimlock and Luthiel would bath it with blinding radiance. They continued in this way for some time and as the cave grew narrower, and the hiding places fewer, the shadows dwindled.

Finally, they came to a place where the cavern was no wider than about fifteen feet. It continued on in a narrow shaft for some hundred feet or more before disappearing into darkness. At the edge of the darkness, Luthiel could see a raised mound. As she approached, she noticed that the mound was made of expertly cut and polished stones. The stones were silvery but upon them were sigils and swirls of some strange black metal. At the place where the mound rose, the walls of the cavern bowed out forming a chamber. In the walls, Luthiel could see empty sconces set for flir bug bulbs or some other light.

Luthiel and Othalas stopped before the mound. On top was a stone sarcophagus that was intricately carved in the form of a noble elf. A crown of flame burned at his brow and a light like a star was depicted to shine at his breast. He was arrayed all in leaf mail. At his feet there was a stone basin. Within the basin lay the crystalline shards of a shattered sword. Beneath the basin, inlays of black metal formed a jagged script set within the stone.

The sound of breaking glass was louder here. Her eyes fell to the splintered shards of crystal. In the light of *Methar Anduel*, they seemed to ignite with the fires of a hundred small stars. She picked up the white and silver hilt in her left hand and the fires blazing in the crystal shards brightened even as the sound grew louder. Beneath the sound of breaking crystal, she could hear an undertone like a joyful song in harmony with the one she was singing. But the new sound was very faint and the sound of breaking crystal was giving her a headache. She put the shard back into the basin and turned her eyes to the inscription beneath.

"What does it say?" she asked Othalas.

"It is in the tongue of the Vyrl. What it says is. *Here lies Vlad Valkire. I, Lord of the Dark Forest, slew him. His bones I took for my own device. But his likeness is here—a reminder that I will bear no slight to my lady, no matter how noble or well intended. The shards of his sword—Aeowinar—are at his feet.*"

"So that is *Aeowinar*—Cutter's Shear?" she said, looking once more at the fragments that lay before her. "And here lies the likeness of Valkire, alone among the shadows where the Dark Lord left him. I wonder what the Lord of the Dark Forest did with his bones?"

"Rendered them into a powder which he sowed into a blade of Darksilver. The blade, it is said, holds the spirit of Valkire even in death. *Mgaurhauth*, the blade is called—Oblivion's Edge. It serves the Dark Lord now and is said never to leave his side."

"But why did the Dark Lord attack Valkire? He stayed out of Valkire's wars with the Vyrl and even gave aid to the side of elves from time to time."

"Long ago, Valkire made Wyrd Stones as gifts for the Lady and Lord of the Dark Forest. These were taken to the heart of the great wood where they were received with gladness. And the Lord placed his about his neck and it gleamed like sunlight. But when the Lady touched her Stone, it gleamed like the light of Silva and she immediately fell into a deep sleep. Nothing the great Lord could do would wake her. Thinking Valkire had cursed his love, the Lord led his armies out into the land. Riding at their head, he made ready to do war with Valkire. But Valkire ordered all who followed him to surrender. So the great Lord made his way to Valkire unopposed. When he came to Valkire and demanded that he break the spell, Valkire shook his head saying—'She has chosen this course for the good of all, for in dreams she saw the black moon rising and to dreams she has gone to face it so that the world will be saved from eternal winter.' But the black moon hadn't yet risen, and the great lord thought it was deceit and that Valkire attempted to usurp him, as was foretold. So he had Valkire put in chains, but Valkire gave no resistance saying 'do as you will, my father.' Then the great lord was enraged for he thought Valkire mocked him and he beat him into the ground with his fists. So passed Vlad Valkire, the greatest hero of an age and the son of the Lord of the Dark Forest who slew him. It is said his rage will not be eased until the Lady of the dark wood returns. To this day, the great Lord still hunts all who were dear to Valkire, seeking to do vengeance for his loss."

"Valkire's family?"

"Yes, and his friends as well—Merrin, Zalos, Mithorden. The Dark Lord's fey have hunted them for thousands of years."

"What happened to them? I know Mithorden and Zalos still live. But what of Merrin?" Leowin would have known and Luthiel had heard this part of the story before, but she wanted to hear what the wolf would say. He seemed to know a great deal.

"It is said that Merrin fell into a torpor brought on by her grief for the death of her husband. It is also said that she sleeps still—carrying an unborn child in her womb. The only child of Vlad Valkire. Others say that Merrin awoke recently and is living in secret with Zalos in Ashiroth. These tell of a child who was born of Merrin only to be lost once more."

"I've never heard of that rumor. How do you know such things?"

"I've heard whispers in high places and, for a time, I hunted Merrin for the Vyrl. They were curious and they have ever lusted after the blood of Valkire. But I was unable to confirm any of the rumors and my way in Ashiroth was harried. Zalos makes no secret of his hatred for Vyrl. I was lucky enough to escape with my pelt." The werewolf's eyes bored into her. She saw both mocking and curiosity in them. He looked as though he would say something else but then stopped himself.

"So we are the first to come here since the Dark Lord made this tomb?"

"The first I know of."

"Not even the other Vyrl?"

"No, even they fear the shadows that live here."

That gave Luthiel pause. "Even the Vyrl fear them," she whispered to herself. And well they should. But she still couldn't grasp that she'd entered a place where even Vyrl feared to walk. She stood there for an indefinite time musing on everything the werewolf said.

Othalas waited, sitting patiently on his haunches. A part of him wondered at everything that was happening but he kept that part tucked away and watched on.

Who is this Luthiel who holds Methar Anduel? he thought to himself.

Luthiel stood for a long time looking at the shards of *Aeowinar* and finally made her decision. Kneeling before the likeness of Valkire, she held the Stone high over her head and sang out into the cavern.

"Ghost of Valkire, if any of your spirit remains in this foul place, I beg your forgiveness for what I am about to do. There are others in the world who were your friends that may still have need of what you left. So I ask your permission to take the shards of *Aeowinar*. I don't have the art or skill to know if they can ever be used again. But I know one who does. So please forgive me for taking them and before I do, hear me! I am taking them to Mithorden who knew you well!"

As she said this, a great wind rose in the cave and it carried upon it the scent of roses and incense. The wind rushed through the chamber and swirled around her. In the world of dreams there was no other sound but the wind. Even her singing was momentarily hushed. Then, on the wind she heard a voice. Othalas must have heard it too, for his hackles were raised and his teeth bared.

As was my dying wish, so shall it be!

The wind about her felt as warm as sunlight and she almost laughed from the joy that welled up within her. For a moment, she forgot she was in a dark, cold cave, surrounded by shadows of the dead and fancied that she was sitting in a warm glade at the height of summer. But as the wind ebbed from the cavern, so too did her joy. Soon, she was alone again with the werewolf in that chill cavern. Yet it was a sensation she would never forget. For an instant, for perhaps the first time in her life, she had felt as though she belonged.

Luthiel stooped and picked up the shards of *Aeowinar*, gathering them carefully into the folds of a leather wrap, which she tucked into one of her pouches. As she did so, she became aware of the growing cold. She lifted her eyes and noticed that the darkness at the edge of her Wyrd Stone's light was deepening. Othalas growled again.

Then, like a great wave, the shadows rushed into the light. Luthiel held it aloft in her trembling hand like a great beacon and Othalas stood beside her. Many of the shadows diminished to nothing before they reached her. Others, sheltering in their self-made darkness, clawed at her with their black talons. The chill in the air had grown unbearable and the skin on her forehead pinched as if her sweat had frozen.

She touched the first shadow with her Stone and it erupted into fire. But where there was one, two sprang up and she danced round trying to avoid the one while striking the other. Beside her, Othalas was a blur of tooth and claw. Shadow or not, his fangs found them. His eyes blazed with fury. Soon, a dozen lay fading and motionless beside him.

Luthiel, though nowhere near as fast or violent, was armed with a light deadly to shadows. She flicked it from side to side and spun it around even as the shadows tried to bear her down. One grabbed her leg and three others piled on top of her. She fell, but as she did so, she touched all three with her Stone. These disappeared. But another grabbed her arm. She switched her Stone from one hand to the other and swung it through what must have been its face. Then, a wave of ten or twenty rushed over her, pushing her to the floor. Still she clutched the Stone and still she sang until one managed to get its hands around her throat. For a moment, her song grew still and the light within the Stone faded.

Then, Othalas was upon her and one by one the shadows fell. She sang once more and the light grew again. All at once, the shadows took to flight. The wave had broken over them, tried to pull them under, but now the tide of darkness was ebbing away from the light she bore. In the back of the cavern, the darkness swelled again and with a cry to Othalas, Luthiel turned and fled.

She did not need to look over her shoulder to know the shadows were right behind her. She could feel the cold and the dark pressing in upon her, grasping at her legs. She ran and sang and then she was out, running among the mists upon the hail battered earth. Othalas stood beside her. His tongue hung over his jowls but he wasn't panting. As usual, in the world of dreams, she felt no fatigue. But she knew she must stop singing. She'd stayed in the world of dreams for longer than she cared to. So she concentrated and after three tries, she slipped from it. She felt her bruises again and the places where the Dimlock had scratched her with their claws. Raindrops fell all about her. Far away the lightning flashed. At least the hail had stopped.

Before she could stop herself, before she could even think, she turned to Othalas, threw her arms around his neck, and gave him a big hug.

"Thank you," she whispered.

Taken aback, the wolf stumbled away from her, and then shook himself.

"It is I who should thank you," he said grudgingly.

A Castle in the Mists

In a moment, she was on his back again and he padded silently through the misty wood. By the green firelight, Luthiel was able to see much of her surroundings. She noticed that the mists seemed to come from holes in the ground, or from the lake, or the pools of standing water that seemed to speckle the Vale. Once, when they stopped, she plunged her hand into the water and found that it was warm, almost hot, to the touch. As she rode, she noticed that the trees were all twisted into flowing shapes that wound up and about in spirals or threw their branches out in bows and swirls. The trees reminded her of so many wooden snakes. Their leaves were of every color. Some were black; others red, silver, or green, and the moss that hung from their branches looked like blue smoke. After a time, they came to a large expanse of water.

"This must be the Miruvoir," she said.

Othalas nodded in silent reply as he padded along around its edge. She was growing drowsy and when they finally came to a halt, her head was nodding. They stopped in a ring of standing stones beneath a castle that looked as though it were carved from gray glass. Its many towers mounted up through the mists, their tops crenellated with glistening spikes. Smog rose continuously through the many holes and vents that crowned the keep. A hot wind seemed to issue from it and the smell of ash was heavy about the place. An iron statue stood silent watch before gates that looked like interlocking teeth. The statue was in the shape of a giant, his helm in the shape of a dragon's skull—the eyes of which were a pair of diamonds, each with a coldly glowing star at its heart.

"Gormtoth will let none enter or depart by night. We must rest in the ring of standing stones. Do not worry, for they will shelter you from the mists while you sleep."

When Luthiel looked again at the ring of standing stones, she noticed that, indeed, the mists did not pass the borders of the circle. Exhausted, she clambered down from Othalas' back, laid her bedroll on the soft grass and was soon fast asleep.

Othalas moved into the standing stones with her. By now, all his wounds were healed and the ache was rapidly fading from them. For a time, he sat there, watching the elf as she slept.

"Little elfin star, how I wonder who you are," he mused. Then he turned to look at Ottomnos. The Vyrl there had left many like her broken or dead. He didn't hold out much hope for this one. "Breaking the Vyrl's laws!" He harrumphed. "Star or no, tomorrow's light is likely to be the last you ever see."

It made him feel sad.

He growled to himself and settled down into the grass to sleep. It was long in coming, and the night seemed to pass too fast.

In the middle of the night Luthiel awoke and stared up into the stars. Her throat was hurting her and her body had become a mass of bruises and scratches. As she rubbed her neck, she remembered something Mithorden had told her. Taking her Stone from its pouch, she softly sang the words *Nin Alhandra*. Slowly, the light in her Stone went out. It made her feel even more lonely and afraid. Before her, the obsidian fortress loomed, and before it the dragon-helmed guard. His white diamond eyes reminded her too much of the Dimlock. With a shudder, she turned onto her side and tried to go back to sleep. She had difficulty, and the night marched on slowly toward the daylight she feared.

THE VYRL

Luthiel woke well before sunrise. She had fallen into brief fits of sleep. But she couldn't remain asleep for long without the nightmares. She kept waking up grasping at her neck and gasping for air. In her dreams, the Vyrl hunted her, their mouths dripping with her sister's blood.

"You failed!" they would cry to her. "We found her first and now we're coming for you!"

As they advanced toward her, she could see their mouths were thick with clots which they crunched with their teeth. She woke with a cry, chill sweat stinging the scratches on her arms, chest and neck. Afraid to sleep, she lay still upon the grass. High above, through the mists, moons and stars peeked. Othalas was awake too. She could see him watching her with his great yellow eyes.

She tried to remember the smell of Winowe's almorah bread baking or the sound of Leowin's soft singing. But no matter how hard she thought about it, she couldn't quite get the memory right and she found herself thinking again of the strangling hands on her neck or of the mouths from her dreams—filled with blood.

It was almost over. The Vyrl were coming with dawn. Would they take her instead of Leowin? She realized now how foolish a hope it was. Why had Vanye let her go? Silently she cursed him for not telling her more—about Othalas, about the Vale, about what they would do to her. But she knew about Vyrl. Every elf did since a tender age. Creatures of endless hunger, they would devour her as punishment for her misdeeds. Then they would send Othalas for her sister.

And if they accepted her? They would devour her then as well. A very few were set free. And those who would talk of the horror described the hard bites, the endless days of bleeding, the terrible pain when the blood was sucked out.

For her, there was no hope.

Mithorden was wrong. Vanye was wrong.

When did she start believing she was different? Was it when Leowin gave her the Stone? Was it before? Sure, she'd always felt that secret hope, deep within her, that she was more than she appeared. She always fancied that she was one of those great heroes in the tales that Leowin told. That she could stand alone and never know fear or weakness. But she'd learned that she was little more than a frail girl. Were it not for her Wyrd Stone, she'd be long dead. And Mithorden thought she was a sorcerer!

Soon to be just another victim of the Vyrl. That's it for you, Luthiel.

But even as she thought these things, she felt angry—angry for the law that would send her sister here, angry for never knowing her real family, angry for having to face all the dangers alone or among enemies. She glared at the wolf. For a time, she thought darkly of killing him where he lay. He'd never reach Leowin then. But the yellow light of his eyes let her know, all too well, that he was still awake.

Sitting guard over me until his masters come.

Even as she thought these things, she wondered if she could bring herself to murder, even if it was to murder a monster. Wasn't he once an elf or some similar creature when the Vale changed him in the great long ago before even Vyrl came to the Vale of Mists?

So, as Oerin's Eye rose, her anger and fear smoldered. But as the light grew, her anger receded and her fear grew until her stomach felt as though it had turned to water.

Then, by the growing light of morning, she saw a great flame rise up from the highest tower of Ottomnos. With the sound of metal grinding on metal, dragon helmed Gormtoth stepped aside. Great winches screamed as the portcullis rose and a drawbridge rimmed in glistening teeth slowly opened.

From out of the fortress came three riders. They were tall, taller than any elf, and the horses that bore them were eyeless giants. Their hooves were cleft—the tips shining like knives. One was red with black flecks, the second was paler than bone and the third was as the color of smoke. Seeing them, Luthiel was reminded of blood, death and burning. The riders were cloaked in black, but the hoods were thrown back revealing faces both beautiful and terrible. Hair the color of blood spilled over ageless skin, gushing down toward eyes blacker than the sea at night. Within them were dim white lights like stars that seemed to drift and swirl. To Luthiel, those eyes were hungry, seeming to suck the daylight. The terrible eyes held her and she couldn't look away. Her terror grew until she felt like crying out. As she watched, one of the motes drifting in the Vyrl's eye winked out. It was as if some hungry shadow dwelling in the Vyrl's eyes had devoured it. She had to remind herself over and over that Valkire took away the Vyrl's ability to eat dreams.

The Vyrl guided their horses into the ring of standing stones. Their eyes never left her throughout their long advance. Beneath their gaze she trembled. She'd never felt so afraid. Her eyes darted back and forth. Fear seemed rise off the Vyrl like smoke off a smoldering log. She wanted to run and hide where those terrible eyes would never see her again.

"So are you the whelp Leowin?" the first Vyrl asked. His voice was the soft, confident sound of a predator taking account of his prey.

Luthiel opened her mouth to say *no lord!* But she could not speak. Her mouth seemed to have dried up. Why couldn't she speak? Her mouth opened and closed but no sound came out.

"She is the daughter of Winowe and Glendoras," Othalas said with a nod.

"Then bring her inside!" the second Vyrl said in her darkly musical voice.

Othalas lay down upon the ground.

"Get on!" he said in his gruffest boat-bottom across rocks voice.

She was so dumb with terror that she walked numbly toward Othalas and was clambering onto his back before she realized what had happened.

They think I'm Leowin.

"*You* lied!" she whispered to Othalas as she climbed up onto his back. But the great wolf only growled to cover her whisper.

Upon Othalas' back, she was nearly eye to eye with the Vyrl. They stood around her so that wherever she looked she was confronted by those terrible eyes. They made her feel sick in her stomach, as though she were staring down into a great depth.

"Come, Othalas, bring the Chosen. We wish to begin as soon as possible." His voice was old, the voice of terrible wisdom.

One by one, they turned their horses and walked down the road to the fortress of charred glass. As they advanced, the heat grew and she could smell the scent of scorched air. As she drew still closer, she realized that Gormtoth was radiating heat like a blast oven. But his armor remained dark. Only his whitely burning eyes betrayed any hint of the great flames that rose beneath the layered plates. With a gasp, she realized that the armor was made all of dragon hide and what she thought was a helm was actually a blackened dragon's skull.

What are you, Gormtoth? She wondered as his white flame eyes followed her. Riding upon this werewolf, among Vyrl, past this strange burning creature whose every inch was plated in dragon hide, she felt as if she'd ventured into an alien place filled with secrets that time long ago forgot.

They continued past the gates and into the belly of Ottomnos. As they passed, strange, white-skinned creatures, with only blackened hollows where their eyes should be, spun the winches. Their movements were convulsive. Other creatures of this kind moved throughout the fortress, jerking even when they stood still. Their flesh seemed to have turned into paste for it lacked definition or any hint of blood. Though they had no eyes, it seemed that they could sense her for they flocked around the wolf, their cold hands grasping to touch her. Their mouths seemed to pant and they whispered something under their breath.

"What are they saying?" she whispered to Othalas.

"Eyes. They hunger for eyes."

She recoiled from the creatures even as they continued to grasp at her, raising their hooked fingers, drawn by some sense beyond sight, toward her eyes. They were all around her now, grasping at her, clutching, trying to pry her off Othalas.

Then, the werewolf let out a great growl and the creatures scattered from him. Still their hands quested toward Luthiel. She shuddered.

The first Vyrl laughed, his soft predator's voice echoing through the fortress.

"Othalas has taken a liking to this little one!" He laid a great gloved hand on the wolf's broad head. "My hunter," he said. "You know as well as I that even wights must eat. Is it kindness to spare her? Or cruelty? Now she knows. Why torture her with fear of what will be? Or are you so foolish to think we will let this little bird go?"

Othalas stared ahead but did not answer.

Now all the Vyrl's eyes were upon Othalas. Despite their stares, Othalas kept quiet, continuing his slow advance into the fortress.

"He *does* like her," the second said with dark music that seemed to get caught up in the smoke rising off the towers. To Luthiel the whole place smelled of smoke and blood. Everywhere she looked, she could see carcasses hanging from chains—bears, beasts, elves—it made no difference. They'd all been sucked dry of blood and every one had its eyes plucked out. But the meat was left to rot.

It is a slaughterhouse, she thought. She glanced at the wights dancing their terrible death dance and shuddered. *Except some of the slaughtered still walk. I have entered a place on the border between life and death where nothing is as it ought to be.*

"Othalas," the third Vyrl said with old-wise chanting. "The time for mercy is gone. You know this. The madness is upon us and with each passing day it grows. If we do not feed, the hunger will consume even our minds until we become little more than ravening beasts stalking the land." He motioned to Luthiel. "And this poor fare is barely enough to sustain us—who once dined upon the rich blood of dreams. Only Valkire's blood could compare to it! Now we wither. Why should she not give us her heart's life-blood? It is only for the safety of her kin, which we could take at a whim. By our honor we starve. So she will pay dearly for our hunger—daughter of the elves who trapped us! And yes, her eyes will feed my wights!"

He stepped closer to Othalas, "You think she is different than the others?"

At this question Othalas growled and met the gaze of the elder Vyrl. For a moment his anger was naked in his eyes, but then he caught himself and bowed his head. Too late! For the Vyrl's great arm snaked out with a speed Luthiel's eyes could barely follow and latched onto her neck.

"My kin!" he called madly in his terrible-wise voice. "Othalas has found someone *special!*" He hauled her from the back of Othalas by the scruff of her neck. She felt her vertebrae popping as he held her in the air in front of him, forcing her to stare into his black whirlpool eyes.

"What makes *you* special?" One handed, he shook her as a child might shake a toy doll. Then, he pulled her close to his face. She was so close she could smell the blood on his breath. His mouth smelled like a barrel brimming with it. "*You* think you are something now that you were Chosen? I'll tell you what sort of something you are. You're meat!"

With that, he tossed her to the ground.

"Come my wights! Let's show Othalas what we do to meat! There's two eyes for the taking, if you can snatch them from her!"

Luthiel couldn't help herself. She was crying. But it wasn't out of grief or fear any longer. It was out of rage. Driven by desperate anger, she scrambled to her feet. The wights were still some feet away from her when she stood. But they were rushing in on her in a convulsive wave. Her hand found the hilt of her knife—the *Cauthrim* blade Hueron had forged her—and with a loud *snick* it sprang from the sheath. It seemed an alive thing in her hand.

Small, overwhelmed, and helpless, she fought as might some poor cornered creature armed with only its teeth against some great and terrible predator. In desperation, she struck out with all her fear-driven strength.

"Monster! Monster!" she yelled as she drove the blade, sparking with the blue fires of Cauthraus, at the face of the Vyrl who bent, gloating, over her.

Too late, the Vyrl saw the fang in Luthiel's hand as she made for *his* eyes. He sprang back, an angel twisted horribly into one of the most terrible creatures in nature. Now his predator's reflexes—long neglected by overconfidence and letting others do the hunting—failed him as he jerked away from the burning knife.

The blow, though it missed his eye, cut a deep furrow into his brow, scored across his temple and lopped off the tip of his ear.

Roaring in pain and surprise, he kicked at the madly cutting Luthiel.

The great foot struck her in the chest, sending her flying in front of his horse, but not before Luthiel sliced a scorching ribbon across his shin. Screaming in rage, he ripped his great sword *Ombrallix*, from its sheath. Its black metal hissed like a snake and smoke rose from the rill.

It whipped out, striking Luthiel, who was, at the same time, trying to stand, with the flat upon the crown of her head. She crumpled to the ground. Her blade flew from her hands, skittering out of reach and her arms seemed to turn to mud as they flopped about her. Blood flowed into her eyes and she could smell her own hair burning. The wights rushed in, their hooked fingers clawing. But the terrible voice of the third Vyrl rose above them in command.

"Wait!" he cried. "I want her to see what I am about to do!"

He rose into her field of vision and he showed her his teeth. They were a nest of points and they were all covered in blood. He must have been devouring the blood of any creature he could catch—bears and boars, rats and cats, any poor thing hapless enough to cross the Vyrl's path. But now he had his eyes fixed on finer prey.

He raised one of her arms in his great hand, then flayed the vein in her wrist with his needle teeth. The pain was greater than anything she'd ever experienced and she cried out as fire leapt through her body. The other Vyrl were upon her in an instant. They bit her on her other arm and upon her neck. Then her world became a red haze of agony. Her stomach clenched against the sudden blood loss, trying to halt the flood going into the open mouths of the Vyrl. They took a pull as an elf might take a pull off a flask of honey mead and she trembled as her heart raced.

This is it! Oh, Leowin, this is it!

She'd succeeded and she'd failed. Leowin would live and she would die. She wondered how many times the Vyrl could suck her blood before she faded and finally died. It couldn't be many more times; three, perhaps four. Their hunger seemed bottomless. She waited for the second pull, steeling herself against the pain.

But the second pull never came. Through the red haze, she thought she saw the Vyrl rock back as if in a daze. The wights came forward again but this time Othalas pounced upon one, sending the rest to flight with a great howl. They fled to the shadows beneath the burned glass where they cowered.

"Madness take you Vyrl! You are *fools!* Don't you know who *she* is!" he rumbled.

The blood oozed from her veins, pumped from her neck.

"I'd forgotten what it looked like," the second Vyrl spoke with her dark music. "How it blazes like gold in sunlight."

Then she saw rainbow wings above her and a shape like a thread of mercury braiding the air.

"You are all idiots! She's going to bleed to death if you just sit around in a stupor."

It landed and tore a patch from her cloak. She knew she was hallucinating now, for the creature tying knots around her wounds was a dragon in miniature. Its body was a silver river and its wings were of gossamer filigree that bent the light into rainbows.

Then, shock took her and she lost sight. Distantly, she felt her body carried for a ways and then laid down. There was talking around her. But she no longer understood it. There were touches on her skin, pressing against her wounds. Soon, even the sounds and touches faded and she was alone in the darkness.

BOOK II

The Mists' Changing Magic

Luthiel awoke to find herself lying in a soft bed. Her wounds were all bound in silken cloth and her clothes lay folded in a pile on her pack which rested upon a bone chair beside her bed. Strange, soft light filtered through the blackened glass of the room. Globes on the wall encircled blue flames. Mists lay thick about the room, swirling in a cloying cloud. As she sat up, they seemed to draw closer, pressing in upon her.

With the sudden movement, a sharp pain shot through her head and her vision blurred. She spent a few moments cradling her head before she could see again. Careful not to make any sudden movements, she looked around her, trying to make sense of her strange surroundings.

In that moment, she couldn't remember where she was. The blackened glass walls were wrought with long, ribbed shapes that made her feel as though she were in the guts of some vast living creature. Like the chair, her bed was made of the bone of some giant creature and the white sheets were stained in places where the blood had oozed through her bandages.

But for her bandages, she was completely unclad. It made her feel particularly vulnerable as she lay there, trying to recall how she had come to this strange place. The mist was growing thicker now within the room. It seemed to be flowing in through the slit windows, pushing through the crack beneath the great bone door. It pooled upon the floor where it rose and swelled like a sea.

Was there something she should remember about the mist? The way it seemed to move like a living creature made her begin to feel afraid, but she couldn't quite recall why.

Then, as long fingers of mist began to push up from the swelling mass around her bed, she began to remember.

I went to the Vale of Mists!

With this recollection, panic began to set in. She jerked away from the grasping hands of mists that were now rising up from the pool on the floor to circle her in a cage of swaying arms. She pulled the covers over her head. But she could still feel the damp touch of it through the sheets.

Then she remembered her Stone.

The Stone! Of course, how could I be such a fool!

She clutched for the pouch around her neck only to find that it was not there. Now she began to panic in earnest. What had happened to her Stone?

Vyrl.

With that thought, she suddenly recalled everything—Othalas, the Cave of Painted Shadows, her struggle with the Vyrl. She glanced down at her naked body.

They looked through everything!

Her heart quailed.

What if they took it?

The sheets grew damper and mist started seeping in through small openings. Thin fingers stretched out toward her. She recoiled, but there was nowhere to hide. Where the mist touched her, her flesh seemed to writhe and twitch.

Desperate, she flung the sheets aside.

Now the mist was all over her. Great ropes of it wrapped around her. Everywhere, her flesh was writhing as though worms were swarming beneath. She leapt from her bed, and scampered to the bone chair. Her head reeled and the place where the Vyrl struck her throbbed. She had to steady herself on the bed before continuing. The writhing beneath her skin grew with each passing moment. Finally, she made it to the chair. Tossing her clothes aside, she searched desperately. Her pack, her map, some scant amount of food, socks, her leather case containing the shards of *Aeowinar* all ended up on the floor as she dug. But no matter where she looked, she couldn't find it.

"Where is it? Oh where is it!" she cried as she threw her clothes on the floor.

Now she could feel the change starting. Something had gotten into her. It wormed its way deep into the caverns of her mind, searching, moving things around. She shuddered to think what would happen when it found what it was looking for. The change began to take control and it wasn't gentle. Her legs writhed so much that she fell the floor. The joints in arms and legs made loud popping sounds. She desperately pawed through her things with fingers that seemed to be shrinking, drawing together. But she couldn't find her Stone no matter where she searched.

"Looking for this?"

The voice came from one of the small slit windows at the far end of the room. There she saw a creature that looked like a dragon in miniature. His silver body sprouted wings like gossamer that caught the light and turned it into rainbows. In his hand he held her Stone.

Luthiel's heart raced. She only had a few moments.

"Please, give it to me!" she cried. Her lips seemed clumsy and her voice seemed shrill to her ears.

"In a moment. I just want to ask you one thing and if you say yes, then I will give it to you. I need your help, you see, and I wanted to know if you'd help me."

Luthiel was desperate, a horn was starting to sprout from her head and silver hair was springing up all over her body.

"Yes, anything, just give it to me!"

"You must promise."

Luthiel knew she didn't have any other choice. If she wanted to remain herself, she must do as the tiny dragon asked.

"I give my word. Now please, give me my Stone!" At least that was what she meant to say. But the last three words came out like a ghostly neigh.

It was enough, though, for the tiny drake sprang into the air and flew to her, placing the Stone gently in her hand.

"I'm sorry," he said. "I had to have your promise."

She didn't waste any more time talking to the tiny drake. Instead, she cupped the Stone in her hands and sang aloud.

Luthiel!

The Stone, dark before, burst into sudden light as she entered the world of dreams. The mists, caught up in the song, swirled about her. She no longer felt the crawling beneath her skin. Instead, the waves in her flesh stilled and the horn and silver hair melted back into her skin. The breath of air was crisp in her lungs, exhilarating. In a moment, the mists dispersed and she was left alone in the room with the rainbow winged dragon. Luthiel let herself sing for a few moments longer. Her pain seemed so far away and the wavery walls gave her odd comfort. The world of dreams sometimes seemed to her like such a soft place. Looking at the tiny dragon, she saw that he was surrounded by a cloud of light, but the shadows he cast looked long and spindly.

MELKION THE DRAGON

Luthiel had begun to watch the drake with fascination when she remembered Mithorden's words about the Vyrl.

Though many mystical creatures covet Wyrd Stones, the Vyrl above all desire them. If your Stone is open, it is likely that they will discover it and then try to kill you so that they can claim it.

With an effort, she stopped singing. She did it in one try this time.

Then, holding the Stone in her hand, she chanted—*Nin Alhandra.* Slowly, the light in her Stone winked out.

She let out a long sigh as the pain from her wounds returned.

The winged serpent who, a moment ago, had held her Stone for ransom landed on the foot of her bed and stared sharply at her with blazing violet eyes. Self conscious, Luthiel sat down on the bed and pulled the blankets about her.

"Don't you ever, *ever*, touch my Stone or anything else that is mine again, you little thief!"

The little dragon flared his wings out in surprise at her outburst.

"I am sorry about what happened just now. But I needed your assurance. You don't understand."

"Understand! Don't you understand what just almost happened!"

"I understand what didn't happen. Now that is something even I have never seen. It is truly amazing," the little dragon said.

Luthiel took a long breath and tried to calm her anger. She was alone in the palace of the Vyrl and this little dragon must be one of their servants. He must not realize what the Stone was.

If he tells them, then it's certain they'll kill me. They'll want the Stone.

"Just don't you ever take something that is mine again," she said tersely.

"In exchange for your forgiveness and your help, I promise." The tiny dragon bobbed his head.

Luthiel would have nodded in return if her head wasn't throbbing so terribly.

"And one more thing, no one but us needs to know what happened here," she said, thinking of her *Cauthrim* blade.

The dragon nodded. But his purple eyes twinkled knowingly.

"Just so we understand each other," she said. She watched silently as the last of the mists slipped from the room.

"They don't bother you?" she asked.

"The mists? Of course not! I am a dragon! The mists would have more luck changing the wind."

Luthiel sat quietly, then took a deep breath and let it out slowly.

"I suppose I should ask you."

"Ask me what?"

"What I've promised to do."

"Oh that! I'll tell you in good time. No need to worry now—no, you have quite enough to concern yourself with already, I should say."

At that Luthiel gave a short, half-hearted, laugh.

"I'm rude," he continued. "We haven't been properly introduced! While I may know who you are, you seem to be at a loss."

"I've been playing catch-up ever since I left home," she muttered. She wondered if the dragon really knew who she was and, if so, how? Had Othalas told her? Or did he just think she was Leowin?

The dragon continued as if he hadn't even heard her.

"Be that as it may, my name is Melkion," he said with a swish of his rainbow plumed tail and a bow of his silver head. "My lady," he continued. "I am at your service."

"Service?"

"Well yes. What can I do for you?"

Luthiel did laugh this time—but not too loud, for it hurt her head. The laugh was more bitter than happy. A moment ago the little monster had threatened to let the mists consume her. Now he was playing at host.

"Don't be ridiculous!"

"Ridiculous? My dear, I don't understand what you could mean."

Now Luthiel was fuming. He was mocking her, she was sure of it. The little court jester was having his fun as, all the while, Vyrl were coming down the hall to dine on her blood.

"I didn't come here through every kind of trouble—attacked by spiders, threatened by werewolves, strangled by shadows, mauled by Vyrl, and nearly turned into something utterly monstrous by the mists—only to be mocked by some prankster who thinks it's all some kind of joke!"

"I was hoping we could be friends," Melkion said in a quieter tone.

"Friends!? What do you suppose would be the basis for our friendship? Dangerous practical jokes at my expense? Bribery? Blackmail? How about looking the other way as the Vyrl torture and kill innocent people?"

"I understand how you could see it that way," the little dragon said. His head drooped on the end of his long neck and his voice sounded very sad. "Sometimes, you have almost no choice and you are forced to do things you normally wouldn't."

"What are you talking about?"

"Well sometimes, you can't change the way things are. You might be too weak. Suppose a very bad thing has happened to someone you love. Suppose they will die unless you go to a bad place and do bad things. What would you do then?"

Luthiel knew the dragon was being intentionally vague. But she did understand about making sacrifices for someone you love. Still, she didn't trust him.

"Aren't you a servant of the Vyrl?"

"Yes, but not by choice. I came here a long time ago in hopes of finding something to help someone I love very much. In exchange for this small chance, I have served as the Vyrl's messenger for more than a century now," his violet eyes glistened as he watched her. "I don't enjoy serving them.

They are terrible. But if I did something to stop them, they might kill me or cast me out of the Vale where I would have little hope of finding help."

Luthiel was still suspicious.

"Does this have anything to do with you holding my Stone hostage?"

The dragon let out a long sigh and then gave her a toothy grin.

"Well if I couldn't interest you in friendship, then perhaps I could interest you in a bite to eat? This place is not known for its fine food, but I could offer you bread, cheese, a bit of fresh fruit and even something sweet that I've stashed away for special occasions."

Luthiel stared at the little rainbow winged creature with her mouth open. Of all the things she'd expected to find in the fortress of the Vyrl at the heart of the Vale of Mists, this wasn't one of them. To be recited menu items, no matter how scant, by a ridiculous little dragon as the Vyrl were contemplating their next meal was almost too much for her to fathom. But she was starving and she felt very weak.

"Well, if you have some food, I'm not saying I wouldn't eat it."

The little dragon put his hands together. "Now that's a start, at least," he hissed. "I'll be right back!" Then, he turned and, with a flap of his wings, glided out the window.

"Strange and stranger," Luthiel whispered to herself. She sat up, pulling the covers down to inspect herself. Her wounds were washed and wrapped in clean cloth. Even her skin was clean. The bruises on her legs stood out in angry blue but the cuts and gashes were all tended to and covered in bandages. She stood. She had to steady herself for a moment as her head reeled. She raised a hand to her head, feeling another bandage on the place where the Vyrl struck her with his sword.

The way her head throbbed, she was surprised that the blow hadn't brained her. She found her remaining clothes clean and folded. She felt better after putting them on and then went through her things.

Strange, they'd let her keep her knife.

She laughed.

Not like it had done her much good anyway.

She had everything, even the shards of Valkire's sword. She unfolded her leather pouch and looked at the shards sparkling in the firelight. Othalas had known about it, but here it was, still in her possession.

"Not that it matters. I'll soon be dead and they can take what they want."

"Now I wouldn't say such things! You don't know everything that's happened since you fell. You should take heart that you are still among the living. It's not everyday this sort of thing happens." The tiny dragon had come upon her unawares. Miraculously, he had managed to lay everything neatly on the table beside her bed. There was a large loaf of crusty black bread, a good sized hunk of cheese, a black lump that looked like chocolate, a shining green pear and a tall cup filled with a golden liquid.

She moved quickly to cover the shards but the dragon was already looking at them.

"Now there's a pretty thing! Where did you get that?" The dragon said lunging toward the shattered bits sparkling in the firelight.

Quickly, she folded the bits in the leather case and clutched them to her chest.

"None of your business you snooper."

"Snooper?" The dragon looked irritated. "Who cares if I'm a snooper who wants to know interesting things! I just do!" The dragon pointed with his tail at the food. "Well are you going to eat some food or are you going to sit there hoarding your little shiny bits for fear that a dragon might steal them?"

Ignoring him, she folded the shards carefully back into her pouch which she hung around her belt before she sat down to eat.

The food was rough but amazingly good. The pear was juicy and the chocolate was exquisite.

"This is wonderful," she said, around a mouthful of chocolate. "Where did you get it?"

"Oh, the girl is not the only one with treasures. Any dragon worth his scales knows how to find precious things and keep them. Here in the

Vale of Mists, chocolate is more precious than gold. For there's only I who knows how to get it."

She bit another piece off, savoring the taste as it melted over her tongue. With some food in her stomach, she felt her mood rising a little.

"Well, if you keep giving me such good food, then you might well have yourself a friend, Melkion. That is, if the Vyrl don't kill me first and if you can keep your claws off my things."

The dragon swished his tail back and forth playfully.

"Leowin, I think there may be some hope for you after all," he said with a smile.

Luthiel smiled back at the little dragon. She was glad Othalas had kept her secret. As she finished her food in silence, she wondered why he lied to the Vyrl. Did he really care about why she came here? Or was he just paying her back for her saving him in the cave?

To think that I could earn the loyalty of Othalas!

She grinned at the thought. As unlikely as such things were, it was nice to think them. Melkion, who had returned to his perch in the slit window, stared at her curiously and swished his rainbow-plumed tail.

Summoned by Monsters

When she was done eating, she lay back in her bed. She felt better now, with food in her belly, her knife in the sheath at her belt and with her Stone, once again, hung around her neck. She'd also tucked the leather pouch containing the shards into her belt. She wanted to make sure, if she lived, that they got back to Mithorden safely and didn't end up in some little dragon's hoard.

Lying there, she felt the ache of her injuries and exhaustion. She tried to stay still, because when she moved, she felt dizzy and her head throbbed. She wanted to keep as much of her strength as she could. She decided to try to get some more sleep.

But as soon as she closed her eyes she felt a disturbance of air beside her. When she opened her eyes again she saw Melkion perched on the chair beside her bed.

"Did you enjoy your food?" he asked.

"Yes, I did, thank you," she replied.

"Good, now I suppose you are ready to go to see the Vyrl."

Even though Luthiel lay still in bed, her head was reeling. It took her a few moments before she could say anything.

"No, I think I'd rather stay here and rest a while," she said.

Melkion looked at her sadly.

"Leowin, I think you'd better come. It is not a good idea to refuse the summons of a Vyrl."

Luthiel was having trouble getting used to being called Leowin. She felt the impulse to correct the little dragon every time he said the name. She tried to gather her wits.

I must go, she thought.

With an effort, she stood, using one to the bed posts for support. It took more effort than she liked to put on her boots. She kept stumbling with dizziness.

No more fighting for me. I'm useless.

When she was steady on her feet she turned to Melkion.

"Lead the way," she said hollowly.

The tiny dragon flew to the door, and opened it with his tail.

"After you," he said.

She went through the door and found herself in a long hall lit by the same blue fires that were in her room. The walls, ceiling and floor were all of black glass. The columns and tube shapes in the walls again gave her the feeling that she was wandering around inside the body of a great living thing. Wights and strange one-armed, one-legged creatures made their way down the hall. The new creatures moved with a grace that was fascinating for Luthiel to watch.

Melkion landed on her shoulder.

"They're called Grendilo," he said, "creatures of the Vale that the Vyrl have conquered."

The wights, though they often turned their heads toward her, shuffled by in their jerking gaits without bothering her.

"They've been told to leave you alone," Melkion said.

"Why?"

"I don't know," Melkion said.

Luthiel wondered if he was lying.

"What are they?" she whispered.

"You don't know? Don't you see they have no eyes?"

"I've only heard faerie tales and myths," she said.

"Three thousand years ago, Vyrl used to possess the ability to devour dreams. This was achieved by some faculty in their eyes. They would hold a creature fast, stare into its eyes. The dreams would be drawn out one by one and consumed by the Vyrl. When the Vyrl was finished, the poor victim's eyes burned into charred husks. Afterward, they roamed the earth as soulless creatures without mind or personality subject only to its hunger and to the Vyrl's will.

"Wights hunger for eyes. It is the only food they will consume. If they don't eat, they fade, slowly turning into shadows. Now the Vyrl can no longer feed on dreams, for Valkire cast a mighty spell that robbed them of this ability. The wights you see here are all well over three thousand years old."

"How terrible," Luthiel said with a shudder. She wondered what happened to the wights after they faded but decided against asking the question.

Melkion bobbed his head but didn't say anything.

"I'm glad they can't do it anymore," she said.

Melkion nodded again.

They spent the rest of their time passing through the halls in silence, with Melkion talking only to give directions. Occasionally, they would pass a wight moving along on some errand or just ambling aimlessly, propelled by some impulse it long ago forgot.

As they continued, Luthiel became more and more withdrawn. She thought that, most likely, she was walking toward her execution. But she didn't understand why the Vyrl had cared for her wounds, let her rest, and allowed Melkion to bring her food.

Perhaps they're trying to make me last longer so they can get more blood out of me.

She kept reliving the events that led up to the Vyrl biting her. She saw again the terrible eyes of the third Vyrl as he held her by the neck, felt the harsh blow of his sword upon her head, the terrible sensation of the Vyrl drawing blood from her body, the pain, and the racing of her heart. Then she recalled how they stopped as if stunned.

Her body started to tremble with fear. She didn't want to go through it again. Would it be better if she'd died? Then her suffering would end. But she didn't want to end, felt determined that whatever it took she would make it through and return to Leowin. She had another vision of the Vyrl biting her, ravenous with hunger, and shuddered. How could she possibly survive?

She wondered if all Chosen shared this experience and if it was worse for them than her. Then, she had a vision of coming here borne on the back of a cold Othalas, marred by mists, blinded by wights only to finally be consumed by Vyrl over the course of days or weeks. Yes, it could certainly get worse.

Outside, the suns were setting. From time to time, they would pass a slit window streaming brilliant red light. The mists diffused the light into a dull red glow that carried far down the halls and passageways deep into the fortress. She wondered if she'd rested all day or if she'd slept through the night and this was the end of her second day in Ottomnos.

Finally, the halls widened and she came to a great gaping pair of double doors. Outside the doors stood two Grendilo dressed in strange armor that made them look like deadly sword-wielding plants. At the sight of her and Melkion, though, they parted and let her enter the great hall.

The charred glass arched up in great buttresses. Upon great flowing columns sat strange carvings—gargoyles, unicorns, werewolves and dragons. Above, on the ceiling, a celestial battle raged—armies of angels and demons clashed, suns bloomed, great ships sailed among the stars or burst into fire. Places in the walls thinned into windows of stained glass depicting noble figures—some terrible, some tranquil and loving. A window in the back of the hall depicted a hunt with Vyrl on great steeds chasing all manner of creatures, including elves, into a burning land.

At the center of the great hall was a long table. In the table were wells of all shapes and sizes. The wells were darkened with bloodstains long made permanent by use and reuse. At the end of the hall were three tall chairs. They sat on the floor level with the table but still managed to dominate the room. The chairs were worked in artistic forms and the charred glass from which they were cut was polished so that it gleamed like black ice. In each of these sat a Vyrl.

The first Vyrl, sleek and predatory, sat in the chair furthest right, the second Vyrl, dark and melancholy, sat in the chair furthest left and the third Vyrl, who had struck her, sat in the center. Before them was a fourth chair. It looked oddly out of place for it was made of a highly polished white wood. A silver metal that could only be *Silen* was worked into its arms and raised back. Othalas sat beside it, a jagged patch of midnight, yellow eyes gleaming as he watched her.

When the Vyrl noticed that she had entered, they rose from their seats. The third Vyrl raised his hand indicating the smaller chair.

"Welcome! Please, come in. We have much to discuss, much indeed."

Luthiel, taken aback by being treated with such formality where she was treated only as meat before, felt her gut tighten.

They're acting like I'm someone important. Why?

"Well, what are you waiting for?" Melkion hissed in her ear.

Spurred by the dragon, she walked down the hall toward where the Vyrl waited. She shuddered as she passed the long table wondering if she'd spend her last remaining moments strapped into one of those reservoirs.

Finally, she came before the Vyrl. She was forced to raise her eyes to look at them. They were an awesome sight. Standing taller than the oldest elves, the Vyrl loomed over her.

The third Vyrl motioned again toward the chair she now stood beside.

"Please, have a seat so we can begin."

Again, Luthiel got a sinking feeling in her stomach.

Why are they being so polite?

She sat down; strangely reassured that Othalas was beside her. Would he help her again or did he consider the debt paid?

After she was seated, the Vyrl sat in their chairs. Even though there was no dais, they towered over her. Melkion flew from his perch on her shoulder and alighted upon the chair's back.

For a moment, there was silence as the Vyrl inspected her. The swirling lights in their black eyes made her feel dizzy, but she forced herself to meet their stares. After they had appraised her, the third Vyrl began to speak.

"Welcome, to Ottomnos and the Vale of Mists—the last place on Oesha where Vyrl still reign. I am Ahmberen, which means memory in the elder tongue, to my right is Elshael, or sorrow, and to my left is Ecthellien, or chance. We are the last surviving Vyrl allied with Vlad Valkire. Together we make up three of the four remaining Vyrl in all of Oesha." He paused before continuing.

Luthiel wondered why they were welcoming her after they had attacked her. She felt very strange and uncomfortable about the way they were acting. Perhaps they'd fallen into madness.

"Now you know us properly," the third Vyrl continued. "But we are at a loss as to who you are. Othalas has told us one tale and then another. It seems, though, that no one is really sure. But, whoever you are, Chosen or not. One thing is certain; you are the daughter of no elf— Glendoras or Winowe or any other."

Luthiel's head was swirling around with the lights in the Vyrl's eyes. What were they talking about?

"So before we continue," he said, "we'd like to know who you really are." The Vyrl were silent as they waited for her reply. Luthiel suspected some trick.

"What do you mean?" she asked.

"Well, you could start with your real name. We know it isn't Leowin, daughter of Winowe. And then, you could tell us where you really come from. For, I assure you, there is no elf with blood like yours from Drakken Spur to Lothyn Aer or beyond."

"I—" She didn't know what to say. She couldn't think of a tale any of these Vyrl would possibly believe. What would happen to her sister if they found out? The uncomfortable silence stretched out. Luthiel lowered her eyes. She could no longer bear to look at them or stare into their eyes. Finally, Othalas spoke.

"I told you, she is afraid for her sister. She won't tell you unless she knows you won't send me for her," he said.

Luthiel's heart quailed. They knew! Othalas told them!

The second Vyrl nodded, then spoke with her beautiful, dark, voice.

"If what Othalas says is true—that you came in your sister's place—then whether or not she is brought here rests entirely in your hands. We know that you are not Leowin, so tell us who you really are."

"How did you know?" she asked, then turned to Othalas. "You told them, didn't you?"

The first Vyrl answered in his predator's voice.

"I have tasted the blood of thousands of creatures and each is different. The moment we tasted your blood we knew that you were no daughter of any elf from Flir Light Hollow. Othalas told us the rest."

Luthiel nodded. That a Vyrl could tell creatures apart by the taste of their blood was something she hadn't considered. But what they said puzzled her. She knew that she was orphaned. But if she was no elf of Minonowe or Ithilden or Rimwold or Ashiroth or any land between the gates of East and West then what was she? Sith? But she looked like no Sith she'd ever seen. They tended to be dark eyed with black hair. She looked more like the elves of the Minonowe, except she was taller than most girls her age, and her skin was fairer, and her hair was silver.

She thought hard about what the Vyrl said before making her reply.

"If I were the one to decide, then my sister would never see this place. My name is Luthiel, Luthiel Valshae, if you must know. You are right that Winowe and Glendoras are not my real parents. I was orphaned at a very young age. They were good enough to take me into their family. Leowin is my foster sister. I don't know where I came from or if it was beyond the Gates of East or West. I was abandoned by someone I can't remember. They found me just outside Flir Light Hollow. A note left with me asked for someone to care for me and gave my name. That is all I know."

"You don't remember anything of the time before you came to Flir Light?" The Vyrl with a voice like sad music asked.

"I was very young, less than one year old. I cannot remember anything of that time. Mother Winowe wanted to keep it secret that I was orphaned. But I found out soon enough. The older children knew and they made fun of me for it."

THE BLOOD OF VLAD VALKIRE

The Vyrl considered her for some time before replying. In the blue firelight, the shadows fell long across the hall. She watched as the lights in the Vyrl's eyes swirled.

"Luthiel Valshae, there are strange things and wonders in this world that even I, who have lived ten thousand years, cannot understand. This is one of them. A day ago I starved and now the blood that is in me—the blood I took from you—is enough to sustain me a month. The hunger is abated and with it, the madness. I am ashamed of what I was, only yesterday. It is a creature I became again three thousand years ago, soon after the death of Vlad Valkire. It is a creature I became first when I dwelt upon the moon Eledweil—before we ruined it—and a black hunger settled upon me. Once, long ago, the blood of Valkire freed me. Now, your blood has freed me from the hunger that devours all."

"As I," said the Vyrl with her dark music.

"And I," said the Vyrl with his predator's voice.

Luthiel stared at the Vyrl amazed at what she was hearing.

"But how can this be?"

"We were hoping you could tell us," the second Vyrl said. Her voice lifted through the hall and, for the first time, Luthiel could hear lightness among the melancholy tones.

Luthiel didn't know how to reply or what to say.

"We have long hoped that someone with the blood of Valkire would return to us and save us from the madness," the second Vyrl continued. "For a time, we had no hope. Then rumor came to us that Merrin, Valkire's beloved wife and queen of the moon that bears her name, had awoken from her ages-long torpor and come to live with the lord Zalos, in the forestland of Ashiroth. We sent Othalas, for we heard that Merrin was with child and we hoped that it was the whelp of Valkire. But Zalos drove Othalas away—for he has grown to hate us over the years. We had once again become the monsters he fought so long ago. We sent Melkion with a message—"

Melkion snorted at the mention of his name and muttered.

"Did little good. Zalos burned the letter and then told his archers to shoot me where I stood. But I am fast when the need is upon me!" Melkion flapped his wings and then settled again onto the back of her chair.

Luthiel brushed her hair out of her face.

The Vyrl continued in his ancient, chanting, voice.

"After Melkion was turned away, we resorted to spies. We had a difficult time. Most were killed and the others fell sick from a strange ailment that twisted their bodies into the shape of giant spiders. Something strange and dark was at work on the eastern marches of Ashiroth and it was preying on our spies. But one got through and found that Merrin, indeed, had borne a child."

"We were filled with hope," said the first Vyrl in his predator's voice. "A child of Valkire was born of Merrin. We had to reach the child. We sent word to Lord Tuorlin of Ithilden saying that we would take no more Chosen if, once the child was old enough, she was sent to the Vale once each year that we might again feed and stave off the madness for a time."

"Tuorlin wouldn't listen," Melkion said. "Zalos denied that Merrin had borne any child of Valkire's line and Tuorlin, who knew us only as monsters, believed him."

"Worse," the lady picked up, "Zalos claimed that Merrin bore his child and he and she were to be wed. There was to be a great celebration. But, only a few days before the wedding, word came to us that the child had passed—the victim of some strange sickness plaguing the elves of Ashiroth. Then, we fell into despair as the hunger consumed us. For without the child of Valkire, we were bereft of hope of release—doomed to days of torturing hunger and of growing madness. With the passing ages we would diminish as the madness of hunger ran its course until we became little more than monsters stalking the land hunting all things that bleed."

"Even after the child's death, Zalos insisted on pressing his suit," the first Vyrl continued. "He and Merrin were wed only a fortnight after the infant's passing. It is said that, now, she is cold to Zalos showing him none of the affections of a wife. So too, it is said, that he keeps her a prisoner in his tower of Arganoth."

The Vyrl fell into silence.

"How terrible that she should suffer so much after all these years," Luthiel said. "First for lost love and now for the child and this terrible lord who has taken her against her will. I suppose Zalos had the little one killed." Luthiel said. She was caught up in the Vyrl's tale. It compelled her in a way she didn't fully fathom.

"Suppose?" It was Othalas who spoke this time, his gravely voice grating through the chamber. "Let me tell you what I suppose. The child was poisoned and grew sicker and sicker. But Merrin, by art or accident, discovered this and suspected that the jealous Zalos wanted her child killed. So she, queen of depthless waters, discovered a means to cure her child and send her in secret to live with the elves ... far from the lengthening arm of Lord Zalos."

"To Flir Light Hollow?" Luthiel asked. Her heart was pounding in her ears like a drum-beat.

"What would be stranger, Luthiel? If some elf from Flir Light Hollow came here and did what you did? Or if the child of Merrin and Valkire, carefully hidden in that happy nowhere, by circumstance and the good of her heart, decided to come to the Vale in hopes of saving her sister? Could any elf you know in Flir Light accomplish all you did?"

Luthiel shook her head in disbelief.

"But I am only an orphan."

At this, the first Vyrl stood. "Indeed! The orphaned daughter of Merrin Valkire sent into exile for her safety. And, wonder of wonders, you came to us in our darkest hour and saved us from madness."

"I don't believe it," she said. "It can't be true!"

The Vyrl only stared at her. Melkion swished his tail irritably and Othalas growled and lowered his head onto his paws.

So many extraordinary things had happened recently that she couldn't keep track of them all—first Leowin's gift of the namesong and *Methar Anduel*, then her night with Mithorden, the Cave of Painted Shadows and now the Vyrl's sudden recovery.

How could she be the daughter of a myth?

If it is true! If it is true! If it is true—oh how I want to meet that poor lady Merrin and ask her! She would know me. She would see HIM in me.

Her head fell into her hands and she grabbed fistfuls of hair.

She was woken from her reverie by a nudge from Othalas.

"There are other things we must talk about. But I think you've been given enough to think about for just one night," he said.

"We will continue tomorrow," the third Vyrl said in ancient, chanting tones. "There is a boon we must beg of you. But it can wait through the night. Sleep sound Luthiel Valkire. May the daughters of the dark lady—the Valkyrie that are your namesake—watch over you this night."

Luthiel stood, and numbly nodded.

"Yes, I'd like to talk tomorrow. I'll want to ask questions about—about everything," she said.

Melkion slipped from his perch on her chair and flew to her shoulder.

"My lady, I'll escort you to your chamber," he said.

"As will I," rumbled Othalas.

The Vyrl rose from their chairs as she walked out of the great hall.

RENDILLO THE GRENDILO

She remembered very little of her walk through the long halls of Ottomnos back to her room. Melkion and Othalas were with her and the wights scampered away from them as they passed. When they finally returned to her room, she was surprised to find that she was exhausted. She'd only been awake for a few hours but the hurts of her long journey were taking their toll. She fell into the bed after taking off her boots and was soon fast asleep.

Othalas and Melkion stayed in her chamber watching over her through the long night.

Luthiel awoke to a soft tapping at her shoulder. It was one of the grendilo. Startled, she jumped.

"Lady, no need to be afraid," he said with a bow. "I am Rendillo, the groundskeeper of Ottomnos. The Vyrl sent me to change your bandages and see that you had something good to eat," he said.

Though standing on only one leg and gesturing with one arm, he possessed a grace that Luthiel had never before seen in a creature. He moved with such deft confidence that Luthiel found herself staring.

"That's alright then," she replied.

He placed a wash basin on the table beside her bed and then began to remove her bandages. His six-fingered hand worked fast but gently and soon all her wounds were cleaned and had fresh bandages on them. Turning on his single leg, he lifted the tray he had placed on the chair and laid it before her.

"We caught some fish for you last night," he said, lifting a cover from the top of a plate. "Here are some eggs too and fruit from the Symbellin trees of the Vale," he gestured toward a lumpy purple ball at the corner of her tray. "Don't let looks fool you, the fruits of the Symbellin are delicious and no two ever taste the same." Also on the tray was a tall glass of pinkish juice and a pitcher of water.

"Now I want you to eat everything," the grendilo said in his thin voice. "You need to recover your strength."

With that he nodded politely and left the room.

Othalas was still asleep but Melkion flew from his perch in the slit window to sit beside her.

The smell of food was overpowering and she tore into it with vigor. When she was finished there was not a scrap left.

Melkion blinked at her. "Well at least you've kept your appetite."

"I'm still hungry," she said. "Do you think Rendillo will bring more?"

"Not till lunch time," Melkion said with a laugh.

"I suppose, now, you would like to take a bath? There are hot springs beneath the fortress. I could take you there if you like."

THE POOLS OF OTTOMNOS

Luthiel had an unpleasant vision of the dungeons of Ottomnos, but the offer of a bath was something she found difficult to pass up.

"Well, if you and Othalas come with me, I think I'd like to take a bath."

Melkion laughed again.

"Alright, get your things and then follow me," he landed on the werewolf's head. "Wake up Othalas, we're taking Luthiel to the springs," he said.

Othalas growled irritably but was soon standing on his massive paws. The room was large, but he easily filled half of it and when they entered the halls, she was forced to walk in front of him.

Slowly, they wound lower and lower, passing wights and grendilo until Luthiel began to hear the quiet dripping of water. As they descended, the air grew damper and the mists thicker. Here and there, clusters of green lights wavered in the clouds.

Soon, the hallways ended and she found herself in a series of natural caves. Ahead of her, the caves wound off into darkness. A fire lamp sat in a recess of one wall. Melkion lit it with a thin breath of flame and Luthiel picked it up before entering the caves. As she followed the tiny dragon, the mists grew so thick she could barely see the dragon's tail swishing back and forth in front of her. The rocks beneath her feet descended, becoming pocked with recesses filled with tiny pools. Finally, a large pool spread before her. Tiny green lights played in the mist that rose off it.

Melkion disappeared for a moment and then returned with a leather pouch.

"There's soap in here and a towel. We'll wait here until you're finished."

Luthiel shed her clothes and was in the water a few moments later. It was hot and the rocks felt warm to the touch. In the center of the pool bubbles rose where the water boiled from underwater vents. She immersed herself, letting the water rinse off the road. Only four days ago, she'd taken a bath at Lenidras. To her, it may as well have been a year. The water stung her battered and cut body that was slowly healing. Her head still pounded when she stood but she didn't feel as dizzy as she had last night.

Letting the soap rest on her stomach, she floated on her back in the pool staring into the darkness filled with mist and green lights. She wondered about Leowin.

Probably worried sick about the coming of Othalas, she thought. She sighed, wishing there was some way she could tell her sister not to fear. Fingering the Stone that hung around her neck she hummed her namesong thinking wistfully of Leowin. She missed talking with her and now she had so much to tell her, so many things that she was afraid to share with Othalas or Melkion or the Vyrl. And what of the Vyrl? She couldn't bring herself to believe half of what they said last night.

"Luthiel Valkire," she whispered. "Did they say that last night or was I only dreaming?"

Since First Summer's Eve, it seemed her life had taken on the quality of a bizarre dream. Now she didn't know what to think was real.

She floated for a long time in the sultry pool, trying to calm her restless mind. Finally, she swam back to the shallow water and scrubbed herself clean. She returned to her pack, found a comb and began the long work of getting out all the tangles. The simple tasks set her mind at ease. She was the slow motion of her arms, the stroke of her hand—up, back, up, back.

When she was finished brushing she pleated her hair into a braid tying it behind her head with a bit of leather cord. She put on cleaner clothes and breathed out a long sigh.

"Now that was nice," she said.

Melkion returned alone.

"Did you enjoy your bath?"

"Very much," she said. "Thank you."

"Now, if you will follow me, the Vyrl want to continue last night's conversation."

ASHIROTH'S ARMY

As she followed the tiny dragon up into the fortress, she noticed for the first time that Othalas wasn't there.

"What happened to the werewolf?" she said.

"Othalas was called by the Vyrl."

"Why?" she asked.

"I don't know," Melkion said. "Could be anything."

Luthiel felt her gut tighten. She hoped they weren't sending him for Leowin. She tried to quiet her fears.

They said it was up to me whether they sent for Leowin.

She couldn't help but wonder if the Vyrl had a change of heart. Perhaps they'd fallen into madness again and last night was only a brief respite.

They continued through the halls of Ottomnos. On the way to the great hall, they passed through the courtyard where she was attacked only two nights before. The bodies that were hung from the walls were gone but the smell of blood still lingered in the air.

Probably will last for years.

As they walked to the opposite end of the yard, she noticed wights cranking the gates shut.

"Someone came or went," Luthiel said.

"They sent the werewolf somewhere," Melkion replied.

"My sister," Luthiel thought aloud.

"No, I don't think so. The Vyrl wanted to speak with you about your—condition before they made any decision about what to do with your sister. This is something else." Melkion hopped off her shoulders and flew until he was above the walls.

"I can see him!" he called down to her. "He's heading toward the Withywraith falls!" He flew around in a circle looking in all directions, then launched himself into the air.

She watched on as his tiny silver form shrank and then disappeared into the clouds that always hung low over the Vale. She waited for long minutes, wondering whether he would come back or whether she would be left to find her way to the Vyrl alone. The wights in the courtyard went about their business, but a few here and there stood still as stones, peering at her. It was as though some desire had overcome them but a greater will held them fast. She knew what they wanted, and shuddered when she saw their hooked fingers clutching, releasing, clutching, releasing.

Finally, Melkion became visible in the sky again. Slowly, the silvery fleck grew until she could again see the tiny rainbows in his gossamer wings.

"What did you see?" she cried to him when she thought he was within earshot.

"It's not good. There's an army gathering in the north—wolfriders and Urkahrim from Ashiroth. I could see a great cloud of dust. They will reach the borders of the Vale within a day."

"But the spiders, how will they get through the spiders?"

"Seven riders move ahead of the vanguard. The spiders are letting them pass! Othalas is going to meet them at Withywraith."

Luthiel blinked as she took in this news. She stood still remembering the words of Mithorden.

Seven, who are still called fair by some, hold Wyrd Stones that were taken and corrupted by black art.

"Come!"

Luthiel walked briskly into the charred glass halls of Ottomnos.

"Hurry!" Melkion urged.

Her head was spinning, but she moved as fast as she was able. Still weak, she was forced to pause often to catch her breath.

"Who are they?" she asked while leaning against one of the walls.

"They're from Ashiroth, Zalos sent them."

"Why have they come here?"

Could they be the seven Mithorden spoke of? she thought.

Melkion laughed grimly. "An army of wolfriders is behind them. Isn't it obvious?"

Luthiel, knowing little of the ways of violence in the world, shook her head.

"No, I don't understand," she said, breaking into a run.

"The Seven are coming to give the Vyrl terms. If the Vyrl don't agree to those terms, then we will likely see an army of Wolfriders attempt to invade the Vale."

"But invading the Vale, that's mad! The mists—"

"Will change them," Melkion said.

They both rushed down the halls in silence. Wights and grendilo hurried past them through the strangely twisting corridors, their metal-shod feet clanging against the floor. They bore weapons and armor of strange design—swords with blades like waves or saws, armor crowned in spines. Shadows danced above and below them through the opaque structure. To Luthiel, it seemed the walls were filled with rushing smoke. In the depths, she could hear a drum beating.

"The elves are fed up. The Vyrl took too many Chosen. Now they've finally gathered the courage to do something," Luthiel said, bending over to gulp the air.

"Zalos has always hated Vyrl," the dragon said. "If the high lords had let him, he would have attacked them long ago. He couldn't do this without support from the other Faelands. This is war."

Luthiel thought about her sister, about the way the Vyrl had attacked her, about the laws that legitimized the Vyrl's atrocity.

"Good," she said. "They deserve it." There was a sense of elation, of freedom.

Melkion swung his head around and glared at her with his amethyst eyes.

"They have shown you mercy! After all that happened last night, don't you understand how they've suffered?"

"I understand the suffering they've caused! Me, my sister! We could both still go to their larder should they slip back into madness or if I do not give in to their demands. What sort of mercy is this?"

Melkion nodded stiffly.

"To think I respected you for your kindness."

"There's a difference between kindness and weakness," she said.

The dragon turned his head and snorted out a cloud of smoke.

"Move faster," he commanded.

"I can't fly," she snapped.

"Learn to," he hissed.

They hurried down the hall in silence for a while.

Well what did you expect? That Melkion or the Vyrl would just let you go? she thought. They had run for a while longer before her anger started to cool.

"Who are these Seven?" she said, after stopping once more to catch her breath.

"You feel like talking now?" Melkion said.

"I'm curious. Who are they?"

Melkion swished his tail irritably.

"They are the champions of Zalos—each a powerful lord and sorcerer in their own right."

Luthiel felt a strange fear come over her and she thought again of Mithorden's words.

"Powerful?"

"Yes, powerful. They are Zalos' warlords. His defenders and champions."

"Othalas is going to meet them alone?" Even as the words left her mouth she wondered why she felt concern for this werewolf who might yet take her sister.

He helped me. He saved my eyes and perhaps even my life.

Melkion chuckled.

"Othalas can take care of himself," he said. "And there are grendilo who go with him. They stay hidden in the mists. If these Seven wolfriders try to harm him, they will be met by a hundred grendilo. There are other creatures, giants of the mists, with skin of bark and hair of moss who also serve the Vyrl. Don't worry about Othalas."

Luthiel nodded, but she felt a lingering concern. Her head was pounding terribly, but, at Melkion's urging, she ran on down the endlessly winding halls.

LUTHIEL'S PROMISE

Finally, they reached the great hall. The Vyrl were sitting in their tall thrones. Gathered all around them were about twenty wights and grendilo. Some of these scampered into and out of the hall on this errand or that. Now that she could see through the hall's great windows, Luthiel noticed that all of Ottomnos was swarming with activity.

They continued past the blood-stained table. Beyond stood the whitewood chair.

Grateful to have a chance to rest, Luthiel sat down.

The Vyrl were occupied giving instructions to their underlings. As Luthiel watched, she realized there was an uncanny coordination in the way the Vyrl communicated. Each, though involved in a different task, seemed to be building off the efforts of the last. It was as though they shared some common will or thought that allowed them to synchronize. Luthiel fancied, for a moment, that she was watching a strange dance.

Soon, all grendilo and wights were dispatched—each to its own task.

The Vyrl turned their eyes to Luthiel.

"You look better," Ahmberen said in his chanting voice. "I apologize for the wounds you suffered at my hand. But those were not your only hurts. It is good to see that they are all healing."

"I—thank you," Luthiel said awkwardly, thinking of her words with Melkion. Ahmberen's own hurts had already mended; even the tip of his ear had grown back. Luthiel didn't feel the need at all to apologize for them.

He deserved it.

The Vyrl watched her for a moment with their swirling eyes. She felt as though she were staring into six gaping pits.

"Many things are happening," said Ecthellien. "Zalos sends his Seven. Widdershae surround the Vale and we are cut off from all contact with the elflands except by creatures on the wing."

"Zalos, who has long harbored hatred for us, has brought an army to our very doorstep," said Elshael with dark music. "Perhaps he has found support in Ithilden for the war he wishes to bring upon us. But of all troubles, Ashiroth may be the lesser. The shadowspiders of the mountains, who long ago closed the Gates of the East and devoured the elves of Elgaldas and Imrahil, may prove to be far worse foes than the jealous lord Zalos. We do not know why or how they came into this world. But it seems, to me, that they are kin to the great spiders of Gorthar—Ingolith they were called. If Ingolith have come to Oesha then the jealous lord is the least of our worries. I do not wish, again, to become a servant to the will of Gorthar."

"You are right to fear them," said Melkion. "I know what they can do, even to dragons. They are terrible hunters and they revel in the suffering of all creatures."

To Luthiel, Melkion's voice sounded sad. She glanced at her left shoulder where he perched. His claws were strong as any eagles', but they grasped her gently.

"Why do you call Zalos the jealous lord?" Luthiel asked. "And what of Gorthar? I know little about him."

"Child, that you know little of Gorthar is a blessing," Elshael said. "I will not trouble you with stories recounting his deeds. It is enough to know that he is terrible."

"Is he an elf?" she asked.

"An elf? No, he is many ages older than any elf. He is Elohwë and his hand was in many works that went into creation. But his masterpiece was death and all the ways that a thing might end. When the time of elves was dawning, Gorthar suffered a grievous wound and fell like a star on the face of the moon that is now called Gorothoth. Ever since, he has lain there, dreaming strange dreams. It is said that the mind of Gorothoth is the dreaming will of Gorthar. Spiders and all things dark, cold, and hungry were his creatures. We fell to his will by trickery long ago. Now we suffer the curse of hunger that he set upon us."

The Vyrl stared at her with their black eyes, each swirling with a hundred lights. She wondered if their eyes were always dark or if some hungry thing inside them had consumed the color until there was nothing left but black and a few small glimmers.

"As for Zalos, he was the greatest sorcerer of all elves," she continued in her dark, musical tones. "He grew used to his stature. But, when Valkire came to the elflands Zalos met his better. Taking this as failure, he became resentful of Valkire. But Valkire sought and won Zalos' friendship. In spite of Valkire's high regard, Zalos often fell into fits of jealous melancholy. Worse, he loved Merrin despite Valkire's friendship and even though that love was not returned. Yet Valkire embraced Zalos, entrusting him with more than any of his other companions except Merrin. Still, Zalos strove in secret to become greater than Valkire and to steal the heart of his beloved Merrin."

"That poor lady! Why doesn't he just leave her alone? Hasn't she suffered enough?" she said.

The Vyrl didn't reply.

"We hoped to spend more time with you, so that you might understand us more before you made a decision whether or not to help us," Ahmberen said. "Now, it seems, we may have only days. So our hand is forced and I must ask you now.

"Luthiel, we need *your* blood. There is no one else who can give what you have. In return, there are things we possess that may help you. Will you hear what we have to offer?"

Sitting before them, dwarfed by their size and intimidated by their terrible eyes, she found it difficult to recall the anger she'd felt in the hall.

"I will hear what you have to say," she said.

Each Vyrl nodded before Ahmberen continued.

"Though your lineage may seem mysterious to you, to us, your blood is proof enough. That blood is something we must have to stave off the hunger and the madness. It is precious to us—of greater value than any-thing else in all of Oesha."

Luthiel trembled.

They'll never let me leave.

"Over three thousand years ago, we made a pact with Vlad Valkire. We would not drink the blood of any other living creature so long as Valkire fed us his own blood. Once a year, he would return and let us con-sume enough of his blood to sustain us. Eventually, we became as we were before the fall. In return, we were his protectors and patrons. We would offer the same to you, if you decide to help us."

She shook her head in disbelief.

They're offering me what they offered Valkire?

The Vyrl, seeing her expression, mistook it for rejection.

"If you do not," continued Ecthellien, "we will return to our old ways." His eyes seemed to grow darker and he thumbed the hilt of his sword as though in an afterthought. "Your sister is Chosen. Though the blood we took from you may sustain us for a month, eventually our hungers will rise again. When it does, Othalas will be sent for her."

"You must understand that, for us, it is not a question of what we want to do," Elshael said. "It is a question of survival. The curse of Gorthar would, in time, consume us utterly."

"We will give you one day to think about our offer," said Ahmberen.

Luthiel looked at the Vyrl, stared into the sinking abyss of their eyes.

I could wait and see what these seven do. Ashiroth may save my sister.

She opened her mouth, about to take their offer under the pretense of delaying them further. But something stopped her.

Fearing and hating them for so long, she pitied them now. If what they said was true, if she didn't help, the hunger and madness would slow-ly consume them until they were little more than wild beasts. They were victims as much as they were monsters.

Then she had a vision of needle teeth biting into her neck. It was enough to raise gooseflesh upon her skin.

I should be happy, she thought. *They've given me Valkire's bargain. My sister's going to live. I'm going to live.*

With that thought, her anger faded and she shook her head, ashamed.

"Melkion, I'm sorry about what I said earlier. I should have listened to you. You were right. Though they are terrible their offer seems more than fair."

Melkion nodded.

"You may, one day, find out that the lord of wolfriders is not so kind. Hope that Zalos never discovers you for who you really are. Indeed, the Vyrl seem terrible—as terrible as Zalos seems fair. But I fear the jealous lord would offer more terror than you could find even in this Vale of Mists."

He's right. If Zalos ever found out about me, I may one day need the protection of Vyrl.

"When I came to the Vale," Luthiel replied. "I had little hope of living, and even less of helping my sister. To see her alive and to live as well, that is all I ask. I don't need a day to consider your offer. It is more than I hoped. I accept."

Again the Vyrl were silent. This time, Luthiel got the impression that they were communicating with one another.

"There are other things to consider," Ahmberen said. "If you accept our offer, you must understand that we will want you to stay alive. We could enslave you, keeping you here for all time against your will. But I don't think it would be wise. The day may come, soon, when we will need your friendship."

"Luthiel, we depend on you to stay alive," said Elshael.

"I came here expecting you to take my life," Luthiel said. "Now you offer to protect it?"

"We grow tired of life as monsters," Ahmberen said. "Your blood gives us the freedom to choose. It is not a hard choice to make. Of our kind which once numbered in the thousands, there are only four left. Three sit before you and one reigns alone in the Dark Forest."

"See how great our wars made us?" said Elshael.

"We wish to become the friends of elves again," Ahmberen continued. "You could help us teach them that they have no reason to fear us anymore. Blade Dancers will stop plotting our overthrow. Even Zalos may, one day, be appeased. If you learn to love us, then you could be our ambassador. If we treat you poorly, then that chance will be lost and our time here will end.

"One day, perhaps very soon, the elves may try to rid the world of the last Vyrl. Even now, clouds of war gather. It is a war we must escape; a war we cannot win."

"Long ago, before Gorthar turned us to ill, we worked alongside the mother and father shaping the first living things that grew on Oesha," Elshael said. "Even the Dark Lady Elwin, spirit of mother Oesha, loved us then. Perhaps, one day, she will wake and we can return to our old labor. But before that happens, we have much to relearn about life and the living. It starts with you."

Luthiel was struck by their words. Relief flooded into her. These were the monsters she'd feared since childhood. But they only wished to live and to make peace.

"How could I not?" she asked. "If my blood makes it so, then I will suffer a little to help you."

She stood and placed her hand over her breast.

"I swear by my heart and by all things good and full of light that I will help you as best I can. If you are good to me in return and hunt no other creatures, I will do my best to make the elves see that you are no longer monsters."

"And to become the mother of many children," Elshael said.

Luthiel was taken aback. She'd not, in her wildest imaginings considered children. Her face flushed.

"Children?"

"Think of what it would be like to live a life filled with endless hunger, living for thousands of years in torment until the curse devours you. If children are born with your blood, we are safer."

As she said this, a wight walked into the great hall. Luthiel's eyes were drawn once more across the chamber, over tables with their hollow bloodstained basins, to the jerking form that was the victim of the Vyrl's atrocities so long ago.

What have I done? she thought. *My children?*

How could she defend these Vyrl who caused so much suffering, who by all rights deserved to die many times over?

Or was it as the Vyrl claimed? That they were victims of an uncontrollable hunger, a madness set upon them by the Lord of Death? Wasn't it their choice in the beginning? Her head spun. She didn't know. Even Leowin wouldn't know.

How was she going to convince others if she doubted? Her gut sank as she thought of the impossible task she'd sworn to.

"I—" Luthiel stammered. "The wights," she said. "Is there some way to restore them?"

They seemed such hollow, soulless things. Was there any hope for these wights?

Dear Ëavanya! Could even you heal these poor creatures?

"Valkire asked the same thing," Ecthellien replied and then grinned his predator's smile.

"There is little hope for them. Unless you can do what Valkire could not," Elshael said.

"I am afraid they are lost," Ahmberen said. "When we devoured their dreams, a large part of their spirit went with it. All that remained were the dark parts—hunger, anger, despair."

Luthiel sat down again. She was starting to feel tired and dizzy.

They did this! These creatures lived in torment every day for thousands of years because of them!

"I wouldn't know where to start or even how to try," she said.

Melkion flew from his perch on her chair back and landed before the Vyrl.

"Can't you see, she's exhausted? Do you expect her to fix all your wrongdoing in one day? That blow to her head didn't help either! She needs to rest and, I think, she needs a place that doesn't look, smell and taste like a slaughterhouse! You have a long way to go before elves or any-one will think you're anything less than monsters! You're lucky she's not from Rimwold or Ashiroth. They wouldn't care one bit for your meager, ages-late, gestures!"

"Melkion, stop," she said. "It's all right." Using the arm of her chair for support, she stood. "They're taking the only chance they have."

She turned to the Vyrl.

"I think I will rest some more, though."

"Then rest well," Ahmberen said. "The night after tomorrow we are going to the Miruvoir. You will need all of your strength."

Luthiel nodded but didn't ask what would happen at the lake. By the way he looked at her with his hungry, swirling eyes, she already knew.

Without another word, she stood and walked down the long hall past the bloodstained table. The Vyrl rose from their tall seats, inclining their heads to her as she departed. She felt odd, having the Vyrl, who towered over her, bow to her.

Melkion followed her, landing on her shoulder as she passed the gates.

SEVEN RIDE TO OTTOMNOS

She returned to her room as fast as she could. It was the only place in the entire fortress that didn't seem as though it were crawling with creatures out of nightmare, the only place where she felt something akin to normal.

"Could you let me know when Othalas comes back?" she asked Melkion, who'd returned to his perch at the slit window.

"Of course," he said.

She was exhausted. The long road and all her hurts were still exacting a heavy cost.

"I'm going to take a nap now," she said. "Wake me up if anything happens."

With that, Luthiel was soon fast asleep in her bed. The late morning soon became noon. The grendilo brought in a lunch of fish stakes, cheese and vegetables.

Still Luthiel napped. The light through the window grew pale as it stretched across the room.

It wasn't until early evening that she woke up, stretching groggily.

"Is he back yet?" Luthiel asked.

"No," Melkion replied.

She picked up a plate of food and began wolfing it down.

"How long do you think it will take for him to return?" she asked in between mouthfuls.

"I don't know," he said. "He's normally very fast."

She nodded and Melkion hopped from his perch at the slit window and landed on the back of her chair.

"I'd like to go outside the gates for a look around. Will you come with me?"

"Of course!" she said, quickly wolfing down the rest of her food. She wanted nothing more than to leave this palace of charred glass and feel the living earth beneath her feet once more or to look up and see an open sky with only leaves and tree branches to frame it.

She slid out of her bed, careful not to move too quickly. She noticed that she was feeling a little stronger, and if her head still spun a little when she moved, it didn't bother her as much as it had the day before or even this morning.

Luthiel took a moment to adjust her belt before following Melkion into the hall. They made their way quickly through the winding passages of charred glass and into the courtyard. Outside, Soelee had already set and Oerin's Eye was hanging low in the western sky. A few of the brightest stars were visible as wan pinpricks and Merrin and Somnos rode at mid-sky and on the eastern horizon. The wight's eyeless heads followed her as she approached the gates.

"Open the gates!" Melkion cried.

The wights hesitated at first as though considering some silent instruction and then went to work on the wenches. The gates parted like the many-chambered-jaws of some strange monster.

Luthiel and Melkion walked past the wights. She again noticed the burning smell as she passed the giant Gormtoth who stood in a pool of white light cast by his eyes. He stood still as a statue, giving no sign that he noticed their passing. Soon, they were on a path beside Miruvoir. The mists, for once, seemed to have retreated back into whatever crack they issued from and she could see the entire Vale from end to end.

Great cliffs and steep hills ringed it in all directions and wild, misshapen forest grew everywhere in a great tangle. In Miruvoir she could see a chain of islands made up of the same charred glass as the fortress Ottomnos. The surface of Miruvoir was flat—a perfect reflection of the sky above.

"This way," Melkion said, gesturing with his tail.

She took the right bend of a crossroads that led beneath a thick canopy of growth. Most of the branches were stripped bare from the storm of a few nights ago. But here and there leaves shaped like hands, fingers or teardrops stretched out to her from the woodline. She had to pick her way through debris as she made her way down the trail and deeper into the wood.

"Wait here, I'm going to have a look," Melkion said.

Luthiel nodded and with one flap of his wings, he was climbing through the thick canopy and into open sky.

Luthiel was alone. With a sigh, she sat down on a log. Time dragged on. The light was dimming and Oerin's Eye cast thin shadows as it set. She grew restless.

"Where is that little dragon?" she said to no-one in particular.

Finally, tired of waiting, she sprang up into the branches of a nearby tree. Ten-legged white insects covered its bark but they jumped to other places on the tree or scurried into hollows as she passed. Jumping and climbing, she made her way into the top of the tree in only a few moments. Her hair was a mess of leaves and cobwebs and she spit out a twig that had somehow fallen into her mouth. Wrapping her arm around the trunk, Luthiel took in her surroundings. She noticed that, in this forest, no two trees were the same. One bore leaves the shape and size of her finger; another had red and golden colored bark; a third was covered in thorny protrusions the length of her arm. An ominous quiet seemed to have fallen over the wood. A flock of green, four-winged bats shot past her. Her ears twitched at their twittering song. Far off she could see a bear with a wolf's head rooting through the brush. In another direction, a creature with a body like a horse but with great wings sprouting from its back and the head of a leopard galloped through a clearing. Peering still further into the far south of the Vale, she noticed that the shadows there seemed to bend in upon one another at odd angles.

Her skin prickled at the sight.

Spiders, here?

She peered at it for a long while trying to make sure her eyes weren't fooling her in the twilight. But the more she looked, the more she was reminded of the cunning maze of shadowebs she'd passed through on her way to the Vale.

Suddenly, she felt very alone and vulnerable. Remembering the speed and brutality with which she'd been attacked the first time, she wondered if a great spider wasn't even now stalking her. She clambered back down beneath the canopy, careful to be quiet and to keep herself hidden. Silently, she settled herself into a nearby bush and waited for Melkion to return.

"Hurry up Melkion," she whispered, making certain her *Cauthrim* blade was loose in its sheath.

It seemed forever before Melkion came back. When he finally did, she stood up from her hiding place.

"There you are!" she said, trying to keep her feeling of relief out of her voice. "Did you see him?"

"I did," he said.

"So how far away is he?"

"Not far at all, he's just over the next rise. He should be here shortly."

Luthiel let out a breath. She was more worried about the werewolf than she cared to admit.

"I'm glad he's back," she said.

"You may not be," Melkion replied.

"What do you mean?"

"He's bringing the Seven with him."

For a moment, Luthiel only stood there.

"Zalos' Seven are coming with him?" she asked. Again, she felt a sharp sense of anxiety. There was something about the way Melkion talked about them that gave her a strong sense of foreboding. And Mithorden's warning weighed heavy in her thoughts.

Melkion nodded.

"Why would they come here?" she whispered.

"Perhaps they are coming to give Zalos' demands in person. I don't understand why, though. They're taking a great risk. The mists could change them."

Luthiel shook her head.

"There's something strange happening that we don't understand. Melkion, I think that Widdershae have entered the Vale." The last she said in almost a whisper.

Melkion's violet eyes glowed in the low light.

"How? Why?" the dragon said.

Luthiel pointed toward the south.

"I climbed this tree while you were gone. Far away in that direction I noticed a place where the shadows seemed to bend together. That's what their webs look like. It's easy to miss if you don't know what to look for."

Melkion flew from his perch and landed on a branch near the treetop, then swung his head around in a slow arch. He noticed it almost immediately, his keen dragon eyes taking in the unnatural bend to the shadows. He let out a long hiss and a plume of smoke rose from his nose.

"Let's get out of the undergrowth. Though the web is far away, I don't want to take any chances. I've never known such vicious hunters."

Relieved, Luthiel followed Melkion back toward the fortress.

"How do you know so much about Widdershae?" she asked as they walked.

"My father's lair was in the mountains near Elgaldas. From our mountain we witnessed firsthand what happened to the elves who lived there."

"It must have been a terrible thing to see."

"It was," Melkion said and then fell into a brooding silence.

Luthiel kept quiet until they cleared the underbrush.

"The Widdershae came a long time ago, but you're still quite small for a dragon. Why haven't you grown?"

Melkion swished his tail in irritation.

"Dragons grow when they sleep. Over all these years I've had little time or luxury to have a proper dragon slumber. These little nightly catnaps elves are so fond of are barely enough to sustain a dragon, much less allow him to grow."

"But what has kept you from sleeping?"

"My service to the Vyrl of course! Don't ask silly questions."

Luthiel looked at the dragon who was still swishing his tail irritably and decided against pressing him further.

They stopped just short of the gate beside the ring of standing stones.

Oerin's Eye descended below the horizon and darkness fell over the Vale before they saw any sign of Othalas. Luthiel was beginning to grow restless again when eight shadows emerged from out of the twisted wood.

Before them jogged Othalas—a great ripple of black streaking across the field. Behind came seven wolves and riders. The wolves, though smaller than Othalas, looked no less fierce. They were grey as old snow and their ice-blue eyes gleamed in the moonlight. As they drew nearer, she could see their riders more clearly. Each wore segmented armor of some dark metal and cloaks of midnight blue fell from their shoulders. They still wore their helms so she couldn't see their faces. Each bore a great war-board bearing a symbol—a golden crown in a wreath of crimson flame. To Luthiel, the crown seemed a twisted tangle of metal from which crystals protruded like red thorns. It was brutally beautiful, as of something forced into shape by a masterful craftsman whose sole design was the discomfort of the wearer.

"It is the symbol of Zalos," Melkion whispered to her. "The golden crown of Ashiroth."

"Does he wear it? It looks like an instrument of torture."

"Yes, always. But it is only visible by moonlight. It is said that Zalos had it made before he accepted the rule of Ashiroth. He said that a crown should remind the king that rulership is a dangerous, bloody business."

Luthiel frowned, staring at the brutal ring of gold and fire.

"He must be mad."

"Mad he might seem, but all his people respect it as a symbol of his sacrifice."

"Sacrifice? He is one of the most powerful and respected lords in the land."

Melkion only nodded.

As the riders drew closer, her unease mounted.

The ice-blue eyes of the wolves seemed hollow, and their smooth movements seemed beyond the grace of a normal living creature. Their mouths were closed and no breath came from their nostrils.

"Are they alive?" Luthiel whispered to Melkion.

Melkion swished his tail. "I don't know."

"They don't breathe," she said.

"I know," Melkion replied.

Growing frustrated with Melkion's half answers, she turned her attention once more to the approaching riders. Her unease was growing into fear as they advanced toward her. Finally, Othalas came to a halt before them.

Lowering his great body, he growled. "Get on. I suppose the Vyrl will want you to hear what *they* have to say."

Grabbing a handful of his hair, she nimbly swung herself across his back. Melkion flared his wings and gripped tight with his claws but still managed to remain perched upon her shoulder.

"Why are they here?" she whispered.

"They refused to give me Zalos' message and insisted on delivering it directly to the Vyrl, You probably know as much as I do about it," he growled as he walked past Gormtoth and into the open jaws of the gate.

Luthiel kept her head low and didn't look behind. The riders behind her were quiet as ghosts, but she could feel their presence by the prickling of skin upon her neck.

They passed beneath the portcullis and entered the courtyard. Ranks of Grendilo and wights waited for them. Interspersed among them were twelve-foot-tall giants with skin of bark and hair of moss. Each carried a great hammer with a stone head the size of a small table. Their green eyes flickered in the fireless light of Ottomnos. Othalas turned so that his back was to the gathered force as he faced the riders.

"Leave your wolves here. The Vyrl will receive you in their great hall," he said.

The Seven sat upon their wolves, taking in the force assembled before them.

"Leave the gates open," their leader said.

"It is you who decided to come here. While you are here, the Vyrl will open or shut their gates as they please."

Silence stretched out across the yard and then, with a screeching of metal, the gates clanged shut.

The leader of the riders laughed. The sound held no mirth as it echoed hollowly off the walls.

"Very well, we will warn the Vyrl ourselves what will happen to them if any harm comes to us," he said in his cold voice. He slid from the back of his great wolf and pulled off his helmet. The other riders followed.

The elf who looked up at her had brown hair streaked with gold and russet. His eyes were green. At some time, he may have been handsome but his face was pale and the flesh seemed to stretch tight across his bones, accentuating the shape of his skull. It was as though the layer beneath the skin had been stripped away and only thin strands of muscle and sinew lay atop bare bone. His face was pale and bloodless and his eyes sparkled coldly. At first, it seemed he looked only upon Othalas. But for a moment his eyes flashed over her. His hollowed face, for a moment, seemed to register surprise and in that instant some of the chill seemed to melt from his features.

"Lady," he said with a stiff bow. "I did not expect to find one who possessed such beauty in a place so terrible. I would swear that I've seen your face before, but it was in Arganoth and the lady's face was marred by grief, while yours is pure. Will you tell me your name? I did not think that the Chosen, Leowin, had come to the Vale."

Luthiel found herself unable to speak. It seemed as though some great pain lay behind his eyes, it was the very pain that hollowed out his features. To her, it looked as if the pain was very close to overwhelming him. She did not know how she knew this. But she sensed it as clearly as if she'd seen him in the world of dreams.

She wondered what he would look like without his suffering, and felt pity for him as someone would feel pity for a person who has lost a limb or who is wasted by some terrible illness.

These sensations rushed over her as she tried to find her voice. The words of Mithorden came suddenly into her mind:

A sorcerer's name has special significance you see. It should not be given freely, nor should it be taken lightly.

She couldn't tell him her name. Zalos must never find out who she was. But what could she tell him? She wanted him to know something about her. But why? Perhaps it was because his eyes seemed so hollow only a moment before and that now, as he watched her, a feeble flame seemed to flicker within them.

"Lord of the Seven," she found herself saying. The words and the way she said them sounded strange to her ears.

I don't talk like this, she thought. *Vyrl talk like this.*

"My name is not something I can reveal here," she said awkwardly. "But I can tell you what I am, if you will hear me." Her mind snatched upon the first thing she could think of—"I am the singer in dreams!" she sang out with a force that surprised her. At her words, the light in the lord's eyes seemed to grow brighter and a thin smile seemed to fall upon his lips. She was encouraged by the change in his expression and thought of her struggle with the Widdershae and the wound she'd inflicted.

"I am the bearer of light in dark places, the web foiler!"

She paused for a moment.

What would the sorcerer say?

"Some have sung that I am graceful as willows and wise as the sea—though I would not claim it. I am a werewolf tamer, a saver of Vyrl and slayer of shadows! I am hope unlooked for by those I hold dear, the Stone wielder, steward of the broken blade, and secret daughter of the moon queen! I am all these things and more but they are both more and less than the name I am called by." The last words, she knew, were a version of those Mithorden once told her. She looked around, glancing from face to face.

It couldn't have worked, she thought.

The leader of the seven stood before her as one held in reverie. His eyes held the look of a man, who, having woken from a nightmare, has just been confronted by a vision of that which is most good and wonderful in the world.

"Lady, you have said many things I do not understand, but I know goodness when I see it. If you are Chosen or if the Vyrl hold you against their will, I swear that we will see you safely from this forsaken place."

Luthiel almost wept for the life that had risen again in his eyes. She felt as though she'd just witnessed a miracle. The life returned to his face, his cheeks seemed to fill and his eyes came alive with light. For a moment, she thought longingly of leaving the Vale with him. But she couldn't forsake her promise to the Vyrl and leave her sister at risk. Even if an army was gathering to confront them, she did not wish to risk her sister's life to the uncertainty of war. A deeper part of her, one she had not yet fully come to terms with, felt an odd sense of loyalty toward the Vyrl and gave them grudging respect for their attempts at restitution. This same part felt pity for the Vyrl akin to the pity she felt for this strange lord. Though she didn't realize it, these deeper feelings had already taken hold of her.

"Lord, I am afraid you are mistaken. I am not held here as a prisoner, but came of my own free will. Nonetheless, I appreciate your kind words."

As she spoke, one of the other seven, a tall elf with severe features, placed his hand on his leader's shoulder.

"Vaelros, I would be careful of this lady—'saver of Vyrl?' How can you trust someone who won't even give you her name?"

Another rider, this one whip-thin and sickly stepped forward and whispered something in Vaelros' ear.

Luthiel could barely hear him.

"Listen to Balgaer, Vaelros, her fair-seeming may be nothing more than glamer."

"Aye," Vaelros said. But his eyes never left her.

Luthiel looked on, terrified by the wan, death-mask features the other riders wore. All seemed lost to the same torment that had, only a moment ago, troubled upon Vaelros. It seemed to Luthiel that they had been robbed of all but the most token semblances of a living thing. They didn't move quite—stiff, yet snake-quick. She had a vision that they were already dead. That by some black art a dark and tortured spirit animated lifeless flesh which had become, to it, little more than a convenient disguise.

A few of them had turned their lifeless eyes toward her. She shuddered, shrinking from their gaze.

"Lady, shall we enter?" Othalas said under his breath.

Luthiel slid off his back and patted his flank with her hand.

Melkion, somehow, managed to keep hold of her shoulder.

"They're worse than before. The last time I saw them was fifteen years ago. Vaelros wasn't with them then, but the rest had already started to take on that look—like dead men walking. They look much worse now," Melkion said.

"What is causing it?" she whispered.

"I don't know!" Melkion hissed. "How should I know?"

Othalas led the way into the fortress. Luthiel was glad to see that Vaelros followed directly behind her with the other riders after him. They followed Othalas through Ottomnos' twisting passages until they finally came to the great hall. Luthiel, shuddering at the long, bloodstained table with its body-shaped recesses, realized she'd never get used to this place so long as she stayed here.

Perhaps, they will, one day, remove the table.

As she walked down the table's length, she noticed that her chair was now placed to the right of the Vyrl's three chairs where the Vyrl were now sitting, watching them with their swirling eyes.

Luthiel, took her seat. Othalas sat down beside her turning around so he could keep close watch on the Seven. As no seats were left, they were forced to stand. Looking at them, Luthiel wondered if they cared anything for comfort.

Faced with the Vyrl, Vaelros turned his attention away from Luthiel. Sitting in their chairs, the Vyrl gave no indication that they had recognized the Seven. There was a long silence in the hall. One of the seven whispered something in Vaelros' ear. Vaelros nodded and clenched his jaw.

"Vyrl of the Vale," he said. His eyes glided over her before returning to the Vyrl. "We have come to you to present the terms of Zalos, Lord of Ashiroth and of Tuorlin, High Lord of Ithilden and warden of the Faelands. These terms are representative of the will of all lords within the Faelands—of Rimwold, Minonowe, and Himloth. Do you understand this?"

Ahmberen spoke.

"We do," he said, his chanting tone filling the hall.

"Then here are the terms of the elf lords," Vaelros pulled a scroll from his belt and broke the seals. Luthiel noticed there were five seals on the scroll, one for each of the elflands. When he was finished, Vaelros began to read.

"We, the lords of the elves, charge the Vyrl with breaking the compact of Valkire and of abusing those laws meant to protect elves sent to the Vale as Chosen. Chosen have died where they were meant to be spared," Vaelros glanced meaningfully at the table with its bloodstains and straps. "And the Vyrl have demanded more Chosen than the agreed to number—one a year—under the implied threat of war. Further, the Vyrl have gathered a host of Widdershae—the treacherous spiders of the Drakken Spurr about the Vale. In recent days, these spiders raided the community of Deldrannor, carrying off twenty of its inhabitants. The bodies of the abducted have since been found—desiccated husks every one."

Luthiel shuddered at this.

I could have been one of them.

"In response to these tyrannical and evil acts, the lords have decided to meet the Vyrl's threats in kind. Upon the reading of this decree, the armies of Ashiroth, Ithilden, Rimwold, Minonowe, and Himlolth march upon the borders of the Vale. The Vyrl will have the war they threatened for so long unless *our* demands are met. First, the Vyrl will surrender unconditionally to lord Zalos of Ashiroth. Second, the Vyrl will remove all Widdershae from the elflands immediately. Third, the Vyrl will never again take an elf for Chosen and will be forced to subsist on what blood they may take from creatures of forest and field. Fourth, the Vyrl will be held captive by Ashiroth for a time not less than one hundred years in recompense for the crimes they have committed against elves. During this time, the Vyrl will be subject to all the laws of Ashiroth and to the will of its lord Zalos. Fifth and finally, the Vyrl will stand trial for their wrongs before a court of lords and agree that any punishment, even death, is fair and just as dictated under the laws of the elflands. If any of these demands are not met, the Vyrl will face total war with the elflands and will be subject to destruction at the hands of the elflords if defeated in battle."

When Vaelros finished reading the edict, he turned it around so that the Vyrl could see the elf lords seals stamped at the bottom.

"I am instructed to give you two days to consider these demands. If, upon the morning of the third day, you are still undecided, we will consider it a refusal and act accordingly. If you wish to decide now, then we can begin the process of bringing you into the custody of Lord Zalos or return with news of war."

The Vyrl sat still and silent as Vaelros' voice faded from the chamber. Silence stretched out for long moments. The Seven fingered their weapons and their bodies tensed—anticipating attack. But the Vyrl only sat still in their thrones, staring with those maddening eyes.

"You must understand," Elshael said finally. "That the terms you have given us are terms we cannot accept. There is no elf who would not have us killed if we fell under the mercy of your laws. There must be some other way."

Luthiel could tell by the looks the Seven gave one another that this was not the response they expected.

They expected the Vyrl to attack them, she thought.

"These are the terms of Lord Zalos and the High Lord Tuorlin. There is no other way," said one of the Seven.

"This charge, that we have brought the Widdershae to the borders of the Vale, is without cause. We have never had dealings with them. The only creatures we associate with are those that are of the Vale of Mists itself. But this is our right, for we have ruled here for thousands of years. How dare you blame us for what the Widdershae have done!" said Ecthellien.

The seven tensed again. Hands drifted toward weapons. Legs flexed slightly, bodies lowered into a predatory crouch.

"Lord Zalos has evidence that you were the ones who brought the spiders here. Are you saying that Zalos is a liar?"

"When lies have served him, yes," said Ecthellien.

An angry silence fell over the hall. The Seven fingered their weapons as they eyed the Vyrl. Ecthellien grasped the hilt of his own sword—by itself as long as Luthiel was tall. Othalas growled and his hackles rose. Luthiel found her fingers tightly encircled around the hilt of her *Cauthrim* knife.

"Enough! Enough!" cried Ahmberen.

"As the demands call for our unconditional surrender," he continued, "and you are little more than emissaries, then there is nothing we can resolve tonight. We will accept your offer of two days to consider these demands and then send our answer to the lords of the elves. Until that time, you are free to stay here. We will have rooms made ready for you presently."

The tension in the room seemed to bleed away.

"Now, if you will allow, we would like to talk this matter over in private," Ahmberen said. "If you will follow Rendillo, he will show you to your rooms."

The grendilo hopped gracefully from the corner of the room where he stood and bowed to the Seven.

"Lords, if you will please follow me," he said.

Luthiel watched as the Seven left the room. Vaelros met her gaze and nodded once before stepping out into the hall. Not knowing what else to do, she nodded back to him.

With the Seven finally gone, the tension of a few moments before evaporated. Luthiel let out a sigh. She looked over at the Vyrl questioningly.

"What now?" she asked.

"We were to ask you the same thing," Ahmberen said.

"Me? How could I know what to do?"

"Does this change your decision to help us?" It was Elshael who asked this time.

Luthiel stared at the ground blankly. She felt as though she'd been struck over the head again by Ahmberen's blade. She didn't know. Could she just leave now and abandon the Vyrl to their problems? If all the elves were joined against them, what choice did they have but to surrender?

Or could the Vyrl defeat all the elflands together?

Even as she thought these things she realized that she'd already made her decision. Perhaps it was this morning, perhaps while she was napping. But at some time, recently, she had resolved herself to help the Vyrl.

"Our bargain still stands," she said.

"Then there may be some way out of this trap the Lord Zalos has set for us, after all," said Ecthellien.

"Trap?" Luthiel asked.

"Oh yes," Ecthellien said. "A very clever trap to catch three Vyrl in. But I don't think he realized you were a consideration. Perhaps he even expected us to attack his Seven. But now that we are not overwhelmed by the madness we can act in ways that he does not expect. There is even a chance we might avoid this war."

"How?" Luthiel asked. "You heard their offer, if you can call it an offer at all. They want unconditional surrender."

"Yes, that's what they said. But what if we sent you back with a message from us saying that we pledge to never take a Chosen again, so long as you or your children live and that we agree to pay each land and family restitution for their losses?" asked Elshael. "Then, some of the lords might not think this war is worthwhile."

"True!" said Ahmberen. "The only reason they are all coming to fight us is that Zalos has them believing they have no other choice. If we give them a way out, some of the realms will want to take it. Luthiel, if *you* give them this message, they might listen. Would you be willing?"

"Well I suppose I would," she said, trying to keep the apprehension out of her voice. "But I don't know how to find Tuorlin, or even what he looks like."

"We were thinking of sending Othalas and Melkion with you," Ahmberen said.

"What about Miruvoir? The night after tomorrow?" She felt a little ashamed about asking this question. But she'd been dreading what might happen at Miruvoir. She kept imagining the Vyrl biting her, reliving the pain when the blood was drawn out of her.

"We still intend to meet you at the lake. Would you be willing to come tomorrow night?" Ecthellien asked.

"I admit I am terrified of what may happen there. But I promised to help you didn't I? Sooner would be better."

"Very well, then." Ahmberen said. "Now why don't you retire to your room and have supper. There are many long days ahead and though you've rested, your wounds still need more time to heal. We will talk about the finer points of our plan after our meeting at the lake. Until then, save your strength."

A DARKNESS IN DREAMS

Luthiel thought about what had happened as she returned to her room. It seemed that, with each passing day, her life and those of the Vyrl were becoming more deeply intertwined.

Now they want me to bargain with the lords. To defend them against the families of those they devoured. Am I doing the right thing? Trying to save Vyrl?

For some reason her gut kept telling her yes. She shook her head.

Maybe I'm the one falling into madness.

The macabre wights and alien grendilo passed by on this errand or that; but, otherwise, she was undisturbed. Othalas walked with her and Melkion kept his perch on her shoulder. Melkion's head swung back and forth, his violet eyes peering into every shadow. She realized they were there to protect her as much as to ensure she didn't run away. It gave her an odd sense of comfort.

The Seven disturbed her—more than the Vyrl and, perhaps, more than the wights. She didn't understand what was wrong with them. But looking at them, they appeared wasted as though by some disease that left their faces cold and hollow masks. Vaelros, their leader, was also affected, though somewhat less so. When she spoke to him, his face recovered some of its life. But it still seemed to her as if he struggled with some great pain that was slowly wearing him down.

"What could cause it?" she whispered.

"What was that?" Melkion asked.

"I was just thinking about the Seven. About the way they looked as if they were—how did you describe it?"

"Dead men walking," Melkion said.

"Yes, that's what you said. About how they looked like walking dead men and about how Vaelros seemed in pain. Do you know anything about this?"

Melkion shook his head.

"I do," Othalas said. "But only in hints and rumors."

"Could you tell me?" Luthiel asked.

"I'll tell what I know, but I'm afraid it isn't much." He growled.

"Long ago, the first of the Seven—he is called Evaldris—became Zalos' lieutenant. He is the oldest and, perhaps, mightiest of the Seven. Though Vaelros is their lord, Evaldris is the one who is closest to Zalos. It is said that Zalos shares all his devices with the Dread Lord as Evaldris has become known. The others followed, chosen by Zalos once every twenty or so years. They are named—Balgaer of swords, Gharam the hunter, Kharik the killer, Torlith the warlock, Eldrik of shadows, and Vaelros the mad. As the captains and lieutenants of Zalos, they have fought and won many victories for their Lord. And if the victories were bloody, the savage people of Ashiroth revered them more. The Seven are from many lands. Evaldris is Sith and only two—Vaelros and Balgaer—are from Ashiroth."

"But what has happened to them? Can so many years of warfare cause them to look like the dead?" she asked.

"Zalos has always been a master sorcerer. To achieve his devices, he will use any lore, art or object—no matter how terrible. It is rumored that the Seven are under some black spell that Zalos wove over them—a spell that consumes them as it continues. It has made them mighty and fearless in battle. For wounds that would kill a normal elf are only minor hurts to them and they are tireless—continuing to fight long after others succumb to exhaustion."

"How do you know this?" she asked.

"For many years, my kin—the werewolves of the Vale—spied on the land of Ashiroth. Zalos has never loved the Vyrl and I thought it best to keep a watch. They brought me news of the Seven now and again. What I have told you was pieced together from their accounts."

They came again to her room.

She walked over to the slit window and peered out into the night. In the courtyard below, the grey wolves prowled. She turned back and found that her dinner was waiting for her. She picked up the tray, brought it over to the bone chair and sat down.

"Why do they call him the mad?" she asked after having a bite of the delicious bird they'd cooked for her.

Othalas, who'd settled to the floor next to the door, raised his massive head to look at her.

"He is the grandson of Zalos and it is said that he is prone to fits of rage. His father, Zalos' first son, was sent into exile many years before. There he died under mysterious circumstances. Some say that his anger is for his grandfather and for the injustice of Ashiroth and its lord. Others say that his anger is for the treatment of Merrin, whom he is fond of. He has been heard saying that there is none more beautiful than Merrin and that all other stars pale before her as the dim lights of night pale at sunrise."

"You know much about him," she said between mouthfuls.

"He is a hero to the elves of Ashiroth and they are free with their rumors and storytelling."

"He doesn't seem like the others among the Seven. He is brighter—more alive. It doesn't look to me like madness at all. Only anger at wrongdoing. It is sad what is happening to him. This curse or whatever it is—there must be some way to break it."

"Why are you so concerned about him?" Melkion asked.

"The others, to me, seem lost. Yet Vaelros still has some life left in him. But I don't think he has much longer. I fear that soon the spark will fade from him and he will become like the rest—a walking dead man. I wonder what horrors visit him and if he can feel the life slowly ebbing from him."

Melkion blinked and Othalas let out a low, gravely chuckle.

"I told you she was a sorcerer," he said to the little dragon.

"I never said I didn't agree with you," the dragon replied.

"What are you talking about?" Luthiel said.

"Well, you *are* a sorcerer aren't you?" Melkion asked.

She considered his question.

"Someone else said the same thing once," she said, thinking of Mithorden. "But I don't see how it could be true."

"You sensed something about Vaelros that we could not," Othalas said. "Before he spoke to you, he appeared, to me, as dead as the others. But after, I could see that there was some life still in him. Something about you—in your voice or your presence—brought that out. Sometimes magic is so subtle that the sorcerer doesn't realize she is using it. That is the best kind of magic."

"I don't see how it could happen."

"That's what makes it magical."

Luthiel finished the rest of her dinner in silence. It was growing late, so she made ready for bed. But she had difficulty falling asleep. Every time she closed her eyes she kept having visions of the dead faces. The more she thought about them, the more they reminded her of wights, except that their faces were forever etched in masks of pain—windows to the unseen tortures they suffered. When she thought of Vaelros, she felt afraid for him.

Without knowing, she slipped into sleep.

She saw him standing on the beach in the place where water laps the sand. Far out over the ocean she saw a small smudge of black in the sky. Slowly, the darkness grew until it covered the entire ocean. Beneath its shadow the ocean became inky black. Still the darkness grew until the only light came from behind the sand dunes in the west. It was a wan, white shaft against the colorless sky. The ocean receded, until only a thin strip of sea was visible in the distance. Above her, she could see a black hole in the inky sky. Its surface was fissured with cracks the color of old blood.

"Gorothoth," she whispered.

Then, the ribbon of black water on the horizon rippled, growing as the sea came rushing back in a vast wave. She ran toward him; grabbed his arm.

"Run!" she cried.

But his face, half-dead, only stared into the onrushing sea.

She grabbed his arm and tugged it. He wouldn't budge.

Now the wave was fast approaching—an oily mountain rising high above them.

She tried to lift him. He was too heavy. She stumbled under his weight and they both fell into the sand. The wave towered over them, uncanny in its silence. She draped his arm over her shoulder and made one last attempt to lift him.

Then the inky waters were upon them. He was torn from her. She was lifted high, higher and then she fell, spinning deeper and deeper. All she could see was darkness. It crushed in on her, filled her nose, forced its way down her throat invaded her lungs. She tried to breathe. But it was strangling her—like a thousand tiny hands crushing her neck, her chest.

She awoke with a start, sitting bolt upright in her bed. The sheets were damp with her sweat. Her breath came out in short gasps as she hungrily breathed in the air.

There was a flapping beside her as Melkion alighted upon the bed.

"Luthiel what's the matter?" Melkion said.

"They're strangling him!" she cried.

"Who is strangling him?"

She didn't understand the question.

"They tried to strangle me!"

She could still see the dream, but slowly the nightmare melted and the black charred walls of Ottomnos came into focus. They were too much like the inky waters. She could feel them closing in on her.

"Luthiel what happened? What's wrong?"

Luthiel shook her head and blinked her eyes.

"I had a nightmare," she said.

The dragon spread his rainbow wings and fanned her with them.

"It's over now. It's alright. It's only a dream."

"Is it?" she said, trying to calm her breathing. "It seemed so real."

"Shhh, it will be alright, you're not alone."

Luthiel looked around the room. The werewolf was gone.

"Where is Othalas?"

"Gone out to hunt. He gets hungry in the late night. Don't worry, he'll be back soon," the tiny dragon said. "Just lie down, breathe easy and try to forget."

She didn't think she could ever forget. She could feel the hands on her neck, her chest, even now. Suddenly cold, she pulled her sheets, damp with sweat, back over her. After a while, she calmed down and the memory of the dream faded. But she would never forget the color of that inky sea and how she failed to save him from it.

"Melkion, do you think he can be saved?" she asked.

"Vaelros?"

"Yes."

"I don't know."

"There has to be some way."

"Luthiel, you should sleep."

She nodded.

"Alright, I'll try."

"I'll stay here with you."

"I'd like that."

It took Luthiel a long time before she could gather the courage to close her eyes again.

A BLACK CURSE

Luthiel was awakened by bright light shining in through the slit window. She sat up in her bed. Melkion was curled up in a ball, fast asleep on the window ledge. Thin wisps of smoke rose from his nostrils. Othalas had returned sometime in the night and was now sleeping beside the door.

She slid off the bed and picked out a clean change of clothes.

When she was finished dressing, she spent some time with her hair and then sat back down on her bed.

Othalas and Melkion didn't look like they were about to wake up anytime soon.

Luthiel stared about the room. But there was nothing there that captivated her.

"Perhaps I should just go back to sleep," she whispered.

But for some reason, a restlessness had fallen over her. She slid off the bed and rummaged through her pack. There were a few odds and ends— the map she'd taken from her loft was still there, the length of rope, the flask Lorethain gave her, a couple of wind charms, food and provisions from home and from Lenidras. On a whim she picked up the flask, undid the cap and took a whiff. The sweet aroma of honeywine filled her nostrils.

Redoing the cap, she looked at the door.

In a moment, she'd slipped past the sleeping Othalas and out the door. Once in the hall, she stopped the first grendilo she saw.

"Where is the chamber of Lord Vaelros?" she asked.

The grendilo blinked in surprise.

"His is over on the east wing. But he's not there right now if you're looking for him. He and the others are sparring in the yard," he said.

"Thank you," she said.

The grendilo nodded. "My pleasure," he said before hopping off down the hall.

She made her way down the winding corridors for some time before finding a way out to the courtyard. Outside, a bank of clouds had covered the sky, blocking the suns from view.

In the yard, the wolves had formed a rough ring. Facing inward, they watched as the seven practiced swordplay. To Luthiel, they seemed swift and tireless. Standing in the doorway, she watched for a few minutes as blow after blow fell. It was obvious, even to her untrained eye, that they were all masters. Their speed and power were difficult to follow. But what made her feel a chill ascend her spine, was that though they practiced furiously none had broken a sweat or were even breathing hard. The only one that seemed to breathe at all was Vaelros. They were fighting in turns, so she waited until Vaelros stepped aside before walking toward the ring of wolves.

"Lord Vaelros," she said, waving at him. "Could I talk to you?"

One of the grey wolves turned its head and growled at her—flashing his teeth.

Stopping in her tracks, she raised her hands and backed away.

She didn't really know what she was doing or why. She just felt an unexplained urge to go to him. She was curious. There were questions she wanted to ask him. But she was also afraid. There was something terribly wrong about these men—who spoke and moved with the quickness of the living but who, in every other way, looked like dead men.

When Vaelros saw her, his hollow-eyed face seemed to brighten.

"Lady!" He said as he strode toward her. "What are you doing here?"

"I came to talk, I wanted to ask you about—about things," she said the last in a lower voice.

When he looked at her, she noticed his eyes. The pupils were so large that they seemed to swallow up all the color. Looking into them was like looking into a black pit. She was reminded of her dream. Her breath caught in her throat. But as he watched her, the pupils seemed to shrink some and she could see the color—grey green—like a sea in a storm. His bloodless lips formed a wan smile.

"Lady, I will talk to you about anything."

His voice seemed to come from some far away place.

"Well, could we walk away from—?" she glanced at the deadmen in their swordplay.

His black pit eyes scanned the battlements.

"We could sit upon the wall."

"I'd like that," she said.

So they made their way up to the battlements of Ottomnos. The charred glass glistened in the morning sun—darkness and light played together in those dim, reflective facets.

They found a low place on the wall between the battlements and sat down. For a while, Luthiel sat in silence unsure what to say. She looked at him as healer might, taking him in from the top of his head to the end of his toes. He smelled of blood and polished metal. The grey armor laid over him like ice over stone. Even his face seemed to be frosted and mask-like. Far more pale than the natural color of flesh. His breathing was very slight and those pit eyes seemed to hold nothing.

The way he looked terrified her. Everything that made him look as though he were living seemed to be fading from him.

She pulled the flask of honeywine from her pouch.

"This was a birthday present from my brother. Would you care to share it with me?" She undid the stopper and held it out to him.

"I would, lady," he said. That slight smile touched his lips again.

What happened to him? she thought. *Yesterday he seemed so much more alive.*

He took the bottle from her hand and brought it to his lips. For a moment, confusion passed over his eyes. It was as though he'd forgotten how to drink. Then recognition awoke in those dark eyes and he took a swallow.

"That's good," he said, the wan smile on his face grew brighter. He handed her back the bottle.

When she brought it to her lips, the place where his mouth had touched it was cold. She shuddered, but forced herself to swallow the golden liquid.

Luthiel was unable to contain herself any longer.

"Vaelros, what is the matter with your men? They seem as if they've died. They don't draw breath and their eyes seem like dark pits. You don't look much better."

Vaelros laughed. It was a grim, half-hearted sound.

"You are as lovely and nearly as wise as the lady Merrin of Arganoth. But she is much sadder. If I didn't know better, I'd think you were her younger sister. The eyes are different and the hair. I can't believe it. If you won't tell me your name, then will you at least tell me where you come from?"

Luthiel bit her lip. She noticed that some of the life was again returning to Vaelros. His eyes held her as if she were a blazing beacon. But what could she tell him? What if the Vyrl were right about her heritage? What if Zalos found out?

"You asked me to tell a secret. It is one I am afraid I must keep," She said.

"Aye, and what you have asked about is secret as well."

They sat in silence for a few minutes each gathering their thoughts.

"Would you sing a song for me?" Vaelros asked.

Luthiel almost gasped.

"Why?" she asked.

"Sometimes, singing makes me feel—better. Merrin used to sing to me."

"What song would you like me to sing?"

"There was a song I heard in dreams. It must have been more than a fortnight ago now. But it was the most beautiful thing I'd ever heard. It goes something like this—" Vaelros hummed the tune to her namesong. "I couldn't quite hear the words. Do you know this song?"

Luthiel took another drink from the bottle and passed it back to him. She looked at him out of the corner of her eye. She didn't see anything sly about the warming smile on his lips. But in his brightening eyes there was a curiosity she couldn't understand. To her, it looked as though he were slowly coming out from beneath a dark and cold shadow.

"If I sang *that* song, I may as well tell you my secret," she whispered, staring at her hands.

He laughed again, and then took another drink from the bottle before passing it back to her.

Unthinking, she took a drink. This time, the mouth of the bottle was warm.

Below, a couple of wolves were staring up at them with their ice-blue eyes.

Vaelros noticed this and took Luthiel's hand. His hand was cold.

"Lady, I think we're being watched. Why don't we find some place a little more private to continue our conversation?"

Luthiel nodded.

"This castle is so dark," she said. "Why don't we go over there?" She pulled her hand out of his and pointed toward the lake.

"A fine place," he said.

Without saying another word, they walked side by side down the stairs and out the small door beside the gatehouse. They made their way toward the Miruvoir following the path that wound about the lake a ways before sitting down on a boulder. Out in the lake, mists rose from the water riding in tiny wisps over the slate surface. They sat in a patch of sunlight but the mists swirled around them in a cloud.

He drew his cloak about him, and pulled the hood over his head to shade his face from the sunlight.

Without thinking, she lifted her hand and drew the hood back again.

He flinched, then sharply raised his hand to bring the hood up again.

"What are you doing!" he growled.

Luthiel stumbled back in fear.

"I only wanted to see your face in the light," she whispered.

She almost walked away right then. But something kept her.

"Does it hurt you?" she asked.

When he turned his eyes toward her again there was madness in them.

"Yes! It hurts! It feels like fire!"

She reeled, shuffling back.

"I'm sorry, I didn't know," she said.

The madness seemed to fall from Vaelros' eyes as soon as it had come on.

"No, it is I who should be sorry. Please forgive my outburst."

Luthiel didn't know what to do. She felt both afraid for and of him. He seemed to be vacillating between humanity, warmth, death and madness. It was a terrifying thing to watch.

"It's alright," she said.

What can I say? she thought. *There must be something.* Her hand roamed to the Stone at her neck. She wondered what he would look like under its light. He'd already asked to hear her song. If she used the Stone maybe she could find some way to help him. But could she chance it?

"Vaelros, can I keep you to your word?" she asked.

Vaelros looked at her for a moment. Something seemed to flash across his eyes—eyes that were drinking her in the way a parched man might drink water.

"No, I'm afraid you cannot."

His response jarred her, both with its bluntness and its honesty.

Now it was her turn to become angry.

"Are you saying that you are unworthy of trust, Lord Vaelros?"

He let out a sigh.

"You don't understand."

"I'm trying to," she replied.

"There are many things in this world, lady, that are better if they stay hidden from the light of day. I am one of them."

"If I can't trust you, then why should I sing you the song?"

He lifted a gloved hand, opening it, palm-up, beneath the sunlight, letting its brilliance play over the dark metal.

"Because, lady, of all last year or the year before I can only remember a few days. The rest is all a cloud of endless nightmares and terror. But since hearing the song, the dark dreams have fallen away somewhat."

Luthiel couldn't find her voice for a few long moments.

"Are the others like you?" she whispered.

"Worse," he said. "When they heard the song, it drove them into a frenzy. They called the wolves. We rode long and hard, trying to hunt down its source. They were going to murder whoever sang it. But they never found her. All they found were some tracks beside the river Rendalas. Tracks that led into the Vale."

"And did you—did you want to murder the singer?"

His fading eyes found hers again.

"No, no. I wanted to thank her. You see, the song helped me, made me feel alive again. For a few nights, there were no nightmares."

"Then why did you ride with them?"

He tore his gaze from her and stared at the ground.

"Because I am compelled."

"What compels you?"

He looked at her again. This time his eyes were both longing and suspicious. He looked left and then right. His face bled from one expression to the next. To Luthiel, he seemed a man at war with himself.

Then, with a shaking hand, he undid a clasp at the neck of his armor and reached his hand beneath. Slowly, trembling, he drew out a long, black chain. Fastened to the chain was a box of some strange, dark metal. The metal was etched in runes the color of blood. Reminded of her dream, she shuddered.

Vaelros held the chain with the box in front of him. His hand trembled and the box swayed before them.

Luthiel reached a hand out to touch it, but Vaelros drew it away before she could.

"This compels me."

"A box?"

"No, the thing in the box."

"What is it?"

"A Stone, blacker than pitch."

"Why don't you just get rid of it?"

Vaelros laughed. "It's not so easy."

Mechanically, his hand put the Stone back beneath his armor.

"Is it a Wyrd Stone?" she whispered.

"Yes."

"They're not supposed to look like that, are they?" she said, remembering Mithorden's words about the lost Stones and recalling Leowin's words about how Elag was trying to make her own Stone darken.

"Every one I've seen looks like that.

"Except Merrin's. Hers looks like a patch of the ocean under moonlight. She keeps it hidden. But I think Zalos knows."

"I don't think they're meant to look like yours. How does it compel you?"

He brought his hand to his face. There was sweat streaming from his forehead.

"It kills me faster if I don't follow it. It kills me more slowly if I do. If I die, I become its creature—like the others."

Luthiel took his hand in hers. She wanted to give him some comfort. But she was also afraid.

"Who gave it to you?"

"My grandfather."

She shuddered.

"Zalos," she whispered.

"Yes. Lady, could you please sing the song now?"

Luthiel nodded.

"Of course," she said. But she thought for a few moments about the darkness in Vaelros' Wyrd Stone. Leowin's voice came back to her:

I saw him trying to use it, over and over again. But so long as he held it, it darkened. He was doing it all wrong. He needed to sing to it and then give it away freely to the right person before it would work properly. Instead, he kept it locked in an iron box and never let even the dimmest light touch it.

"Vaelros, if you give me your Stone, I think I might be able to help you."

It was amazing the change that came over Vaelros. Fear flashed in his eyes and again, his face seemed sunken, dead. But within those eyes, the conflict still raged. With a trembling hand, he reached within his shirt and drew the chain out once more.

He held it tight, seeming unable to let go.

Without realizing what she was doing, she snatched it out of his hands.

His other hand clenched at his sword hilt, trembled there, but made no move to draw it.

"Poor warrior, weary of the long road and of wasting shadow, rest your hand a while," she said. Something in the quality of her voice seemed to calm him. Still, the struggle went on behind his eyes.

She turned her attention to the box that held the Stone. There was a catch on its side. She worked the catch but the box wouldn't open. She tried again. Nothing happened.

"It doesn't work that way," he said in a quavering voice. But his eyes still held her and there was light in them when he looked at her. His body was hunched, though, and he pulled his cloak about him as a man caught in the grasp of a death-chill.

"Then how does it work?" she asked.

"You must use my name."

"Vaelros?"

"My proper name."

"And what is your proper name?"

"Vaelros Morithingol," he whispered.

So that is the second name of Zalos—Morithingol, she thought. *It is strange that no-one knows this.* But Luthiel, remembering Mithorden's words about sorcerer's names wondered if it was by design that his sur-name was kept secret.

She held the box in her hand and whispered as much as chanted the name—"*Vaelros Morithingol.*"

With a 'snick!' the lid snapped back. A cold mist poured out of the box. Wreathed in the mist was a perfectly round Stone. It was black. Blacker than any thing she'd ever seen before except, perhaps, the face of the dark moon.

Then, she started to sing her namesong.

The sunlight fell on it. Some of the cold and the shadow seemed to melt away. A touch of color returned to the Stone. It seemed a swirl of black and violet.

But it was brief. For within Vaelros' Stone, the gloom gathered again. From out of it a tendril snaked, touching her on the neck.

A song she heard
Of cold that gathers
Like winter's tongue
Among the shadows
It rose like blackness
In the sky
That on volcano's
Vomit rise
A Stone of ruin
From burn to chill
Like black moonrise
Her voice fell still…

Luthiel choked, her song ended. Her ears filled with dissonance that rose from the black Stone like flies from a corpse. Vaelros stiffened, and his hand jerked back toward his sword's hilt.

His eyes hollowed as they followed her.

It compels him, she thought.

She turned her eyes back to the Stone.

There is my enemy.

The dirge rising from it was overwhelming. Her hand was going numb with chill. Despair fell on her. It seemed pointless to even breathe.

In a gesture that seemed futile, she raised her hand to her neck and lifted *Methar Anduel* from its pouch.

Blackness rose from Vaelros' Stone. Tendrils oozed out of it clutching at her like spider legs.

But her eyes were on the tiny spark at *Methar Anduel's* heart.

What now? Even her thoughts seemed faint—like a gentle voice in a loud room.

Sing! The voice commanded. *Sing or be lost!*

She opened her mouth. In response, the dark song grew louder until the sound was so violent it rattled her teeth. Against it stood only the gentle voice.

The black Stone trembled as if in anger—

Down! Down! Deep you go!
Tumbling, descending!
Foolish life ending!

—came its song.

There was a fluttering in her chest and her eyes became dim and clouded. The world spun about her and she had the brief sensation of falling. But the gentle voice rose up to answer it.

In the depths a light will grow
A silver shine no shadows know
Like wings unfolding in the sky
That circle round a gleaming eye

Faintly, she realized that the voice was her own. Heartened, she sang out stronger. Light returned to her eyes and the vertigo faded. There were more words to the dark Stone's song. But her song covered them. It rushed from her like wind—building at the last into crescendo.

> *Turning darkness all away*
> *Even depths will know their day*
> *For every shadow has its end*
> *In light!*
> *Life will return again!*

Silence. For an instant all was still.

Then, upon an impulse, Luthiel touched her Stone to Vaelros'. When the two met a ringing rose up like the distant tolling of bells. The tendrils lifted from Vaelros' Stone like smoke.

Vaelros, who stood before her with his sword half drawn, collapsed to the ground. With a hacking cough, his mouth opened. Black smoke oozed out and with it came the trickle of old blood. He gasped, took a deep breath and hacked again, this time vomiting a gout of the black stuff. It splashed into the lake where it spread through the water like a cloud.

She sang on. Now the words were ones she couldn't understand.

Vaelros' Stone grew warmer. The wisps rising off it were changing from black, to grey to white. Finally, there was no smoke at all and the color slowly returned until it blazed with golden fire. In her hand, it looked like a small sun.

She was finished.

The light shone on for several heartbeats then faded.

There was another sensation of dizziness. She clutched a nearby tree for support. But it soon passed.

Vaelros slowly stood and wiped his mouth. His face was flushed and pale but very alive. The darkness in his eyes melted away. With his left hand, he unclasped his cloak and flung it from his shoulders, letting the sun fall upon his face. For a moment, he winced but then the shadow was completely gone and he spread his arms as he looked up into the sunlight sky.

"It is so warm—almost as warm as your song in my ears."

He looked upon her with eyes no longer filled with desperation, but with wonder. He took a step forward and then came to his knees before her.

"I forsake everything that I was gladly. For sunlight has again come into my world and her name is Luthiel. Take me with you and I promise I will do all I can to serve and protect the fairest of all ladies to ever walk upon the face of mother Oesha."

Luthiel smiled at him and laughed.

"Stand up, Lord Vaelros, kneeling does not become you."

She helped him to his feet placing the Stone in one of his hands. Raising both Stone and hand to her lips, she kissed the Stone and then curled his fingers around it.

"You and it are free from the darkness in dreams now. Use it well and in your own way."

The look he gave her was one of reverence.

But then, a hollow cry rang out from Ottomnos. It was the howl of seven wolf voices. But to Luthiel is sounded like the onrush of the winds of winter. There was a clamor in the courtyard accompanied by the harsh bark of command.

At the sound of the wolves, something seemed to break within him.

"Luthiel!" he cried out as if in pain.

Before she could do anything, his arms were around her. It was as though he could barely stand without the support.

The wolf voices cried out again. Among them, she could hear the hollow calls of the riders.

"Vaelros! Vaelros!" they chanted.

Hearing those fell voices, Vaelros cried out again.

"They're hurting you! You must leave. Can you run?"

Vaelros nodded.

"I can certainly run from them!" He stumbled away from her making his way toward the woods.

"Thank you!" There were tears streaming down his cheeks. Whether they were pain, happiness, or both she couldn't tell. Luthiel felt tears welling in her own eyes in answer.

"Your life and spirit restored is all the thanks I need. Now get out of here!" she said.

There was a commotion at the gates. It sounded as though they were trying to break out from the inside.

"They are coming to murder me!"

With that, he plunged into the Vale of Mists. The mists closed in behind him.

"Fly Vaelros! But come back when this has passed!" she cried.

From out of the Gates of Ottomnos, six dark figures rode. But behind them came Othalas. Soon, he outdistanced them, coming to stand beside Luthiel.

"Get on!" he growled at her.

She bounded onto his back.

Melkion shot out of the mists, tilted up on a wingtip as he turned and then landed upon her shoulder.

"A fine fix you've gotten yourself into now!" he cried.

The Six came to a halt before them.

"Leave her to us," Evaldris said, pointing at Luthiel with his sword tip. Her skin prickled and she felt a sudden, overpowering urge to run.

"If you give her up and tell us where he went, we may let you live."

"You will not have her," Othalas growled, then tilted his head back and let out a howl that mounted on the very walls of the Vale, spilled over and then came rebounding back almost as loud as the first time. From the gates of Ottomnos rode the three Vyrl. They formed up on either side of Luthiel—Ahmberen and Elshael to her right, Ecthellien to her left. Their monster horses snorted and pawed the earth.

"The Lady is not to be harmed," Ecthellien said. "Unless you wish to begin your war now. Then you would face all the might of the Vale. As it seems you've already lost one of your number. I am afraid that the odds would be very long."

The cold wolves growled.

"The negotiations are over," Evaldris said in whisper that seemed to carry far through the mists. "By treachery you have turned Vaelros and now we must see to him. But your acts won't be forgotten."

"Turned! I say saved!" Luthiel cried. "Vaelros escaped a nightmare of lingering death. It is one you should know well—for you live there. Would that you had the chance he did. But, alas, there is no hope for you."

"Vyrl, whatever tortures you have performed on this girl have surely driven her mad. It is a shame that you have resorted to such base acts. One thing is very clear to us now. She is your creature and she has done great harm to our captain. This aggression will not be without an answer."

With that, they turned their wolves and bounded into the Vale. Soon, she couldn't tell their shapes from the swirling clouds.

Her heart sank as she watched them.

"How long before they find Vaelros?" she asked.

"Even if they are great hunters, they will have trouble in the Vale. It is teeming with creatures. If you wish we can send word—they will help him," Ahmberen said.

"Yes, please," she said. "Whatever ill he has done was under terrible threat. He is a kind man, and gentle-natured. If he were not, I think he would have long ago become like the rest of them." She nodded in the direction of the Six.

Ecthellien pulled a horn from his belt and blew four times. Four great blasts rolled across the Vale. From both the wood and the fortress poured grendilo and other creatures of the Vale—werewolves and giants with skin of bark and hair of moss and eagle-headed lions and lion-headed horses and birds whose wings burned and other much stranger beasts.

They formed in a great company before Ecthellien and he rode his monster horse back and forth before them.

"Six riders on fey wolves hunt a lone man on foot in our Vale!" he cried. "We would not have this man be taken! Go now! Tell your fellows! Give him whatever aid you can and hide him from their eyes!"

He brought his horn to his lips again and let out four more peals. As quickly as they had formed, the company broke, melting again into the mists.

"Thank you," she said to Ecthellien as he returned to her side.

"I think we should thank you," Ahmberen said. "You have already turned one who would have killed us away from that path—though he may not yet know it."

Luthiel nodded.

"I didn't think of it that way."

"No, I suppose you wouldn't," Elshael said. "It was a good-hearted thing. But it was also very reckless. You could have been killed or taken."

"Lady, I am sorry. I will try to be more careful," she said.

"Elshael, don't be so hard on her. She will have to take many more risks, I am afraid. And most of those will be far more dangerous than what happened here this day," Ahmberen said.

Elshael nodded to Ahmberen.

"You're probably right. I don't have to like it, though."

"Nor do we all," Ahmberen said. "But remember, Luthiel didn't choose this."

With that, they rode single file, back through the yawning gates of Ottomnos.

LADY OF OTTOMNOS

Luthiel spent the rest of the afternoon sitting atop the battlements. She'd already eaten the lunch Rendillo had brought her and now she sat staring out into the mists worrying about Vaelros. She could hear the wintry howl of wolves far off. The answering calls of werewolves comforted her somewhat as did the horn peals of Ecthellien—who'd ridden out to help find Vaelros and return him safely to Ottomnos. As she sat there, hoping to see Vaelros emerge from the mists, the day darkened. Soon Soelee set and Oerin's eye followed after. Stars winked into view and, in far too short a time, she found herself confronted with the night.

As Silva rose, she saw Ecthellien returning alone. Her heart sank.

"Did you find him?" she called from the gates.

"No, lady, we did not," he replied.

"Oh," she said.

"Don't be afraid, Luthiel. His hunters are lost in the mists now. The Vale is not a place for tracking. Scents drift through the mist and are carried on invisible rivers through the air in all directions. Worse, you often cannot see the hand in front of your face, much less the prints on the ground."

Luthiel felt little comfort, but thanked him for his reassurance, nonetheless.

"Dinner is waiting for you in the Great Hall," Ecthellien said. "We wanted you to sit with us before tonight."

Luthiel felt cold and anxious. She didn't know if she'd be able to eat anything. The hall, with its long, blood-stained table, didn't appeal to her as a place for dining. But she climbed down from the battlements and fell into step beside Ecthellien despite her misgivings.

What choice do I have? she wondered.

When she entered the great hall she found that a long board had been laid over the table covering the blood-stained holes. The floor space around was wet and showed signs of scrubbing. Throughout the hall, flir bug bulbs were hung and flower petals lay scattered over every surface. The air smelled of flowers, fresh grass and open air. But she still thought she could catch a whiff of blood and metal.

Melkion, who'd kept watch upon her from a distance for most of the day, winged his way into the chamber. He landed on the back of her *Silen* and white-wood chair which was at the far end of the table. A flir bug bulb rested in the table's center casting its dancing light across the polished board.

Ecthellien walked before her, leading her to the chair. He slid it out for her, inviting her to sit down before he returned to his place among the other Vyrl. For once, the Vyrl were silent, seeming content to gaze upon her. Othalas came into the room last of all, padding on quiet feet till he reached the end of the chamber. She hadn't seen him all afternoon and wondered where he'd gone.

Then the grendilo came out of a door at the far end of the chamber. They were carrying covered plates, each balanced precisely on their heads as they hopped toward her. When they came to the table they laid the plates out in front of her. Each plate was artfully decorated with garnishes of flowers, butter, honey, or jelly. One was arranged with cuts of fruit in the shape of a flower, a second held slices of some delicately carved meat in a glaze of orange and red, a third was piled with steaming vegetables glistening with butter and honey. Slices of black bread were laid out upon a plate beside her.

She opened her eyes wide at the feast laid out before her.

"Thank you," she said. She was again amazed at the civility of the Vyrl, who still seemed to her as savage, dark creatures.

"You are welcome," Ahmberen replied. "We wanted to let you know how much we appreciate what you have done for us."

As she looked over the food, she wondered if Vaelros would find any-thing to eat this night. Or was he still running—cold and alone—through the Vale of Mists? Looking at the food, she felt a moment of guilt for her relative comfort.

But how long will it last? she thought. *How comfortable will I be when they drink my blood again?*

Her head still ached a little from when Ahmberen struck her. Her bite wounds were healing as well. Soon, she would no longer need her bandages. But they said they would take enough blood tonight to last them a year.

She shuddered, suddenly feeling not at all hungry.

"Luthiel? Are you well?" Elshael asked.

"I was just thinking about Vaelros," she said.

"Put your worry aside," Ecthellien said. "His six companions have lost him as have we. But there are hundreds of grendilo and thousands of eyes on the wing who will bring word of him to us, once they find him."

"Listen to Ecthellien," Ahmberen said. "And please try to enjoy your dinner. It is a gift, the first of many that we have for you this evening."

"Gifts?"

"Yes. To demonstrate our admiration of you and to serve as proof of our good intentions."

Reluctantly—for her stomach still felt tight—she took a small bite of the glazed meat.

It was delicious!

She cut off another piece and soon that was gone as well. Her appre-hension faded as she enjoyed her meal.

"It *is* good!" she said between mouthfuls.

For once, the Vyrl smiled at her. She quickly averted her eyes but it was too late for she caught a glimpse of wicked teeth. Taking a deep breath, she returned to her delicious meal.

They're just fattening me up, she thought. But she found herself carried away once more by delicious enchantment.

When she was finished with the main courses, the grendilo brought out a black cake covered in melted chocolate with a hollow reservoir in the center filled with some golden liquid.

"This one is mine," Melkion said. Leaning over her shoulder, he stretched out his long neck, opened his mouth and let out a thin tongue of flame. The flame licked the liquid's surface, setting it alight. The flame's heat melted the chocolate coating causing it to run all over the cake.

"Now, blow it out," Melkion said.

She filled her lungs and exhaled. The flame extinguished in a wisp of smoke. It looked so good, her mouth watered. Delicately, she cut a small slice off and brought it to her mouth.

"Get some of the liquor on it. It tastes better that way," Melkion said.

She dipped the cake in the golden liquid and then put it into her mouth. The liquor, warmed by the flame, melted into the cake which, in turn, melted on her tongue.

"Mmmm!" she said, hungrily cutting another piece off.

"Glad you like it!" Melkion said with a wink.

Hungrily, almost soundlessly, she devoured the rest of her cake. As she ate, Ahmberen spoke.

"Tonight is very special to us," Ahmberen said. "We intend to make it so for you as well. We welcome you, Luthiel, to become as one of us. For though you are not a Vyrl, your blood is of closer kin to ours than to any elf. For the blood that we will take tonight we will honor you as we honor each other. You will possess a full fourth of all that is ours. Each year that you grant us blood, we too will grant you tokens of our riches. Further, you will command our minions as we do. From this day forward, wights, grendilo and other creatures of the Vale will know you as queen. They will answer your call, ready to do your bidding."

Ahmberen paused, allowing Luthiel to consider his words.

"Melkion," he said, after waiting a few moments. His voice echoed through the chamber which was slowly filling with a multitude of strange creatures. Ravens with feathers of green, gold or silver perched in the windows. Perched beside them were orange birds with flaming wings and eyes like rubies. The grendilo were joined by wights, giants and strange chimera creatures. Even the mists seemed to gather in that chamber, the green lights flooding in through doors and windows until all the air was aglitter with them.

Melkion hopped from the chair's back and onto the table. He dipped his head in a slight bow.

"Yes, Ahmberen?" he said.

"Long ago you came here searching for someone. In exchange, you pledged to serve us as our messenger. Is Luthiel the one you sought?"

"She is," he said, turning his head to glance at Luthiel. "She has the broken blade—Cutter's Shear."

Luthiel looked at him curiously.

"Then we release you from our service. You may go where you wish, but for your good service all these long years, we grant you our friendship. You may enter the Vale whenever you choose without fear of its creatures. You are welcome in our fortress and we grant you three boons to ask at any time of your choosing."

Melkion bowed again, this time deeper.

"Ahmberen, you have become gracious—it suits you," he said, then turned to Luthiel. "If you will have me, lady, I would like to stay with you. There is a boon I would ask of you when the time comes. Until then, will you have me?"

A dragon asking to serve her? She didn't know how to reply.

"It would be an honor, Melkion," she said.

"Now that that's settled," Ahmberen said. "We each have a gift for you—tokens of our love for you."

As he spoke, Elshael stood and walked toward Luthiel.

"Stand up," Melkion whispered in her ear.

She glided out of her chair and turned to face Elshael who held a velvet case before her.

"Of old in the days when Eledweil was still new and full of life, the Aedar who lived there crafted of *Eledril*—the moonsteel of Eledweil—crowns for their lords and ladies among the Elohwe. These circlets were of the finest make—light as air upon the heads that bore them. Woven within that precious metal were *Esilis*—tiny stones that shone with the light of stars. By craft that is now lost, the crowns could be made to appear as only a thin thread of silver or to shine brightly like a crown of stars. In later days, during the ancient wars of heaven and Oesha, the crowns were worn by the greatest heroes among angels and elves. For creatures of the void feared the lights when revealed in their fullness." She opened the box and within lay a crown of impossibly thin filigree. Trapped within the weave were lights that burned like the brightest stars of night. "It is akin to Wyrd Stones—that contain the spirit of Lumen who was the first light of creation—for stars are the children of Lumen. Spirits of the void have always feared stars, for it was with their light that Ëavanya built the walls of night that were meant to ward them from creation."

Luthiel stared at it in wonder.

"It is so beautiful," she whispered.

"Go on, take it from the box," Elshael said.

Luthiel lifted the glistening crown from its box. It was light as a cloud in her hand and its brilliance chased the shadows into the far corners of that great chamber.

"This is the last of the *Neltherduel*—the crowns of light. Here, let me help you." She lifted the crown and placed it gently on Luthiel's head. Luthiel could barely feel it. It was lighter than gossamer but its radiance made everything around her stand out in soft relief.

Elshael grasped Luthiel's hand, bringing her forefinger to the center of her forehead.

"Blink your eyes," she said.

Luthiel did as she asked. When her eyes fluttered open, the light was gone.

"Do it again."

Luthiel obliged her and the light returned.

"If you don't wish to reveal the light, just touch the crown and blink your eyes. If you want to bring it back, just do the same thing again."

Luthiel nodded.

"Thank you lady, I will treasure it always." Luthiel didn't know what else to say.

Luthiel placed her finger to her forehead and blinked. The bright light faded.

Elshael kissed her forehead and then backed away.

As she returned to her throne, Ecthellien stood. He held before him a long, black bundle which he presented to her. Undoing the cloth, he withdrew the arching curves of a bow. Strung, it reached her chin.

"This is one of the bows of the Aedar. Fashioned of the heartwood of a life-tree it is very difficult to break and if cloven or fractured will mend itself."

He ran his finger along the string.

"This is the hair of a Keirin—a spirit of light, air and storm. And these," he produced two quivers full of long, black feathered arrows, "are bolts from the armory of Ottomnos. They are old and of the finest make. The heads are all moonsteel."

Luthiel accepted the bow from him. Its wood was white as that of her chair and within it were etched subtle designs of stars and moons. A wire of Lumiel was twisted around the midpoint forming a handle. Its ends were plated in grey Somril and a two pronged guide of blue Meril protruded from the handle.

"Thank you," she said bowing to him as he knelt and kissed her on the forehead.

Ahmberen was already standing beside Ecthellien. In his hand he held a tiny pouch which he gave to Luthiel.

Luthiel opened the pouch to find a beautiful platinum ring set with white stones. The pattern was of waves and a shape like a whirlpool swirled around a signet stone.

"This ring is a Kelebrith—a key to Ottomnos. It was Valkire's once, now it is yours. Touch it to any door in the fortress and it will be open to you. Library, treasury, armory, they are all unlocked by this key."

She held the ring in the palm of her hand.

"It is too large," she said.

"Put it on," the Vyrl replied.

She placed the ring on her finger and gasped as it shrank to fit. She turned her hand over looking at the band in amazement.

Ahmberen handed her a bag of coin that had hung around his waist.

"A fourth of all the wealth of Ottomnos is yours, of which this is only a small part."

Then, he bent and kissed her upon the forehead.

When Ahmberen returned to his throne, Othalas rose from where he lay at the head of the table.

"Though I have long served the Vyrl," he said. "I am my own creature and ultimately choose who I will have. They now recognize you as both a partner and an equal; I offer myself and my kin to your service and protection. If you must ride into danger or to war, I ask you to take me— for I sense that your road will be long and difficult running through many dangers before reaching its end."

"Othalas, greatest of all wolves, if I have you with me then I don't know how any danger could touch me. This is a gift far greater than any I would have thought possible."

Othalas laughed in his gravelly way.

"Aye, lady, I may be great. But do not be deceived. There are some creatures in this world and the other that are my equal or better in might, cunning, or terror."

"If it is as you say, then you will be very welcome to come with me. Though I hope I will not have to face any more terror. I have seen enough, I think, to last a lifetime or more."

Othalas chuckled.

"I hope so too. But if it does not happen as you wish, then I will come when you call me."

Ecthellien was standing again and he gave her a small silver horn.

"Othalas asked me to give this to you," he said.

"Sound it and I will come as fast as I am able to," the werewolf growled.

Luthiel looked at them each in turn, then walked up to clasp the werewolf around his great neck.

"I don't know how I can ever thank you all for what you've done," she said.

"What you will give tonight, will more than repay us. I will not lie. It is not an easy thing to give," Ahmberen said.

Luthiel looked at her feet feeling the lump growing in her throat.

"I understand," she said.

"Then come," Ecthellien said. "We may as well begin."

They stood and advanced until she was surrounded. Melkion assumed his perch upon her shoulder and Othalas rose, stretching his great bulk before he fell in beside her.

"There is one more gift—the gift of the bond. But that is for after," Ahmberen said. "Are you ready?"

"I don't think I'll ever be ready for what is about to happen," she said. "But I agree with Ecthellien, the sooner this is finished, the better."

"Then follow me," Ahmberen said.

GIFT OF THE BOND

He walked down the hall until he came to one of the doors opening to the courtyard. After spending some time in the charred glass tunnels, they emerged into a star-lit courtyard. The mists hung low to the ground, swirling around her feet and legs, but the sky was clear above them except for the occasional swell of mist which would arch up like a grey hill beneath the night sky before sliding away again.

The gates opened to their approach and then closed again as they passed through.

They continued down the road until they came to the lake-shore. In front of her, the Miruvoir was still. Occasionally, the mists would break, revealing a perfect sky reflected in the water.

The Vyrl stopped on the lakeshore.

"We're not going to mislead you, Luthiel. There is still some danger," Ahmberen said.

"Though your blood helps us to hold the madness at bay, while we are feeding, there is always—the hunger. There is a chance it might overcome us all and we won't be able to stop feeding."

"But you stopped the last time," Luthiel whispered.

"Yes, hope that we are able to stop again," said Ecthellien.

"Did Valkire suffer the same risks?"

"Yes," Ahmberen said.

"It is only a small risk," Ecthellien said. "Your blood is very potent."

"We just wanted to be completely truthful with you about the danger," Elshael said.

Luthiel nodded. Her heart pounded like a drum in her chest. She had begun to believe that the Vyrl had, somehow, been completely turned by some quality in her blood. But now, doubt was again casting its chill over her.

The Vyrl's black eyes swirled with slowly dwindling lights. This time, she didn't turn her eyes from their gaze. She wanted to see them, to stare deep into their abyss and puzzle out their dark mystery. They drew endlessly in on themselves, devouring lights and blackness alike. Was the Vyrl's control only a façade for the hunger that burned like an all consuming cold within them? For a moment, she stared into the empty eyes of creatures who were once angels and wondered at the terrible might of the thing that had brought them low, making them slaves to hunger. Was it some hurt inflicted on their spirits long ago? Or did some spirit of darkness live within them still, seeking ceaselessly to bend them to its terrible will?

Unable to bear it any longer, she tore her eyes away.

Remember, Luthiel, she reminded herself. *They ravaged Eledweil. What is my blood compared to the life of an entire moon?*

"This is already decided," she said. The certainty in her voice belied her terror. "I accept the risk and hope that you are stronger than the darkness within you." She wondered, for a moment, at what she was saying.

Ahmberen nodded. "Good," he said. "Now, it will be easier for you if we do this in the water. It numbs the skin, deadens the pain."

Luthiel looked over the misty lake and then began to undress.

"I hope it works," she whispered.

When she was finished, she stood before the Vyrl, naked but for the Wyrd Stone hanging from her neck. There was a chill in the mists about her feet that climbed into her legs and made her shiver. Slowly, she entered the cold water letting its shock rise up her legs, over her pelvis, stomach, chest and finally her neck. Completely immersed but for her head, she shivered as the Vyrl entered the water beside her. The waves they set off lapped over her body.

In the east, she could see the pale sliver of Lunen rising. It made a silver pathway over the lake. Within the pathway, was the black outline of a small island.

Ecthellien raised his hand and pointed toward the island.

"There, see how the light of Lunen makes a path through the water?"

"Yes," she whispered through trembling lips.

"Swim toward the island. We will be with you."

She pushed off the bottom and started to swim. For a few strokes, the Vyrl glided through the water beside her—black shapes in the moon-kissed water. Then, she could feel their hands upon her.

"Keep kicking your legs," Ahmberen whispered in her ear.

She did as she was told, gliding gracefully out into the water. All about her the dark night lay in stillness as if it were a predator waiting to pounce upon a trembling prey. To her, a shadow seemed to glide across the moon and the mists seemed to deepen. On the shore, she thought she saw a black cloud rising up among the mists to stretch its inky fingers out over the water. Toward her. Toward the Vyrl.

For a moment, she froze in fear. Her whole body quivered with anxiety. She forced her legs to move. Then the black mists were upon her. They swirled around the Vyrl rushing in through their mouths and nostrils. Hanging in a cloying shroud over the water.

Just think about swimming. Just think about swimming. She repeated the thought to herself over and over in time to the kicking of her legs, trying to move out from beneath the cloud. The Vyrl were staring at her with their hungry eyes now. In them she could see nothing but madness.

Then she felt a searing pain in her neck. She gasped. The pain was *severe*. She felt herself starting to struggle. The hands gripped her tighter. The water splashed. Her face slid below the water. In a panic, she pushed her head above the water again and gulped down the air in hurried gasps. She tried to focus on the island, tried to keep swimming. A second pain seared through her right arm and a third through her left. The Vyrl at her left arm clamped its teeth, shaking its head from side to side driving its teeth deeper. A second panic came over her and she struggled again, kicking her legs hard this time. But the Vyrl's grip only tightened.

The Vyrl pulled blood from her in long draws that made her heart race and her vision blur.

A sickness rose in her stomach, growing until all she wanted was to curl in a ball, sink to the bottom and there be forgotten. But she kept kicking—more to struggle against the creatures that were now drawing the blood from her in great sucking pulls than to move herself any closer to the island.

She was already growing confused and disoriented with fear and blood loss. The water was black with the night, black with the Vyrl's bodies and black with her blood—pumping into the Vyrl's mouths and oozing beyond them into the water. Her hands, wrists, and neck burned but her legs and toes felt as though they were freezing. The coldness crept up her body until it reached her hips, then flooded into her gut and chest. Still she thrashed, but with each passing heartbeat her struggles grew weaker. After a few minutes of struggle, most of the strength had drained from her arms and it was all she could do to keep her legs moving.

It was a good thing the Vyrl still held her, for she felt certain she was no longer strong enough to swim on her own. She could no longer feel her limbs or even tell if they were moving. A piercing cold settled into her chest.

For a moment, she passed out. Then, a few seconds later, her eyes fluttered open and she found herself lying upon her back in the water. The black shapes of the Vyrl were still hunched around her body. She forced herself to look away from them. What they were doing was too terrible to watch.

Slowly, the mists cleared and she found herself staring into the depthless nighttime sky. Lunen shone over the lake's mirror face. Far to her left, both in the water, and in the sky, she saw the dim orb of Somnos. All of her body felt heavy with fatigue and her stomach was crumpled into a useless bag. She felt both thirsty and nauseous at the same time. Some of her feeling returned. Her neck hurt, her legs hurt. She realized, almost absently, that the Vyrl had moved and were now feeding from different places. One had moved to the other side of her neck. Another was sinking its searing fangs deep into her left leg. The third floated in the water beside her, staring with his mad and hungry eyes. In that moment she felt with certainty that she was lost. The Vyrl's mouth was a rictus of blood-lust. But he just floated there staring. The battle was going on inside of him, behind the hungry swirl of his eyes. Meanwhile, the other two Vyrl sucked ravenously at her veins. Her heartbeat became a throbbing pang and she struggled against fatigue just to keep her eyes open.

She realized she was going to die.

She wanted to live, tried to live, gave one last feeble attempt to throw the Vyrl off. She thrashed, kicked and cried out with a voice that sounded, to her, as though it was very far away. The sickness in her stomach spread and the pain in her chest grew until they were all she could think of. She was so weakened by blood loss that, soon, all she could manage were a few feeble splashes. Somehow, in the struggle, she was twisted around so that her face ended up in the water. She tried to lift her head but found that she lacked the strength. Her hands fell limply in front of her face. Her eyes were still open and she could clearly see the bottom. She might have stood and walked to the far shore if there weren't two Vyrl latched onto her.

She was no longer afraid. Instead, she let go. She felt entirely relaxed, even comfortable. It wasn't so bad now. All the bad parts were over. Most important of all, Leowin was safe. But somewhere in the back of her mind something cried out that she didn't want to die. Oddly, in the cold of the water, in the cold of her lack of blood, she felt warm. She drifted and she knew, but it didn't trouble her—except for the part in the back of her mind—that she was very close to dying.

Around her, the water splashed and she felt herself being jerked back and forth. It was as though two of the Vyrl were fighting over the prize of her body and what paltry bit of blood remained to her. Even now, she could feel the heartbeat in her chest quavering like the wings of a wounded butterfly. Suddenly, another mouth left her and finally the last. It was as though they were grabbed and then forcibly pulled off.

She felt hot hands lifting her out of the water. Her head bobbed at the end of her neck for she no longer had the strength to support it. But she did manage to open her eyes. She saw the rocks and roots of a bank passing beneath her feet. A rising Cauthraus spilled its red light over everything. To her delirious eyes it looked as though the world was bleeding. In front of her something flickered and she felt warmth on her forehead.

"What have you done! Look at her, she's dead!" She could hear Melkion's voice as though from a long way off. *Why was he so far away?* she wondered.

Beside her, Ahmberen growled savagely. "Fool of a dragon! You could never know the way it takes hold." His breath wistled through bloody teeth. "This time was worse than ever. But it is gone now! And the girl's not dead yet. Out of my way! She needs to be warmed!"

The Vyrl's voice also sounded far away and it dawned on her that something was wrong with her ears.

She was laid down beside the fire upon a mound of blankets. Another pile of blankets was cast on top of her. Despite the fire and the blankets she shivered uncontrollably. Blood oozed in dark ribbons from the wounds in her arms, legs and neck. She watched on dully for a few moments and then let her eyes close. Her heartbeat alternated between thumping and racing.

Beside her, she could hear the sounds of bickering.

"I'm not going to let an *elf* drink my blood!" said a loud voice. To Luthiel it sounded like Ecthellien but the voice was so savage and so far away that she couldn't be certain.

"She is no mere *elf*! If you don't, then she may die and we will surely fall into madness. Ecthellien, you must remember your oath!" Ahmberen growled.

"Oath? Is it worth bearing the pain? We could have it now—*all* of it."

Then, in a lower voice.

"Ahmberen, you know what I'm talking about. Heart's life's blood. We could *share* it, you and I."

She blinked her eyes open again. Slowly, Ahmberen and Ecthellien came into focus. Ahmberen was standing over her with his back to her. Ecthellien faced him. His eyes darted between her and Ahmberen. Away and to the left of Ahmberen, Elshael stood as one in a daze. But she ignored the two. Her black eyes were fixed on Luthiel.

Ahmberen trembled at Ecthellien's words. He clenched his fist and then, with what seemed a supreme effort, drew still.

"Never utter those words again," Ahmberen said in a low and dangerous voice. "Not in her presence."

Despite Ahmberen's words, the madness was still in Ecthellien's eyes. In his face, Luthiel could see none of the nobility she'd grown accustomed to. His lips drew back from teeth caked in blood—her blood.

"It is not enough!" he snarled.

"Aye, if you listen to the hunger, it is not. But if you only took a moment to think on what you need, you would realize that it is more than enough. You've been bewitched."

They turned and Luthiel saw that each one held a naked blade. Smoke rose from Ahmberen's and in the low light she could see its faint red glow. Ecthellien's was black as night itself but she could see its tip pointing at Ahmberen's eyes. It quavered, and then it faltered.

"She's our last chance to lift the madness," Ahmberen continued. "Do you know how difficult it was for me to tear myself from her? If I hadn't, we'd almost certainly have lost her. But now that we've taken her blood, we have a year. A whole year, Ecthellien!"

At that, Ecthellien's sword point dropped.

"Just as it was in the days of Valkire?" he replied. The savageness faded from Ecthellien's voice and was replaced with confusion.

"Yes," Ahmberen replied.

There was another short period of silence.

"I think I am well. It is passing," Ecthellien said at last.

"Good! Quickly now! We don't have much time!" Ahmberen said, motioning to Luthiel.

Now that the danger had passed, Luthiel's strength failed and her sight grew dim.

A long period of silence followed. It was broken occasionally by low grunts. Throughout this time, her shivering became uncontrollable and her heart raced violently. This scared her terribly. She rocked back and forth, humming to herself, thinking of home and how she'd probably never see it again. What would Leowin think? What would Winowe, Glendoras and Lorethain think? They were the only family she knew. She didn't want to die here in the Vale of Mists and be forgotten.

Her chest spasms had just stopped when a cup was placed in front of her. Its contents were hot and the steam of it warmed her face. The cup was thrust into her hands. Its metal felt so hot that she almost dropped it.

"Drink," Elshael said with soft melancholy.

She suddenly felt very thirsty and realized that it was, indeed, a good time to drink. Tilting the cup forward she put her lips over its steaming rim and took a few large gulps. The liquid was hot and it burned her throat at first. It was thick, salty and some of it stuck to the roof of her mouth. Her tongue became alive with a strange, metallic flavor that she found delicious. After a few swallows, though, the burning in her mouth faded to tingling. But, wherever the liquid passed, it left a sensation of warmth. It was as though she were gulping down sunlight. It dripped through her like hot honey. When the flood touched her chest, her heart calmed. The beat paused for a moment, as though taking a breath. Then it resumed its normal course. She felt refreshed—as one waking from a deep sleep.

With each gulp, her thirst grew. Too soon, the cup was empty and, with a sigh of regret, she placed it on the ground. But before her hands left the first cup, another was held in front of her. She was amazed at the ferocity with which her hands latched onto it. Her mouth was greedy and she gulped it down.

The tingling sensation grew until it felt as though a hundred small fires were dancing beneath her skin. Her heartbeat strengthened and she could hear her pulse like drumbeats in her ears. If her senses were dull a moment earlier, she felt at the very peak of alertness now. Indeed, a sense of clarity fell upon her. Immediately, she felt embarrassed at the loud slurping noises she was making while drinking.

Though she was still very thirsty, she paused. What was she drinking anyway? She looked down into the cup and saw that it contained a substance that looked like blood caught on fire. Golden flames licked over a deep red substance that swirled and boiled within its container. She felt disgust and held the cup away from her.

"It's blood!" she cried out.

"Yes, and it's saving your life," Ahmberen said.

She nodded and slowly brought the cup back to her mouth.

As she put her lips to it, she noticed a reek rising from the blood like the burning of subtle incense. The odor was not unpleasant. She closed her eyes and tried to imagine that it was water, or some exotic wine. When the blood touched her lips, she felt another onrush of overwhelming thirst. Before she realized it, the cup was empty. She put it down. Immediately, a third was placed in her hands.

She stared up in amazement.

"This is the last," said Ecthellien.

She nodded and picked it up. She was ready for the thirst this time. Nonetheless, its intensity surprised her. Her lips locked onto the cup and all she could do was gulp blood as fast as she could swallow. The sensation that was first a tingling and then a flame stopped. An instant later, she felt a jolt like lightning. Her whole body convulsed. Involuntarily she stood up.

She dropped the cup. It rolled on the ground leaving a thin rill of blood where it passed.

One.

Two.

Three.

With each heartbeat she saw through new eyes, heard through new ears. She saw herself, she saw Melkion, she saw Othalas, she saw each of the Vyrl in turn. She reeled, suddenly overwhelmed with vertigo.

She's going to fall. The thoughts were not her own.

She felt two sets of arms shoot out before she felt them catch her.

What's happening to me? She thought.

It is the gift of our blood. The gift of the bond. She realized that the words were coming from Elshael but her lips didn't move.

"I can hear you. In my head. How?" she whispered.

The blood we gave you, the blood that saved your life causes it. This is called the gift of the bond. Ahmberen thought.

Luthiel closed her eyes and shook her head trying not to see from so many different points of view. Trying not to feel as the Vyrl did. But she couldn't help it. She felt the power of their bodies, perceived the insights of their minds, felt the madness of hunger like a shadow in the back of her head. Even now, she could feel them wanting more blood; feel herself hungering for blood in sympathy.

And they've just fed upon me. I wonder how terrible that hunger must become after a year, she thought.

Or three thousand years, Ecthellien thought in reply. *This hunger is a weak and pitiful shadow compared to what we will feel by the end of this year. But still it will be bearable. Indeed, we could last for many years before the madness began to truly set in.*

But what happened on the water? The frenzy? Luthiel shuddered to remember it. The Vyrl shuddered in empathy. She realized now, they were feeling the fear and pain that she felt. She could also feel their corresponding guilt and remorse.

A shadow on the night, Ahmberen thought.

There was a fell mist, Elshael thought.

It came upon us like a dark enchantment. It drove us mad with hunger. We are fortunate that Ahmberen broke the spell. Otherwise, things would be worse, Ecthellien thought.

As the thoughts entered her mind she felt the remembered pang of hunger that the Vyrl experienced. Even the memory was severe enough to make her bend over double. She should be angry. They'd almost killed her. But it seemed impossible for her to rage at them now. Slowly, the hunger faded.

How can you stand it? she thought.

Fight with all of your heart and mind. Sometimes even that is not enough, Elshael thought.

But why would such an enchantment come upon you? she thought.

What I wonder is who? Who could do such a thing and are they hiding somewhere just beyond the lakeshore? Elshael thought.

I saw something there, Luthiel thought. *It was like a shadow in the mists. It came when we first swam out.*

The memory of it flashed through her mind and she knew the Vyrl shared it.

"Othalas!" Ecthellien called. "Search the far lakeshore. Be careful. Something very dangerous could be hiding there."

"Othalas, stay here," Melkion said. "I'll go. If something is there then it will be less likely to see me."

Melkion sprang into the air and soon disappeared into the night. She sat down on the log. Cradling her head, she tried to sort through all the things she was sensing. Closing her eyes made it worse—she kept seeing things through one or all of the Vyrl's eyes—so she kept them open.

Her senses remained at knife-edge clarity. The depthless sky slid by in tiny ticks. It was deep—a well in which stars were mere raindrops—and her stomach spun. She marveled. The greatest depth of all was above and she'd never realized. She imagined falling up into the endless dark and shuddered. The night was a hungry pit filled with lights. It reminded her of the Vyrl's eyes and she shuddered to think that she was seeing through those eyes even now.

After a short time, Melkion returned gliding to a graceful landing on an out-thrust branch above her.

"There's nothing," he said. "If something was there it is gone now."

The Vyrl's thoughts were revealing. They worried about Gorothoth. They worried about creatures from the depths of night that they last saw more than six thousand years ago. One by one, they dismissed these worries and left them in some dark corner of their minds.

At least it is gone now, whatever it was, Elshael thought.

What if this happens again next year? We have to find out before then. We came too close to losing Luthiel this time to risk it again, Ahmberen thought.

The world is becoming a very dangerous place, Ecthellien thought. *That shadow reminded me of enchantments I haven't seen since the days of the great betrayal.*

Nor I, Ahmberen and Elshael both thought in concert.

As she listened to the Vyrl's troubled thoughts, Luthiel heard words that she didn't understand, felt sensations that she had difficulty comprehending. But she was able to pierce a bit of the mystery surrounding the Vyrl and their past.

The Vyrl's fear was deep, feral, unreasoning. It troubled Luthiel that creatures as great as Vyrl could know such fear. But what disturbed her most were the brief flashes. Images of death and burning, the feelings of hunger, torment, isolation and the shrinking of minds by madness and depravity. She realized then that the Vyrl were victims of a devastating and ongoing spiritual torture. It was this process that had turned them into monsters. It was a process she had interrupted and she could feel their gratitude for her, their protectiveness and even adoration. Yet, in the hunger that had afflicted them that night, they sensed something akin to the spiritual weapon that had left them wrecked and broken creatures compared to the angels they once were in the great long ago.

Under her blankets, Luthiel shivered as her wounds began to throb. She sighed wondering—*Must I always suffer harm of some kind or another?*

"Could we please go back?" she asked before the Vyrl could respond to her thoughts. The normal sound of her voice reassured her somewhat. It was a sound she liked. The rich emotions and shades of meaning in the mental landscape made her head spin. When combined with the intensity of the Vyrl's fear, it was just too much for her.

"I don't think we'll solve this mystery tonight," she whispered. "But I feel very hurt and I'm afraid my wounds need tending to."

She again felt the swell of sympathy and admiration coming from the Vyrl.

"How could we be so careless?" Elshael said, as she moved to help Luthiel stand. "Come here. There's a boat."

The rest of the Vyrl joined in, guiding her to the boat. She was amazed at how weak she still was. The blood the Vyrl had fed her had brought her back from the borders of death, but her body ached with pain and exhaustion.

Once in the boat, a grendilo with a long pole brought her swiftly back to Ottomnos. Othalas swam alongside and Melkion and Elshael sat in the boat with her. Ecthellien and Ahmberen took a second boat but stopped short on the lakeshore. As she entered the Gates of Ottomnos they began picking through the woods, searching for any signs they could find. They were joined by werewolves and some of the Vale's chimera creatures.

Luthiel was rushed to her room. They built a fire for her and stripped off her blankets to tend to her hurts. Rendillo boiled water on the fire and made her cup after cup of hot tea and honey. She gulped it down, letting the warmth seep into her bones. Melkion, Othalas and Elshael stayed with her all night. It was in the early morning when she finally fell asleep. Even then, her dreams were troubled by the sights, thoughts and sensations of the Vyrl. Later on, she had a dream of Vaelros. He was among grendilo and bark-skinned giants. They were on the move and mists swirled about them. But he was happy since, for the first time in many long years, he was free. Still he kept moving, driven by some unreasoning fear of the six who pursued him. She sensed, in her dream, that his fear of them was enhanced by having been one of them. It was their state he feared—a state of perpetual torment on the border between life and death. For within him, there was a deep hurt that may never fully heal— a wound left by the curse that nearly killed him. Even in her dreams, she marveled at the likeness of his thoughts to those of the Vyrl.

A BRIEF REST

When Luthiel awoke, her entire body felt stiff and battered. For a long time, she just lay in her bed, staring up at the charred glass ceiling. Melkion fluttered into view, then landed on the bed beside her.

"Are you all right?" he asked her.

"It hurts to move," she replied.

"Well, you have certainly earned your rest. I think it would be wise for you to stay in bed for a while."

Luthiel swallowed. The wounds on her neck—old and new—made it hurt.

"I'm afraid you're right. Even if I wanted to, I don't think I'd be able to stand."

"You lost quite a lot of blood last night. We're lucky to still have you with us. Wait here while I have Rendillo bring you some breakfast."

"Thank you Melkion," she said.

But before Rendillo arrived, she'd fallen asleep again. Outside, rain began to fall and she slept through the morning and into the afternoon as the pitter-patter whispered over Ottomnos.

She awoke again to the smell of steaming tea and of lunch.

Melkion was insistent.

"You need to eat!" he said. "If you don't, you won't get your strength back." He flapped his wings in exasperation.

"Melkion," she said. The words came out soft and her throat hurt but she still chided him. "You're acting like a mother willow-jay brooding over chicks!" She laughed but not too much, because it hurt.

Melkion swished his tail in exasperation.

"You! You need a little brooding over! Now sit up and eat your lunch!" A thin wisp of smoke rose from his nostrils and swirled into a ring around his head before drifting out the slit window.

Laughing softly, she sat up and ate her food. When she finished, drowsiness settled over her again and she was soon drifting off to sleep.

Now and again, the Vyrl's thoughts would enter her dreams. But they were distant and difficult to understand. She could sense their fear, though, and during these times, she would wake up staring at the ceiling for long periods until the whispers in her mind faded.

At other times, she was disturbed by nightmares. At first, the dreams were about drowning in Miruvoir, too weak to swim from loss of blood. In her dreams the Vyrl didn't stop drinking her blood. They were overcome by hunger and the dark enchantment in the mists. But as time wore on, her nightmares changed. Widdershae hunted in the Vale of Mists. Sometimes it was her they hunted, sometimes it was Vaelros. Worse, Dimlock seeped out of the Cave of Painted Shadows at night. They hid in the dark places—the depths of the wood where even the noonday sun was enfeebled by the dense canopy and the mists and in the deep crevasses from which the mists seeped. There they waited, ready to leap upon the unwary and strangle them. Still worse, six half-dead wolfriders prowled through the Vale, their cold eyes flashing in the smoky mists. In one dream the six confronted her again.

"Where are the Vyrl? Where is Othalas? What will you do now that you are all alone?" Evaldris hissed.

In the dream, the six drew their swords in unison, the wolves they rode upon unhinged their breathless jaws, and they slowly advanced upon her.

During dreams like these, she awoke with a start.

"Luthiel, are you alright?" Melkion would ask.

"It's nothing, just dreams," she would reply.

Despite the intermittent nightmares and the rare intrusion of Vyrl-thoughts, she rested, letting Melkion and Rendillo nurse her back to health. She continued to doze for the rest of the day, eating when food was brought to her, then falling asleep again. The rain fell throughout the day, into the night and through the next morning. She'd fallen again into napping when a calm, familiar, voice stirred her.

"Luthiel Valkire! My, my! Who would have ever thought it?"

Luthiel's eyes fluttered open at the sound. Standing over her, robed in grey-green and wearing a wide-brimmed brown hat was a wet and travel-stained Mithorden.

"Mithorden!" she cried in surprise, and then immediately regretted her exuberance as pain shot through her throat.

His eyes sparkled and he laughed.

"You've come far since we last met. If I recall correctly, you were quite hopeless. Though somewhat battered, I'd say that now you are certainly better off than hopeless!"

The sorcerer chuckled as he sat down on the bed next to her. "Now, let me have a look at you."

He inspected the wounds on her arms, her neck, her head and glanced at the older scars.

"Well, it seems you've had a very rough time of it. I see the Vyrl still haven't learned how to treat a lady," he said while turning her arm to inspect the bite marks. He brushed the circlet on her forehead. "At least they give you gifts that suit you."

She watched him in wonder. There was a comfort in his presence that reminded her of home. His steady, perfectly sane eyes held in them a light that seemed to brighten even the charred glass walls.

"Mithorden, what made you come here?"

"Why you, of course," he said. "If you remember, I promised I would help you as best as I could. Well now that my business, and a very nasty business it was, in Ithilden is finished, I've come to lend what aid I can. From the look of you, it seems I've arrived just in time."

Luthiel remembered the spell that hid her from the Widdershae.

"You've already helped me, Mithorden. Were it not for you, I'd be stuck in some spider's larder, or worse." She shuddered when she spoke of the spiders. They had haunted her dreams ever since her encounter at the river. But they weren't alone. The Dimlock of the Cave of Painted Shadows and the half-alive, half-dead wolfriders of Ashiroth had all visited her in nightmares lately.

"Hush! Don't speak of such things!" He laid a hand upon her head. "I know it has been very difficult for you and there will, indeed, come a time when we must again speak of them. Sooner rather than later, most likely! No matter how much we wish it, they won't go away! But do not burden your mind with the thought of them. Now is the time for rest and healing."

With that, he sat down in her chair and pulled out a bag which he placed before her.

"It's Yewstaff fruit. Eat it all! I'm not going to leave this room until every last piece is gone."

"What if I want you to stay?" she asked.

"Then eat slowly." He laughed. "But eat them all the same. They will help you get well."

And with that he launched immediately into a droll tale about Mad Mazriel the Mazecrafter who built every variety of maze both cunning and dangerous. This particular tale started with Mazriel outsmarting himself by crafting a maze, that even he, the master could not escape. He built it working from the outside in. When he found himself in the center, he realized he was lost. Then proceeded a perilous but often comical adventure as he attempted to escape from his twisted creation.

Luthiel ate the Yewstaff fruit as she listened. Now and again, she broke into fits of laughter. When the tale was finished, so was the fruit. Afternoon had blended into evening and evening into night. Rain still whispered as it fell over the fortress.

"Now, wasn't that fun?" he said. "I haven't had the opportunity to tell old Mazriel's tale for some time now."

"It's a fine tale," she said. "Do you know any more stories about Mazriel?"

"Of course."

"Would you please tell them?"

"Ohoh!" Mithorden exclaimed. "Not tonight! Time to sleep and let the fruit do its magic. But I promise you, if you like, I will tell you another tale tomorrow come morning!"

Luthiel nodded. She was still exhausted from her ordeal even though she'd slept for the better part of two days.

"Will you stay here with me?"

"Of course! This chair is quite comfortable to sit in and I've asked Rendillo to bring me a cot if he can find one."

Assured by the sorcerer's presence, she fell into a deep sleep. This time, there were no nightmares. Only the occasional thought of a Vyrl disturbed her rest. But even these seemed dim and distant, like flashes of lightning that are barely visible on a far horizon. When she sensed them, she would stir, coming up through the layers of sleep to almost waking. But as soon as she sensed them, they faded and she fell back into her dreamless rest.

She awoke late the next morning to the smell of breakfast—eggs and warm bread. Rendillo had left a tray on the chair beside her bed. In another chair sat Mithorden. He was sitting next to the slit window, staring out into the misty morning. In one hand, he held a cup of steaming tea which he was sipping. Melkion was curled up on the bed beside her, blowing long wisps of smoke with each breath. Sometime late in the night, Othalas had returned from wherever he'd been and was now sitting beside the door. His great golden eyes flashed at her movement.

"Ah! There you are!" Mithorden said. "I was beginning to think you'd sleep through the day."

She yawned and noticed that her throat felt better.

"I think I needed the rest. You and Melkion said as much. But now, I think I feel much better. Othalas, do you think we could go down to the baths today?" Rendillo had come to sponge her off and to change her bandages from time to time but she felt as though she needed a good bath.

"Of course!" Othalas growled. "Anything to get you out of that bed you've laid in these past three days."

Stirred by the noise, Melkion opened an eye.

"She's not like you, werewolf. It takes her some time to get over her hurts," he said.

Othalas laughed. "There comes a time when resting helps not at all and a body needs to stretch itself, to work the muscles and to feel the wind in its face."

Mithorden winked at her.

"He's right, you know. I think a journey to the baths would be good for you. It will get you ready for tonight."

"Tonight?" she asked. Her throat was getting better. The Yewstaff fruit Mithorden brought was really helping.

"Yes, Tonight." Mithorden replied. The steam rose off his teacup and swirled around his face. "The Vyrl have called a council. The first council of Ottomnos. Vaelros has returned. Othalas brought him last night and I am here. There are many things to discuss. I am afraid the Faelands are entering a very troubled time. But there are things that can be done and many who are here have the ability to do them—including *you*."

Luthiel sighed.

"I promised the Vyrl I will do what I can. But I don't understand how I can change the mind of Zalos or the other lords."

"Alone—you cannot. But here there are some who might help you."

"Would you?" she asked.

"I may indeed!" he said. "It's not going to be an easy thing, though. Not easy at all! But enough of this! We'll talk more about it tonight. For now, I think you should enjoy your breakfast before it gets cold."

Luthiel looked at the piece of bread she'd been holding in her hand but that she'd forgotten about as she spoke with Mithorden and took a bite out of it.

"I'm off to tend to a few things before our meeting. I want to have a chance to talk with Vaelros."

Luthiel's ears pricked at the mention of Vaelros' name.

"He's here?"

"Of course he is! Didn't you hear me before? Othalas brought him back with him last night. The Vyrl were wise to bring him back. There are many dark things out there hiding in the mists and not the least among them are the six."

Luthiel breathed a sigh of relief. She'd felt concern for Vaelros ever since he'd fled from his six companions only days before.

"Well, at least he's safe for now," she said.

Mithorden nodded.

"Yes. For now." He rose from his chair, laid his tea cup on her tray and collected his staff. "I will see you this evening," he said and then was gone.

Luthiel found herself wishing he'd stayed. She finished her breakfast, then slowly eased her aching body from the bed.

She slid into a set of clothes Rendillo had left, cleaned and folded, on a trunk beside her bed.

Othalas and Melkion led her to the springs. They waited patiently in the mists as she bathed.

After washing, she floated for a long time in the steaming water, staring up into the mists. First, she thought of the Vyrl's gifts. They made her feel uneasy, reminding her of her bond with the Vyrl. It was a bond she wished she could be free of. Deep in the caves beneath Ottomnos, she could not sense their thoughts—only hints of the darkness that always lurked in the depths of their minds. She worried that sharing those sensations for too long would make her like them—creatures driven by hunger and fear.

Then she thought of the night the Vyrl fed upon her. She recalled the intense pain of their bites, thought of how they almost killed her and of the shadow in the mists that drove them to frenzy.

Will it happen next year? she wondered.

The darkness of the cave seemed to close in on her and she suddenly felt very alone in the black waters.

Touching her fingers to her forehead, she blinked her eyes. Starlight filled the cavern, diffusing out into the mists. It wasn't the uncanny light of her Wyrd Stone but the mists gave this place a wavery quality that reminded her of the world of dreams. Lifting her hand, she looked at the ring *Kelebrith* sparkling in the light. The white gems captured the starlight then threw it back so that spots of light fell into the water or motes traced white lines through the mists.

"The key to Ottomnos," she whispered. "They *do* want to make me one of them."

Or perhaps they only wanted to make her understand. To know their hunger, to feel the deep need that drove them to such terrible acts.

Opening the pouch that hung from her neck, she pulled out *Methar Anduel*.

She no longer feared that the Vyrl would try to take her Stone. They needed her. That much she knew now. And, if Mithorden was to be believed, they couldn't take it from her without breaking or killing her.

"*Luthiel!*" she sang.

Brilliant silver light erupted from the Stone. Where it passed everything seemed to waver and she found that she no longer felt the water on her skin. There was also a sense of lightening as of a weight being lifted from her. Oddly, the bizarre world of dreams seemed less threatening to her now. Instead it felt comforting to drift here in the water, bathed in *Methar Anduel's* strange silvery light.

Then she noticed that she could no longer sense the Vyrl's fear and hunger.

Why would it cut them off?

She recalled the way it had destroyed the Dimlock and wondered if it had a similar effect on the shadows within the Vyrl's mind that were now encroaching upon her every thought.

Drifting in the world of dreams, she thought of Leowin. The Stone was her gift and the gift of her mother—Merrin—if the Vyrl were to be believed. She held the Stone in her hand and stared deep into its light. Whatever gifts the Vyrl gave her; they could never replace this Stone.

She let herself drift in the world of dreams for an undetermined time. Then, remembering Mithorden's warnings about lingering, she forced herself to stop singing. It was more difficult than she anticipated. She struggled. But on the third try, she stopped singing and the light in the Stone dimmed to a spark.

As she swam back to shore, she wondered if she would ever leave the Vale or see Flir Light Hollow again. Was she trapped with the Vyrl by the armies encircling the Vale? Would the elves send her into exile, banishing her forever to the Vale of Mists? The thoughts caused a brief but sharp pain in her chest. She wanted to see her family again. She wanted nothing more than to see Leowin.

It's all right Luthiel, she reassured herself. *Mithorden will help you.*

When she reached the lakeshore, she toweled herself off, braided her hair, and donned her clothes before walking up the path toward the fortress' lower levels.

Melkion and Othalas were waiting for her.

"What took you so long?" Othalas growled.

"Long? How long did I take?" she asked.

"I'd say three hours at least," Melkion snapped.

"Three hours?" she said.

"Yes," Othalas growled. "We were about to go in to see whether you were all right. What were you doing in there?"

Luthiel flushed.

"I had a lot to think about," she said.

"We saw lights," Othalas said.

"And heard singing," Melkion said.

She stared at her feet but didn't reply.

They stared at her for a moment longer before turning around.

"Well, I hope you're ready," Melkion said. "The council begins in an hour."

"I'm ready," she said.

As they exited the caves and ascended into the fortress, the fear and hunger of the Vyrl returned. She shuddered, wondering if it was a sensation that she would carry with her for the rest of her life.

CUTTER'S SHEAR ~
THE SWORD OF VLAD VALKIRE

As she walked, she thought of the shards of *Aeowinar*.

They were Vlad Valkire's.

Her thoughts lingered.

When I took them at the Cave of Painted Shadows I promised to give them to the sorcerer.

"Where's Mithorden?" she asked them.

"He's with the Vyrl now," Melkion replied. "They're getting ready for the council."

"Would you mind bringing him to my room?" she asked. "I have something to show him before the council."

"I don't know, he seemed busy," Melkion said.

"Tell him it's important," she replied.

Melkion looked at her curiously for a moment and then, with a flap of his wings, he was flying down the corridor.

"What was that about?" Othalas growled.

"It's about what we found in the cave," Luthiel said. "The shards of *Aeowinar*."

Othalas turned his head and looked at her with his great yellow eyes.

"Your father's sword?" he growled.

She shivered when he said it.

"Yes," she replied.

They walked the rest of the way to her room in silence. When they arrived, she sat down on her bed, looking over her things.

"Othalas, would you mind leaving me alone?" she said.

The werewolf looked at her with his great yellow eyes. She thought she saw concern in them. It was odd coming from the face of a creature so obviously built for violence.

Without a word, he left her.

Numbly, she took out the leather pouch containing the shards of *Aeowinar*, unfolded it, and arranged them on the bed beside her. As her hands moved, her thoughts drifted.

She felt uncomfortable talking about Vlad Valkire. And each time she learned more about him, the more difficulty she had thinking about it.

If he is my father, then I will never know him.

Even her mother, if what Vaelros said was true, was locked away in the fortress of Arganoth.

How would I go to visit her with Zalos there?

She felt the Wyrd Stone about her chest, then lifted the hilt of *Aeowinar* and stared deep into the clear metal of its blade. Tiny motes of light flickered within. But she had to strain to see them as they seemed to slip from under her gaze.

His Wyrd Stones, his sword, his ring, even his friends are all around me. I may know them. But I will never know him.

When she was finished, she sat quietly on the bed, staring down at the broken bits of Cutter's Shear laid out before her.

Mithorden came into the room quietly. She ignored him, still staring at her father's sword.

"Melkion said it was important that I come."

"It was important to me," she said.

"Then it is important."

She motioned to the shards.

"What is this?" she asked.

Mithorden's eyes fell upon the broken pieces of the blade. He walked over to them as though drawn. She picked up the hilt and handed it to him. He held it close to his eyes.

"Othalas told me you went to the Cave of Painted Shadows. He never told me about this."

"What is it?" she repeated. For some reason, she wanted him to say it. It had been tucked away in her pouch and the events in the cave seemed so unreal, so like a dream to her now, that she craved some affirmation.

"These are the Shards of *Aeowinar*. The Cutter's Shear of Vlad Valkire," he said. "He made it. It was his masterwork. You didn't know?"

"I knew," she said.

"Then why did you ask me?"

"I couldn't believe it."

Silence passed between them for a time.

"Who was Vlad Valkire?" she asked finally.

Mithorden looked at her. His clear eyes shone at her from under his dark brows like stars beneath a thunderstorm.

"Luthiel, what do you mean?" he said gently.

There was a fierceness within her she couldn't understand.

"I've always been an orphan," she said. "But I felt something in the cave. It was like the sound of a summer wind through the trees. Belonging, I think it was. I was going to the Vyrl. I thought I would die and was grateful for the moment. But now, I want to know more."

She clutched Mithorden's wrist.

"What was he like?"

Mithorden nodded his head sadly.

"He was a great man," he said. "He was an even better friend."

She didn't understand why, but the way he said the word friend with such admiration, struck her. She felt tears rolling down her cheeks.

"Please, tell me more," she whispered.

"Well, he was about my height," Mithorden said. "But his hair and his eyes were like yours. His face was kind and he had a ready smile. He had a way about himself that I admired. He was brilliant, yes, but ready to laugh at himself when he made mistakes. You may not believe it, but he made mistakes often."

"Why?" she choked around her tears.

"Because he tried to do great things. Anyone can succeed at easy things. But the things Valkire tried were very difficult. He wanted to make things better for people of all races—for he saw the good in them."

It was almost too much for her to bear. She cried uncontrollably.

"But why me? Why all of this?" she motioned to the shards, to her Stone, to the ring on her finger. "How could I help Vyrl? How could I come here and survive!"

She picked up the hilt of *Aeowinar* and looked at him over its cross guard.

"Who was he?" she whispered.

"I think I understand now," Mithorden said. "I'm sorry I didn't see it before. I should have. But the cares of the old often forget the cares of youth."

He walked over to her and put his hands on her shoulders, looking deep into her eyes.

"There can be no doubt, Luthiel. Vlad Valkire was your father."

"I can see it in your eyes and in the warmness of your face. I can see it in your grace and in the way you find the good in things."

He laughed and his eyes glittered with water.

"I can see it in the way you try to do the damnedest of things."

"I don't believe it," Luthiel said stubbornly. But a part of her did and this part of her hurt worse than Vyrl's bites.

"I do," Mithorden said softly. "I said it before and it is true. You are Luthiel Valkire. The Wyrd Stone, the Vyrl, *Aeowinar's* shards—they are all a part of who your father was, a part of your heritage."

Luthiel took a deep breath. She knew the things Mithorden said were true. She knew now that her stubborn disbelief was not so much rooted in the improbability of these things. It was, instead, rooted in the pain of never being able to know her father, to never have a normal family.

A part of her still thought of Glendoras and Winowe as her mother and father. But she'd always felt a barrier between them. It was as if they didn't know how to treat her. Only Leowin had known.

She took a deep breath and sighed. Even though it was painful, she realized she still wanted to know everything about them.

"Who are my relatives?" she asked.

"Well, Merrin of Waves, queen of the moon that bears her name, is your mother. Your grandmother is the lady Elwin of the sacred dark, spirit of Oesha, mother of Valkyrie and queen of unicorns. Your grandfather is the great lord of the Dark Forest whose name has been hidden. Your father was their only son and you are the only daughter of Merrin and Vlad Valkire."

The room seemed to be spinning about her. She was glad that she sat on the bed. She motioned to the broken sword.

"Othalas told me what happened to Vlad—to my father. How the dark forest's lord broke Cutter's Shear. How he—how he killed my father."

She choked and tears ran from her eyes. Mithorden embraced her. Finally, she pushed herself away from him and wiped her eyes.

"I know the council starts soon. I just wanted to ask you now. It's important for me to know the truth. It may even be important for me to know it for the council."

"You're quite right about that." Mithorden said calmly.

"Will you promise to tell me the whole story of my father one day?" she asked.

Mithorden smiled at her.

"I do. But I hope to find your mother so that she can help me do it," he said.

Luthiel choked back the rest of her tears.

"I'd like that," she said.

"Well, you'd better gather the shards of your sword now," he said motioning to Cutter's Shear. "The council is going to start soon and you shouldn't leave them here unattended."

"My sword?" she whispered, looking at the shards.

"Yes," he said. "As your father willed it."

"He willed it to go to me?"

"He confided it to me and Merrin the month you were conceived."

Then he rose, nodded to her and left.

"I'll see you soon," he said as he departed.

For some reason, it gladdened Luthiel that her father would will it to her. She took her time gathering the shards of Cutter's Shear—the masterwork of her father. She looked at each fragment, at each perfectly formed inch of blade.

My father's hands made this, she thought.

When she was finally done gathering the pieces she rose with a sigh and left her room.

Melkion and Othalas were waiting for her outside.

They seemed to sense her need for quiet and didn't speak as they walked down to the courtyard.

"I need to stand in the sunlight for a bit," she said. "Then I'll be ready for the council."

ARMIES GATHER

Luthiel spent the rest of her time wandering the grounds of Ottomnos with Melkion and Othalas. She noticed that the Vyrl had cleared the courtyard of bones and carcasses. She could see a few wights and grendilo scrubbing the charred glass of the fortress.

"Getting out the blood," she whispered.

Melkion glanced at her.

"What?" he asked.

"It's nothing," she replied.

All throughout the fortress, she found signs that the Vyrl were trying to make the place look more inviting. The halls were better lit. Silver or white basins of water were placed at intervals throughout the fortress. Here and there censures of incense burned filling the air with sweet aromas.

In stark contrast to these efforts, Luthiel noticed other work being done—the work of war. Barrels filled with arrows, javelins or spears were being placed at intervals across the battlements, and upon the towers great engines of war were being constructed by bark-skinned giants. The machines looked alien—like giant insects made of wood and metal. But, even to her, their intent seemed clear enough—they were killing devices.

Iron trap doors in the base of the courtyard were flung open and from their depths a great smoke rose and she could see the flickering of firelight within the darkness. From out of the pits there came a clangor of metal upon metal. The forge masters of Ottomnos were hard at work turning out weapons of every kind, readying for a war the Vyrl no longer wished to fight.

The wights that scurried to and fro were now clothed head to foot in armor; and upon the battlements great watch fires blazed even though it was still afternoon. The sky was filled with birds. A great cloud of them circled over Ottomnos. But from this cloud outriders swarmed over the land, hugging the hills, dipping beneath treetops. As she watched, a silver feathered raven broke from the flock and winged his way toward her. She cried out, startled, when it landed on her shoulder.

"Report!" it cawed. The sound, loud in her ear, made her flinch. She noticed that its glittering eyes were fixed on the ring she wore.

"Report!" it cawed again.

"What does it want?" she asked Melkion who was perched on her other shoulder.

Mirthful smoke curled from Melkion's nostrils.

"It wants to give you a report," he said.

"Report?" she asked. "What do you mean?"

The silver feathered raven who had been watching her with one eye took her 'Report' as a cue and immediately burst into cawing speech.

"South and east we flew! Through mists! Under leaf and branch! All the way to rim and back! Spiders in shadows! A flock, a pack, a swarm! Out along the rim! One, two, a few! Deeper in the Vale!"

Not waiting for any reply, the raven launched itself into the air where it joined with a flock of hundreds before winging off to the north where they disappeared into the mists.

"What was that about?" Luthiel asked, startled by the noise and movement.

"That was a Khoraz—a raven of the Vale," Othalas said. "By the look of him, it was Mindersnatch, one of their chieftains. He was telling you what he and his kinsfolk discovered on their flight to the southeast."

"Spiders? Widdershae?" she whispered. "Melkion, then what we saw a few days ago was a shadow web?"

"I'm afraid so," Melkion replied. "While you rested, the Khoraz have given a hundred reports like the one you just heard. It seems that the

Widdershae are gathering just inside the rim. But some have moved deeper. We've sighted them as close as the near lakeshore."

He looked at her meaningfully.

She trembled, remembering the black mists that had driven the Vyrl mad with hunger.

"We found spider tracks on the lakeshore the night you gave blood to the Vyrl." Othalas growled.

"Could they have done it?"

"There are some among them who know the dark arts." The dragon replied. "Their queen is a master of such enchantments."

"I'm glad Mithorden and Vaelros have come to Ottomnos," she said.

"They're not the only ones," Othalas said, bounding up the stairs toward the battlements. "Come up here and take a look."

She followed the great wolf up the steps. Her legs ached with stiffness and pain but she ignored it. When she cleared the final stair, she turned her head, looking out over the land surrounding Ottomnos.

All the way to the lake and out to the forest's edge she could see grendilo, giants, chimera creatures and other strange beasts she couldn't put name to. Tents of hide or makeshift wooden structures filled this area as cook and watch fires burned, adding to the mist with their long tails of blue smoke. A group of well ordered grendilo and giants were busy constructing palisades.

Luthiel didn't know what to say at first as she looked out over the gathering. There were thousands of them. Finally, she found her voice.

"I guess this means there will be war," she said.

"No, not yet," Othalas replied. "Sometimes the best way to prevent war is to show your strength. This lets the enemy know what he's in for. Sometimes, it's enough. In this case, the Vyrl ordered the mobilization when they first heard word of Widdershae in the Vale. Those spiders are not to be trifled with."

Luthiel nodded.

"No, they are terrible," she said. "But do you think a great army, sitting in one place, would be the best defense against spiders? I wonder if it wouldn't draw them here. To me, they seemed like hungry creatures."

Othalas snorted.

"The spiders are cowardly," he growled. "They will strike from darkness and then let their foul venoms do the dirty work. After the victim has passed, or is helpless, then they'll return to feed. If we stick together, it's more difficult for them to pick us off one at a time—as is their way."

Luthiel felt fear pricking up her spine.

"I see," was all she could bring herself to say.

The widdershae who devoured the elves of the mountains, she thought to herself.

"We'd better get back to the great hall," Melkion said. "The council should be starting any minute now."

Luthiel took one more look at the thousands gathered around the fortress of Ottomnos before following the werewolf back down the stairs and into the black glass fortress.

A SECRET COUNCIL

They entered the great hall to find Mithorden, Vaelros, and the three Vyrl waiting for them. With them was a great giant who, sitting down, was taller than the standing Ecthellien, who, in turn, was seven feet. A smell like burning metal filled the room and Luthiel noticed that Gormtoth was standing to the left of the Vyrl. His eyes blazed white in the pits of his dragon-skull helm.

As Luthiel entered, her mind suddenly became filled with the Vyrl's thoughts.

There you are! Ahmberen thought. Then, looking her from head to foot. *That will not do.*

Ecthellien, taking his queue from Ahmberen, turned to Rendillo.

"Bring Luthiel's weapons and the armor we set aside for her. If this is to be a council of war, then we will have her dressed for it," he said.

It was then that Luthiel noticed they were all girded as if for battle. The Vyrl Ahmberen and Ecthellien wore great hauberks of black *Narmiel* and Elshael wore a mail shirt of smoky *Sorim*. In Elshael's hand was a spear of *Silen*—coming to a graceful, if wicked, point. Ecthellien and Ahmberen's greatswords hung from their belts. The giant wore a studded leather shirt and resting across his legs was a black iron hammer. Even Mithorden wore a sword. The scabbards of both Ahmberen's and Gormtoth's blades leaked smoke.

"I am sorry," she said. "I did not know this was a council of war."

"No matter," Ahmberen said. "You were resting."

"Now, we can begin once Vaelros returns," Mithorden said.

"Luthiel, please have a seat," Elshael indicated her *Silen* and white-wood chair. When she sat down, a grendilo brought her a steaming cup of tea. She noticed that a map was laid out on the table in front of her. It was a map of the Vale and the surrounding lands. She felt a slight twinge in her chest when she noticed that both Lenidras and Flir Light Hollow were on the map. Glass markers of every color were scattered over it. She guessed they were meant to show positions of forces. But she couldn't make out what was what.

Rendillo returned with her bow, quiver and a mail shirt of white *Lumiel* balanced in a pile upon his head. She already had her *Cauthrim* long knife and the shards of *Aeowinar* tucked into her belt. Rendillo helped her into the mail shirt, as she refastened her belt. The mail was light and she could barely feel its weight. Then, Rendillo slung the bow and quiver over her shoulders. Uncle Hueron had taught her how to use a bow when she was only five. For an instant, she felt the urge to test the bow Ecthellien had given her.

Melkion watched her from his perch on the back of her chair.

"Now *there's* a fierce Fae princess," he said. "You have the look of a Valkyrie."

Luthiel laughed at the compliment even as she felt a twinge in her chest. She'd heard myths of the Valkyrie and always thought of them as fine bits of fancy—a happy tale to tell children. But she'd never believed in Vlad Valkire either, much less thought that she might be his daughter.

My grandmother is the mother of all Valkyrie, She thought. The Vyrl turned their heads toward her, nodding their affirmation.

"Better than any Valkyrie, I have Melkion of Dragons as my friend and advisor," she said.

Melkion grinned, showing his needle-sharp teeth. Smoke leaked between the gaps. Then, he swung his head around to stare at Othalas with his violet eyes.

"Valkyrie ride unicorn. You'll have to go without."

Othalas mock growled at Melkion's jibe.

"She has better than unicorns. If we go into battle, she'll ride with me! The eldest werewolf!"

"Eldest and toothless!" Melkion replied.

"What do you think these are?" He flashed his teeth at Melkion.

"A fine collection of ivory," Melkion said, showing off his own collection. In the light, they shone like steel.

Luthiel couldn't help but laugh. After all that had happened, she wanted to laugh. Chuckles rose from Mithorden and even the bark-skinned giant laughed. But his laughs sounded more like the low rumble of thunder. Still, there was a dark undertone in her mirth. Ride to battle?

Am I ready for war? she thought.

"The dragon speaks truth!" the giant roared. "The lady looks as fearsome as a Valkyrie."

"Only nobler!"

The voice that sounded from the great hall's entrance was crisp and direct, bearing no hint of mirth. She turned her head to see Vaelros striding toward her. Like the others, he was dressed head to foot in armor. Its overlapping plates sparkled in the blue firelight.

He stopped in front of her. Then, in one crisp movement, fell to a knee. With an equally precise movement, he drew his long, black, sword; kissed it, and presented it to her.

"Vaelros, what are you doing?" she said. "Stand up."

"Not until you accept this," he replied.

For a moment, she was paralyzed. Accept his sword? The sword of Zalos's captain?

"Why? Are you—?"

"If you don't, I understand," he whispered. "I was a monster. But not anymore. Since we met I've had the life I forgot. Death would be clean now—a good ending."

He raised the blade to his neck.

"If you wish, I will make my end now."

She looked down at Vaelros. His sword, inches away from his neck, trembled. When her eyes met his, he looked away.

This is the old way, Ecthellien thought. *The way elves once offered themselves to Vyrl.*

She reached down and gently pushed the sword away from his neck. Then, she put her fingers under his chin lifting until their eyes met.

"Vaelros, there is no reason," she said. "I am not a Vyrl."

"No reason?" he said. "After all that I've done?"

Her voice caught in her throat, she didn't know what to say.

He turned his eyes from her.

"I did terrible things."

"You were driven to do them," she replied. "I know this."

"Then take my sword."

"Dear Vaelros," she whispered, laying a trembling hand across the guard. She had to concentrate to make it steady.

"Take it, or I end this now."

Finally gathering her resolve, she lifted his blade. It was cold and she trembled when she touched it. She noticed that the metal, which she thought was only black, contained swirls like billows of a cloud. It seemed to hint at shapes that her eye could not quite distinguish. A chill fell over her. It drew her eyes and the more she looked the more she saw that made her afraid. Tearing her eyes away from the metal, she pressed her lips against the place where he had kissed it. It was cold and there was frost where his lips had touched it.

Hastily, but carefully—as though she were handling a live and dangerous snake—she returned the sword to his hands. Then, bending over him, kissed his forehead.

"I pledge my life to you," he said. "And I swear to serve and defend you with all that I am."

"Noble Vaelros, I accept your pledge and in return I promise to protect you, as best as I am able. Stand now and know that to serve me requires no kneeling or bowing—only honesty and a good heart."

Vaelros stood and returned his sword to its sheath.

"Thank you lady," he said then turned and took his place at the table across from her.

"Now that was a heartening thing to see," Mithorden said. "Though unexpected, I think it is an excellent beginning." He rose from his seat and walked toward the head of the table.

"For those of you who do not know me, I am Mithorden, friend and, very briefly, tutor to the lady Luthiel. And, for everyone's benefit, this is Vaelros, former Captain of the Seven of Ashiroth, and, as you just witnessed, knight and protector of the lady Luthiel. Beside him are the three Vyrl—Elshael, Ahmberen and Ecthellien, the last of their kind; they are the great and terrible masters of the Vale. They are now also pledged, if not to serve Luthiel, then to protect her. Here is Othalas, the first werewolf born of mists, greatest of his kindred, cohort of Vyrl and, recently, of the lady Luthiel. Here too is Melkion of dragons, son of Faehorne the terrible, now also bonded by boon to the lady Luthiel."

"You're forgetting me!" the giant in the corner grumbled. "And though she's fair, I have no loyalty to this lady. Today's the first time I've seen her."

"I was just getting to you," Mithorden replied, somewhat exasperated at the interruption. "The impetuous brute before me is Norengar, king of the giants called Maltarmir who live in the Vale of Mists and who are sworn, by blood pacts made long ago, to serve the lords and ladies of Ottomnos."

Mithorden turned to Luthiel.

"Show him the ring *Kelebrith*," he said.

She raised her hand, displaying the brilliant ring with its white stones to the giant, who gazed at her in amazement.

"The Vyrl have again accepted one as their equal, Norengar. I am afraid that you are indeed loyal to the lady."

Mithorden smiled mirthfully.

"If you had grace, you would ask her forgiveness for your impertinence."

"Hmph!" the giant replied. "I, King of Giants, ask forgiveness of this tiny creature? I'd rather ask forgiveness of a flutterfler! Or of one of these flir bug bulbs—which I'd sooner sit on!"

Mithorden turned to Luthiel.

"Lady, they're mighty and brutish—impressive to look upon—but don't call upon even their king for wit, or tact, or any other grace."

Despite herself, Luthiel laughed.

The giant harrumphed again, but this time there was mirth in his eyes.

"Now we come to Gormtoth," Mithorden continued. "Narcor of Eledweil and before of starlight. I have not forgotten that you once served both Malcor and dark Vyrl before Valkire turned you. You too owe this lady your allegiance, for she is the daughter of the one who freed you."

To Luthiel's surprise, the Narcor nodded.

"I knew this," he said. His voice was deep and filled with the sound of fire on damp coals. "For eyes of flame pierce even the flesh, laying spirits bare." He paused before continuing. "All spirits," he said.

Mithorden nodded.

"Good, very good," he said. "Now that we are all introduced—"

"All but one," Vaelros interrupted.

"Now that we are all introduced," Mithorden continued more firmly, "all but one. I must ask each of you to swear secrecy to what now is about to be revealed. Some of you know of it, others may have guessed. But from this point forward, no one but these here should know the true identity of Luthiel until we decide to reveal it."

Luthiel, guessing what Mithorden had in mind, didn't quite understand the reason for secrecy.

"Why can't we talk about it?" she asked. "What about family? Surely, they can be trusted."

"No, not even they can be trusted," he said. "The fewer who know now, the better. I am less afraid of your loved ones than of the ears that might catch a few wrong words carelessly whispered. Then what would happen to them? There are terrible things walking in the world, beneath both suns and moons; and a black will of ancient evil stirs where it once lay dreaming upon Gorothoth."

At mention of the word—Gorothoth—a shadow seemed to fall over the already dark chambers. The Vyrl frowned and Melkion sharpened his claws. Even Norengar looked nervous—shifting his iron hammer from one hand to the other.

"Many of you were once its victims. But no longer! Now you have a chance to protect your last best hope—this seeming elf who is little more than a girl. So swear your silence until the day comes when she must be revealed."

The Vyrl looked at each other. Luthiel could sense the half-thought question that passed between them. Then Ahmberen nodded.

"We swear," they said in unison.

"I swear," Vaelros followed.

Melkion, Othalas and even Gormtoth swore. Norengar grumbled but finally swore at Mithorden's urging.

"You as well," Mithorden said to her. "You cannot tell anyone, even your sister, you understand this?"

She nodded.

"I think I do," she said reluctantly. "I swear not to give my true name or identity to anyone other than those who are here with me now."

Though I don't know what good it will do me. Zalos' six champions may already have guessed who I am. She thought of her last encounter with them and trembled.

Mithorden let out a sigh.

"Good, good," he said. "Now we may continue." His voice softened as he walked toward her. Gently, he drew her from her chair and walked with her until they stood at the center of the hall.

"Now at last we come to *you*," he said. "You know who you are, don't you? After everything that's happened?"

She cast her eyes downward for a moment. In that instant she thought of *Methar Anduel*, of the Cave of Painted Shadows, of how she freed the Vyrl and Vaelros, and of her conversation with Mithorden less than an hour ago. She didn't understand so much of it. Of the magic or of the darkness. A part of her still stubbornly denied it. But there was too much evidence now to reject who she was. She didn't need the Vyrl's thoughts whispering in her mind to tell her.

"Yes, I know now," she said with a smile to Mithorden. "You helped me remember?" she whispered to him.

Mithorden put a gentle hand on her shoulder.

"Then tell them," he said.

She took a deep breath and nodded again. She looked out across the room into the swirling eyes of the Vyrl, into Vaelros' troubled yet happy eyes, into Melkion's violet orbs and Othalas' golden ones, into the giant king's pine-green eyes and into Mithorden's clear ones and finally into the flaming eyes of Gormtoth.

He knew, she thought. *Except for the giant, they all knew. But at first I did not. Oh, Leowin! I hope I remember the myth right this time!*

"I am the daughter of my mother and of my father too," she said. It didn't quite make sense, but it helped her to start talking.

"She is Merrin of Waves and he was Vlad Valkire," she continued with more confidence. "She is Elohwe and the blue moon bears her name. He was the first man Valkyrie—son of the nameless lord of the Dark Forest and of Elwin the dark lady, blessed spirit of Oesha. Together, my father and mother broke the Tyranny of Dreams and freed the elves from the Vyrl.

"I am Luthiel Valkire.

"I am an orphan and I do not know my mother or my father—whose tomb I saw in the cave with shadows painted on the wall."

The words made her sad but she did her best not to show it in front of those gathered before her. They sat or stood in silence, watching her. She could feel their eyes on her but she would not turn her face from them.

Mithorden patted her gently on the shoulder.

"Very well said," he whispered to her. Then he faced those gathered in the hall.

"Many of us may have guessed this. But we must remain fully aware of *who* it is that stands in front of us and of the great risk both we and she must take. As she said, she is the child of Valkire. And she brings with her a hope that many of us thought had died long ago. It is a hope we *must* protect."

He glanced at Vaelros.

"We would do well to follow this young lord's example.

"The Vyrl have already made a pact with her, asking her to go to the lords that now stand, ready to do battle, just beyond the rim of the Vale. They would send her into great danger, risking even their newfound solace. Yet she has graciously promised to go and to try to turn the elves from a war that they are now resolved to fight. In this task, she must not fail.

"This council was called to discuss *why*. For the danger is more than just that presented by the armies surrounding this Vale. The real threat is hidden. But signs of it may be found in the actions leading up to this war and in many of the dark things that have happened throughout the age. It is this hidden danger that most concerns us. For it may become greater and more terrible than any trouble since the dawn of this age.

"And this council was called to discuss *how*. For we must have a plan or we will surely fail."

He looked at them each in turn.

"Do you understand, fully, who it is that stands before you? And do you accept that we must now set aside all our differences and, if need be, follow her into great danger?"

Those assembled nodded.

"Good," Mithorden said. "Now we may begin this council in earnest."

Slowly, Luthiel and Mithorden returned to their seats at the table.

"Well, I suppose we should start with why?" Melkion said.

"Yes," Othalas said. "Why is this danger here? Could the spiders that have crept into the Vale have caused it?"

"In this danger," Mithorden said, "the spiders may play a part. But I do not think they are the reason for it." His eyebrows were raised but he provided no other answer.

"Or is it the sudden fury of the elves?" Ahmberen said. "They have tolerated us for so long, it seems uncharacteristic of them to risk so many over so few of their kind."

"The elves' fury was warranted," Mithorden said, "and long overdue. I do not think that they are the cause. But they are coming! Their anger has grown for centuries and now they come to deal punishment for their loss."

"So are they all coming?" Luthiel asked. "All the armies of the Fae?"

"Yes, Luthiel," Mithorden replied. "Himlolth and Ithilden, Rimwold and Minonowe, Ashiroth and Khargalast. Six armies of Fae stand beyond the rim and one of Widdershae is beneath it."

Luthiel breathed out a sigh and shook her head in amazement.

"But what if they enter the Vale?" she asked "The mists would change them." She remembered how the mists had almost changed her. "What would they become?"

"What indeed!" Mithorden said.

Norengar shifted his hammer on his lap.

"The sorcerer talks but he doesn't give any answers, only more riddles. If you know the why of this danger, then why don't you tell us?" The giant grumbled.

"I wanted to hear what you know first. True, I know some. But it is only part of the story. It is enough for me to be very concerned, mind you. But I don't know everything. Nor can I confirm half the things that I have guessed. I was hoping that you would shed light on things by sharing your experiences."

He looked at each face in the room.

"I think many of you here could shed light on something that has lain hidden for far too long. We should lay bare the identities and intentions of all our enemies if we are able to. Then, we may have a clearer understanding of *why*."

His eyes turned to Vaelros.

"I think it would be best to start with you. As one of the Seven, I'm certain you have seen much that may help us understand our danger.

Zalos was my student and I know he used the Wyrd as a means to gain power. I fear he has delved too deeply into the black arts."

Then his eyes shifted to Othalas.

"Or, perhaps, it is best to start with you. You have traveled much— both in the woods of Ashiroth and upon the slopes of Ghul Shalar. What have your wolf eyes seen that we should know?"

VAELROS'S TALE

Vaelros and Othalas exchanged glances.

"I will start," Vaelros said. "Though it is not an easy thing for me to speak of Zalos or of my time as his captain."

Luthiel quailed when she saw that hollow look cross over his face. But it was just a shadow of the thing that was killing him only a few days before. It passed like a thin cloud that momentarily blocks the sun but is then carried off by the wind. He looked at her and gave a wan smile. His left hand lifted to the bag that hung from a chain about his neck and encircled it.

"It is easiest for me to start at the beginning. For my memory of the middle years is fragmented and unreliable.

"Many years ago, my grandfather, Zalos, drove my father from the fortress at Rildenscol and banished him from Ashiroth. Zalos does this every few hundred years to keep the lords in line. As was his custom, Zalos offered me my father's lordship. But I refused and resolved myself to go into exile with him.

"On the night before we left, I was visited in my dreams. A lady, both beautiful and terrible, came to me. She seemed so real. I can still remember her smell—earth and lilacs. In my dream, the lady took my flesh. She was consumed with unnatural fire. It burned through me, sinking into my bones till they ached with heat and exhaustion. The dream lasted all night and just before I awoke she took the chain which hung around her neck and fastened it to mine. Fastened to the chain was a black box with discolorations the shade of old blood. Within the box was a stone the color of pitch.

"When I awoke that morning, I was exhausted. It was as though I'd not slept at all. Even worse, the box was real."

Vaelros stood and pulled something from the pouch at his belt. He tossed it onto the table where it rolled about like a dice before coming to rest on one of its faces. Luthiel recognized the black box.

"This is the box," he said, staring at it a moment before he continued.

"As we traveled, I became sick with chills. I shivered so much I could barely stay atop my wolf. The cold seemed to come from the box. So I cast it off a high cliff into the sea. I saw it splash into the troubled water and sink like a stone. I thought I was done with it. But that night, I was visited again. When I awoke the next morning the box hung from my neck.

"This happened for many days. I would cast the box away, or bury it. One day I even tried to burn it. But each night the lady would return it to me and each morning I awoke to find the box slung from its chain on my neck. Then, one night, the dark lady told me the truth. She had slowly withered until that night it seemed I lay with a skeleton. Just before morning, she stopped riding me. Rolling over to her side and gripping me with her gaunt fingers, she said that she was the spirit within the Stone. Each night, as I slept, she was taking my life away. If I did her bidding, the leeching would be slow and I would live longer. If I fought her, the leeching process would quicken. But one day, sooner or later, my life would be spent. I would not die as men or elves do. Instead, I would linger on the borders between life and death—my body and spirit a vessel that she and her master would control. There was no escape. Suicide or death in battle would complete the process.

"From that point forward, I was completely beholden to the Stone's compulsion.

"The first compulsion was to kill my father.

"It came as desire. I hated him and I thought, endlessly, of killing him.

"At first, despite the spirit's warning, I fought these desires. For three nights, I forsook sleeping. For I knew that she was waiting to punish me with nightmares. But, on the fourth night, my strength failed and I slipped into sleep. The nightmares were even more terrible than I imagined. But I couldn't awake to escape them. When my sleep finally ended, I felt cold and everything seemed dim to my eyes. Even though it was summer, I began to see the ghost of Gorothoth in the sky.

"Worse, the compulsion to kill my father became a pounding war-drum in my head.

"Finally, I could not fight any longer. When I gave in, drawing my sword, the relief was so great that I think I laughed out loud.

"I don't remember much of it and I think I hesitated, for I suffered terrible wounds from both him and his guard. But a keening arose from the Stone and it cast a shadow as a torch might cast light. Beneath the Stone's spell, I entered a world of nightmare where the air seemed to waver as though from a great heat and always the moon Gorothoth hung in the sky. When this happened, few things could harm me. Even if I was wounded, the Stone sustained me and I continued. These hurts, I think, sped me on toward the half-life.

"After I killed my father, the Stone compelled me to return to Ashiroth, where I became one of Zalos' Seven. Each bore a Stone like the one I wore. Each had descended into the half-life. I was the only one that remained.

"It is with a sense of bitter irony, I think, that Zalos made me their captain. I could no more refuse him than I could refuse the Stone. And I guessed that it was he who made or found them.

"For many years, I bought my life with terrible deeds. Most, I cannot remember. Life and sleep blurred together. For as I slept, nightmares haunted me. Slowly, the nightmares crossed over into my waking thoughts. Eventually, I could no longer tell reality from a dream.

"My life was nearly spent when the lady Merrin came to me. To my eyes, it seemed as though she were robed in light and song. And by her song, the nightmares retreated. It made me feel more alive than I'd felt in many years. I had become so accustomed to the terror that its absence left me stunned and confused.

"But I was not the only one in danger. Even though Merrin was with child, Zalos held her as a prisoner in Arganoth for he wanted to make her one of his wives. I do not know how she possessed the presence of mind to recognize my condition. Nor do I know how she managed to slip beneath the watchful eyes of Zalos' servants and heal me.

"But she did. My doom was delayed and I returned, for a time, to the world of the living. While she was near, the nightmares seemed far off. When my wits returned, I learned that she was using a bright Wyrd Stone to help me. She would come to me under the gentle darkness of night, sneaking into my chambers, and there, very quietly, she would sing to me.

"Later, she told me that she was overcoming the effects of the curse. Which she said was coming from my Wyrd Stone. For a time, there was hope. For she thought that if she could open the box, then she could break the enchantment that had turned the Stone to darkness. But even though I knew the words that would cause the box to open and grant her access to the Stone, I could not say them. The compulsion upon me was too strong and even Merrin could not overcome it.

"It was then that she showed me *Methar Anduel*. I do not know what art she used to hide it from Zalos for he was always searching. He did not suspect. He *knew*. Yet it was as though he was blinded either by her art or by some flaw within him. So even though he searched he never found *Methar Anduel* or Merrin's own Stone *Ethel Bereth*.

"She told me that *Methar Anduel* was the greatest of the Wyrd Stones. Its magic could break my curse. Merrin could not use it. But the child that grew inside of her could. She told me to have hope and that she would not let me go over to darkness.

"During our time together, she taught me ways to resist the Stone and to extend my life even when we were apart.

"I still don't understand why she helped me or what reason she would have to forgive my terrible deeds. I was a monster and yet she understood that I was also a victim."

He looked into Luthiel's eyes. The look was so intense that she had difficulty meeting his gaze. But she held it.

"You saw it too," he whispered. He took a deep breath and rubbed his eyes before continuing.

"Eventually, Zalos grew wise to my improving condition and, always suspicious of Merrin, he sent me away more and more often. The past few years I have spent without returning to Arganoth once. I think it was Zalos' plan to let me slowly fail, even if it took a hundred years.

"Then, by happy accident, I was sent here on a mission to lure the Vyrl into war. When I saw Luthiel, I was drawn to her. She reminded me so much of Merrin. And, somehow, she knew how to break both the Stone's compulsion, for it would have had me kill her, and the curse.

"So now I am here. I hope that my service to Luthiel can, in part, make amends for all the evil I've done."

For a long time, there was silence in the room.

Luthiel's emotions were conflicted by the story. The terrible violation of the Stone and the doom he faced were things she had difficulty understanding. Still, she felt a deep sympathy for him.

Also, when Vaelros spoke of Merrin, Luthiel was captivated. She wanted to ask him a hundred questions –

What was her voice like?

What did she smell like?

Did she really look that much like her?

Yet the one thing that she came away with was an overpowering sense of anger at Zalos. It was so intense that she could not contain herself.

"How dare he!" she muttered.

Who is this Zalos? Why does he think that he can use people this way? Merrin suffers, Vaelros suffered, how many more?

But another part of her was afraid.

How could anyone challenge him?

She could sense the Vyrl's minds but, for the moment, they were silent.

A Piece of a Shadow Crown

Mithorden was looking at Vaelros from his seat across the table. His eyes shifted to the black and blood colored box.

"You were very fortunate," he said.

"I know," Vaelros replied.

"Your tale bears out what I've feared for many years, but could never prove," Mithorden said.

"And what did you fear?" Ecthellien asked.

"That Zalos was using the black arts to corrupt the Wyrd Stones. I do not know why or how. I certainly did not teach him to do such things," Mithorden said. "But when I met Evaldris many years ago, I knew that something terrible was happening to him. There were dark things afoot in the black of his eyes. But at that time I could not guess its cause. Even later, as more joined Evaldris and I saw them ride to battle beneath a black cloud that seemed to lift off of them like smoke, I did not guess the true nature of their affliction.

"It was not until much later that I began to suspect. There were other rumors as well—tales that grew in odd and unexpected ways before they reached my ears. It was difficult for me to tell what was true, for the tales always seemed to be tangled up in lies."

"You taught Zalos?" Luthiel asked.

"I have not stopped regretting it for almost three thousand years. For a time, he was my finest student." He stared at the table for a while as the others sat in silence.

"Vaelros," Mithorden continued after a long pause. "There is no reason for you to feel responsible for the things you were compelled to do. You preserved your will, and now you are free."

"Not altogether free," Vaelros said. "Though the darkness is very distant now, my dreams are still haunted by nightmares. But it is a small thing when compared with before."

"In your time as one of them, did you see anything else?"

"I saw much, but none of it is clear to me," Vaelros said. "I cannot tell my remembered nightmares from what actually happened. Nightmare or dream, it is difficult to recall anything other than flashes and moments. Except for my time with Merrin and, later, with Luthiel. I remember those times as clearly as a midsummer night with all the moons in the sky."

Mithorden nodded.

"The mind craves comfort and will shy away from that which it fears or cannot understand," he said. "What you have already said reveals enough. Much I have long suspected without proof. We have to wonder, then, whether Zalos has other reasons for wanting war with the Vyrl than simple revenge. Though he may be unscrupulous, he is cunning. He has a power in his voice that allows him to compel others to aid him. Much rides on us countering Zalos' influence over the elves. It would help us to know why he wants this war."

"He has always sought rulership," Ahmberen said. "Perhaps he is trying to cement a claim to the starlight throne."

"His designs may fall much deeper. It has long been my fear that he serves a greater, darker will than even his own."

He lifted the black and blood colored box off the table.

"This box is proof that my fears were not without reason."

"How?" Luthiel asked.

"It is made of *Narmiel*," Mithorden continued. "But not just any *Narmiel*. This metal is far more pure than even that within Ecthellien's sword." He held the box to his eyes. "This metal has been reworked. But if you look closely you can still see some of its original design. This one, it seems, still bears some of its original markings."

He pointed to some runes, that, though distorted, were still visible upon the box's surface.

"This one says:

"Beneath my will"

"What does it mean?" Luthiel said, leaning closer.

"It is only one part of the eight part saying:

"Beneath my will, Under my gaze, Compelled by blackness, Under my sway, Hunger to devouring, Ambition to burning, Satisfaction to emptying, Ease to yearning

"This incantation was carved into a crown of shadow. *Netharduin*—they were once called."

"This is a piece of a *Netharduin*?" Vaelros asked.

"What is a *Netharduin*?" Luthiel asked.

"They were made over six thousand years ago by Gorthar. Within them were trapped spirits of the void that would influence or dominate all who wore them. Gorthar used them to corrupt the angels. By them many beautiful things fell from grace. Among them were Vyrl, who were consumed by hunger and the Narcor who were consumed by madness and lust for burning. Their fall brought much suffering to this world. Not the least of which was the ruin of Eledweil which became Gorothoth."

Mithorden held the piece before him and Luthiel gazed at it apprehensively.

"This is a piece of a shadow crown?"

"Yes," Mithorden replied. "But not just any *Netharduin*. This is a piece of the master *Netharduin* that Gorthar used to ensnare Chromnos the first and mightiest of the Elohwë. For many years, Chromnos was influenced by the shadow crown. But Chromnos, whose spirit is the very flame of will in this world, could not be wholly overcome. When he discovered Gorthar's plan, Chromnos struck the *Netharduin* with a mighty blow. It shattered into eight pieces, freeing him of its influence. Then he cast Gorthar from heaven, tossing the broken crown after him. Gorthar fell onto the moon that was then named Eledweil and is now called Gorothoth. The pieces of the crown must have fallen somewhere nearby.

Somehow, Zalos has recovered at least seven of them and reworked them into boxes.

"This little box has revealed more to me than a hundred years worth of searching. Even a fragment of a Netharduin is very potent. Its use confirms that Zalos is serving Gorthar. The stakes for Zalos will be high—much higher than if he were acting out of his own interest. Under Gorthar, it is likely that Zalos's goal is to break the Faelands."

They stared in silence at the box in Mithorden's hand.

OF THRAR TAURMORI
THE DEMON LORD

"But I doubt that he is the only one we should concern ourselves with," Mithorden continued. "No, I am afraid that others, though less visible than Zalos, may be equally dangerous."

"Thrar Taurmori," Ahmberen said.

"He is one," Mithorden replied.

"The Widdershae," Eshael whispered.

"Yes, they are indeed dangerous! Do any of you here know anything about them?"

"We know of Thrar Taurmori," Ecthellien said.

"As do I," said Gormtoth.

"He was with us on Eledweil," Ecthellien said. "There, he was the lord of the Malcor. When the war was lost he fled to Ghul Shalar in the Rimwold. There he rules over all the lands within sight of his iron tower. Many among the goblins serve him. Trolls have also come to him from Cauthraus and a few Malcor still walk behind the walls of his fortress."

Luthiel knew of Thrar Taurmori only as one of the lords of the Fae. For he was the most influential lord in Rimwold.

"He is a demon?" she asked. "But how could he be a Faelord?"

Ahmberen turned toward her.

"He turned the tide of battle against the Vyrl and joined with Valkire on the condition that he keep his fortress, lands and power. Valkire agreed, so long as Thrar forfeited his *Netharduin* and would never again set fire to the land. For a time, Thrar Taurmori was true to his word and we kept his crown here in the Vale of Mists."

"But a hundred years ago," Eshael continued. "Someone entered the Vale, slipped into our fortress and stole the *Netharduin* from our vault."

"I hunted the thief for many days," Othalas growled. "But he was quick and cunning. Though I found his trail many times I could never catch up with him. The goblins had left fresh mounts for him along the way. He would ride one at full gallop until he reached the next, where he would change and then ride on. But I stayed close behind him, in some cases within hours. He must have sensed me, for he rode as if death itself were at his heels."

"It was," Melkion hissed.

Othalas ignored the dragon and continued.

"I kept going south, past the lands of Minonowe and into Rimwold. Finally I came to the iron tower of Ghul Shalar. It was then that I knew who had stolen the crown."

"We sent messages to High lord Tuorlin of Ithilden," Ecthellien said. "But we received no answer. They would not believe the word of a Vyrl against the word of Thrar Taurmori."

"So he has his crown of shadow again?" Luthiel asked.

Ecthellien nodded.

"How many crowns were there to begin with?" Luthiel said.

"Only four," Mithorden replied. "Three for the Elohwe and one for lord Chromnos."

"Chromnos broke his and Thrar Taurmori stole his back, but what happened to the other two?"

"What indeed?" Mithorden said with his bushy eyebrows raised.

She knew the sorcerer was holding something back and it irritated her. But before she could come up with a retort, Ahmberen spoke.

"Valkire kept the crown that was taken from the Vyrl Glauroth. But this one has since passed to Zalos. The last crown has been unaccounted for since the great betrayal."

Outside, the suns had set and only moonlight, dimmed by the mists, filtered in through the painted glass. As they sat in silence, Luthiel wondered what it meant that Zalos held the pieces of one crown as well as a whole one. She also wondered about Thrar Taurmori. He wasn't the kindest of lords but she'd never thought of him as a demon.

It could explain Vane and his family, she thought.

Before she could follow this line of thought for much longer, Mithorden spoke again.

"Now that it seems you have exhausted your knowledge, I will tell you what I know. But I think we should eat first. I find it better if such business is dealt with on a full stomach," he said.

Do No Harm Without Need

Grendilo brought in foods of all types as well as wine and water. Mithorden ate like a man possessed of great hunger but he wouldn't eat any meat. When Luthiel asked him why he never ate meat, he replied, "I have vowed to do no harm without need. If I am starving in the woods, then I would take a beast as I would a root. But, given a choice, I would let live. I get enough from fruits and honey, from breads and cheeses."

Luthiel nodded but she found herself wondering if she could ever give up eating meat. She fancied herself a huntress and felt no wrong for her taking life for food. She understood, too, that the wild creatures had a will to live and to hunt and that, to some, she might also be taken for a predator like the wolf or the bear.

They are like me, she thought. *They take life to live.*

We are like the wolf and bear. We are like you as well. The Vyrl thought to her in reply.

At first she was startled by the sudden intrusion of the Vyrl's thoughts. But she soon calmed, thinking about how the Vyrl almost consumed her. How they almost certainly would have killed Leowin.

Is this the way wild creatures view me? As a monster?

The thought was unsettling and she put down her fish for a moment.

But you were not always this way. You did not always consume the blood of elves, she thought.

Oh we did. But before we never consumed enough to kill. In those days some of us took elves as lovers. These gave us both blood and passion. Later, the dark desires came upon us and we killed many of those we adored, Ecthellien thought.

What you became was beyond nature, Luthiel thought. *You fed upon all you could devour. Your hunger was never satisfied.*

True, Ecthellien thought. *When our might was limited, first by the depravity of false leaders, then by guilt, and finally by the division that comes with lack, our strength waned and we grew mad with hunger. We, with the Ingolith, turned all of Eledweil into our larder and, together, we devoured most of the creatures that lived there. In the end there was nothing left but lifeless waste. We were the few who ate many and we could not control our hunger. Soon, we had no one left to devour but one another. But elves might also ruin a world if you lost or failed to use those greatest gifts of life and intelligence— invention and advancement. If false leaders led you astray; if you were made to feel guilty for using the arts and powers that sustained you; you might also fall first into decline and finally into war and madness. Are we really all that different, you and I?*

Luthiel considered Ecthellien's thoughts as she ate. Though she felt there was a difference between elves and the Vyrl, she realized that the difference was less clear than she had originally believed.

Could we really ruin this world as the Vyrl ruined Eledweil? she thought.

What in nature could not, through misguidance and failure to properly develop the strength to which it is due, become dangerous? Dangerous even to itself. Life often does what it can. It is the way of life to seek power, to survive by that power, to exploit through that power and finally to develop into something far beyond what it was before, something greater. It is when life becomes limited that depravity sets in. The end for those who cannot escape is always the same—a bitter struggle and finally death.

What Gorthar did to us was to take away those things that made us strong—our connection to dreams, to inspiration, and to our will to make our own future. We were limited, driven to desperate hunger. And it is when the great races are compelled to commit violence or to do harm out of desperation— when they think they have no other choice—that abomination arises. Some call this evil. Having suffered it, I know it as weakness.

But am I right to think that affliction isn't the only thing that causes it? Luthiel thought. *What about those who choose to deny something from a creature so that it becomes desperate or broken or both?*

This is worse still. Those who inflict deprivation are the authors of evil.

But what if, by restraint, you deprive yourself? Luthiel thought.

This is the greatest evil. For what a creature will do to itself it will not hesitate to do to others, Ecthellien replied. *But what you have described is not restraint. For restraint results in a benefit. Gluttony is harmful because it makes a creature weak, sickly, vulnerable to outside influence. Restraint results in strength of body and mind. Deprivation is what you are describing. It is always harmful, stifling what a thing needs to become greater.*

So when do you know you have taken too much from yourself? When does self restraint become deprivation? Luthiel thought.

You will know, if you are truthful to yourself, the difference between deprivation and restraint. The counterfeit of restraint is denial of personal truth. In this denial lies the seed of depravity.

Luthiel's head was spinning. She was finding the twisting meanings difficult to grasp. The Vyrl's thoughts didn't make sense. There was so much more to it. It couldn't be so easily described.

But what about intentional wrongdoing? Theft, murder, tyranny for power's sake?

It becomes clear when you understand that intentional wrongdoing is denial of personal truth. For when you harm others you deprive the most important part of yourself. It is the part of you that hungers for love and to give love. Many do not think of it as a need. But it is as necessary as air and light, as essential as earth and water. It is the very design of life to support other life and to grow greater by the support of other living things, Ecthellien replied.

These are the great, unspoken, laws that are woven into us all—heart and hide, blood and bone. If we break them or if others, who have power over us, break them then the result is evil. It is both very simple and very difficult to understand. But the pattern is within us all and we must keep our eyes open to the truth to understand it. Believing alone is not enough. We must each find it. And once we do, we must never lose sight of it.

You know a lot about good and evil for one who still suffers from depravity, Luthiel thought.

I was pushed into darkness and with your help I climbed out again. I know the way both falling down and climbing out. Now I am stronger. With your help I will grow stronger still. It is my hope that with my help you will also grow in strength even as you lend that strength to others.

"Do no harm without need," she said to herself.

"That's what I said," Mithorden replied.

"But what if need drives you to harm something?" she asked.

Mithorden looked at her and his eyes became very serious.

"Now that, Luthiel, is a very wise question," he said. "Need, perceived or otherwise, or any other kind of desperation, is the chief reason for harm in this world. What made you ask me?"

"Something the Vyrl said to me," she replied.

"Good, they would know much about need."

She looked at her fish and, deciding that she didn't need it, reached for the cheese instead. The rest of the meal she spent in silence listening to the conversations at the table but too wrapped up in her own thoughts to contribute. Finally, when dinner was almost finished she opened her mind to Ecthellien again for one last question.

Ecthellien, I just remembered something from the old tales that I never understood. I was wondering if you could answer a question I've had since I was very young?

If I know the answer I will tell it.

What did Gorthar do that was so terrible? she thought. *Before the betrayal, before Chromnos? What did he do that made the great mother and father cast him beyond creation and into the void?*

For a while, Ecthellien was silent. When his thoughts returned again they were edged with a fear she could not put a name to, but somehow understood.

He made death final.

The words rolled through her like a long rumble of thunder.

Death final? she thought.

Yes.

Her heart quailed at Ecthellien's thoughts. She had always believed that the spirit found new life after death. It was what she'd been taught since childhood. After death, the spirit returned to the great well of all souls. There, they waited to return to the world. It was a comfort to think about it this way. But she'd always questioned how they knew. And with the questions came doubt. Still, she couldn't accept what Ecthellien said as truth.

But what of the things that come back? Dimlock? Wights? Or those afflicted by the black Stones?

Only abominations remain after they should have passed. Parts of them are dead, but some parts of them—the worse parts—live on. They are very close to death. So they fear it more. Until fear and its mirror—rage—is all that drives them.

Luthiel ate the last of her dinner in silence keeping both her mouth and her thoughts quiet. Still, in the back of her mind, she wondered what the world would be like without fear of death. She remained silent until the last of the plates were cleared from the table and Mithorden was, once again, walking to the head of the table.

"It would be a far better place," she whispered to herself.

How The Widdershae
Came to Be

"Many of you have spoken about the dark things and of the danger we face," Mithorden said when he reached the head of the table. "Now it's my turn. I will start with a tale of how the Widdershae came to be. Some of you may already know this tale. But I will tell it to you in its entirety. Some of the details you may not recall. For I had the opportunity to speak with those unfortunate enough to have witnessed these events first-hand and the rumor that some call history has left most of the more important details out.

"Many years ago, after the time of Valkire, but before our current day, there lived a race of elves called the Delvendrim. They inhabited the northern peaks of what are now called the Drakken Spurr Mountains. A peaceful if somber people, the Delvendrim knew much about the secrets kept in deep and hidden places at the roots of the mountains or in the depths of night beneath the stars. For beneath the mountains they delved out great warrens and these were connected to Oesha and its moons by Lilani. Also, upon the mountain peaks they erected rings of stones to catalogue the movements of moons and stars. The Delvendrim were a people who treasured the knowledge of hidden lore and of ages long past.

"Their queen—Keldara—was no exception. So when she received a Teluri—a mirror that opens a gateway to other places—as a gift from an anonymous benefactor, she was delighted. For the Teluri was useful both as a window and a gateway. Her excitement was so great that she didn't question the identity of her benefactor and began using the Teluri immediately.

"But there was something wrong with the Teluri. Something that Keldara didn't notice at first. For, when left alone, it would darken and in its window glittering clusters of eyes would stare out.

"Keldara's daughter, Ninowe, was the only one to notice the eyes. But Keldara dismissed it as a child's fancy. Nonetheless, Ninowe would sneak into her mother's chambers, covering the mirror when no one was looking.

"Then, one night, something dark crossed into our world. The cloth Ninowe had used to cover the mirror had fallen away. It crept through the mirror and onto Keldara's bed. The form it took was small for the world could not yet bear all of it. It only paused long enough to sting Keldara's leg before it scurried back to the darkness behind the mirror.

"The sting was enough to awaken Keldara. In an instant, she sat upright, opening her eyes just in time to see the thing scurry back into the mirror. She only glimpsed it. But she said it looked like a spider, barely larger than a clenched fist. To her eyes it seemed black as night itself.

"It was then that Keldara began to wonder about her mirror and to fear that she should have listened to Ninowe. Who *had* it come from? And what was the dark spider that had bitten her?

"She cried out and other elves soon came to her aid. She had them take the mirror to a secure place far beneath the fortress were it was locked into an iron box. Healers also came to tend to her. The wound was barely visible. And it only hurt Keldara a little—itching more than it stung. But the healers, urged on by Ninowe, did what they could to draw the venom out.

"Yet that venom was beyond the art of even elves to heal and, over the days, it began to fester. First a yellow ring formed around the bite. The ring slowly grew until it covered her thigh. Then, within the ring, near the bite, all the flesh became black and mottled.

"After a week, Keldara's eyes became glazed. The whites turned a yellow-green and the pupils began to distort into a jagged shape.

"During this time, Keldara began to fall into fits of raving. The fits grew worse and worse until the healers who attended her feared they would have to bind the queen to her bed. Then, on the eighth night after Keldara received the bite, she sprang from her bed and fled from the city. Ninowe never saw the mother she knew again."

Mithorden paused and Luthiel noticed that she was sitting on the edge of her seat and that her hands were tightly gripping the table's edge.

"What a terrible story!" she said. "How do you know this?"

"I learned this account from Ninowe," Mithorden replied.

"Fearing for her mother's life," Mithorden continued, "Ninowe and the healers journeyed out into the mountains to look for her. By this act, she, and those who went with her were the only elves to survive what happened.

"They followed Keldara into the mountains, tracing her tracks along the streams and springs that fed into the river flowing beneath the city— providing it with both water and a roadway to the world beyond the mountains.

"They tracked the queen for nearly a week. And they were troubled. For the marks in the earth became strange. Her footprints seemed to narrow. And then it appeared as though she went on all fours. But there were other marks along her trail that disturbed them more. Indentations, like those made from a pointed stick, pierced the ground.

"Had the tracks not changed over the course of many days, they would have lost the queen's trail entirely. The change was slow enough that they were certain it was the queen they tracked. But they greatly feared what was happening to her and many times the healers urged Ninowe to go back. But Ninowe wouldn't hear them. She was determined to find out what terrible thing was happening to her mother and, if possible, to save her.

"In the end, the healers decided to go with Ninowe. Again, their decision to persevere was what saved them.

"For one night, they happened on the poor creature that was once the queen of the Delvendrim. And they were terrified, for in peeking through the trees they beheld a creature that would live on in their nightmares from that day forward. It resembled the elf-queen they knew very little. It had the body of an insect and great black legs—each tipped with a point like a spear—protruded from that body. Its original arms and legs had changed almost beyond recognition. But they could still tell it was the queen for her face, though horribly misshapen and ringed with clusters of black eyes, was still recognizable. Bits of cloth still hung here and there from its misshapen body and occasionally it would click to itself.

"When they saw it, it was crouched over a spring lowering its mouth to the water as if to drink. But, instead, it was vomiting into the water. The black detritus spilled through the water like ink, snaking down into the stream the spring fed. They followed the creature for three days. And each day was the same. The creature would stoop over whatever spring or river it could find and then vomit into the water. On the third day, the healers had seen enough. Fearing that whatever the creature had vomited into the water might also poison the Delvendrim, they hurried back to their city.

"It took them three days to make their way back through the mountain passes. But water travels much faster than a group of elves afoot, especially when journeying down the steep and jagged slopes of the Drakken Spur Mountains. So when they returned to the city, they found that all of their brethren had fallen ill. Their eyes had turned green and their pupils were slowly becoming misshapen. Some were developing black splotches upon their skin.

"All too familiar with what had happened to the queen, they fled from the place in terror. I came upon them on my way into the mountains one year. They'd taken up residence many miles away from the Gates of the East. But even then, they were considering moving further west for rumor of dark things was already reaching the foothills and this was only a year after the terrible event occurred.

"I felt particulary sorry for Ninowe. For seeing her mother in such a state had unhinged her mind and, periodically, she fell into fits of madness. I did what I could to help them and I urged them to move on. For the Drakken Spurr mountains were very close and I feared that these spiders might set upon them. But I knew very little about Widdershae then and I was, perhaps, careless. For I wasn't as firm as I might have been.

"A few years later, I returned to see if they were still living in the shadow of the Drakken Spurr. The lands about had grown wild and terrible for the Widdershae, as the spider-elves became known, were ranging out into the foothills now. Their terrible shadow webs were cast in cunning places and most beasts had long since fled to the safety of Minonowe.

"Killed or fled, the last survivors of the Delvendrim were nowhere to be found. I fear they may have been devoured, for I have not seen them since. But I hope they were wise enough to leave before the spiders came upon them. Perhaps they still felt the call of the mountains and their deep mystery. Perhaps it was too strong for them to leave sight of those great peaks standing beneath the stars and moons.

"But one thing is certain. The Widdershae did not devour the Delvendrim. The Delvendrim became Widdershae. They were poisoned by a black spider that slipped into our world through a Teluri."

"But what was it?" Luthiel asked. The hands with which she was gripping the table had broken out into a sweat. "What was this tiny spider that slipped through the mirror?"

"I don't know for certain. I can only guess. There is but one creature that lives among the stars that could do such a thing. And they may yet inhabit the black moon Gorothoth. I do not think that it is a coincidence that the Delvendrim became spiders."

"Ingolith," Ecthellien said.

"Yes. I fear that by some black art the spiders of night have cursed the mountain elves to become Widdershae in their likeness."

"But the rivers Rendalas and Gwithemlo," Luthiel said. "They are also fed by springs in the mountains. Wouldn't the elves of Minonowe and Ashiroth also become poisoned?"

"We only know that they did not. Perhaps the vomit of the creature Keldara became was too diluted when it joined with the great rivers. And perhaps she could only infect other elves while she was still partly elfin herself. What we do know is that no more elves have fallen to this terrible illness."

"That's not entirely true," Othalas growled.

"What did you say?" Mithorden's eyebrows lowered in concern.

"Some elves in Ashiroth turned into Widdershae. There it is a rare illness. But it happens now and then."

A silence fell upon the room.

"This is terrible news," Mithorden said. "But there is little we can do about it now other than remain vigilant."

"Why didn't you tell Tuorlin the truth about the Delvendrim?" Luthiel asked.

"I did," Mithorden replied.

"Then why don't we know the truth?" she said.

"Lord Tuorlin decided that it was too terrible. He thinks that some things are best kept secret. I don't agree, but I must respect his rule."

Silence, once again, fell over the gathering. The blue lights of Ottomnos and even the yellow lights of the flir bug bulbs were not enough to comfort Luthiel. Somewhere, perhaps close by, were creatures that once walked the face of Oesha as elves but were now Widdershae. For some reason, the fact that they were once elves made them seem more horrible to her. She remembered their pointed ears, the almond shape of their eyes, and shuddered.

Escape Plans

"Why are we talking of these things now?" Luthiel asked. "Vaelros, the elves of the mountains, the demon Thrar Taurmori, the betrayer Zalos. Why?"

"Because we must know what we face!" Mithorden said sternly. "We cannot afford to delude ourselves. Nor can we let the elves fall prey to lies. There is a common thread that runs through all these tales and its leads back to the Black Moon. For hundreds of years, its influence has grown in secret. It cannot continue. We must resolve ourselves to do what we can to stop it and its agents—Thrar Taurmori, the Widdershae, and even Zalos. For now, the war against the Vyrl must be stopped. I don't know why Zalos has pushed this war upon the elves. But I don't trust that he intends only to remove the Vyrl. The Widdershae are here and the mists of the Vale are here. I fear that this is some ploy to weaken or break the elves ere winter falls."

"All this talking of dark and terrible things grows tiresome," Norengar muttered. "You remind me of children trembling in fear of the shadows that come with sunset! I thought this was a council of war!"

"I agree! Enough trembling and whimpering. If it lives it can also be killed," Othalas growled.

"It *is* a council of war," Mithorden said. "But only because war has come to us—a war we *must* avoid."

"But the spiders? What about the spiders?" Luthiel asked.

"Once we have peace with the elves, then we'll deal with the spiders," Mithorden said.

"But they're all around us," she said. "How can we escape?"

Mithorden looked back at her in surprise.

"How did you know?" he asked.

"A crow told me," she said.

"Well, I see that you've settled in," he said glancing at the Vyrl. "Don't get used to it, though. We're leaving."

"You still haven't answered my question," she said.

"I'll let the Vyrl answer for you," he replied.

For a moment, the Vyrl's thoughts were confused.

"We know of no way to reach the rim without first going through the Widdershae," Ahmberen said.

"No other way?" Mithorden replied. "What of the Lilani that lies in the heart of this castle?"

"The Lilani? But it leads to Cauthraus," Elshael replied.

Mithorden shuffled through some of the maps that were piled upon the table.

"Never rely on the wisdom of Vyrl, for it will fail you," he muttered as he unrolled the map he had picked out. It was an odd drawing that Luthiel didn't recognize.

"This is the moon Cauthraus," he said. "Here is where the Lilani beneath this castle opens." He placed a finger upon the map. "And this is another Lilani that leads back to Oesha." He pointed to a place that seemed nearby on the map. "It opens here." He pointed back to the map of the lands surrounding the Vale. The place his finger marked was just behind the bits of colored glass. "It should let you in directly behind their armies."

Luthiel was looking at the map of Cauthraus. When she noticed that the edges curled in, she had a sinking feeling. Leowin had described maps like this to her once, long ago.

"Is this a map of all of Cauthraus?" she asked.

"Yes," Mithorden replied.

"Then how far is it between the two Lilani7

"About three hundred miles," he said.

Luthiel stared at the map in disbelief.

"Three hundred miles? How are we going to ever make it in time? That'll take weeks. And what if there are trolls? Don't trolls live on Cauthraus?"

"You have a talent for asking two questions at once don't you?" Mithorden chuckled. "In answer to your first question, Othalas can make the journey in little more than a day. And in answer to your second question—yes, trolls do live on Cauthraus. You'll have to avoid them. They're vicious."

A sudden and overpowering sense of dread came over her. Her skin raised up in gooseflesh. It wasn't Mithorden's talk of trolls that had frightened her. Rather, it was a sense of something terrible.

Then, in the map, she had a vision of a wall of fire rising up, up—climbing high as a mountain. Behind it hung the black moon in the face of a pregnant sun. The flames raced toward her and then the vision faded.

She stood, unable to tear her eyes from the map, trying to breathe evenly. It was only a flash but it seemed so real.

"Could we not take the other road?" she said.

"The spiders may spot us. They have set a watch. And the path will be far more difficult now that they've had time to thicken their webs."

"You want me to go there alone?" she said tilting her head toward the map of Cauthraus.

"If you were listening, you'd know that Othalas would go with you."

"I *know* Othalas would go with me!" She was becoming exasperated with the sorcerer's word games. "But would anyone else come with me as well?"

"The werewolf is fastest," Mithorden said. "It would be safer to make the journey alone."

"Alone." She said it more as a statement than a question. She wondered why it seemed that she must do everything alone. The vision of fire flashed in her mind again. She wiped her brow. Her hand came away sweaty.

"I don't wish to go at all. Alone is far worse," she said.

"Mithorden, shouldn't Luthiel bring someone with her?" Vaelros said. "Couldn't Othalas carry more than one?"

"I certainly could," Othalas growled. "But I'm not a pack animal."

Mithorden considered Vaelros as he stroked his beard.

"Perhaps it is a good idea to send someone along with Luthiel. But I don't think it should be you, Vaelros. Zalos and your six former comrades must be considered. If they saw you, they might not let you leave unpunished. One of the Vyrl, though, might help things. That is, if one of you were willing to take the risk."

The Vyrl exchanged speculative glances.

"But what of the elves? They might imprison the one that comes," Elshael said.

"They might," Mithorden replied. "But if you came in a show of good faith it would strengthen Luthiel's plea."

Vaelros laid his hand on his sword hilt.

"I made a promise. I'm with Luthiel," he said.

Mithorden stared at Vaelros under lowered brows.

"It would be a terrible waste if you were taken again so soon," he said. "You'll have other, better, opportunities to help."

Vaelros brooded.

"I'll do as Luthiel says. Not you."

"If she values you, she'll ask that you stay here," Mithorden replied with a glance at Luthiel.

But Luthiel was lost in her own thoughts. She still wasn't convinced that the journey to Cauthraus was a good idea. The fire, this time a tall red flame with a black crown of smoke, rose in her mind again.

"Mithorden, didn't you pass through the Widdershae on your way here? Surely, you know of some magic that can hide us from them?" she said.

"I *did* pass through them on my way into the Vale," he said. "But I was alone. It was a dark and dangerous path—strewn with webs of shadow. Likely it has grown worse. Their web-spinning is ceaseless. I would rather not risk it with a larger group."

"But isn't Cauthraus also dangerous?" Luthiel asked. "You helped me the first time, couldn't you do it again for the rest of us?"

"I could. But it wouldn't guarantee our secrecy. You were found. Even I was stalked by one of the more cunning among them. A very near thing, but I was able to escape. They are sly hunters —very difficult to fool. Alone, I might hide from most. But a group? I could try to hide us, but I am afraid we would draw their attention once we came into their midst. Nor do I wish to risk sending us one at a time through so many. If I had known their numbers, I would have thought twice about sending you the first time. I will pass that way again, alone. And I will meet you at the Lilani."

"But why won't you come with us?" Luthiel asked. She didn't like this idea at all. "Shouldn't we go together?"

"The elves do not know that I came to the Vale. I don't think it wise that we arrive together through a Lilani known to come from Ottomnos. It is very likely to be guarded. I should return alone. That way, I'll have a chance to meet with Tuorlin and the other lords first.

"Also, my support for you will mean more if you 'convinced' me to bring you to them." He said the last bit with a wink.

Ecthellien, who was quietly listening to the conversation, leaned forward.

"It is an awful place, Cauthraus," he said. "Wars are as common there as the poisonous gas that rises from the ground. At day, the very air burns and all creatures who live there must flee from the dawn into night."

"The air burns?" Luthiel asked with dread in her voice. "Mithorden, do you know when we will arrive?"

Mithorden's brows lowered.

"The Lilani opens in a place that is on the far side of Cauthraus this time of year. Dawn will come there in a few of Oesha's days. It is growing hotter. Oerin's eye is visible and light from Soelee is streaming into the sky. But it should still be safe. The second Lilani lies closer to sunrise. By the time you reach it, you should see Soelee's rim on the horizon. The heat will be uncomfortable, no more."

"Are you certain? What if we arrive there when the sun has already risen?" she said. The more she heard about Cauthraus the more she thought of her dreadful premonition. But did she want to risk slipping through the spiders again? She didn't like either but she wanted nothing more than to return home. She missed Leowin and her family and the happy leisure of her days in Flir Light hollow.

It was the best time of year. The berries would be ripe for picking. She and Leowin would be waking up in the early morning to make the two-hour journey. And then they would be out among the fields, feet and clothes muddy with the wet loam of early summer. There, the only spiders she would have to brave were the relatively benevolent garden variety with beautiful designs of white and gold upon their backs. They seemed almost kind, these spiders. And when they ended up on your clothes when you accidentally blundered into their webs, they would politely drop off, crawling away in search of better places for web-building.

She sighed at the memory, but it was short-lived as Mithorden was talking again about the red moon.

"You won't arrive when the sun has risen," Mithorden said sternly.

Luthiel still felt ill at ease. The vision of fire was still fresh in her mind. And, since she left Flir Light, she'd learned to trust her premonitions.

I fear the red moon for a reason, she thought.

"When was the last time you were there?" she asked. "Do you have a better map? This one is not very detailed."

"It was a few hundred years ago," Mithorden said. "And of course I have another map! Don't be silly."

"A few hundred years? What if the way has changed? What if the Lilani has been covered up by something? What will save us then?"

"And what will save me from a hundred silly questions!? Luthiel Valkire, there are more things to know than you can learn in so short a time. Trust me! If you haven't learned *that* already, then it will save us both a lot of worry once you do!"

Luthiel blinked her eyes.

"I fear that there is great danger," she whispered.

"Danger? I daresay there is. But sometimes you must do things despite it. The greatest danger of all is to sit here while events overtake us. You should know this. You went into far greater peril when you journeyed here."

"I thought it would be the last big risk I would have to take."

Mithorden looked at her and there was sympathy in his eyes.

"Luthiel, I am sorry. But the danger is growing for us all."

Luthiel thought about the stories, the dark tales told in the evening in the flicker-glow of fire or flir bugs. She knew now that they were true and she would not be able to listen to them again without a tightening in the gut or a prickle on her skin.

I've changed, she thought. *And I'll be restless until I know the dangers have passed.*

Yet they might never pass.

"Luthiel *has* risked much for us," Ecthellien said. "It is unfair, I think, that she also risk this journey alone. I will go with her." The lights in the Vyrl's eyes swirled as he stared at her. Was she seeing things, or did they seem brighter to her now? The change was very slight, but the smaller lights didn't seem to be shrinking anymore and the larger ones were growing. They were all still tiny, like a collection of small and large pinpricks, but the black that they swirled among seemed less sinister to her now.

"She wouldn't be alone," Othalas growled.

"Even Othalas might be overcome by the terrors of the red moon," Ecthellien said. "There are worse things than trolls on Cauthraus. You will need my help."

Gormtoth nodded but didn't say anything.

"Good," Mithorden said. "Then the number is set. Three will go by way of Cauthraus and I will slip, once more, through the spiders' webs."

"Now, for the rest of you, I advise that you continue to make ready for war."

"Wait!" Luthiel said, louder than she intended to. They all stared at her. "Must we decide so soon?"

"You never answered her question," Vaelros said. "How do you *know* for certain that the moon isn't already burning on the Lilani's far side? At least we would have a chance to make it through the spiders. If the air burns, no-one will survive."

"Nothing has changed on the red moon, Vaelros," he said.

"Do you really know? Are you willing to stake Luthiel's life on what you think you know?"

Mithorden stared at him under his brows.

"I know," he said. "and my heart tells against bringing her back through the spiders. But I cannot, beyond any doubt, prove to you that day has not come to Cauthraus."

"So you *don't* know. You would send her there on a guess? While you pass by some other way?"

Mithorden's eye's flashed but he didn't reply. Instead, he turned to Luthiel.

"I've given my council. The way I would choose for you is to go with Ecthellien and Othalas to Cauthraus. I would be lying to say that way isn't dangerous. But the spiders, I fear, may prove worse."

"Then why would you go alone?" Luthiel said. "What if they were to take you? Without aid, you would be lost to us. I understand what you are saying. But I am also afraid. Afraid for you going alone into danger. Afraid of the hidden dangers that may lie in wait for us on the red moon. Whatever path we choose, I think we should not separate and, if need be, face the danger together."

Mithorden smiled at her and a lightness seemed to come into his eyes.

"Then I leave the decision to you, Luthiel."

"In this, at least, we are agreed," Vaelros said.

Luthiel sighed as she considered her choices.

What do I risk? Spiders or fire?

"I would not have *any* of us go alone into danger," she said after sitting silent for a time. "Nor would I have us take a path that, for a poor guess, would end in fire. That way, I would choose last and only in desperation when all other ways were tried. So though Mithorden's council is against it, I would have us try to make it through the spiders. More of us may go that way and what we cannot win by stealth we might still take by might of arms. The Vyrl are here and they are mighty. Gormtoth is here and he is mighty. Mithorden, Othalas, Norengar—there is strength here to rival all the Fae Lords together. If you will come with me, then I think it is our best chance."

"I am with you, Luthiel." Vaelros said.

"And I," said Ecthellien.

"As am I," said Othalas.

Elshael and Ahmberen exchanged glances.

"Gormtoth, though strong, is about as subtle as a thunderstorm," Ahmberen said. "You'll have a better chance at slipping by without him and the rest of us. We'll stay to safeguard Ottomnos. But we will keep contact through the Koraz and we'll gather a force to come to your aid if trouble finds you."

"Best keep that force ready!" Mithorden said. His eyes rested on Vaelros for a moment before returning to Luthiel.

"The sooner we leave the better," he said.

"Is first light tomorrow soon enough?" Luthiel asked.

"It will have to be," Mithorden replied.

Luthiel sighed with relief. But in her thoughts, the vision of flame lingered.

FAREWELL TO OTTOMNOS

For another hour, they talked over the finer points of their journey and of how best to prepare Ottomnos for a battle against Widdershae, elves or both. When they were done, more food was brought and beer and wine with it. Creatures of the Vale filtered in, joining the drinking and conversation. Mithorden grabbed two beer mugs and took Vaelros by the arm, pulling him over to a quiet corner. Luthiel watched them discretely. Vaelros' body language was stiff but his eyes were resolute.

"Melkion," Luthiel whispered to the dragon on her shoulder.

His violet eyes gleamed.

"I'm curious what they're talking about," she motioned to Vaelros and Mithorden. "Would you mind listening in for me?"

"You want me to eavesdrop?" he hissed.

"Yes," she said simply.

She didn't like the way Vaelros and Mithorden had conflicted. Nor did she care for Vaelros' distrust of the sorcerer. But she understood the fear that Vaelros was coming out from under. It made her even more concerned.

I wonder what rash thing he may do for a threat he perceives?

The more she thought of the nightmare world he'd lived in for so long, the more she wondered if he'd lost his ability to distinguish between real and imagined threats.

"Why?" the dragon said.

"I'm concerned about Vaelros," she said.

The dragon nodded and with a flap of his wings he was flying across the chamber. He landed on a small table near Mithorden, where he appeared to occupy himself with tearing apart the roast haunch of some wild beast.

Then the singing began—the mighty voices of giants combined with the reedy voices of Grendilo in a rolling ballad. Even the chimera creatures sang with them in chorus.

It was a warsong. Its loud, powerful notes filled the great hall.

Luthiel was both startled and impressed by its force as the faces of those in the hall fell into grim resolve as they watched the singers or sang along.

When the song was done, there was a loud cheer and the clamor of mugs pounding on the table.

"Another!" Norengar shouted, pounding his stein—the size of a small barrel—hardest of all. "Another!"

And so the giants began again. This time the tune was about a different kind of battle entirely—of sailors fighting a storm at sea. The ship Eleth Migaellen, was the greatest of its day, and it struggled for nigh unto a week against a storm that pushed it ever closer to the Knife of the Ocean, until finally her mainmast was broken by a mighty blow of wind and wave and she was driven onto the shoals where she shattered.

The song awoke within her a longing she could not explain. In her mind's eye she could see the ocean's ever changing face and she felt a pang in her heart that was beyond words, as of one who pines for love never requited. It was as though the ocean called to her through the song.

Talk of the sea affected her this way and though she'd never seen it, she often had visions of it in dreams—both waking and sleeping. Once, when the longing took her, she wrote a poem about the ocean. Seeing it, Leowin had promised to take her to Ithilden and to show her the majestic ships the Ithildar shaped out of Aerinwe—trees that grew as saplings on shore. As they aged, Aerinwe roots ever sought the sea. And when they were large enough, a storm swirling out of Lothyn Aer would catch them, pulling them out to open water. There they drifted for the rest of their days. Forever riding the ocean's wild waves—be they gentle or riled with passion.

Perhaps it was this passion that called to her through the song. And when it was done, her voice was among the ones raised in cheering.

So the songs of Ottomnos continued long into the night as more and more creatures of the Vale came to listen or to talk with one another.

Many of these gathered close to talk with Luthiel. Many more peered at her curiously or whispered questions to their neighbors while they watched her. She was amazed to find that most of them were once elves who had come to the Vale in search of treasure or adventure, or were lured by the Vyrl's enchantments. Many were conquered long ago by the Vyrl and some, like the giants and the grendilo, had served them since the time of Valkire. Though the masters of Ottomnos still intimidated them, they spoke in whispers of Luthiel's influence and of how the Vyrl now seemed fairer.

Luthiel looked out over the bizarre gathering. There were bark-skinned giants, lions with elfin heads, and elves with lion heads. There were birds with burning wings and the one-armed, one-legged grendilo. There were wights and giant serpents. Even the werewolves had come—their sleek predator shapes glided quietly through the gathering. She felt oddly at home among them.

After a time, Melkion returned to her.

"He spoke of Vaelros' wound," Melkion hissed.

"Wound?" she asked.

"Yes, Mithorden says that he has been 'heart wounded' by his corrupted Wyrd Stone. Though now free of its influence, he says that Vaelros is likely to spend a long period of time recovering. This period, he warns, could be dangerous."

Luthiel looked at the dragon, remembering the pain Vaelros felt when his six fellows had come for him.

"He asked Vaelros to request boons of the Vyrl."

"What boons?" she asked.

"He asks that Vaelros request to stay at Ottomnos and—"

"And?" Luthiel prodded.

The dragon looked away.

"To give him a replacement for his sword. Mithorden says that it is cold and that the dark metal—Narmiel—seems to have taken on the dreams of Gorthar. It could slow his recovery or hurt him further."

"What did Vaelros say?"

"He mainly listened. He said he'd consider giving the sword back. But he said that, no matter what, he's going with you."

Luthiel nodded.

"Thank you Melkion," she said.

The dragon only swished his tail in reply, then flew off to perch among the eves. It looked to Luthiel that he brooded up there—watching the gathering restlessly as his rainbow plumed tail slid back and forth.

She sat quiet and alone for a time—thinking about Vaelros.

Mithorden was probably right. Vaelros shouldn't be journeying with them so soon after coming out from under the Stone's darkness.

If the sorcerer has reason to worry, then it's to be taken seriously. But if Vaelros won't listen we'll just have to watch over him.

She wondered if Melkion would help her.

A flame-winged bird and a werewolf approached and politely asked to join her. She smiled at them.

"Nothing would please me more," she said.

The drinking, singing, and tale-telling lasted well into the night. As it grew late, her thoughts turned toward morning and to what lay ahead. She dreaded another difficult and dangerous journey.

The dangerous part was supposed to be getting into the Vale, not leaving it, she thought. *But it looks like getting out may prove even harder.*

Though she was loath to leave, Luthiel bid farewell to the kind old bird and werewolf who were sharing a tray of fruits and smoked fish with her.

As Luthiel left, Othalas and Melkion joined her.

"They didn't mention you coming with us," Luthiel said to Melkion as they walked through the charred-glass corridors.

"Well, then, I guess he'll have to stay here," Othalas said with a gravely chuckle.

"It doesn't matter what they say or don't say. I do as I please," Melkion replied.

"I'd be glad if you came," Luthiel said to the dragon.

"Good," he said.

The dragon didn't speak again that evening. Instead, he brooded. Occasionally, thin streams of smoke would rise from his nostrils. Once, he flew out into the night and returned with blood on his claws and snout.

Othalas ignored the dragon. He fell to the floor and in no time was slumbering.

But Luthiel's mind was too alert to fall into sleep immediately. Instead she walked over to the slit window and stared out into the night. Ottomnos brooded among the mists and flickering watch fires. There was something both strange and familiar about its gracefully sloping walls and towers, the dull gleam of its charred glass.

She'd experienced much here and, strangely, there was a part of her that felt melancholy about leaving.

My father once called this place home, she thought. *Could I come to think of it that way?*

She looked at the slumbering Othalas—his predator's body lay in still repose. She watched his powerful muscles ripple with the rise and fall of his breath.

"I remember a time, not too long ago, when you were ready to kill me. Now you growl if I suffer so much as a scratch."

Looking back out into the night, she wondered at how she was no longer afraid of the Vale.

Now that I know your secrets, you're not so terrible.

Was there something about this place that had changed—or was it her? Its ever-changing mists, its creatures who were once elves, goblins, or even men seemed compelled by her in a way she didn't quite understand. Now that she'd come and the Vyrl no longer hunted them, there was less fear—unless it was of spiders or of war.

Instead, Ottomnos and the Vale it ruled seemed a melancholy place to her—brooding on its dark past, reluctantly readying for war. Those arching spires thrust their mighty defiance high, and yet the place seemed more ready to return to happier times.

"Farewell Ottomnos," she whispered into the night. "You've become a place of unexpected welcome to me."

She reveled in this thought, trying to remember if she'd ever felt so wanted, or even needed, among the elves.

No, she thought. *I only felt different. But here all are strange.*

From out of the night, a cloud of mists rose up. A swarm of green lights drifted in through the slit window, catching in her hair, tingling upon her skin, or dancing about her.

Startled, she jumped back. And then, realizing what they were, returned to the window. She let them brush past her face, enjoying the sensation of them touching her skin.

Can they hear me? she wondered.

Looking out into the night one last time she said —

"Vale of Mists, I think we have come to terms, you and I."

She gazed over the watch fires, into the Vale's swirling mists and beyond.

The spiders were out there, weaving their shadowebs, waiting. And the armies of the elves were there too, waiting in their camps among the Mounds of Losing. Her eyebrows lowered and her face became resolute.

I made my way here; I'll make my way out again.

"I'm coming home Leowin," she whispered into the night.

Then Luthiel returned to her bed and tried to sleep. She found it difficult. Instead, she lay awake thinking of the council, of the stories told there, of Cauthraus burning, and of the Widdershae. Last of all she thought of leaving the Vale and returning to Flir Light Hollow. The conflicted feelings stayed with her until, in the late night, she finally drifted into slumber.

As far as she knew, for the rest of the night, the lights stayed with her.

APPENDICES

APPENDIX I:
THE ELFIN RUNES

The elfin runes were characters drawn to represent shapes in nature—the curl of a wave, the silhouette of a fish in deep water, the body of a serpent threading between two stones. To the elves these characters have special significance, for they understand them—their shapes and sounds—to be the very language of creation. In them, there is the most basic magic of forms and definitions. But also in them is the deeper understanding of spirit. For while the runes describe shapes and sounds, they also hold deeper meaning and are the key to understanding both the mysteries of the self and of the boundless universe. So here, in these motes and marks, in these slashes on the page, in rock, or earth, is the language of stars and moons, of wind and water, of wyrd and dreams.

	ELFIN	ENGLISH
LEOWE		A
RAE		B
BELIR		C
VALA		D
NIN		E
FEHRIS		F
WINAE		G
SHAELYN		H
MELLWYTHE		I
LILANI		J

NOS		ß
LIEL		L
TIRNA		M
FAE		N
OMAH		O
TOSH		P
ZAE		Q
RILNO		R
AELAS		S
ELOH		T
ENRIS		U
VALKIRE		V
WELOWEE		W
DIRNA		X
ERNON		Y
KIRNA		Z

APPENDIX II:
THE SUNS AND MOONS
OF OESHA

Soelee: First sun of Oesha. Soelee is slightly smaller and dimmer than the day-star of Earth but is by far the brightest object in the skies of Oesha. A white-yellow star, Soelee rules the skies of day.

Oerin's Eye: Second sun of Oesha. Bright enough to dim most stars, Oerin's eye rises first and sets last extending the time of gloaming both morning and evening. Oerin's eye is an almond shaped white-blue star.

Lunen: The first moon of Oesha is the color of pearl. Associated with peace and wisdom, Lumen's glow softens the skies of Oesha at night and in the hours of gloaming.

Merrin: The second moon of Oesha is the color of ocean waves. A wild and mysterious moon, Merrin is the patron moon of sailors and of storms.

Silva: This moon shines like a bright silver penny in the sky. The third moon of Oesha is associated with grace and goodness.

Sothos: Somber grey, Sothos is associated with dreams and sleep. The fourth moon of Oesha is sometimes difficult to find in the sky as its dim disk often blends well with the background. Also called the sleepy eye, Sothos is sometimes associated with the magic and mystery of dreams.

Tiolas: The fifth moon of Oesha is banded yellow and green. A wild place, Tiolas is associated with the primal spirit of nature. The Tyndomiel claim Tiolas as their patron moon.

Veolin: Wrapped in rainbow hues, Oesha's sixth moon is the one most often associated with the mysteries of wyrd and magic.

Cauthraus: The color of blood, Oesha' seventh moon is considered the patron of warfare and bloody conflict. The harsh moon seems to burn with deep red fire as it shines down upon Oesha. It is the brightest of the eight moons and is easy to see during daytime.

Gorothoth: The eighth moon of Oesha lurks like a shadow in the sky. Veins the color of old blood cross its face and cold seems to radiate down from it. Gorothoth is visible in the sky only for half of the year—from late fall until First Summer's Eve. The black moon is associated with all things ill upon the world of Oesha.

GLOSSARY

Aelin—(the elves) Aelin represent the first born of the thinking races and make up all the elves that dwell upon Oesha or elsewhere. They include Ithildar, Sith, Valemar, Tyndomiel, and Gruagach.

Aëdar—also called angels, the Aëdar were among those spirits to aid the Elohwë in the great works that shaped the world. Of the Aëdar there were the Ahrda—the spirits of the elements that make up the worlds which are earth, air, water, fire and spirit; the Melear—the spirits of life; the Maehros—spirits of the void; and the Minowe—spirits of light and music. Dragons were among the Ahrda and Narcor (Malcor when corrupted) who are spirits of fire and Keirin who are spirits of storm and many more who are not named here. Vyrl, who were the masters of life and blood and of the dreams of living things, were among the Melear as were the Elvanna who were the spirits of all things good and growing, as were the Mordrim who were the spirits of new life and of changes in form and function. Of the Maehros little is known except that they were dark and strange and that they hungered to devour all things and ever they held the expansion of the world in check for their gluttony was boundless. Keirin were also counted among the Minowe for though they were spirits of air and storm granted to them too were the lights of rainbows and of stars. The Elkala were also among the Minowe and these were spirits of song and of inspiration and of good dreams—both waking and sleeping. So too were the Anari who were the great spirits of stars and the Elune who were spirits of moonlight, gossamer, and sleep.

Aeowinar—also called Cutter's Shear, this mighty blade was the masterwork of Vlad Valkire. It was said that *Aeowinar's* sharpness was unmatched and that there was not a thing which it could not cut.

Ahmberen—one of the three Vyrl in the Vale of Mists. The name Ahmberen means memory in the elder tongue.

Almorah—cakes of dense bread filled with oats and honey. Almorah are often used as a staple by Valemar, Ithildar, and Gruagach.

Arganoth—the fortress of Zalos that lies at the head of the falls that form the river Gwithemlo.

Ashiroth—the Land of the Gruagach that lies to the north of Minonowe.

Black (references to and meaning of)—the evil associated with shadow. For example: the black moon Gorothoth.

Blixx—a race of goblins and the cousins of the Red Caps. Blixx hold a hatred and resentment for all things elfin. They have a long-standing alliance with the Trolls and often fall under the Dominion of Thrar Taurmori. But their chief lord is Korde Morgurlag. Blixx live in tribes in the badlands of the Rimwold.

Bwandirin—the giants. These include the tree folk and the blue giants of Maltarmireth who were servants to the Vyrl.

Chosen—children sent to feed the Vyrl in the Vale of Mists.

Dark (ith. Neth) (references to and meaning of)—"dark" in elfin has a dual meaning. In its first reference, it can be associated with blackness or evil. But in its second it is associated with those things hidden or concealed. Dark, this sense, is the beauty of mystery and of all things wild or unknown. It is the dark of twilight which is filled with stars. Ironically, the dark is full of lights yet to be revealed.

Dark Lady—*see* Elwin.

Detheldris—the Paths of Terror. A region of the Drakken Spur Mountains that are now inhabited by Widdershae.

Dimlock—during the Age of Dreams, Vyrl ruled over all of Oesha feeding on the dreams of men and elves. The dreams were drawn through their eyes which fell away like brittle ash. Those devoured in this way became wights, serving only the will of the Vyrl, lusting after eyes which were their only food. Deprived of this food, the wights would become shrunken and twisted, eventually fading into shadow until they were never seen again. It was not known what became of these creatures until the dark moon rose and beneath its orb black goblins slinked from the shadows. These are the Dimlock, natives of the moon Gorothoth and who have life only beneath its darkness, upon its face, or with the other nightmares in the world of dreams. For in the sunlight they are only shadows but in the darkness of deep winter they appear, ambushing the unwary, carrying them off to the black moon where their flesh is subjected to unspeakable tortures or they are tossed into the great fires.

Drakken Spur Mountains—the mountains beyond the Gates of the East. Long ago, elves would travel through the Drakken Spur and into the lands of Sith and Humans beyond. Now the Mountains are inhabited by Widdershae and passage to the lands beyond is only possible by sea or through the scorched lands to the south of Felduwaith. Few other than Sith and sailors have made this journey.

Ecthellien—one of the three Vyrl in the Vale of Mists. The name—Ecthellien—means chance in the elder tongue.

Elohwë—mighty beings who were the first offspring of the creators Ëavanya and Ëavanar. Each represented a spirit essential to the forming of the world. Aehmiel Eversong, Lumen of Light, Gorthar of Death, Chromnos of Will, and Eldacar of Sight are but a few Elohwë. Also called archangels, the Elohwë have ever had a hand in the shaping of the world and in the commitment of great deeds within it. Both the Aëdar and Elohwë live with one foot in the waking world and the other in the world of dreams.

Elshael—one of the three Vyrl in the Vale of Mists. The name, Elshael, means "sorrow" in the elder tongue.

Elwin—also called the Dark Lady, she is the spirit of Oesha given flesh and form. Perhaps the greatest of the Ahrda, she is also the wife of the Lord of the Dark Forest. For thousands of years now, she has slept—much to the grief of her lord.

Fae— (also known as Elder, and Valas) A family of magical creatures including, elves, trolls, goblins and faeries.

First Summer's Eve—the first day that Gorothoth is not present in the sky. It also represents the beginning of summer. Among the elves, First Summer's Eve is the most holy day of the year.

Glendoras—Luthiel's foster father.

Gorothoth—the terrible moon that rides in the skies of Oesha from late Fall to early Summer. Gorothoth is the source of terrors that walk the face of Oesha including the Widdershae, Dimlock and many more. Also called Lunmir or Shadowmoon.

Grendilo—strange one-armed, one-legged creatures who possess a grace and agility greater than any creature that walked on two legs. Natives to the Vale of Mists, the Grendilo serve the Vyrl who live there.

Gruagach—the physically powerful and wilder cousins of the Ithildar. They were the third-born of the Aelin. Blood of sap, flesh of wood, the Gruagach are a hardy breed who have formed a pact with a tribe of dire wolves, the Urkharim, who live among them as equals.

Himlolth—the land of the Tyndomiel that lies to the north and west of Minonowe.

Ithildar—first born of the Aelin—High Elves. Fair of face and form the Ithildar are the most beautiful and magnetic of the Fae. The glory of their presence is such that men and goblins have worshipped them as lesser gods and of all the elves they are the most advanced in art and knowledge. Ithildar learned the elder language from Aëdar—dragons and spirits of light and song—they have since been its keepers among the elves, teaching it to their kin and children alike. For that reason, the elder speech bears their name—Ithildar (ith). Ithildar is also the name of the great tree of life at Ithilden's heart. The tree is often referred to as Great Ithildar in speech.

Ithilden—the land of the Ithildar that lies to the west of Minonowe.

Leowin—Luthiel's foster sister. Daughter of Glendoras and Winowe.

Lilani—magical gateways that allow passage between Oesha and its moons. Lilani form where wyrd, the magic of dreams, concentrates into vast streams flowing over far greater distances than any of the rivers on Oesha.

Lorethain—Luthiel's foster brother. Firstborn of Glendoras and Winowe.

Melkion—the Vyrl's dragon messenger.

Merrin—queen and spirit of the ocean moon that bears her name. Merrin was also one of the companions of Vlad Valkire and, later, his wife.

Mithorden—(Spiritwatcher) he was summoned by Elroth long ago on an errand of which he will not speak. He is a mysterious sorcerer wandering the lands, consorting with both the strange and powerful. He has been known to appear during the direst of times and some have said that his appearance is a sign of ill things to come.

Moons of Oesha—silver Silva, pearl Lunen, blue Merrin, green and gold Tiolas, smokey Sothos, rainbow Veolin, red Cauthraus, and black Gorothoth.

Moonsteel—metals from moons of Oesha, often thought to have magical properties. Silva—*Silen*, Lunen—*Lumiel*, Merrin—*Marim*, Tiolas—*Tiloril*, Sothos—*Sorim*, Veolin—*Viel*, Cauthraus—*Cauthrim*, and Gorothoth—*Narmiel*.

Neltherduel—the crowns of light. Shaped by Aëdar, these crowns were light as gossamer upon the brows that bore them and woven into their silvery metal were lights like stars.

Netharduin—the four crowns of shadow. Forged of old by Gorthar from *Narmiel* (shadow-steel), these fell crowns are invisible except when touched by the shadow of Gorothoth or of the void itself. Then, it is visible as a dark metal of shifting hues like smoke cast off by a smoldering fire. Each crown houses a spirit of want, rage and bitterness bent to the will of Gorthar, which soon corrupts any who wear it, twisting their lives until all their works result in death and ruin. The ruling *Netharduin* was worn, for a time, by Chromnos until he broke it. The shards of this crown were later reforged by Zalos who used it to corrupt the Wyrd Stones which were, in turn, used to ensnare the Mirghast.

Nethril—the blood silver of the dark forest. This metal grows out in spiral veins from beneath the great tree of life Anaturnar. Sometimes the Dark Fae forge Nethril into terrible weapons. But the metal is difficult to work.

Oesha—the world. According to ancient myth, Oesha was the first living world conceived among the stars. The same myth states that Oesha was the proto world after which all other living worlds were crafted. But only on Oesha, it is said, can dreams be brought to life through the magic of wyrd.

Othalas—eldest of werewolves, Othalas serves the Vyrl in the Vale of Mists.

Ottomnos—the Vyrl's Castle in the Vale of Mists. First ruled by Vyrl and later by Vlad Valkire, Ottomnos was returned to the Vyrl three thousand years ago. There they reign over that misty land and all creatures that dwell within it.

Red-Caps—a kind of goblin friendly to the elves and living among them. Red-Caps are known for their fiery red hair, strong jaws and pointed teeth. Though friendly to elves in general, they harbor a great hatred for humankind and have been known to attack them whenever they perceive advantage.

Rendillo—a grendilo who serves the Vyrl in the Vale of Mists.

Rimwold—a land of elves and goblins to the south of the Minonowe.

Shadow (ith. Nar) (references to and meaning of)—an aspect of evil. Shadow is associated with the drawing of precious warmth away from life. It is the cold of death and of unnatural life beyond death. It is also associated with lies, deceit and treachery. Shadow is the black of evil.

Shadow Webs—these are the dreaded webs of the Widdershae. They are spun of the black that lies in the wells of night. An ancient darkness that, but for these webs, is known only in what can be seen between the stars after both suns fall.

Sith—second born of the Aelin. Elves of the Dark Forest who serve the lord there whose name must not be spoken and who also serve the Dark Lady who sleeps there.

Teluri—small Lilani that were fashioned into mirrors. It is said that a great sorcerer could use them to watch things from afar or to transport themselves to any active Lilani. It is said that those possessing the Teluri may use it to communicate with one another over great distances. The lords of the elves are in possession of four of the original seven Teluri; the other three were lost.

Tuorlin—Lord of Ithilden and High Lord of all the Elflands. Tuorlin is one of the few surviving Chosen who went to the Vale of Mists.

Tyndomiel—of all the elves, Tyndomiel are the strangest as they each possess the ability to shape-change. Tyndomiel group themselves into clans of like kind. All varieties may be found—bears, wolves, dogs, cats, lions, birds, dolphins, sharks, and many others— throughout the lands of Himlolth and the water surrounding it.

Trees of Life—great and ancient trees that have been growing on the face of Oesha since her birth. Many of these trees have died off or been killed over time. But three are still known to remain— Anaturnar in the Dark Forest, Ithildar in Ithilden, and Yewstaff in the Minonowe. Others may grow in hidden places, for some were uprooted by the dragon Faehorne during the strife of the treekillers.

Valemar—an offshoot of the Ithildar, the Valemar are the youngest of the elves. Feet as nimble as the breezes, forms as flowing as water, the Valemar are the most graceful of the Aelin. The Valemar have taken Minonowe for their home.

Vanye—A Blade Dancer of Ithilden, Vanye has been sent on an unhappy mission to name a Chosen. Renown among the Blade Dancers for defeating the leaders of Nine Trolls Army, and the grandson of High Lord Tuorlin, Vanye would rank higher among the Blade Dancers were it not for his sometimes failing to follow the rules.

Veil—the border that separates the world of dreams from the physical world.

Vlad Valkire—the great lord who broke the Vyrl's Tyranny over elves. The name Vlad Valkire, in the elder tongue, means "a lad Valkyrie." For he was the first male born of the Dark Lady Elwin, who was the mother to all Valkyrie. Vlad is also the son of the Lord of the Dark Forest, who killed him.

Vyrl—of old, they were Aëdar, before they were corrupted by the dark will of Gorthar. Once angels, they are now demons of hunger and malice. It is rumored that only three Vyrl remain alive on all of Oesha. Three rule in the Vale of Mists. Each year, according to an ancient promise, a child must be sent to feed the Vyrl. These Chosen seldom ever return.

Werewolves—elves who were transformed into wolves by the changing influence of the Vale of Mists. Werewolves possess incredible vitality and are nearly impossible to kill, recovering from all hurts unless their bodies are entirely destroyed.

Widdershae (Widd-ur-shee)—spider-elves. A branch of elves of the middle house called the Delvendrim (deep-elves), who were wiped out by a terrible plague that turned them all into giant spiders. The Widdershae succumbed to the poison of Saurloth, queen of the

Ingolith and so they were twisted in form to resemble those spiders of the great void. The wise count them among the Ingolith. For their forms have been twisted by spirits of the void which possess them. Great magic may still drive these spirits out and restore the Delvendrim who were thus twisted. Delvendrim returning to the world in this way can recall their lives as Widdershae only through nightmares.

Winowe—Luthiel's foster mother.

World of Dreams—a place parallel to the real word and overlapping it. This place responds to all desires, fears and dreams of humankin and the greater spirits. Only sorcerers can sense the existence of the world of dreams and the only physical beings who can look into it are those who possess a Wyrd Stone. Of late, the world of dreams has become a dangerous place, populated with Dimlock and other nightmares.

Wyrd—a word that stands for both dreams and magic. It represents the deep connection between dreams and the mystical arts.

Wyrd-Stones—thirteen Stones fashioned by Vlad Valkire while under the instruction of Mithorden at Lenidras. They are crystals that have within them each a bit of the song of Aehmiel and the light of Lumen. Powerful aids to sorcerery, the Wyrd Stones transport their users into the world of dreams which is the world from which all things spiritual and magical come. Wyrd Stones wholly reveal what sorcerers must sense in order to practice their art—the raw stuff of creation—true dreams, making it readily available for use in magic. When activated, the Wyrd Stone causes its user to become ghost-like and semi-solid. Things of the physical world other than moonsteel or nethril affect them less, passing through them with only slight resistance. Great wounds become minor. Hunger, fatigue, pain, all become insubstantial while in the world of dreams. On the other hand, creatures of nightmare and dream may directly affect a sorcerer traveling through the world of dreams, making use of a Wyrd Stone very dangerous in the current day.

Zaelos—The Lord of Ashiroth. Also former companion of Vlad Valkire.

ACKNOWLEDGMENTS

When I undertook the task of writing a female epic, I was foolish enough to believe that I would be writing an epic rather than going through an epic adventure myself. As I soon found out, the journey is both long and very difficult, putting livelihood, sanity and happiness at risk. So much so that it would have been impossible to complete without the aid, indeed, the rescuing, of others time after time.

In most books, this section begins with the phrase—*so many people have helped me in my work that it would be impossible to print the list here.* For my part, I will do my best to recall and give credit to everyone who helped me in putting together Luthiel's Song. This is my chance to pay some small part back to them, although they are all deserving of much more.

Special thanks are due to:

My wife—Catherine. This amazing lady has stood behind me ever since she first learned of Luthiel. Since the beginning, she has encouraged me to 'just keep submitting it.' Often, she believed in the strength of the story more than I. In many ways, Catherine has inspired the character Luthiel. But more so, it was Merrin—the great love of Valkire and the spirit of the ocean moon. For she is my ocean lover—as wise as the sea and as passionate as any storm that ever rose over depthless waters.

My good friend Matthew Friedman. Were it not for him, Luthiel would still be wallowing helplessly in a box tucked away in a dark and, yes, spider-infested closet. It would seem that, even in this world, the Widdershae hunt her. But thanks to Matthew's stalwart friendship and literary expertise I have found a great many ways around and through the ephemeral webs and foils of writing. In addition, Matthew aided in the layout of the cover and content of the book both in its electronic and hard copy forms. In many respects, the dragon Melkion was inspired by Matthew. I wish you all friends as capable and constant!

My mother who is deserving of thanks for a million and one things. Not the least of which was reading to me every day of my childhood life. But also of great importance was allowing me to have a Snow White lunchbox as a child. Never was there a parent so good at allowing me to find my own way and make my own mistakes. I think there's a lot to be said for this gift. My own pioneering spirit owes much to her subtle influence. In some ways, Luthiel draws from her, for she struck out on her own path—much like Luthiel—some twenty odd years ago. There is a strength and spirit in her that many see and those who are blessed enough to receive her aid in counseling can join with me in attesting to her caring and kindness.

My father. He has suffered, in life, the suffering of Vlad Valkire and bore wounds that would wreck a lesser man. For me to say that his story has not affected my own would be shallow and a lie. I admire both his strength and his humor. But a greater trait, I think, is his love of beauty in the world and of stars. Though he may not know it—to me, his heart is both elfin and fair.

My grandfather Edwin Page Preston. Born of an ancient line of Kings, he had a nobility about him that I both admire and miss. There was a deep love in him for all people and his gift was in making you feel as though you were the most important person in the whole world to him. In his passing, I resolved myself to finish this tale, if only in the hopes of making his spirit proud.

My cousin Lawson. Without him, my tale would have likely surrendered to a Disney-like sappiness and lack few shreds of real grit. There is much to be said for having honest friends and family. Lawson was given, first, the difficult task of dealing with my grandiose delusions and, second, of telling me, nicely, that the first draft of my book sorely inadequate. In the end, he had an open enough mind to pick up later drafts and appreciate them. I know none of these tasks were easy, and I thank him for it. It is fair to say that the character Vanye is largely inspired by the character of Lawson. Those of you in need of strength, leadership, and decisive action hope that you have friends and family like Lawson.

My good friend Benjamin Baugh. A great friend from college, Ben has been with Luthiel from the start. It was through role playing with Ben, that I was able to flesh out the character traits of Luthiel and begin to solidify her in my mind. In ways, his ideas provided seeds for the setting of Oesha—especially the Dark Forest. May you all have friends as creative as Ben.

My good friend Jonathan Finn. I think my fancy with elves was, in large part, facilitated by Jon since the fourth grade. If Ben helped me solidify Luthiel, then Jon helped me conceive her. In one form or another, the World of Dreams has been made real through our discourse over time. In fact, my first foray into novel writing 'The Great Adventure' was co-written by him in the fifth grade. But we've been swapping stories since the first grade. I think our dialogue, which has often been one of the strength of spirit, belief, intuition, and emotion vrs the strength of practical thought, logic, reason and knowledge has provided me with a balanced view of the world and, better, sharpened my mind. In many ways, ours is the discourse of Apollo and Dionysus. This discourse taught me resolve, which was essential to the completion of this work and many others. I wish you friends as strong willed and minded as Jonathan Finn.

My grandmother, Jeanne Preston (whom I know as Memom). A wonderful lady who truly believes in the good in all people she has stood behind me in everything that I've done. Foremost, though, when I was considering entering the military directly after High School, she came to my rescue and convinced me to apply to Flagler College. Though I did not have the wisdom, or foresight, to see with eyes unclouded, she did and set me on the path toward a respectable education in writing. May you all have grandmothers as lucid, wise, and caring as Memom.

My good friend Campe Goodman. Campe introduced me, long ago, to the creative process of role playing, which, in large part, is storytelling. The elements of storytelling, if practiced well, facilitate a wonderful game. But the art of free association, improvisation, and description necessary to execute a game in an enjoyable and entertaining fashion also feeds into writing. In a subtle, yet strong way, Campe has aided me in this. Campe is also an amazing friend, and one of the most intelligent people and creative people I know. May you all have friends as brilliant, helpful, and incisive as Campe!

My good friend Robert Friedman. Robert has provided me with amazing access to the literary world. I am more than appreciative of his aid with introductions and submissions which have been benevolent beyond compare. Robert has introduced me to numerous writers and literary agents including, but not limited to, Simon Lipskar and Danny Lliteras. Robert has also provided gentle, yet firm, writing criticism. May you all know people as open minded as Robert!

The gamers—who include a number mentioned above: Campe Goodman, Jonathan Finn, Lawson Fannéy, Matthew Friedman, Benjamin Baugh, Rafael Chandler, and Rick Courtney.

Bill Jackson, my brother in law, for his amazing music and for also aiding in the development, conception and execution of a pheonomenal web campaign. He designed and launched the Luthiel's Song Website and has written the theme music to many sections in the novel. He has also stood behind the story since it began. May you all have brother-in-laws as talented and capable as Bill!

My sister Mary Page for giving me inspiration in what it means to be kind, loyal, loving and heroic. For believing in me even when I did not deserve it and for being the best sister a brother could ever wish for.

My sister-in-law Martha Vinson for sharing a passion in writing and for all the interest and kind words.

Elizabeth Spooner for coming to my rescue. The Valkyrie would be proud to know one such as you in their ranks. I have seen unicorns and have it on the highest authority that one awaits you in dreams.

Jim and Marth Lynch. For happy homes, warm fires, steady support, for a quiet, comfortable place to write, and more love and smiles than a son-in-law could ever ask for.

Siya Oum for her wonderful artwork and for her constant aid and admiration for the story. She has believed in it since day one and has provided support other writers could only dream of. I've never worked with someone with both the professional and creative energy of Siya. May you all find people to work with who are as awesome as Siya!

My college professors for providing me with an amazing foundation in writing:

Dr. Darien Andrew—for teaching me that to write simply is to write well, for being the best first year college writing teacher any poor student could hope to have, and for trying to keep me out to the military (a noble task doomed to failure).

Dr. Karl Horner—for teaching me that you need to revise it all again, and again, and again, for his wonderful essays and writings on *The Boy Inside the American Businessman*, for constructing a fabulous creative writing program, for bringing Tim O'Brien to Flagler College for colloquiums, symposiums, readings and courses, and for letting me write fantasy while at school.

Dr. Robin King—for teaching me the fundamentals of great thinking. For his wonderful lectures on truth in fiction. For his challenging, rigorous, humorous, beautiful, and entertaining dialogues.

Dr. Andrew Dillion—for his amazing poetry and for his beautiful soliloquies on Shakespeare.

Jim Tinsley, Rennie Campbell, Jessica Duda, and **Paul and Stacy Rickets** for their continued faith and support.

Lucia, Nichole, Nate, Jessica, Harvard, and Mamimi and everyone else from Myspace for providing constant feedback and support.

It is possible that I have forgotten someone. If so, please bring it to my attention and I will remedy the problem upon reprinting.

Sincere thanks to you all! Luthiel and all the world of Oesha owe you both their thanks and gratitude.

May you ever walk in the light of two suns. May the moonshadow never fall on you.

Robert Marston Fannéy

ABOUT THE AUTHOR

Robert Fannéy's abiding love of fantasy began as a nine year old boy when he was first introduced, by happy chance, to *The Hobbit*. He has been hopelessly lost in the World of Dreams ever since. He began writing *Luthiel's Song* at the age of 22, while at Flagler College in St. Augustine, Florida. After numerous careers and many stolen hours on nights and weekends, the first part of the tale—*Dreams of the Ringed Vale*—is finally complete. He is currently working on the second Luthiel's Song book—*The War of Mists*.

Robert lives in Virginia with his wife, Catherine.

You can find out more about Robert, *Luthiel's Song* and the World of Dreams at **www.luthielssong.com**.